THE
RETREAT

Also by Henry Denker

NOVELS

I'll Be Right Home, Ma
My Son, The Lawyer
Salome: Princess of Galilee
The First Easter
The Director
The Kingmaker
A Place for the Mighty
The Physicians
The Experiment
The Starmaker
The Scofield Diagnosis
The Actress
Error of Judgment
Horowitz and Mrs. Washington
The Warfield Syndrome
Outrage
The Healers
Kincaid
Robert, My Son
Judge Spencer Dissents
The Choice

PLAYS

Time Limit
A Far Country
A Case of Libel
What Did We Do Wrong
Venus at Large
Second Time Around
Horowitz and Mrs. Washington
The Headhunters
Outrage!

THE
RETREAT

Henry Denker

WILLIAM MORROW AND COMPANY, INC.
NEW YORK

Library of Congress Cataloging-in-Publication Data
Denker, Henry.
  The retreat.
  I. Title.
PS3507.E5475R47   1988   813'.54   88-23194
ISBN 0-688-08306-4

Printed in the United States of America

First Edition

1 2 3 4 5 6 7 8 9 10

BOOK DESIGN BY BRIAN MOLLOY

53467

To Edith, my wife

PROLOGUE

The airport tower radioed permission for the private jet to make its approach from the north. The plane banked gracefully in the cloudless blue sky over the southern California desert.

Inside the luxuriously appointed cabin, Kitzi Mills stared out the window at the bare, scrubby mountains that rushed by, but unaware of their primitive beauty or of the vast stretches of desert below.

Blond and beautiful, Kitzi had become a stage star when she was so young that now she was only in her mid-thirties, but people assumed she was older. Prolonged bouts of drinking and pill-taking had not helped. Though still beautiful, her famous face was pale, and thinner than it had been. She gripped the hand of the man who sat opposite her.

Suddenly she cried out, "Tell him not to land!"

"Kitzi, honey, please . . ."

"I want to go back to New York!"

"Don't be frightened, baby. Look at this as a new beginning," he tried to reassure her.

He was Marvin Morse, her agent and manager since the beginning of her career. In times past he had also been her lover. Although only in his late thirties, he already bore the service stripes of his high-pressure profession: gray streaks in his curly black hair.

Morse pressed Kitzi's thin, graceful hand. He was startled at how cold it felt. This woman who once had been so warm in his passionate embrace was now icy with fear. She began to tremble. He released his seat belt, dropped to one knee beside her, and took her in his arms.

"Kitz, darling, have I ever let you do anything that wasn't best for you? Have I?"

She shook her head and began to weep silently. When she pressed his hand to her breast, he could feel every thrust of her beating heart.

God, what she's done to herself, he thought.

The plane's wing dipped, bringing into closer view the mountains that thrust up from the windswept desert floor. Stretches of the sand below were relieved by man-made oases, towns consisting of precisely laid-out streets, bordered by houses with roofs of terra-cotta shingles. They were surrounded by green lawns and golf courses, all carefully tended and watered. Thousands of swimming pools reflected the brilliant afternoon sun. Above the houses towered tall palms and other desert trees, all trucked in and arranged at the direction of fussy landscape artists.

The plane descended.

"They'll all know me," Kitzi suddenly cried. "I'll be a freak."

"They treat everyone the same. Liz Taylor said that. And Bob Mitchum. He took the treatment there."

"Four weeks . . . four whole weeks . . . that's forever," she lamented, still weeping and shaking her head.

"Alice can visit you from time to time," he reassured her.

"I don't want Alice to see her mother in a place like that!" she insisted.

"Okay, okay, whatever you say." Marvin pretended to agree, but he had seen Kitzi in the grip of such panic attacks minutes before going onstage for first previews of what later had turned out to be some of her greatest hits. Always she was terrified the show would fail, she would fail, the critics would hate her, the audience would reject her. The audience and the critics always loved her. Yet she suffered the same terrifying anxiety each time.

Except, of course, Marvin had to concede, *this time is different. If they can't cure her here, where else can I take her?*

The wheels of the plane touched down with a slight bump. The pilot reversed the engines' thrust to slow the speed. Instead of making the usual run the length of the field, then doubling back to the modest terminal building, he steered the white-and-blue jet toward the far corner, where a long white limousine waited.

"We're here," Marvin Morse said as the plane jolted to a stop. Kitzi Mills clutched his hand even more tightly.

"One drink, Marv?" she pleaded. "One drink before we get off?"

"No, honey, no," he forbade, kindly but firmly.

The hatch was opened from the outside, and folding steps were lowered to reveal the uniformed chauffeur who awaited them.

Morse tried to assist her down to the car. As if making an entrance onstage, Kitzi brushed past him and pulled herself erect, determined to deplane on her own. But on the third step she faltered and would have fallen had not both Morse and the chauffeur leaped to her aid. Morse embraced her and guided her down to the ground and the limousine with its dark, tinted windows. Declining the chauffeur's assistance, Morse eased her into the cool interior of the luxurious car. He was relieved to discover that the bar was bare of bottles and glasses.

Thank God for Tony Frascati, Morse thought. It had only taken a single phone call. Once Morse had explained the problem, the singer responded, "A great lady like Kitzi Mills deserves her privacy at a time like this. Just tell me when. My plane will be there."

With his meticulous concern for detail, Tony had made sure that the ordinarily well-stocked bar of his limousine was empty for this particularly sensitive journey.

There was no need for Morse to instruct the chauffeur. Without a word, the large limousine pulled out of the airport and raced swiftly along a highway flanked on both sides by immense tracts of raw desert. Occasionally a garish billboard advertised some new condominium development.

Kitzi saw none of this, for she was in Morse's arms, her face pressed against his chest, her eyes shut tight to deny what awaited her.

The limousine passed a hospital complex with stately buildings of white stone and sun-proof amber glass, surrounded by green lawn and accented by tall palms precisely arranged. Once beyond the medical center, the limousine turned left past a white granite stanchion on which large bronze letters announced: The Retreat. The simple name had been chosen to avoid the stigma invoked by "Sanitorium" or "Clinic" or "Treatment Center."

The limousine proceeded slowly along the winding road toward a small complex of four white, one-story buildings, all with red-tiled roofs. Three were free-standing dormitories, each of which might have housed twenty college students instead of twenty addicted patients.

The fourth building was the Administration Hall. The limousine pulled to a stop there.

"Darling, we're here," Marvin announced softly.

Kitzi hesitated before pulling away from him to look out. When the chauffeur opened the door, the sudden flood of sunlight and hot desert air was a shock to her frail body.

"Okay, Kitz," Morse said, assisting her out of the limousine.

She stood beside the car, unsteady, and stared at the building, blinking as her eyes adjusted to the bright sunlight.

"Come on, honey." Morse started to lead her toward the entrance. She would not budge. "Kitz, you've come this far . . ." he started to plead.

She removed his hands from around her arms.

He was fearful that at the last moment she would refuse treatment. "Kitzi . . . you promised Alice . . ."

"God damn you," she said in a low, harsh voice, "stop using her to blackmail me. You son of a bitch, you're responsible for this. You've driven me, exploited me, forced me to work, lived off me for years. Like some . . . some pimp! You greedy bastard! You . . ." She groped for words of invective, finally exploding. "You . . . you fucking Jew!"

Even in her distraught state she was aware. At once she began to weep.

"Marvin . . . darling . . . No, I didn't mean . . . I don't know what I . . ."

He embraced her. "It's all right, Kitzi. I understand. This is a rough time."

Through her tears she said, "I've never said anything like that before, never even thought it. Honest, Marvin. Please say you forgive me. Say it?"

"Of course I forgive you. Now let me wipe your eyes. And stop crying. You've got an entrance to make. A very important entrance. You don't want to make it crying, do you?"

He used his silk pocket handkerchief to dab her eyes dry. She sniffled back her remaining tears but felt compelled to ask, "You do forgive me, don't you?"

"Of course. Now, come."

He put his arm around her to guide her to the door.

"I want to do this on my own," she said.

She freed herself and started for the door. When she overtook the chauffeur, who was carrying the single piece of luggage she had been instructed to bring, she took the bag from him to continue on toward the entrance. Alone.

She pushed open the tall, bleached-oak-and-glass door and stepped into the quiet reception area. At the front desk, she hesitated, then announced softly, "I'm Kitzi Mills. I think you're expecting me."

Marvin waited outside the Administration Building of The Retreat.

He watched through the amber-colored windows as Kitzi engaged in brief conversation with the receptionist. Saw her sign a document. Saw a male attendant take her bag and lead her away.

The chauffeur waited silently at Morse's side until Kitzi disappeared from view.

"Don't take any offense," the chauffeur said. Marvin looked at him, puzzled. The man explained, "She's not the first I've brought here. Just before they go in, most of them get scared, say all kinds of nasty things. It's their last chance to fight the treatment. She didn't mean it."

"I know," Marvin said. But the hurt was there. If he had loved her less it would not have been so painful.

"If you have the time, Mr. Frascati'd like you to spend the rest of the week at his compound. Said you could probably use it."

"I'd like to, but I have to get back to New York."

"His plane's heading back to New York early tomorrow, if you'd like to spend the night."

"Good idea. I could use a break," Marvin said.

He was shown to a small bungalow in the Frascati compound. There he found everything a man might need to spend a comfortable

11

night, or even a week. Robe, pajamas, swim trunks in all sizes, fresh shirts, light, colorful linen slacks, also in all sizes, razors of two types, electric and blade, toiletries from Dunhill, and, as always, unopened bottles of Johnny Walker Black, Jack Daniels, Tanqueray, and Absolut, with ice cubes, soda, tonic, sliced fresh lemons and limes.

He did not pause to have a drink but started for the main house. He found Tony in his soundproofed studio listening to his latest recording before approving its release. Frascati saw Morse, and gestured him to be seated while he continued to listen, his body rhythmically swaying to the music. Until something he heard disturbed him. He snapped his fingers impatiently and shut off the recording to make a note. Marvin Morse's ear had not detected any flaw, but evidently Frascati's had.

"Son of a bitch," he said softly to himself. "Why didn't I feel that when we cut it?" He finished making his note, then half-turned to Morse. "She get here all right?"

"Yes. I never could have gotten her to go on a regular passenger plane. Thanks."

"As long as she got here," Frascati said, embarrassed to be thanked. "Drink?"

"Not yet."

Frascati poured himself one. Straight Johnny Walker Black on the rocks. A waterglass full.

"Nice of you to do this. Especially for a woman you've never even met," Morse said.

"We did meet once. At a USO benefit in the Hollywood Bowl. She was on just before me. When she came off we passed in the wings. I grabbed her hand and said, 'Doll, you are great!' She looked up at me like a kid in a fan club, blushed, and asked, 'You really think so, Mr. Frascati?' "

"Shy. She was always really shy," Marvin said. "Yet she had confidence. From the very first day I saw her."

Frascati looked at him over the top of his glass. "You're in love with her."

"*Was,*" Morse protested, then admitted, "*am.* Always will be, I guess."

"Does she know?"

Marvin nodded.

"Tough," Frascati said.

"Tougher than you think," Morse said. "Once you've made love to her . . ." He did not complete the thought.

"I know the feeling," Frascati said. He took another swallow of Scotch. "Think she's going to make it?"

Morse shrugged.

"Half of them don't," Frascati warned.

"I've heard," Morse admitted grimly. Suddenly he exploded, "God, if I'd known, or even suspected, the day I first saw her. . . ."

He felt the need of that drink now. Frascati sensed it, poured for him.

"I never would have let her go into this lousy business! I would have taken her down to the bus station, put her on a bus back to Minnesota, and said, 'Go home, kid. Forget about show business. Even if you make it, it'll break your heart.' "

Tony smiled. "You think that would have done it? Once you've got that bug up your ass it won't let go. She'd have come back. Even if she did break her heart trying."

Morse nodded. He knew. He had handled too many young talents not to know. He held out his empty glass. Tony filled it again. They touched glasses and drank.

"That first day," Marvin Morse began. "That first day. . . ."

Part One

1

Oh, what a beauty she had been when, young, fresh, eager and keen-eyed, she first appeared in his office, asking for a chance. Only a chance.

She had been working as a waitress in order to afford acting, singing, and dancing lessons.

At the time, Marvin Morse had been a novice himself. Twenty-two. A mere kid, in Broadway talent agency terms. He had been just months out of City College when he started at the George Gordon Agency. They assigned him to the mailroom, delivering inter-office memos and scripts from one office to another. He was referred to as "boy" and "kid" and "hey, you." He did not mind. It gave him a chance to sneak looks at inter-office memos. To gossip with secretaries. To eavesdrop on agents' conversations. He learned how deals were made, then unmade, only to be improved. How clients were placated and sometimes double-crossed to the advantage of the Agency or more important clients.

Soon he was ready for the first important step up the ladder. Assistant to an agent. Usually it was a slow process, unless an act of God intervened. One did.

One of the triumvirate who ruled the New York office of the Agency was having an afternoon dalliance with a young, aspiring, untalented actress in his apartment at the Dorset Hotel on Fifty-fourth Street. In the midst of one enormous thrust, he lunged forward, sprawling across her young body. Unable to move or talk, though conscious and staring at the startled young woman, he could not explain or even gesture for help. She did not understand the catastrophe that had occurred. She only knew that, as far as her budding career was concerned, this was one wasted afternoon.

She did pay him the courtesy of phoning his secretary to suggest that someone look in on him at once. Then she dressed quickly and departed discreetly.

By the time word raced through the office, things were already in a state of change. A younger executive was moved up to fill the vacancy. The executive's assistant was made an active agent. And, as an agent, he needed an assistant. He chose to interview Marvin Morse, whom he referred to as "That nice-looking kid from the mailroom. What's his name? You know, the tall kid with the black, curly hair."

Young Marvin Morse was prepared for his crucial interview by Sarah Blinkhorn. A woman in her early sixties, small, seemingly frail, gray-haired, neatly dressed, Sarah had the endurance of a marathon runner.

She had been with the Agency for more than thirty years. In terms of service, corporate know-how, and intimate gossip, no one at George Morrison outranked her.

On the day Marvin Morse had his interview for the position of assistant to Irwin Fleischman, old Sarah Blinkhorn took him aside.

"Marvin, I talk to you like only your mother would. You go in there. Be polite without groveling. Be interested without appearing anxious. Listen a lot. Say very little. Don't admit to any lofty ambitions. Fleischman suspects anyone with big ambitions."

Marvin got the job.

Near the end of his second year as Fleischman's assistant, Marvin was promoted to the rank of agent and transferred to the Talent Department, which meant that he would represent actors and actresses for Broadway shows, summer theaters, and what little television was still being done in the East.

He was given his own private office—small, windowless, but his own. And his own secretary, who would sit just outside his cubbyhole. He requested Sarah Blinkhorn. His choice surprised Management. But since at the moment Sarah was not attached to any specific job, Marvin was permitted to have her.

At first he regretted his decision. There was hardly a move he made that old Sarah did not comment upon or criticize. When he sent a young actor over to a producer's office for an audition, Sarah would stand in his doorway and shake her graying head. Ever so subtly, but making very sure Marvin noticed.

"Okay, Sarah, what did I do wrong this time?"

"Abe Furstburgh didn't get to be president of the George Gordon Agency this way. He would never have sent that young man."

"Yeah? And why not?" Marvin would challenge.

"Because, sonny, he is not a Whitehead-Stevens type. Terry Fay won't like him."

"So who should I have sent?" Marvin would ask sarcastically.

"You know that young Hale Sanderson? He's the one."

The damned trouble, Marvin eventually learned, was that Sarah was almost always right. Through his own enterprise and energy, combined with Sarah's know-how, he slowly built his career.

In less than six months he was promoted to an office with a window. Sarah was given a large outer office.

On that day, that first day he ever saw Kitzi Mills, Sarah had waited anxiously for Marvin to return from a business lunch at Joe Allen's. She drew him aside so as not to be overheard in his inner office.

"Marvin, there is a girl in your office. I don't know what her name is—Katherine something—but she has that look."

"Look?"

"Hepburn had it when I first saw her. Barbara Bel Geddes when she was only seventeen. Jean Arthur——"

"Talk about yesterday's mashed potatoes—" Marvin tried to interrupt. Sarah seized him by the chin. "Shmuck, listen to me! Go in there. See for yourself. But don't let that girl get away without signing her up."

Sarah was straightening his tie, hand combing his curly hair as she said, "Just promise me one thing—you won't fall in love with her."

"What kind of crazy thing is that to say?"

"She is the girl that every Jewish mother warns her son not to bring home else she will kill herself," Sarah said before she stood aside to let him enter his own office.

At a single glance, Marvin Morse knew exactly what Sarah meant.

Seated alongside his desk was a girl he judged to be no more than nineteen. Blond hair hung loose down her back. When she turned to face him, he found that her hair framed a face which was pale and delicately shaped. *Angelic,* was his first and instant thought.

She was angelic—slender, beautiful. He revised his estimate. Very young—seventeen. No more.

She rose quickly, as if she had trespassed upon his office by sitting. She was somewhat taller than he had anticipated, but she filled her jeans nicely, so he knew she had good, strong legs.

"Marvin Morse?" she asked. "Are you he?"

"Yes," he said, echoing her words, "I am *he.*"

He smiled. She smiled shyly, apologizing. "Back in Minnesota I won a speech contest. Because I talk that way naturally, I guess."

"You're from Minnesota, are you?"

"Yes."

"And you've come to the Big Apple to become a star on Broadway," he chided in friendly fashion. "You realize you're not alone. There are thousands of you. All working tables at Jackson Hole and O'Neals. Just waiting for that one big break. Which, for most, will never come. You're aware of the odds, aren't you?"

She drew herself up a bit taller and straighter.

Regal, Marvin Morse said to himself. *She has a regal carriage that reminds me of some British actresses I've seen. Maggie Smith. Vanessa Redgrave.*

"Mr. Morse," she responded, "those odds do not include me."

"Really? Okay. Convince me," Marvin challenged. "I'm a producer. You've come for a reading. Show me this unusual quality you're so sure you have."

She rose from her chair, went to a corner of the room, and faced the wall. Minutes later she turned back to him. The intensity in her eyes made everything else fade into the background. She was no longer a young girl dressed in jeans and denim shirt. No longer with flowing blond hair. Her face was neither pretty nor soft. It was all eyes, blue eyes, but eyes of steel. From her small, perfectly shaped mouth came a voice of such power that it filled the room and seemed to echo as she began the speech of Lady Macbeth, come straight from the bedchamber of Duncan. She pretended to wash her hands with such passion that Marvin could almost see the blood on them.

Not until she had finished was he aware that he had held his breath throughout the entire speech. His first thought was one of regret. *Where, in the American theater as it exists today, is there room for such a talent? Who writes such parts? Worse, in these times, who gets to be a star playing the classics?*

Out of embarrassment for lack of something appropriate to say, his first words were, "You never told me your name."

"Katherine Millendorfer."

He smiled. She smiled in return, her eyes once again that soft, warm, friendly blue.

"I know," she admitted. "It won't exactly fit over the marquee of the Music Box Theatre, will it?"

"Or even on the Radio City Music Hall," he joked. "How about instead of Millendorfer, say, Mills? Katherine Mills. How's that?"

She hesitated a moment, then nodded. He found himself staring and had to break the moment. "What do *I* call you? I mean, what do people call you who are close to you?"

"My grandfather . . . he used to call me Kitzi. Said I was his little kitten."

"Kitzi Mills . . ." Marvin considered slowly. "I like that."

He found himself staring again, and smiling.

"Something funny?" she asked.

He could not tell her that he was thinking of Sarah Blinkhorn's last caution: "She is the girl every Jewish mother warns her son not to bring home, else she will kill herself."

Instead, he said, "I was just thinking. It might sound a little odd . . . 'Macbeth, starring Kitzi Mills.' Doesn't quite go together, does it?"

"Oh, I don't intend to do Shakespeare. Musical comedy."

"You sing?"

"And dance."

"As well as you act?"

"Better," she said.

He contemplated asking her to audition her singing ability, but, considering the power of her voice, he decided not to.

"Do you have a demo of your singing?"

She shrugged her shoulders and shook her head.

"Too bad. They're casting a new musical titled *Oddities.* The part of the ingenue is still open. But the director is a cockeyed genius who says hc has no time to waste. So his assistant weeds out the impossibles by listening to their demos."

"Is it a good part?" she asked.

"Very good. A stepping stone to a big future. You know, since Streisand, we haven't had a really talented new musical comedy star."

"And it takes a demo? Damn!" she said in obvious frustration. "I have one. But it's in my luggage."

"Where's your luggage? Let's go get it," he said, not catching on.

"Can't. Lost by the airline. I came in Tuesday night and they still haven't found my bag."

"Hell!" he said, defeated. But a moment later he said, "Wait a minute . . . just one little minute." He reached for his phone, drummed his fingers on it before deciding. "First we've got to find out . . ." He lifted the phone. "Sarah, get me Stash Burkowski in John Firestone's office."

"Stash Burkowski—— What for?"

"Just get him!" Marvin insisted.

"Marv, don't do anything rash just because she's a pretty girl."

"Get him!" Marvin said more firmly.

"Okay, okay," Sarah agreed reluctantly. "Just dor't get engaged or married before I get him. I never should have had that girl wait, *ne-ver.* "

In moments, Sarah buzzed back. "Marv, I've got Burkowski on the line. But before you pick up, I beg you, don't do anything foolish. There are lots of pretty girls but very few direct contacts to Jock English."

"Okay, *Mother,* just put him on!" Marvin said impatiently. "Stash? Marvin Morse, the Gordon office. Stash, I have an unusual situation here. I was hoping you might help *me* at the same time I help *you.* You see, I have this girl sitting in my office. Just flew in to audition for Jock."

Before Burkowski could interrupt, Marvin anticipated him. "I know, I know, Stash. 'Send over the demo.' "

Katherine shrugged in a gesture of hopelessness, but Marvin Morse held up his free hand to reassure her as he continued, "Stash, that's the problem. You know these screwed-up airlines. They lost her luggage. And her demo's in the luggage."

"Jock won't make a decision till the end of the week," Burkowski said. "By that time her luggage should be here. Right?"

"Right," Marvin had to agree, virtually admitting defeat, until an impulse overtook him. *I can't let this chance go down the drain, not for this girl.* "Stash, she can't wait till the end of the week," he improvised.

"Everybody waits for Jock English." Stash was incensed now.

"Stash, Stash, cool it. No disrespect to Jock. But she has no choice."

"Why not? If she wants the part."

Marvin brought the phone even closer to his lips. He spoke as if imparting a secret of consequence to the nation's security. "Stash . . . don't breathe a word of this. If the office knew I was telling you, they'd kill me. She's in New York on her way to London. They've sent for her to audition for a revival of *No, No, Nanette.* "

"They sent for her?" Stash asked, impressed. "Paid her way?"

"You don't think she'd pay her own way, do you?"

"No, no, of course not."

"Stash, I tell you now, if she goes to London they won't let her come back. So if Jock wants to hear something very special, he better break his rule this one time. Otherwise she'll be gone before that demo shows up."

"I'll talk to Jock and call you back."

Marvin Morse hung up his phone and realized he was sweating. Jock English was one of the Agency's most important clients. If this bit of perfidy became known, well, young agents had been fired for much less.

They stared at each other. Marvin Morse. And Katherine Millendorfer.

Finally she said, "I appreciate what you just did for me."

"I haven't done anything yet."

"You lie very well," she said. "He believed you."

"We'll see how *much* he believed me," Marvin replied.

The wait seemed endless. He continued to sweat.

He stared at her. God, she was beautiful. And that hair. He resorted to another hackneyed phrase: *Spun gold.* It fit this girl as it fit no woman he had ever seen.

Finally his phone rang. Sarah was on. Her doom-filled voice conveyed the best news Marvin Morse would hear that entire year.

"Stash called. Be backstage at the Imperial at four o'clock. And bring the girl."

"Thanks, Sarah, thanks a million," he said with great relief.

"I hope you know what you're doing, *boychick,*" Sarah said skeptically.

2

Marvin Morse and Kitzi Mills waited in a corner of the dimly lit stage of the Imperial. The single worklight barely illuminated center stage. *Hell,* Marvin thought, *if English could see her in a decent light, that would be half the battle.*

Marvin reached for her hand. His was cold. Hers was warm. *Christ, at least she could share my nervousness.*

She walked to center stage, cast a glance at the position of the worklight, a naked bulb atop an iron skeleton that rose from its tripod, then she moved forward to be abreast of it.

Good, he thought, *she's making the most of the light. It brings out that face, that beautiful face. Now, I hope to God she really can sing.*

Peering into the dark theater, she asked, "What would you like to hear?"

"What do you do best?" the voice of Jock English came back from that darkness.

Without an instant's pause, she replied, "Ballad. Rock. Punk. Everything. What are you looking for, Mr. English?"

"I'll settle for rhythm," he said, deliberately choosing a form she had not mentioned.

"Gershwin? Styne? Hamlisch?" she countered.

Christ, Marvin Morse wanted to cry out, *don't play games with*

*him. He loves that. Because in the end he's the boss. He wins, you
lose! So stop fencing and start singing.*

"Bacharach," English called out.

As confidently as if she had auditioned for a hundred shows and
won a hundred roles, Katherine Millendorfer, from Minnesota, half-
turned to the young man at the piano. " 'What Do You Get When
You Fall in Love?' Key of C."

The pianist played an intro of a few bars, then threw her a head
cue. She turned front and center and began to sing.

Her voice filled the empty house. By the fourth bar, she and the
accompanist had begun to play to each other. The young man's face
lit up. She glanced over at him. He smiled, nodded, as if to say,
"You're on a roll, kid!"

Marvin Morse thought, *Whatever sacrifice she had to make to pay
for those lessons, it was worth it.*

When she finished, there was a moment of silence before the
judgment from on high would be rendered.

Marvin Morse held his breath. What would it be? The usual curt
"Thank you very much." Or "Very nice. We'll get back to you,"
when they never intended to. Or the bare truth. "Sorry, but you're
not quite the type we had in mind."

After an eternity of some twenty seconds, English's voice came
out of the darkness.

"What have you done before, my dear?"

To Marvin, "my dear," delivered as it was with a touch of sarcasm,
was the preamble to one of Jock English's famous sadistic turn-
downs. He had crushed many budding young talents, and some older
ones as well, with his biting criticism.

Young Katherine Millendorfer moved downstage to address the
invisible director.

"Annie Get Your Gun, Promises, Promises, and *On Your Toes,"*
she said.

"And what role did you play in *Annie Get Your Gun?"* the voice
came back.

"Annie," she replied forthrightly.

"You?" English called out. "You, at your age, played Annie?
Where?"

Without pause, the girl announced, "Waukesha."

"Where's that?" the voice came back.

"Minnesota," she replied.

"I know every fucking summer theater in this country! There's no summer theater in Waukesha!" English exploded, incensed that a young upstart actress would attempt to deceive him.

"Waukesha High School," she corrected.

Marvin Morse's stomach not only shrank, it puckered. *There goes my job. English bawls the hell out of Nat Cohn for having on his staff an agent either young enough or stupid enough to try to pull a fast one on Jock English. A high school–sized talent for the ingenue role in a Broadway musical. Sarah! How right you were!*

"Waukesha High School," Jock English repeated. He burst out laughing.

"Come on, kid, let's get the hell out of here, Marvin Morse urged silently, *before this gets any worse.*

But the young actress edged down to the very apron of the stage, peered into the darkness, and asked, "Where did *you* start, Mr. English? At the Met? At Lincoln Center? Or at the Imperial Theatre?"

Her challenge cut short all laughter. The young pianist sat up stiffly, expecting one of Jock English's notorious rages.

There was whispered conversation out in the dark, empty house. Marvin Morse took the opportunity to call softly, "Let's go, Katherine."

"Young woman, don't you move!" came the command from the dark.

They heard footsteps come down the carpeted aisle. Jock English finally climbed into view. Even in the dim glow of the worklight he was striking.

Tall, thin, totally bald, bereft of all facial hair, he looked odd, but imposing. His penetrating black eyes reflected his innate impatience with everything but his own desires and demands and, above all, his own success. Those eyes could embrace people or dismiss them at a glance.

Born Jacob Englander, in the Bronx, he had since developed many affectations that gave credence to his assumed name. Today, he wore a khaki bush jacket, slacks to match, and tan suede combat boots. He seemed better outfitted for a safari than a Broadway audition.

English drew close to Katherine Millendorfer. He circled her with condescending contempt, smiled, and shook his head, as if despairing. But the girl continued to hold herself stiffly erect and proud.

"Well now, you want to know where *I* started. Okay, I shall tell you. I started at James Monroe High School. In a skit written by George Kaufman. Of course, you wouldn't know who George Kaufman was. Your generation doesn't know very much about anything, especially the theater.

"The skit was *If Men Played Cards as Women Do.* Very funny. At least when I got done with it it was funny. I had to direct myself. Our idiot dramatics club teacher didn't know her ass from her elbow. That's when I realized I'm not really an actor, I'm a director. And, as always, I was right."

He chuckled, and drew his long, delicate fingers over his beardless face. As he circled her once more, she refused to be cowed and stood even taller. Her beautiful face, with its chiseled features, grew in defiance and strength.

Marvin Morse watched silently. *Give in. Let the bastard think he's intimidated you. He won't give up until you do.*

Still she would not relent.

"So," English resumed, "Waukesha's loss is Broadway's gain. And it seems I'm to have first crack at it. We know you sing. What else do you do?"

"Act," she said.

"Oh." He glanced out into the dark house. "Did you hear, Stash, not only sings but acts. "Okay, so *act!*"

There is no worse cue for an actor or actress, even one with years of professional experience.

But there was a limit to the cruelty that Marvin Morse would allow even Jock English to inflict on any performer. He stepped forward. "Katherine, you don't have to put up with this! Let's go!"

English turned on him. "You shut up!" He turned back to the girl. "I said *act!*" He jumped off the stage to rejoin his assistant back in the darkness.

Katherine Millendorfer started upstage to face the bare brick wall.

She hunched over, clasped her hands between her thighs, closed her eyes, and stood that way for several minutes, which seemed like an eternity to Marvin.

Finally, she turned downstage and began to speak lines from the final scene of a play in which she was not a girl of seventeen but a woman in control of her life for the first time.

She was firm and decisive as she began, " 'I was your little skylark, Torvald. No, your doll, which you would in future treat with doubly gentle care, because it was so brittle and fragile.' "

Jock English had directed Ibsen's *Doll's House* in four different productions. He knew the lines. Drawn by her performance, he slowly moved down the aisle until he stood at the foot of the stage.

" 'Torvald, it was then it dawned on me that for eight years I had been living here with a strange man, and had borne him three children. Oh, I can't bear to think of it! I could tear myself into little bits.' "

To Marvin's surprise, English replied with the next lines from the play.

" 'An abyss has opened between us, there is no denying it. But, Nora, would it not be possible to fill it up?' "

English reached up for her hand, but Katherine drew back. " 'As I am now, I am no wife for you.' "

" 'I have it in me to become a different man,' " English responded.

" '*Perhaps,*' " she replied, " 'if your doll is taken away from you.' " Then, deliberately skipping some lines to accelerate the tempo of the scene, she pretended to slip a wedding ring from her finger as she said, " 'Here is your ring back. Give me mine.' "

" 'That too?' " English responded.

" 'That too,' " Katherine said.

English performed the gesture of handing up his own wedding ring. As she pretended to take it, she continued, " 'Now it is all over. I have put the house keys here. The maids know all about everything in the house—better than I do. Tomorrow, Christine will come here and pack my own things that I brought with me from my father's house. I will have them sent after me.' "

" 'May I write you, Nora?' "

" 'No, never. You must not do that.' "

" 'But at least let me send you . . .' "

She interrupted as the lines were written, " 'Nothing . . . nothing.' "

" 'Let me help you if you are in want,' " English continued.

" 'No. I can receive nothing from a stranger.' " She turned from him.

English reached up to stage level to catch her hand. " 'Can I never be anything more than a stranger to you?' "

She stared down at him. " 'Ah, Torvald, the most wonderful thing of all would have to happen. Both you and I would have to be so changed that . . . No, Torvald, I don't believe any longer in wonderful things happening.' "

She withdrew her hand from his grasp, started toward the wings, and gracefully disappeared offstage as English, taken with her total believability, concluded the scene with his own lines, " 'Nora! Nora? Empty. She is gone. Gone. . . .' "

They were walking east on Forty-fifth Street toward the George Gordon office on the Avenue of the Americas when Marvin said, "It's a miracle, that's what it is, a miracle."

"What?" Katherine asked.

"You walking into my office out of the blue that way."

"Maybe," she said softly.

The way she said it made him stop and look into her blue eyes. She returned his gaze. "My grandfather . . . he brought me up . . . he was a minister. After everything I've seen I don't believe in miracles."

"After today, even you have to believe," Marvin insisted.

"Would it change things for you if it wasn't a miracle?" she asked.

"When a girl I've never seen before walks into my office at two o'clock, and by four o'clock is in a big musical like Oddities, that is a miracle, young woman," he insisted.

"You've seen me before," she said.

"Impossible. I'd never forget a face like yours."

They both stopped. He had not intended to make such a frank declaration of his feelings.

"But you did. See me. Before."

29

"When?"

"Today," she said.

"Today?" He was confused. "I saw you today? Before we met in my office? Where?"

"Where you had lunch," she said.

"I saw you in Joe Allen's and never noticed? I don't believe it," he said.

"You were at a table for two. With a man about your age. He had red hair, wiry red hair. Not particularly handsome. Homely, in fact."

"Jules Berkowitz. Another agent in the office. You noticed us?"

"Yes. But you didn't notice me. You were both too busy talking about the part of the ingenue in *Oddities*. About how impossible it was to get an audition with Jock English without a demo."

"You were close enough to hear that and I never noticed you?"

"You ordered a hamburger. Charred. Then you joked that it was from being brought up in a kosher home. You said, 'Kosher meat shouldn't bleed.'"

"How could you possibly know that?"

"I took your order," she said.

He looked into her face to find her blue eyes dancing with delight at his surprise.

"You took . . . no, can't be. I distinctly remember when I paid the check I gave my credit card to a man, a young man."

"Of course. Because by that time I was on my way to your office to be there before you got back."

He shook his head in amused disbelief and took her hand. They had not walked more than three steps when he stopped suddenly.

"Hey, wait a minute! That whole story about your demo being lost in your luggage . . ."

Her smile admitted everything.

"A lie? A complete fabrication?"

She nodded.

"Man, you are something," he said.

"What about that trip to London to audition for the production over there?" she countered. "What would you call that?"

"Agents are supposed to lie," Marvin protested.

"So it wasn't exactly a miracle."

"I guess not," he agreed.

Standing there, hand in hand, in the midst of the traffic on the corner of Forty-fifth Street and the Avenue of the Americas, he said, "I have a feeling we're going places together. The two of us."

The details of Kitzi Mills's contract were settled before the end of the day. Later, English complained bitterly to Nat Cohn. "That smart-ass young agent you sent over with her, keep your eye on him. Too shrewd. Just when I was becoming interested he urged her to leave. Son of a bitch read my mind. He was already prepared to up her price. Well, I have to admit, it worked. He tricked me. Next time you come up with a find like that girl, send some other agent along to represent her."

The very next week Marvin was given a twenty-five-dollar-a-week raise. And he was appointed to handle Kitzi Mills exclusively.

3

Through the weeks of rehearsal of *Oddities,* Kitzi Mills was so busy that she had little time for anything else. Her day was precisely choreographed. Rehearsal of the book of the show with the principals, Lanny Everett and Edie Cullen in the morning. Dance rehearsals with the chorus at the studio over on Seventh Avenue after lunch. And then, before dinner, lessons from a vocal coach Jock had selected.

It seemed to her that she was always gathering up her things in her canvas carryall and racing from one studio to the next, ungathering her things, gathering them up again, and hurrying on. When the day was done she could barely drag herself back to her furnished room and collapse onto her bed.

Then, at around nine, her phone would ring. Marvin would always ask, "Up to going out for some supper?"

Sometimes she was; most times he would bring sandwiches. They would eat in her room and talk over her day. She was so excited that eating seemed unnecessary. For her, each day was a succession of new adventures and new discoveries.

The first time she had a scene alone with Lanny Everett. The first time she did a complete run-through of her dance numbers with the chorus line. Her coach, Boots Ryan, had actually kissed her and told her she was great.

The most important day of all was when Jock English listened to her two songs in the show. He was so delighted that he said to the composer and the lyricist, "She's fine. Just fine. We could use another number for her." Extravagant praise from a man as demanding as Jock English.

Each night, Marvin Morse would watch her, in awe of her beauty as she related the events of her day. He admired her intensity, her beauty, and the way her confidence increased from day to day as she conquered the role and grew comfortable with each part of her role. This was what she had wanted to do ever since she could remember. Now she was doing it. All, thanks to Marvin. In her more enthusiastic moments she would kiss him in gratitude.

Except for one time.

The night she sang for him the new song Jock English had had written especially for her. It was a ballad, a love song.

"During the show I'm secretly in love with Lanny Everett. But I don't dare tell him because my mother's planning to marry him."

Marvin smiled. "Kitzi, I know. I think I know your lines even better than you do. I've heard them so often. Get to the song."

"Well, the way Jock explained it, I'll do this new number in one, all by myself out on stage with just a spotlight on me. Because it's a confession so secret I wouldn't dare make it to anyone else."

"Kitzi, darling, just do the song," Marvin pleaded.

Without any accompaniment, she began to sing. The sparsely furnished rented room on West Forty-ninth Street gradually became her stage. Her voice, strong when it had to be, was now soft and wistful as she confessed her secret love.

At the conclusion, she sank to the floor, slowly, gracefully. He knew that when she did that in front of an audience, there would be a moment of stunned silence before they burst into ecstatic applause.

He stared down at her, she up at him. He reached out to lift her to her feet.

"Kitzi, what 'My Heart Belongs to Daddy' did for Mary Martin, this song is going to do for you."

"Is that all?"

"Isn't that enough?" he asked, puzzled.

"Don't the lyrics *mean* anything to you?"

"They're lovely. Touching. Everybody in this world has had a secret love that for one reason or another they couldn't express to the person they were in love with. That's the charm of the song."

"Marvin, I was singing it to you," she admitted softly.

"Oh, God," he said, expressing in those two words all the difficulties that he was about to admit to himself. "Kitzi, what I'm about to say you're only going to hear once. Then I want you to forget it."

He took both her hands in his.

"I have been in love with you ever since I first saw you. Why do you think I sneak into the theater to watch you rehearse? And when you're rehearsing your dance numbers, are you aware that I stand outside the studio door and peek in through the little glass triangle to watch you? Or that I waylay the stage manager every evening to ask how your rehearsal went? Because I love you. And I always will."

"You want me to forget that?" she asked. "Why?"

"There are reasons. Lots of them."

"Like what?" she asked.

"Business reasons. Agents and clients should never become involved," he said evasively. "Other reasons."

"Name them," she insisted.

Before he could, she kissed him full on the lips. Her open mouth invited his tongue. She enveloped him with her arms, then with her legs. She drew him into her with a fierce hunger. At the instant of entering her, he was startled to discover that she was a virgin. In the passion of her embrace he did not consider why, but he feverishly explored every part of her tantalizing body.

Afterwards, she lay in his arms, spent, panting, but refusing to let him free. She held him tight to her and in her and kept whispering, not to him but to herself, "So this is how it feels . . . really feels . . . really feels. . . ."

* * *

It could not remain a secret. Certainly not from Sarah Blinkhorn.

The next morning when he came into the office, Sarah remarked, "A little late today, aren't we?"

"I overslept."

"Where?" she asked.

He ignored her question.

"Sarah, I've got a lot to catch up on. I want to get ahead on some projects so I can go out of town for two days over the weekend."

"We're going out of town for the opening, are we?"

He wished she would stop using "we" when she meant him.

"Sarah! I have a client who may have a great future, which can mean big bucks to this agency. It is important for me to see how she does in her first professional opportunity."

"I know," Sarah said. "I've seen it happen. I remember the time Carl Horowitz went out of town to 'see' a young star named Anne Foster. A pretty, blond, talented young singer in a Ziegfeld show. Only she wound up pregnant, and he wound up kicked out by Abe Furstburgh. Watch yourself, kiddo."

"I don't know what you're talking about," Marvin said.

"Don't you?" Sarah challenged, as she closed the door so they would not be overheard.

"Sarah, please, today no lectures."

"I've seen it too many times. Agents falling in love with their clients. Always for some damn reason it is a nice Jewish boy falling for a blond shiksa."

"Sarah, let's leave that lecture to my mother," Marvin said.

"Mark my words. This can come to no good, Marvie. The girl is a talent? Okay. Be her agent. Make her a star. But don't ruin her life and yours!"

"Sarah——" he remonstrated.

"I've seen it. Too many times," she warned.

"Sarah!"

"So, shall I make a reservation for you in Boston?" she asked.

"Book me at the Ritz——"

"——with the rest of the cast of course," Sarah concluded pointedly.

* * *

His first impression of the Ritz in Boston was that everyone in the lobby seemed to whisper. He checked in and was given the key to a room on the eighth floor. Before he could ask which room Miss Mills was in, a bellman had taken his bags, and he was on his way to the elevator. There he experienced his second lasting impression of the Ritz.

The elevators were perfumed.

He was unpacking when he heard the door of the next room open and close. He continued unpacking until he heard Kitzi's voice. Then he pressed his ear against the wall and heard her singing her love ballad. She interrupted herself to correct her phrasing of the lyrics, then continued. Just back from rehearsal, she was again rehearsing.

He continued listening, delighted with her voice, her feel for the lyrics, everything. When she was done, he slipped out of his room and knocked on her door.

"Who is it?" she called.

"Room service,"

"I didn't order room . . .," she began to protest. Then, recognizing his voice, she flung open the door. They embraced. They held each other so closely, so tightly, that each could feel the other's heart beat. She drew him into the room and closed the door. They were two young lovers with a single compulsion—to belong to one another. There seemed no end to their passion. One act of love led to another. And another.

The Shubert Theatre was in the usual turmoil that prevails before the first full dress rehearsal of a musical out of town. It is the first time everything comes together—sets, staging, costume changes, music, dialogue, and dance cues.

Jock English was his most sadistic on such days. With *Oddities,* it was no different. The lighting designer, a slight, dark-haired woman, was at his side taking notes as they ran through the light cues. The set designer was torn between listening to English and shouting instructions to his own crew. The production secretary followed English, notebook in hand, jotting down all his orders and suggestions. The young man who had designed the costumes was off in a corner of the theater conferring with his assistant.

Marvin sat in the back row of the orchestra section on the aisle and watched.

The producer, John Firestone, a lanky man in his late fifties with a shuffling walk, made his way down the center aisle, intending to impart a few very quiet suggestions to Jock English. Before the older man could even begin, English exploded. "If there is one thing I don't need right now, it is any advice from any fucking real estate magnate! Get out of this theater! Unless you want *me* to walk out!"

Firestone retreated up the aisle to stand alongside Marvin.

When he became aware of Marvin in the darkness, he asked, "Who are you? What are you doing here?"

"I'm Kitzi Mills's agent. Marvin Morse, George Gordon Agency."

"Oh. Morse. Yeah. I heard about you. You make sharp deals," the producer said, recalling the terms Marvin had insisted on for Kitzi, playing her first role in a Broadway-bound show.

"She's worth it, Mr. Firestone. Every penny of it. She's going to be a star."

Accustomed to the extravagant claims of agents, Firestone replied, "We'll find out soon enough."

They had reached the moment in rehearsal when Kitzi came out and downstage to open the second act with her new solo.

She was five bars into it when suddenly Jock English interrupted in a rage. "Where is that bastard designer? Neil! Neil Angstrom! Forget your little boyfriend and get over here!"

The orchestra stopped playing. The technicians who had been tinkering with the sets stopped working. The dancers stopped stretching and limbering up. In the wings, Edith Cullen and Lanny Everett ceased running the lines of their next scene.

Neil Angstrom, who had won two Tonys in the past three years, confronted English in the center aisle. Very softly in deliberate contrast to English's fury, Angstrom asked, "Something wrong, Jock?"

"Something wrong?" the director bellowed, even more incensed since the designer had upstaged him with his mild question. "There isn't a stagehand or chorus boy in this theater who couldn't tell you what is wrong."

"Well, perhaps I should ask one of the stagehands," Neil Angstrom said, again softly, tongue in cheek. As he pretended to move toward the stage, Jock English seized him by the arm of his jacket.

"Angstrom, are you trying to louse up our most important number? Ruin the one song that will emerge as a hit no matter what happens to this whole goddamned production? Or are you just trying to destroy me?"

"Don't tempt me," Angstrom said, refusing to cower.

English was about to strike the smaller man when both Firestone and Marvin raced down the aisle to intervene. Marvin threw his arms around English to hold him in check. English struggled and shouted across Marvin's shoulder at Angstrom.

Meantime, Firestone tried to usher the designer down the aisle and out into the alley.

"Please, Neil, Jock's under terrific pressure," Firestone cautioned. "You know how it is, trying to put a big musical together. Do me a favor. Wait until he cools down."

"I've tried . . . damn it, Mr. Firestone, I tried to satisfy every crazy idea of his and now . . ."

"I never approved that color for Kitzi's dress in her big number!" English shouted from inside. "The most important moment in the show, and every woman in the audience will be thinking, 'God, what a ghastly color!' "

Jock English had finally verbalized the source of his abusive explosion.

In the wings, the two leads, Lanny Everett and Edie Cullen, had remained silent until Everett whispered, "That prick would beat his own mother for kicks."

"Yeah," Edie Cullen appeared to agree, though actually she was nursing her own private and angry thoughts.

The crisis between Jock English and young Angstrom was resolved when the designer agreed to dip-dye Kitzi's costume for the next night's preview and then design a new one for her before the New York opening.

Edie Cullen's anger was not so easily appeased, however.

That bastard Jock English, she fumed silently. *Twice in his tirade he had the nerve to call Kitzi Mills's solo the most important number in the show. My show! Well, I'll teach that son of a bitch!*

4

The first preview of *Oddities* was scheduled for Saturday night. Everyone in the theater was tense and under great pressure. A first paid performance is always the test of a show's ability to entertain, hold, and satisfy. As John Firestone was always sure to remark, "This is the night the show loses its virginity. You either love yourself or hate yourself in the morning."

To Marvin Morse, there was only one important moment in *Oddities*—Kitzi's big solo. He fidgeted through the first half of the preview, listening only casually to the response of the audience, their laughter, their applause, their silences, all of which were noted by Jock English through whispered observations to his production secretary.

Finally it was time for the second act. The stage remained dark. The curtain did not rise. A spotlight hit the right wing of the stage. Kitzi Mills peeked out, her blue eyes shining. She surveyed the empty stage, looked out at the audience to invite them into her confidence, and began to sing.

At the back of the house, John Firestone whispered to Marvin, "Not since Julie Andrews in *My Fair Lady*. The same clean, honest voice. And her phrasing. Marvelous. Marvelous."

On her last five bars, Kitzi sank gracefully to the stage floor. The follow spot irised down to complete darkness. For an instant the audience remained silent. Then there was such an outburst of applause that it was impossible for the conductor to give the orchestra its next downbeat. Kitzi, who had slipped offstage in the darkness, was forced to return for another bow.

From his seat in one of the back rows, Jock English whispered to his production secretary, "Make a note. Got to give her an encore."

The orchestra segued into the next scene. Lanny Everett and Edie Cullen came on but during their dialogue the audience was notice-

38

ably restless. To make matters worse, Edie Cullen heard sporadic coughing. Jock English whispered frantic notes to his secretary—the entire scene would have to be rethought, rewritten. But that's what previews in Boston are for.

The rest of the show moved along, some scenes playing better than anticipated, others less so. Finally the curtain came down. When the audience had departed, the house lights came up. Carpenters, set dressers, electricians, lighting crew jumped to repair details they had noticed were wrong during the performance. Exhausted, the cast relaxed. Some members dropped into seats in the first row of the orchestra. Some lounged on pieces of stage furniture which had already been draped with dustcloths to protect them. Others lay on the stage floor, stretching to limber up after the tension of a first preview. After a hasty conference with Jock English, Stash Burkowski came down the aisle.

"All right, everybody! Clear stage. Only the cast will remain. Mr. English has some notes!"

After they assembled, Jock English strode onstage. He looked over his cast. "Well now, we've had our first plunge into the icy water. And what have we learned? We're pretty good. They actually liked us. All we need to do now is rewrite the script, redirect the dances, bring some life into the score, act the hell out of this piece, and we might—I say might—have a shot! But without all that we are dead. D–e–a–d. Dead! I have notes for all of you. Lots of notes. But we will start with the lull in the early part of the second act. Edie, my love—"

For the first time, he realized that Edie Cullen was not onstage. "Where is she? Someone fetch Miss Cullen! At once!"

A member of the chorus raced to the wings. In a moment there was agitated whispering offstage. Finally Isabella Sorrentino came waddling onstage. The heavyset Italian woman had been Edie Cullen's dresser in every show she had starred in for the past twenty-six years.

Jock English demanded, "Where is she? Or isn't she feeling well? It wouldn't surprise me, the way she performed tonight."

"She's in her dressing room."

"Doing what?"

39

"Packing! We are going back to New York tonight." With that, the woman waddled off.

For a moment, Jock English was speechless. John Firestone leaped up from his seat in the first row. Marvin Morse did not dare move, but he felt a sudden cold hand grip his stomach. Kitzi's big opportunity to become a star was suddenly endangered, possibly destroyed.

Firestone climbed the three-step rehearsal stairway to the stage. He beckoned Jock English to follow him.

"We'd better talk to her."

When Firestone knocked on her door, Edie Cullen was indeed packing.

"Edie? Darling? John. I'd like a word with you."

"I am not interested in talking. Only walking. Out of this theater. Out of this town."

"Believe me, darling, I won't stop you. I just want to talk to you."

Edie Cullen pretended to reconsider. In a moment she called, "Okay, John." They heard her door being unlocked. She peered out, caught a glimpse of Jock English, and shrieked, "Not him! I don't want to see that bald-headed monster ever again!"

With a single glance Firestone warned English aside. He entered the room alone. He took Edie's hand, kissed her on the cheek. Jock and Marvin remained outside the closed door, listening.

"Darling, you tell John what's wrong and I'll see that it's set right." Edie remained silent. "What is it? Your first scene in the second act? The writers are at work on it right now. You'll have new dialogue for tomorrow's rehearsal, and we'll put it in tomorrow night. Okay?"

"The trouble isn't in *that* scene," she said, as she withdrew her hand from Firestone's. "It's in the scene before."

"Edie, darling, that song is one of the big moments in the show. It gets the second act off to a terrific start," Firestone pointed out.

"It stops the action dead," she contradicted. "Then I have to come on and try to lift the fucking show off the floor and get it moving again."

"I'll talk to Jock. He'll do something about it," Firestone promised.

"That bald vulture! He planned it all along! I'm the star of this show! And he had that number written especially for her because he's probably screwing her every goddamn night!"

"Believe me, Edie, there's nothing going on between them."

"That song was not in the show when I signed to do it!" she insisted. "So either *it* goes, or *I* go!"

"Edie, you can't mean you want me to cut that girl's big solo . . ."

"There's only one star in this show. And I am not going to come on and do a scene after some little ingenue stops the show before me. So it's either-or!"

To emphasize her position, she resumed packing. When Firestone had rejoined Marvin and Jock English outside the dressing room, Marvin whispered, "She can't do that, can she? I mean, she's under contract. She *has* to appear, doesn't she?"

Jock thought for a moment. "If we could find someone, I could get her up in the part in, say, two weeks, three at the most. So we'd have to delay the opening in New York at least three weeks, maybe four, depending on how good she was."

Firestone had been doing his own mathematics. "Jock, you're adding seven hundred thousand dollars to the budget. There goes all our television money. These days you can't bring a musical into New York without half a million or more in television advertising."

"Can you raise it, John?" Jock asked.

"Not overnight," Firestone said, before admitting, "Not even in a week. In fact, I don't think I can raise it at all."

"I know that bitch. I should. I've slept with her often enough. When she says she's going back to New York, she's going back to New York. What do we do, John?"

"What can we do? We cut the solo."

"You can't!" Marvin protested. "It's the best number in the show!"

"Morse," Firestone asked, "have you got three quarters of a million dollars to invest in this show?"

The question was ridiculous.

"So we cut the number," Firestone said. He reached out to rest his hand on Marvin's shoulder. "I give you my word, kid. In my next show I'll make her a star. But not this time."

Marvin shook his head silently, refusing to accept the situation. Then he asked hoarsely, "Who's going to tell her? Who even has the guts?"

Firestone glanced at English, who, by his attitude, indicated that he would not assume that difficult burden. Firestone turned to Marvin. "Kid, it would hurt less coming from someone she loves. You have to do it."

After the rest of English's notes had been given, Marvin waited in the doorway of the small dressing room which Kitzi shared with Vera Adams, the woman who played Edie Cullen's best friend. "Wasn't Kitzi terrific tonight?" Vera enthused. "There's a Tony in that song. Maybe even a movie contract." She reached out to pat Kitzi on the behind. "When you're a big star, don't forget your old friends."

Kitzi was just wiping the cold cream from her face as she smiled back. "Go on, Vera, stop kidding around."

"Kidding?" The woman turned to Marvin. "She thinks I'm kidding. Listen, when Danny Kaye did his number in *Lady in the Dark,* I was in the chorus. Sixteen and scared to death. But I knew he was a star. I got that same feeling tonight. You're in like Flynn, baby!"

Marvin wanted to cry out, *Damn it, shut up! It's tough enough without you going on that way!* Instead, he suggested, "Ready, Kitz? Let's find someplace to grab a bite. You must be starving."

"Starving?" she countered, laughing. "I feel like I don't ever have to eat again. I could live on the applause I got tonight."

"Honey, just . . . just let's go."

They were seated across from each other in a small booth in the all-night bar and restaurant down the block from the Shubert. Kitzi stared across the table at him, her blue eyes bright with excitement and delight. When he reached to take her hand, she clasped his as she said, "This never would have happened without you, darling. And what you saw tonight was nothing. I know a dozen things I can do to make that number even better."

The waitress handed them menus and asked, "Cocktails?"

"Miss Mills doesn't drink, but I'll have a Scotch. Double."

"Double Scotch, you?" Kitzi asked, smiling.

Rather than explain, Marvin said, "I always see Humphrey Bogart do that in those detective films on late-night television." Secretly he hoped it would give him the courage he needed now.

While they waited for his drink, Kitzi continued. "You know, when I came offstage after my number, Lou Pollack was waiting for me in the wings. He kissed me and said, 'When I wrote those lyrics, I never dreamed they would sound so great, so touching.' That's the word he used, 'touching.' He had tears in his eyes. Honest, Marv, real tears. I wonder if any girl in this world feels as great as I feel tonight. To have this chance and to have the man I love all at once. Sometimes I look at you asleep in the dark and I say to myself, I must be the luckiest girl in the world!"

She leaned across the table to kiss him. He returned the kiss, but with less intensity than usual. She detected it.

"There's something wrong," She stared into his eyes. "I've never seen you look like this before. Marv, what is it?"

"Kitzi, I . . ." The waitress brought his drink and he took a burning gulp of it. "Kitz, sweetheart, the show. It's running long. Too long."

"It'll speed up when the scene changes are made," she countered.

"But not enough. Like Jock said before, there have to be cuts," he said.

"I know. That first scene in the second act between Edie and Lanny. That drags. They could cut it in half and still get as many laughs."

"That would help," he lied. "But they decided it will take more."

"Like what?" she asked.

"Well, Jock thought . . . and John Firestone thought . . . well, the second act of a musical must always be shorter than the first act. It gives the audience a sense of accelerating pace. So they decided to cut——"

"I know." Kitzi anticipated him. "The reprise of Edie and Lanny's number. That didn't go too well tonight, did it?"

"No," he admitted. "But that's not it, Kitz. Jock, John, they . . . they decided to cut your number."

She was more puzzled than startled. At first, she did not comprehend. "When you say my number, do you mean . . . No, no, they couldn't! It was the biggest moment in the show tonight. The audience loved it! They loved *me.* "

"Jock says . . . says it stops the second act cold, it destroys the momentum . . ."

Tears overran her eyes and spilled onto her cheeks.

"Kitzi . . . please don't cry. Not here."

"Why not? Who'll see? Who even gives a damn?" she countered, then called, "Waitress! I'll have that drink now! Vodka. On ice!"

For more than an hour, Marvin Morse tried to console her with half-truths and outright lies. She was unmoved. She continued to cry and drink, drink and cry.

Gradually, and with increasing concern, Marvin realized this was not the first time in her life Kitzi Mills had drunk to excess. He had to carry her from the restaurant, lift her into the cab, and take her back to the Ritz. Fortunately, when they arrived it was after three o'clock in the morning. He managed to ease her by the night doorman and into the elevator, which now smelled more of Kitzi's vodka than its usual perfume.

He undressed her and put her to bed. When he lay down beside her, he took her in his arms to comfort her. Soon they were making love. Somehow the alcohol made her even more passionate. She wept, she made love, she was drunk, all at the same time. He even had a most disturbing suspicion that she was unaware of who he was.

5

At one o'clock the next afternoon, the entire cast assembled for rehearsal. Jock English ran through his notes. He made a point of being meticulous and blunt in his criticism of every cast member, with the noticeable exception of Edie Cullen. Whenever it was necessary to correct her, he would blame the script or her musical intro or some other member of the cast for not feeding her her cue quickly or deftly enough. Today Edie Cullen was never wrong.

It was obvious to everyone that there had been a confrontation between the two that threatened the future of the entire production. But none of them was prepared for his final announcement.

"Now, we ran nineteen and a half minutes longer than I had anticipated. I know what you're all thinking. When we play the show in, we'll pick up time. Sure! But not nineteen minutes. So, much as I regret it, there's only one way to get that nineteen minutes out. Block cuts. Cut entire numbers. I have one clean cut that will save us seven minutes."

Sitting out in the dark house, Marvin Morse and John Firestone glanced at each other. Up on the stage, Kitzi Mills, pale, drawn, still suffering the physical effects of excessive drinking, clenched her hands under her script awaiting the announcement.

"A lovely moment," English said. "But in a musical like this, pace, excitement, drive are what we need. So the solo, Kitzi's solo, will have to go."

There was a gasp of surprise and resentment from many members of the cast. But it was quickly suppressed by the fierce glare of Jock English's black eyes. "I can assure you, from my years of directing, that the audience never misses what's been cut, because they don't know. So let's not spend our time bemoaning what's gone and concentrate on what we have left. Now, let's run the cuts, then do a run-through from the top. Let's go!"

The run-through started raggedly, the cast still resenting the elimination of Kitzi's number. But by the time the first act was over, like the good soldiers they were, they had absorbed the injunction and begun to give the performances of which they were capable.

During breaks, other cast members came up to Kitzi to whisper, "Don't let it get you, kid. Your time will come. You'll be a star. You'll bury that bitch one day."

Every night, after each preview, Kitzi left the theater with Marvin. They went to their little restaurant, where he tried to convince her to eat. She chose to drink. At first he tried to keep up with her. After several nights, though, he realized that the more she drank the less he could in order to get her back to the hotel.

Once in her room, there were tears. And lovemaking. He tried to divert her craving for alcohol with plans and promises for her future, with talk of all the things he was going to do for her career once they were back in New York. Especially after the opening-night reviews in Boston, which should be good for her. Not just good, but great! Better than great!

Surfeited with both alcohol and sex, she would lie in his embrace until she fell asleep.

Poor kid, he thought, *who can blame her? To come so close to becoming a star and have it snatched away like that by some over-the-hill bitch who's just trying to hang on by her fingernails. If only there were some way to sneak her solo back into the show, she'd be okay. Better than okay. Great. There must be some way . . . there must be some way.*

6

The night of the Boston opening, the show went well. As the satisfied audience was leaving the theater, John Firestone remarked to Marvin, "Jock was right. The audience never misses what they don't know was cut."

Marvin picked Kitzi up at her dressing room to take her to the after-opening party which Firestone had arranged in the dining room at the Ritz.

There, a mood of cautious optimism prevailed. Those investors who had made the trip to Boston seemed happy with the outcome. There were extravagant predictions of its critical reception. The man from the Shuberts, who were holding a theater in New York for the show's opening, smiled as he ate and drank. He had already phoned in his very guarded opinion: "Edie Cullen's age is beginning to show. But she's a favorite of the New York critics, so I'd say we have a chance. The show itself is so-so. It needs a lift. Maybe they'll find it before they get to town."

Despite Marvin's efforts, Kitzi ate nothing at the party. She kept draining her glass and sending him back to the bar for refills. He tried to space her drinks by loitering at the bar, letting others precede him, or by stopping on his way back to their table to chat with other people.

Nevertheless, before the party was over, Kitzi had downed six vodkas and was insisting that Marvin get her a seventh. He refused and urged her to go up to bed, since there would be no reviews until morning. She snatched her empty glass from his hand and went to the bar herself to demand a refill. Marvin shook his head no to the bartender, who maintained that the bar was closed for the night. Kitzi hurled her glass against the wall behind the bar and started out, shaky, but determined to make a flamboyant exit.

Marvin overtook her at the door just as her legs buckled. As he caught her, Edie Cullen and Jock English passed them and Marvin heard the star say, "You'll have to replace her before New York. She can't hold her booze."

Marvin was tempted to shout after her, *You goddamn bitch! It's all your fault!* He said nothing, except to urge softly, "Come on, Kitz, honey. Straighten up. Lean on me. Let's make it to the elevator. Come on, honey, come on."

He carried her back to her room, undressed her, and put her to bed. He sat on the side of her bed, his feeling of frustration now transformed into fury. *That bitch Edie Cullen! First destroying Kitzi. Now urging that she be fired before New York.*

He turned to his sleeping lover, hesitated for a moment, then reached for her with both hands and abruptly lifted her to a sitting position despite her drunken protests.

"Katherine Millendorfer! No, don't try to turn away. Look at me! Listen to me! You were too drunk to hear, but you know what Edie Cullen said about you tonight? She told Jock English, 'You'll have to get rid of her. She can't hold her booze.' Are you going to let your career go down the drain without even fighting back? I don't know why you drink. Right now I don't care. I only know one thing. It's going to stop. Now! Today! Do you hear me? It's going to stop!"

She mumbled, "My song . . . they took away my song . . ."

"We'll get it back," he promised recklessly. He would promise anything to make her quit drinking, to keep her from destroying her promising life. "We'll get it back." But by that time she had fallen asleep again, and he could not know whether she had heard him or not.

When he woke, it was light. He heard her in the bathroom retching. When he went to her, he found her leaning over the bowl, bathed in a cold sweat. He washed her lips and face with a wet towel and led her back to bed, where he wrapped her in the warm blanket.

"I'm sorry, darling," she said meekly. She was always apologetic after she had spent a night getting drunk. He did not respond. "Did you say something to me last night? Something about Edie Cullen saying something to Jock? Did that happen? Or did I just imagine it?"

"It happened," he said. And he told her again.

"She said that?" Kitzi responded, "I ought to kill her . . ."

"That would certainly be better than drinking yourself to death," he replied angrily.

"I'm sorry about the drinking . . ."

"But it doesn't seem to stop you," he pointed out. "Why, Kitzi, why?"

"Don't hate me. Please? That's one thing I couldn't bear," she begged.

"To let you go on destroying yourself—do you call that loving you?" He picked her up in his arms and held her tightly as he continued, "Darling, don't you see, because I love you I've got to make you stop drinking."

"There's only one way," she said. "My song. I want my song back. I need it."

"Promise me you'll stop drinking, and together we'll find a way."

She hesitated. Finally she asked softly, "Will you love me again if I promise?"

"I will always love you," he said, and meant it.

The dean of Boston drama critics in the 1970s was an erudite man named Chauncey Weems. A New Englander, he appeared at first glance to be a tall, spare academic, possibly a professor of philosophy or English literature at Harvard. He knew everything about the theater, and he was a singular critic in that he loved to see plays succeed, not fail. His interest in a play exceeded his duty to merely watch it and pass judgment.

More than once he had been called in to serve as unofficial peacemaker between warring factions in a production on its way to New York. When a producer failed to reconcile the differences between playwright and director, or playwright and rebellious star, the word would go out, "Call Chauncey Weems."

If there were a way to save Kitzi's number, Marvin decided, Chauncey Weems was that way. Aware of the risk involved in approaching a critic directly, Marvin prepared precisely what he would say to Weems. When he had rehearsed it several times, he placed the call to the newspaper and was surprised to be put right through and greeted with a dry, if preoccupied, "Weems here."

"Mr. Weems," Marvin began as he had rehearsed, "my name is Marvin Morse, and I am the agent for a brilliant young actress who is not being given a fair chance to——"

"Young man," Weems interrupted, "this is not a casting office. I am not in the business of finding roles for young actresses, no matter how brilliant they are!"

"Wait, please, don't hang up," Marvin begged. "You don't understand!" And he abandoned his carefully prepared script.

"Mr. Weems, she has the part. But her song, her big song, the opening of the second act, they cut that out. Just cut it out! And it's destroying her! Please, Mr. Weems, if you have any feeling at all, any sympathy for talent, you have to do something!"

"Exactly what would you suggest?" the critic asked.

"I don't know. I just don't know. But something . . . anything," Marvin pleaded. Then he admitted, "This is all wrong. I had it so carefully planned, what I would say, what you would say, and now I've screwed it all up, haven't I?"

"Let's say you haven't done a perfect job of it. Now, why don't we start all over again. Just tell me what's going on. Slowly. Coherently. Shall we try?"

Marvin drew a deep breath and started again. Slowly, coherently, he explained.

Weems thought for a long moment and then said, "Tell you what. Right now I'm preparing my TV show for PBS this evening. Bring that girl to Studio Two at the Public Broadcasting Station at six o'clock. I do a show in which I rereview plays, performances, and interview people."

"She has to be at the theater at seven-thirty."

"Bring her at six. She'll be free by six-thirty," Weems promised.

They waited in the modest reception room of the PBS television station from a quarter past five until a young female receptionist came out to say, "Mr. Weems wants you to meet him in the studio."

The studio was only large enough to accommodate a low platform and two chairs. Weems sat in one. He rose and greeted Kitzi warmly to put her at ease.

"My heavens, you're even more beautiful offstage than on. Now, just sit down here and relax. Would you like some coffee? Eleanor! Bring Miss Mills a cup of coffee. Now then, let's give our cameramen a good look at you. Come in close, boys. People are tired of looking at my wrinkled old prune of a face. Tonight let's give them youth and beauty."

Marvin remained in the darkness, admiring the way Weems put Kitzi at her ease.

Once Kitzi was comfortably settled with a cup of coffee in her hand, Weems looked off-camera to his producer. "How much time have we got?"

"Two minutes to air," the producer called back.

"Okay. Now, Kitzi, don't be surprised at anything I ask. Just take your time, respond with whatever makes you comfortable. And before you know it, this whole ordeal will be over." He smiled, patted her hand, looked into the camera, and said, "Okay. Throw me a cue when we're on."

There was introductory theme music and then the red light flashed on Camera One. Chauncey Weems cleared his throat and began. He spoke of *Oddities,* the show he had seen the night before, repeating in essence, his mildly favorable notes.

Then, to Marvin's surprise, and Kitzi's, he said, "One of the things that audiences, and even critics, never hear unless they pop up in other shows later on, are those songs that are cut from musicals while they're breaking in out of town. Some of the greatest hits of Rodgers and Hart, Rodgers and Hammerstein, Irving Berlin, Cole Porter, Frank Loesser, and other great Broadway composers were cut out of shows and used later in other shows, and have then become great hits. Irving Berlin's famous Easter song—maybe the most famous Easter song of all time, 'Easter Parade'—was originally called 'Smile and Show Your Dimples,' and was cut, deservedly so, only to show up years later with lyrics that started, 'In your Easter bonnet. . . .' "

Weems turned to Kitzi. "I wonder, Miss Mills, did anything like that happen with *Oddities?* I'm sure my audience would welcome an inside look at what goes on when a show is trying out in Boston."

"Well . . . ," Kitzi began, then faltered.

Every cell of Marvin's body tried to cry out, *Tell him, Kitzi! He's opened the door for you. Opened it wide. Just tell him.*

"Actually," Kitzi began, "we were nineteen minutes over, and we had to cut something. It was my song."

"Your song?" Weems pretended surprise. "My dear, if you don't mind, would you give my audience an exclusive performance of a song they may never have the opportunity to hear anywhere else? Can you do it without accompaniment?"

"That's the way I did it in the show," Kitzi said. She slipped out of her chair, slid to the floor, and, with her legs crossed under her, started to sing.

The camera moved in close. She became aware of it and responded to it. When she had finished, Weems waited until the camera was on him again. He took a pause and then remarked softly, "And they cut such a touching song from the show? Hard to believe. I think that would clear up the reservations I have about the second act. Thank you, my dear."

When Marvin Morse brought Kitzi Mills back to the hotel he found a message waiting in his box at the desk: "I want to see you. At once. J.F."

He discovered that John Firestone was not in his suite at the hotel but at the theater, overseeing some last-minute changes Jock English was making.

When Marvin entered the theater Firestone approached him, grabbed him by the arm, and walked him out to the alley.

"You are one smart son of a bitch, my boy!" Firestone began.

"What do you mean?" Marvin dissembled.

"I saw the Chauncey Weems show on TV. Cute. Very cute!"

"Oh, that . . . ," Marvin pretended to belittle.

"Yes, *that,*" Firestone said. "Now, I want you to disappear."

"You mean go back to New York?" Marvin resisted.

"I don't care where you go. Just don't be around for a few days."

"Kitzi needs me."

"I'll take care of her. But I don't want Edie Cullen to see you around the theater. So go visit museums. Go walk around Harvard Yard. Go see Walden Pond. Do any goddamn thing you want, but stay out of sight!"

John Firestone had not become one of the most prestigious producers in the Broadway theater by the sheer wealth he had accumulated in the real estate business. He was a sensitive man but, above all, an excellent tactician.

He sent word to Edie Cullen, Lanny Everett, and Jock English that there would be a late supper in his suite after the second night's performance.

Once drinks were served and the buffet had been laid on, Firestone not only closed the front door to his suite, he made sure that the others were aware that he locked it as well. With a dramatic turn that would do credit to an accomplished actor, Firestone faced them and declared solemnly, "Edie, Lanny, Jock. . . . We are in trouble. Big trouble."

All three put aside their food, prepared to hear the worst.

"I had a call from the Shuberts today. It's a technicality. But you know the Shuberts. When they want out of a deal, any technicality will do."

"Out? Why?" Jock English demanded.

"Jock, please let me explain. I had a handshake deal with Bernie for the Imperial. I assumed that, as usual, my accountant drew the check and sent it over. Turns out he forgot."

"You're good for the money. Everyone knows that," Edie Cullen protested.

"Of course. But, as I said, when the Shuberts want out, any technicality will do."

"Why do they want out?" English repeated.

"Chauncey Weems. They didn't think his review was particularly good."

"It wasn't bad," Lanny Everett defended.

"Lanny, with the Shuberts, 'It wasn't bad' and 'Not particularly good' add up to the same thing. They won't give us the Imperial unless we do something to improve the show."

Jock English caught on. He'd been in theater far too long not to realize that devious strategies were sometimes necessary. He asked the crucial question.

"Can't we find out what Weems didn't like? Maybe we can fix it, then get him back to rereview the show. Can you manage that, John?"

"I can't guarantee it, but at least I can try."

At rehearsal the next afternoon, Jock English made certain changes in the script which he had intended to make all along. He shortened some scenes. He extended two of the dance numbers. Then, pretending it was an afterthought, he said, "What the hell, let's give it a shot." He reinstated Kitzi Mills' solo. No protest from Edie Cullen. The unspoken threat that an Edith Cullen show would have to close out of town for failure to secure a New York theater had made the star newly pliable and acquiescent.

With the changes made in the three days after the opening, John Firestone invited Weems back to see the show at the Saturday night performance.

When the curtain went up for the second act, John Firestone stood in the rear of the house behind the last row. As he waited for Kitzi to make her appearance, he sensed someone sidle up to him. Without even turning, he asked, "Marvin?"

"I had to be here to see this," Marvin apologized.

"It's okay now, kid."

The follow spot hit the wing. Kitzi entered. The spot followed her to the center of the stage, where she slipped gracefully into a sitting position. She began to sing with no orchestral accompaniment. When she was done, the silence in the theater carried her all the way back to the wings. The applause only broke once she disappeared. They called her back for two bows and an encore.

Then, as instructed by Jock English, the conductor interrupted the applause with a vigorous attack on the next number which brought Edie Cullen onstage with such gusto that the change of pace gave new impetus to the entire act.

John Firestone whispered to Marvin, "A good week's work, my boy. But only half the battle."

As the final curtain came down, Chauncey Weems came up the aisle. Firestone intercepted him.

"Well?"

"You've done it, John," Weems said, at the same time casting a subtle glance in Marvin's direction.

"Only one thing, Chauncey. Would you go back and see Edie? She'd love it."

"Of course," Weems said, fully aware of what Firestone wanted.

John Firestone knocked on the door of Edie Cullen's dressing room.

"Edie? Honey? Are you decent? Someone here who'd love to see you. Chauncey Weems."

"Of course," Edie called back, grabbing her robe from Isabella's hands.

Firestone opened the door for Weems, who went to Edith, took her hand, and kissed it. "Magnificent! Tonight was the most marvelous Edie Cullen I've ever seen! Especially the way you swept on in that second act. Any lesser star couldn't have done it after that girl's solo. But you topped her. In spades! Great. Just great!"

Edie made a pretense at modesty, but her long years of experience made her ask, "John, did you tell him about the Shuberts, those bastards?"

"No, darling, I didn't. But I will."

Weems smiled. "Edie, no matter what trouble John has with the Shuberts, there won't be any after my follow-up piece on Sunday."

"Thanks, Chauncey, thanks so much." She kissed him on the cheek, thinking, *Why doesn't he use a more expensive after-shave lotion than Old Spice?*

As Firestone walked Chauncey Weems out of the theater and down the alley, Weems asked, "John, you didn't use that old line, 'The Shuberts are refusing us a theater'?"

"What the hell, Chaunce. It worked, didn't it?"

"Thank God! That Mills girl, she's worth her weight in gold."

* * *

The show opened at the Imperial Theatre on Forty-fourth Street in New York on a Sunday. By the time the television reviews were in that night, and the reviews came out the next morning in the *Times,* the *News,* and the *Post,* the show was a hit.

Kitzi Mills was a star.

Exercising his considerable diplomacy, John Firestone later convinced Edie Cullen that Kitzi Mills's name should be featured in the ads—under the title, of course, and in smaller type than her own.

7

At the George Gordon Agency, Marvin Morse was rewarded with both a larger office and an increase in his annual salary and bonus. On the show-business social circuit, Marvin and Kitzi became the "in" couple of the season. They were sought after for all parties given by wealthy hostesses who were part of the theatrical scene by virtue of their substantial investments in plays and musicals.

Sarah Blinkhorn watched it all evolve with the satisfaction of a proud parent. But whether it was her natural pessimism, or her long experience as an observer of show-business romances, she remained skeptical.

She feigned happiness when they took up residence together in an apartment on the west side of Central Park. She even permitted herself to participate in the excitement of selecting furniture, carpets, and draperies. But always her silent, private doubts continued to gnaw at her.

It began harmlessly enough. Kitzi and Marvin lay in bed, she in his arms. They were close, warm from making love.

"Darling, are you ashamed of me?" she asked.

"Ashamed? Are you crazy?" he replied. "I'm so proud I must be obnoxious."

"Then why don't you introduce me to your mother?"

"You met her at the opening-night party at Sardi's. She kissed you. Don't you remember?"

"I meant introduce me to your mother and father, like people do when they're thinking of getting married."

He rose up, looked down at her, and asked, "Are you serious? I mean, do you really want to get married?"

"Uh huh," she whispered.

"And I was afraid to ask," he confessed. "I thought you might think it would interfere with your career. If I became too serious, you'd want to break free."

"I'll never want to be free of you, Marv. Never," she said. She embraced him once more, locking her long, graceful legs about him.

When they lay side by side, breathless, he whispered, "When do you want to meet them?"

She responded quickly, "Soon. Very soon."

"Okay, Sunday. After your matinee," he promised.

Sunday dinner at his parents' apartment in Brooklyn was wonderful. Kitzi handled herself magnificently. When dinner was over, she insisted on helping clear the table. She joked about the days when she was waitressing to support herself. The men went into the living room, where his father lit up a cigar, but not before asking, "Marv, the smoke—will it affect her voice?"

"No, go on, Dad, light up," he said, quite conscious of the animated conversation and bursts of laughter coming from the kitchen.

He could not resist recalling Sarah's warning that very first day. "She is the girl every Jewish mother warns her son not to bring home else she will kill herself." *Yet Mom is knocking herself out,* he thought, *to make her feel wanted and loved. Wait till I tell Sarah tomorrow.*

Later that night, when Kitzi was slipping into her nightgown, she asked suddenly, "Are Jewish children so different from other children? I mean, aside from Christmas and Easter, how different can children be?"

He took her by both hands, forcing her to look into his eyes.

"What did my mother say?"

"She isn't against our getting married. But she wants the children brought up Jewish."

"When there are children, *we* will decide how they're brought up," he said firmly.

Kitzi nodded in agreement, without disclosing that she suspected she was already pregnant.

At the matinee the following Wednesday, after the house was dark, an unusually tall, gaunt man, with bearded, concave cheeks and sharp, alert gray eyes, slipped into the theater.

Though he held a ticket for the aisle seat in the third row, he preferred to watch the first act from the back of the house. To avoid being recognized during intermission, he took refuge in the office of the theater manager. He reappeared only long enough to watch Kitzi's solo at the opening of the second act. He left the theater as soon as she finished.

He strolled up Broadway, back to the Plaza Hotel on Central Park South. There, from his large, expensive suite, he placed a call to the George Gordon Agency in Beverly Hills. He asked to speak to Abe Furstburgh. When the receptionist attempted to shunt him off to someone else, the man announced in a deeply resonant voice, "My dear woman, I am Gordon Wainwright!"

"Oh, yes, of course, Mr. Wainwright." The woman was immediately intimidated. "I'm sorry. I'll find Mr. Furstburgh for you at once!"

At that moment, Abe Furstburgh was in his limousine on his way to meet an important client for lunch at the Hillcrest Country Club. He took the call on his car phone.

The moment he heard himself addressed as "Abraham!" in that impressively modulated voice, Furstburgh knew to whom he was talking. No one else, not even his wife, called him Abraham.

"Gordon! How are things? I hear you have a new film going into production."

"Abraham," Wainwright intoned, "I want that girl!"

"Girl? What girl?" Furstburgh asked, taken by surprise.

"Abraham, don't stall me. Don't start scheming how to hold me up. In this instance, money is not important."

At once, Furstburgh's mind raced to structure a deal that would exact an outrageous fee for whoever it was that Wainwright was so desperate to engage.

"Gordon, to me, more important than money is the role. Is it right for her? What will it do for her image?" Furstburgh asked, racking his brain to fathom who Wainwright was so desperate to cast.

"The role will make her a film star! That's all you have to know," Wainwright pontificated. "You're wasting her, Abraham. Ruining her career."

Still groping for a clue to the girl's identity, Furstburgh placed his hand over the mouthpiece to ask his assistant, "Wainwright wants some girl we represent. Do you have any idea who?" The assistant shrugged.

"Abraham, if that girl sings that song five hundred more times, how is that going to advance her career? She's perfect now."

Stalling for time, Furstburgh suggested, "Gordon, why not drop into the office and we'll discuss it? This afternoon?"

"This afternoon?" Wainwright thundered. "I am sitting here in the Plaza. I have just come from the Imperial. And you want to meet this afternoon? Abraham! I want a deal before I leave New York!"

Plaza . . . New York . . . Imperial Theatre . . .

Furstburgh finally had all the clues he needed. To strengthen his bargaining position, he proceeded to invent obstacles to the deal.

"Gordon, right at the top, I have to warn you the girl has a run-of-the-play contract," Furstburgh lied.

"I'll buy her out of it!" Wainwright replied at once.

"Plus, she is under the personal management of one of our agents, without whom she does not make a move!"

"Tell him I'm going to make that girl a film star!" Wainwright dictated.

Sure now that he had interposed enough hurdles to allow him to extract an outrageous deal, Furstburgh promised, "Gordon, I'll do my best."

"I want more than your best. I want that girl!" Wainwright said before hanging up.

Furstburgh hung up the phone, turned to his assistant. "That girl . . . what's her name . . . the girl we have in that show in the Imperial?"

"Mills. Kitzi Mills," the younger man reminded him.

"Yeah. Wainwright wants her. And he sounds hot to trot. Remind me to look into it when we get back to the office."

Wainwright ordered three dozen long-stemmed red roses to be delivered to Kitzi Mills's dressing room at the Imperial. When the clerk asked if a card was to be enclosed, Wainwright replied, "Only a single word. 'Tonight!' With an exclamation point. And send the bill to me at the Plaza." A second later he exploded, "Who am *I*? *I* am Gordon Wainwright, you idiot!"

Damn it, is my voice slipping so that people don't recognize me?

Because she was the third featured player in the show, Kitzi Mills's dressing room at the Imperial was on the second floor. It was a narrow room, with a makeup mirror along one wall and barely enough room to accommodate her costumes and her own clothes. There was a small white porcelain sink in the corner, stained from the years of makeup which had been washed off over it. Aside from her own chair, which faced the mirror, there was one small upholstered chair with a sagging bottom.

Once Wainwright's roses arrived, the call went out for vases. By the time all thirty-six roses had been arranged, her dressing table was almost obscured, and two vases had to be set on the floor. The perfume was almost as overpowering as her curiosity. Three times while making up for her first entrance, she looked at the card which both tempted and frustrated her.

"Tonight!"

These must be from Marvin. And "tonight" must mean something special. The date for the wedding! He's made up his mind that we'll get married right away. Especially after how well things went with his folks. God, I hope so. Then I won't have to tell him about being pregnant. I wouldn't want him to marry me because of that.

She realized she was wrong when Marvin arrived just minutes before the curtain went up and was obviously as surprised and puzzled as she at the garden in her dressing room. And the tantalizing card.

Before she went out in response to the stage manager's call of "Places, please!" Marvin kissed her, careful as always not to smudge her makeup. Then he dropped into the sagging armchair, the card in his hand.

"Tonight!"

Son of a bitch, is this from some admirer who's fallen in love with her from the audience and intends to woo her? There've been more than a few of those. But none so flamboyant or dramatic as to send three dozen roses and such a card. Well, if it's going to be tonight, I am damn well going to wait and see!

As usual, Kitzi had her two encores, and took her bows at the end of the performance. She returned to her dressing room, breathless and excited, began to undress, and was half-naked when they heard a knock on the door. She and Marvin glanced at each other: This must be the source of all those roses.

Marvin went to the door. Gordon Wainwright stood there, tall, gaunt, bearded, imperial in carriage. In his most impressive voice, he said, "Miss Mills . . . my dear Miss Mills. . . ."

He brushed by Marvin, strode to Kitzi, took her hand, and gallantly kissed it. He looked around, pretending dismay at what he saw. "I thought surely a young woman of your talent would have a star's dressing room."

Marvin had recognized Wainwright, but Kitzi had not. It was obvious on her face and in her bright but puzzled blue eyes.

"Wainwright," the man said. "Gordon Wainwright."

"Oh, yes," Kitzi realized. "Now I recognize your voice. From your television commercials."

Resentful at being reminded of his ventures into the lucrative field of television peddling, Wainwright hastened to inform her, "I would prefer to be recognized for my films. I am about to embark on a new one, which is why I am here tonight. If you have no other plans, could we have a bite of supper? I reserved a table in the Oak Room at the Algonquin."

"Mr. Wainwright," Marvin interceded, "we don't talk business after the show. Kitzi's too tired. She had a matinee today. Tomorrow at my office would be better. Or maybe you and I could do lunch."

"No, wait," Kitzi said. "I feel fine tonight. Why don't we go to supper?"

Before Marvin could respond, Wainwright said, "Marvelous. I have a limousine waiting. I'll be at the stage door."

At the Algonquin, Wainwright held court like a reigning monarch. Celebrities who had stopped in for a late snack or a nightcap came to his table to pay their respects. Enthralled as Kitzi was by Wainwright's commanding presence, she was even more impressed by their adulation. Stars whom she had always admired and envied sought to ingratiate themselves with the old master.

Each time another star came to the table, Wainwright introduced Kitzi Mills as the star of his next film appearance. *Landfall.* Marvin saw that Wainwright's praise of her effected a change in her appearance. Her eyes grew brighter and more reverential toward Wainwright, who in turn became more paternal and possessive. He held Kitzi's hand and pinched her dimpled chin, seeking every opportunity to make physical contact with her.

At the evening's end, when Wainwright's limousine drew up at their apartment building on Central Park West, he kissed Kitzi's hand.

"Delightful child. A magical pixie is what you are. I don't know whether to star you or adopt you." He laughed, then asked, "Can I drop you somewhere, Marvin, my boy?"

"Somewhere is right here, Mr. Wainwright," Marvin said, making clear his relationship to Kitzi.

"Of course, dear boy," Wainwright replied, unable to completely conceal his surprise.

As they were undressing, Kitzi said suddenly, "He's an authentic legend, isn't he?"

"He's certainly old enough to be a legend," Marvin pointed out.

"He may be old, but he's a fantastic character," she said. "It'll be fun working with him. They say he's brilliant."

"*Was,*" Marvin corrected.

"You don't like him, do you?"

"I don't have to like him. If the script is right, if the deal is right, we'll do the picture. Otherwise, I don't care if he's Coppola, Lucas, or Spielberg. We only do what's right for you."

He reached out to her, drew her close, and pressed his face between her breasts. Soon his hands were slowly moving up her thighs and between them to where she was soft as velvet. She kissed him. They made love.

Afterwards, lying side by side, they stared up at the ceiling, which reflected the glow of the streetlights.

"It's like a dream," she said.

"What?"

"Me. Doing a Gordon Wainwright film. Just imagine, we'll be in Hollywood together. Hollywood!"

8

At seven o'clock in the morning, Pacific Coast time, Abe Furstburgh placed a call to Gordon Wainwright at the Plaza Hotel in New York.

"Gordon, Abe. How did it go?"

"Nothing ever goes perfectly, does it?" Wainwright said.

"What's wrong that can't be fixed?" Furstburgh responded, too quickly.

At which point Wainwright knew that, for the moment, he held the upper hand in the deal.

"Abraham, you know me. God knows I've directed enough of your stars. I need everything a star can give me every moment. I need total control!"

"So who's saying you can't have it?" Furstburgh asked.

"That young man, that Marvin chap. All the work I do with the girl during the day he'll be undoing at night. She'll be doing the part *his* way, not *my* way. I cannot permit that to happen!"

"I'll talk to him," Furstburgh promised.

"I'm sorry, Abraham, that won't do. Too bad. She would have been fantastic in the part. Ah, well. . . ." Wainwright said before hanging up.

Minutes later, his phone rang once more. He allowed it to ring four times before he answered.

"Yes?" He elongated the word as if it were three syllables instead of merely one.

"Gordon," Furstburgh interrupted, "before you come to any conclusions, let me ask you. If it could be worked out that the young man stayed in New York when Kitzi Mills went to the Coast, would that do it?"

"It certainly would help," Wainwright said, pretending to give the suggestion serious consideration.

"Okay. Done!" Furstburgh said.

"If you can get it all arranged, call me and we'll talk a deal," Wainwright said.

Later that morning, properly briefed and instructed by Abe Furstburgh, Nat Cohn had his secretary call Marvin Morse and arrange lunch at the King Cole Room of the St. Regis.

"Marv, I know how you young turks are. You look up the ladder at us older guys and ask, 'When am I going to have my shot?' Well, don't think us 'old farts' don't appreciate ability. We love the job you've done with Kitzi. So we want to enlarge your responsibility in the Legit Department. We're making you the assistant to Alvin Horowitz."

"Assistant to——" Marvin started to respond with considerable enthusiasm before he realized, "I'll be going out to the Coast, once we make the deal for Kitzi to do the Wainwright picture."

"Marv, Alvin's due to retire in eighteen months. We're grooming you to take over his job. You can't do that and be out on the Coast."

"I don't know," Marvin equivocated. "I'll have to talk to Kitzi about it. She might not feel secure going out there on her own."

"Any girl who can command a stage like she does is secure, believe me," Cohn said, pulling out a long, imported panatella and lighting up. "Marv, this is the chance of a lifetime. Take the advice of an older man. Don't pass it up."

"I'll have to talk to her," Marvin persisted.

"Don't 'talk' to her. *Convince* her!" Cohn urged.

"You won't go with me?" Kitzi asked.

"This is a big opportunity. For you. And for me," Marvin tried to explain. "In the long run, it could be the best thing."

"How could being separated be the best thing?" she asked, her blue eyes filling with tears and her dimpled chin beginning to quiver in a way that unnerved him.

He took her in his arms. Pressing his face against her head, which rested on his chest, he confessed, "Kitz . . . honey . . . I've been thinking for some time now. About us."

"You changed your mind. Is it your mother?"

"It has nothing to do with her. It has to do with us. You. And me. How long do you think we could go on this way? You rising so fast. And me just being your agent. Before long I'd become known as a man who hitched his wagon to a star. That I was living off you. That's not much better than being a pimp."

"Don't say things like that!" she protested, almost in tears.

"Honey, please, listen to me. This is *my* time to become a star. In another eighteen months I can be Vice President in charge of Legit. That's an important title. Men have gone on to head studios or networks from jobs like that."

"Will I get to see you during the two months?"

"Honey, the only reason the jet plane was invented was so I could see you every weekend," he said, smiling.

She smiled. She kissed him. She had agreed.

On Monday, without telling anyone, even Marvin, Kitzi Mills consulted a gynecologist, who confirmed what she had suspected.

She spent the rest of the day walking through Central Park. It was a breezy, sunny afternoon that proved winter was over and spring was only days away. Dressed as she was, in slacks and a big, baggy sweater, she appeared more a high school girl cutting class than a rising young star in show business. She had no makeup on. Her long blond hair was tied back in a ponytail.

To tell Marvin or not? If she did, he would surely forbid her to go to the Coast and make Gordon Wainwright's film.

Worse, what if Marvin said, as he well might, "Choose between being the mother of my child and becoming a star." She could not give up her career. Performing was as much a part of her as Marvin was.

She could become pregnant another time. These days, doctors said any time up until she was thirty-five was safe for child and mother. But she would never again be nineteen and standing on the verge of a great career.

There was no question in her mind.

On the following Monday morning, accompanied by Evelina Downs, the black woman Marvin had hired to be her dresser, Kitzi Mills went to a hospital in the East Sixties which had been converted into an abortion clinic.

While Evelina waited downstairs in the reception area, Kitzi was taken upstairs to the surgical floor. There she was told to undress, slip into a white hospital gown, and wait in Surgery until the doctor was ready for her. She lay down on the table, feeling cold, tense, yet determined to undergo the procedure. Soon she heard the voice of a male doctor down the corridor.

"I'll get the one in O.R. Five," he said.

Suddenly she realized he was referring to her.

Something within her rebelled. *I am not just "the one in O.R. Five." I am me! I am a woman named Kitzi Mills! Katherine Millendorfer! And this is my baby! Our baby!*

She sat up abruptly, swung her legs over the table, and came to her feet. She started across the hall to the small cubicle where her clothes hung. She ripped off the white gown and dressed hurriedly.

As she started out of the room, she collided with the doctor.

"Miss?" he asked. "What's wrong?" As she fled down the corridor, he called, "What happened? Where are you going?"

She did not turn to answer or even wait for the elevator. She ran down the stairs, not stopping until she was back in the reception room. She took Evelina by the hand and raced toward the door.

Loaded down with her carry-on luggage, Marvin brought her to the departure gate at Kennedy International in time to board the 9:00 A.M. flight for Los Angeles. He kissed her, held her, whispered in her ear, "Just think, five whole days. It'll be the longest time we've been apart since the day we met."

"Do you have your reservations for Friday?" she asked.

"Got 'em!" he started to say when he was interrupted by an

attractive but overbearing young woman who was accompanied by a still photographer.

"Sir . . . young man . . . would you step back so we can get a clear shot of Miss Mills? And Miss Mills, would you turn this way, and smile?"

"Who the hell are you?" Marvin asked.

"Mr. Wainwright wants some publicity shots of Miss Mills," the young woman said. "Miss Mills, here, hold these magazines. Mr. Wainwright wants you to give the impression of being a studious young actress. Intellectual. It adds to the character he wants you to project."

"Look, lady, I'm Marvin Morse, Miss Mills's agent. I'll decide what kind of photos, if any, Miss Mills wants to have."

"Oh, yes, I was warned about you," the young woman dismissed him. She turned back to Kitzi as the photographer continued snapping away. "Miss Mills! Mr. Wainwright especially said he wanted you to hold these so the names of the magazines will show."

She arranged them in Mitzi's arms, while the photographer continued his work, until a uniformed airline passenger agent approached to insist, "Whoever is the passenger had better come. . . . We've finished boarding all the others."

Marvin picked up Kitzi's carryon luggage and started toward the boarding ramp. But the passenger agent said, "I'll take those, sir."

Just before they closed the door, Marvin and Kitzi exchanged hasty kisses, between which she whispered, "Friday night! Don't forget!"

"I've already got my ticket!" he called back as the door closed, separating them.

He turned away to find himself confronted by the young woman. She no longer seemed so domineering.

"Sorry. But when Gordon Wainwright says 'Jump!' we ask 'How high?' We do all his publicity in the East."

"I understand," Marvin said.

"She really is something. I don't blame you for being so crazy about her," the young woman said. She stood back a bit and took a long look at him. "I don't blame her for being crazy about you, either."

"We're going to be married as soon as she finishes the picture."

"Good," she said with a faint smile.

"What does that mean?"

"It's good that you're not planning on getting married any sooner. Wainwright is a very demanding director. He wants every moment of his star's time."

"We can wait," Marvin said.

The young woman smiled again. "If you get tired of waiting, my name is Florence Fenton. I'm with the Thompson-Berns Agency. Sardi Building. Tenth floor."

"I'll remember that," Marvin said, smiling back at the young woman, dark-haired and slender in her business suit. "Fenton . . . What was it before?"

She laughed. "Feinstein, of course. Okay, Morse, see you around." She hurried to join her photographer.

9

On Thursday afternoon, at 3:00 P.M., Pacific Coast time, Abe Furstburgh was completing a deal at lunch in the Polo Lounge of the Beverly Hills Hotel when he was interrupted by the maitre d', who approached with a plug-in telephone.

"Call, Mr. Furstburgh. Very urgent! Wouldn't give a name."

With great annoyance Furstburgh lifted the phone. "Hello. Who am I talking to?"

"Abraham," came the sonorous voice of Gordon Wainwright. "We have a problem."

"Problem?" a suspicious Furstburgh asked.

"The Mills girl. Doesn't know the first thing about how to work to a camera," Wainwright said with an air of paternal dismay. "A whole crew standing around, a whole cast, while I have to put her through her lines and moves over and over. I'm afraid, Abraham, very much afraid, we are going to have to send her back to New York."

"Gordon, you can't do that," Furstburgh protested.

"I can't eat all that cost either."

"How about we provide her with a dramatic coach?" Furstburgh suggested.

"Then I'd have to teach the coach how to coach her," Wainwright said solemnly.

"Couldn't you work with her off the set? Say, over the weekend?" Furstburgh improvised.

"She's expecting that young man of hers for the weekend," Wainwright said sadly.

Abe Furstburgh had been in show business too long to miss so obvious a cue.

"Not to worry, Gordon. I'll see to it the young man does not arrive for the weekend. You can work with her to your heart's content."

"Thank you, Abraham, thank you very much. We may save the girl's career after all."

On Friday morning, just before 10 A.M. Eastern time, while Marvin Morse was reading a playscript which had been submitted for Kitzi Mills, he was interrupted by Sarah Blinkhorn.

"Marv, Alvin just called. Wants to see you in his office. Right away, he said. Some kind of emergency."

Little Nat Cohn was in Alvin Horowitz's office when Marvin entered. Cohn was pacing anxiously, exhibiting all the signs of a man wrestling with a momentous crisis.

"I'd be on the plane right this minute," Horowitz volunteered. "But you know what would happen."

Cohn interrupted his pacing to accuse, "Alvin, you never should have double-crossed Roger Stevens on that last deal!" Only then did he acknowledge Marvin's presence. "Oh, hi, kid. Boy, have we got a problem!"

"Can I help?" Marvin asked.

"I don't know," Cohn said. "You're new at this, and young. Believe me, if we had any alternative—but we got a star in the play down in the Kennedy Center. She hates the director. So she wants to pull out. But this is such a great role for her that we don't want her to. What we would like is for Stevens to replace the director. That would solve it all."

"*I* could call him," Marvin volunteered.

"Son, you don't just call Stevens and say, 'Roger, fire the director.' It has to be done with diplomacy. With tact. Say, for example, you fly down tonight. Tomorrow morning you see Roger in his office at the Kennedy Center. That's the best time to get him. Saturday morning. He's alone in the office and there are no phone calls to interrupt. You have a quiet, sincere talk with him. That's the way you deal with a gentleman like Roger Stevens."

"I'm due to fly to the Coast tonight. The ticket's on my desk right now."

"Marvin, my boy," Cohn began as he reached up to place his hand on the taller man's shoulder, "an agent doesn't just 'represent' his client. He has a 'relationship' with his client. He must be available at all times. On call. Like a doctor. When the client hurts, we hurt. Otherwise we can't call ourselves agents in the highest sense of that term."

Horowitz volunteered, "Believe me, I'd go. But Stevens won't even talk to me. We need a fresh face down there. But someone bright enough to talk to a man like Stevens."

"Actually, kid, this is a test," Cohn said. "To see if you're ready to fill Alvin's shoes. Deliver Stevens's agreement to change directors, and you've proved all you have to."

It was 10:15 A.M. in New York when Marvin Morse dialed the number of the Beverly Hills Hotel. He discovered that despite the early California hour, Kitzi had already left for the studio. He was forced to leave a message: "Darling, I can't be there. Will call later."

By four o'clock, Marvin was on Eastern's Washington shuttle. Despondent, he settled down in the smoke-infested cabin, opened his attaché case, took out *Variety* and Hollywood Reporter. He was trying to busy himself with them when he was arrested by a familiar voice.

"This seat taken?"

He looked up into the pretty, provocative face of Florence Fenton. Her dark hair was done in a silky braided coronet that framed her features. She was wearing a strong, tantalizing perfume that helped dispel the stench of cigarette smoke. She slid into the seat alongside him and fastened her seat belt.

"Down to catch the show?" she asked.

"We've got a problem down there."

"We do too," she said. "There's a lot of bad talk drifting up to New York. Once people start saying 'The show's in trouble,' that kills off theater-party business. It also kills off the chances of getting our stars on TV talk shows." Then, as an afterthought, she asked, "I thought you were due to go to the Coast today. Had that ticket right on your desk."

"Couldn't. Because of this." He did not wish to explain any further.

Nor did Florence ask.

The plane took off. They made no conversation for the rest of the hour. When they landed, to be courteous he asked, "Where are you staying? Maybe I can drop you?"

"The Watergate. It's right across from the Kennedy Center."

"Me too. Let's get a cab."

"You pay for the cab, I'll take dinner. Okay?" she said.

"Okay."

"I'll get us a table in the restaurant upstairs in the theater," she said. "The view is great, even if the food isn't."

They saw the play together. When they went backstage to visit the star, they were greeted by a torrent of protest.

Marvin tried to pacify her by assuring her, "I'm seeing Mr. Stevens in the morning. I'm sure once he knows how unhappy you are, he'll do something about it."

"He'd better," the star threatened. "I want that director out of this theater by tomorrow. Else I quit! Got it, sonny?"

Marvin and Florence glanced at each other—she really was ready to carry out her threat.

They were walking across the wide street that separates the theater complex from the Watergate Hotel. It was a clear, early spring night. The lights of a tug towing an oil barge passed by on the river.

Suddenly Marvin said, "I didn't think the direction was bad, did you?"

"No. But some stars, staring a Broadway opening in the face, get to hate everybody. Nerves. But she'll get her way. She always does."

"So a talented young director has to pay for it," Marvin remarked sadly. "Lousy business."

"No," Florence said. "Wonderful business. Just full of lousy people. Go make your Coast call, then let's grab a cup of coffee."

"Look," an exasperated Marvin Morse shouted at the operator on the switchboard of the Beverly Hills Hotel, "keep ringing! Miss Mills may be in the tub. It's her way of relaxing after a tough day."

"I'll try," the operator said, her impatience obvious.

He could hear her ring and ring and ring. Still no answer.

"Sorry, sir." The operator sounded smug.

"Did she leave a message?"

"I'll connect you with the front desk."

The clerk at the front desk did have a message in Miss Mills's box. It said simply that she would be out of town for the weekend.

"That's all? No phone number? Just 'out of town'?"

He hung up reluctantly. He heard a knock on his door. Florence Fenton was there, dressed to go out. She read his face at once.

"Gone for the weekend, is she?"

"You know your trouble, lady, you are too fucking smart!" he exploded. An instant later, he said, "Sorry. Yes. Gone for the weekend."

As he was slipping into his jacket, she asked, "Do you want to know *where* she went?"

"And if I do?"

She went to the phone and dialed a number she seemed to know well. When she received an answer, she asked, "Ah, Francisco. Miss Fenton. May I speak to Miss Mills? Or Mr. Wainwright? Expected any minute. I see. No, don't bother to tell her that I called. I'll reach her on Monday."

She hung up the phone. She stared at Marvin with sympathetic black eyes.

"Come on," she said, "let's go over to Georgetown and get something to eat. Or drink."

The man who took care of Gordon Wainwright's Malibu home was named Frank Ramirez. But it gave Wainwright a certain pleasure to call him Francisco because he enjoyed drawing the name out over three exaggerated syllables. So whenever he called to apprise the man of his plans for the weekend, the conversation always started with a rolling, majestic "Fran-cis-co, we will be having company for the weekend."

Ramirez, a small, lithe man whose age showed only in the deep creases in his mahogany-brown face, could write the dialogue that followed.

"We have a great deal of work to do. So there will be only the two of us. Something simple will do. Beluga caviar and Scotch salmon with cocktails. Rack of lamb for the entrée. I leave the rest up to you."

Wainwright's Rolls arrived, as usual, right on schedule in the driveway of the large, Malibu home. "Francisco!" Wainwright called, though there was no need to: The man was there, and plainly visible. But it fed Wainwright's ego to order him about.

Ramirez opened the door of the Rolls to permit Kitzi Mills to emerge. She stepped out and looked around, impressed by the size of the house and the refreshing aroma of the Pacific.

Ramirez was struck by her pale beauty and her glowing blond hair. The old bastard not only had excellent taste but good luck besides.

"Your bags, miss?" Ramirez asked.

"One bag," she said. "It's in the trunk."

As Ramirez went to secure it, Wainwright came around the car to take Kitzi's hand and lead her into the house. At the threshold he stopped. Then, as if introducing her to the house and the house to her, he pushed the door wide open.

The view to the ocean was unobstructed. Even from the front door one had the feeling of being aboard an ocean liner. Kitzi found the view so startling that she instinctively looked up at Wainwright, as if to ask, *Is all this real?*

With a paternal smile, he took her hand and led her inside. The living room was two stories high, with gray beams that affected the color and grain of driftwood. To one side of the room was a fireplace of rough white stone as tall as the house itself. Two steps led down into the room. At the far end, two steps led up to the deck outside. The deck doors and wall were all of glass and gave

an unobstructed view of the ocean which heaved and fell rhythmically.

"Would you like to go for a swim?" Wainwright asked.

"I'd love it," Kitzi said. "But I didn't bring a bathing suit."

"Not to worry," Wainwright said, calling, "Fran-cis-co!"

Ramirez appeared at once. "Yes, sir?"

"A swim suit for Miss Mills." He pretended to study her before
deciding. "Something that will give Miss Mills all the freedom her
youth deserves."

Ramirez knew that meant the red bikini which was the old bastard's favorite.

Kitzi Mills stood poised on the top step of the steep, weathered
wooden staircase which led down to the rocky sand beach. She
started down the stairs. When she reached the beach, she raced
across the sand toward the restless green waters.

She dove in. Her young body cut the water like a knife. Arms
outstretched, she shot to the surface and began to swim in long,
slow strokes. It felt good to wash away the tensions of the most
difficult week of her young life. A week when everything she did,
every word she spoke, seemed to be under critical scrutiny, from
not only the legendary Gordon Wainwright but the other cast
members.

After every take she had felt the impulse to ask, *How did it go?
How did I do? Was I all right?*

As she swam in the cool Pacific, she felt that her worst week was
over. After a weekend of working with Wainwright on the script, the
coming week should be far less taxing.

On the deck, perched high over the beach, Gordon Wainwright
stood at the rail peering through a pair of high-powered binoculars
as Kitzi Mills emerged from the water.

God, he thought, *the face of an angel, the body of Venus. How
her breasts strain the bra of that bikini.*

He was interrupted by Ramirez, who came out bearing a large tray
with a domed glass cover under which was a riot of color. Thinly
sliced, deliciously pink salmon imported from Scotland, yellow lemon
quarters, mounds of more delicate yellow chopped egg yolk, snow-

white bits of chopped onions, and, finally, large grayish buds of caviar
that glowed like dark pearls.

Kitzi Mills had just slipped out of the wet bottom of her bikini.
She stood naked and damp in the bathroom of her suite. The bathroom door was open. She heard a timid, respectful knock at the outer
door. As she reached for a large coral bath towel to cover herself, she
called, "Just a minute." But the outer door opened simultaneously.

Wainwright burst into the room as if propelled by a most important creative discovery which he felt driven to impart to her. Kitzi
clutched the towel to her chest, but not before Wainwright got a
glimpse of her naked, moist body. He stared for an instant before
pretending to be embarrassed. "Oh, I'm sorry, my dear. Terribly
sorry," he said, and withdrew at once.

She continued toweling her body dry. Wainwright went back to
his own suite to resume looking through the peephole he had had
ingeniously concealed between his own bathroom and the adjoining
visitor's suite.

As he watched, he kept thinking in great anticipation, *God, what
a night this will be. Such beauty . . . such youth . . . such youth.*

10

Marvin Morse and Florence Fenton sat across from each other
over a small marble table in an Italian coffee house in Georgetown.
It was late, past midnight. But the place and the streets outside were
crowded with government employees beginning their weekends.

The two had been silent, Florence out of respect for his pain.

"You knew his home number without even looking it up."

"That was his Malibu number. I know his home number too, if
you'd like."

He pushed back his third drink so hard that it toppled and he had
to move swiftly to prevent the glass from shattering on the tile floor.
"Let's go back to the hotel. I want to try that number again!" he
said.

"You don't want to make that call," she cautioned.

"But I do!" he insisted.

"Take my word, you don't want to make that call!" she insisted, even more firmly but without raising her voice.

They left the restaurant. He looked around for a cab, but she suggested, "Let's walk. It's a nice night and it's not too far."

They walked in silence. When they arrived at the Watergate, they each checked their messages, took their keys, and started up to the fourth floor. They parted at the elevator. His room was six doors to the left. Hers was three doors to the right.

He hung up his jacket, undid his tie, and was unbuttoning his shirt when, on impulse, he decided to go knock on Florence's door. All he could think of was Kitzi.

Florence expected him. She called casually, "Marvin?"

"Yes."

She opened the door wearing a white silk nightgown which outlined her full breasts and the curve of her belly. Her long dark hair hung loose over her shoulders. She slipped into an emerald robe whose color set off her dark beauty.

"I want that number."

"Don't ask me for it. Because I will have to refuse. And you're not a man I want to refuse anything to."

It was a bold, frank admission.

"You'll go to any lengths to protect a client!" he accused in his frustration.

"I'm protecting you!"

"Kitzi and I are going to get married!"

"You still can. This is only a minor episode in her life. And she didn't plan this. You did."

"Me?" he denied.

"Throwing a twenty-year-old girl like her into the same cage with a crafty, lecherous bastard like Gordon Wainwright. That son of a bitch always works things out his way," Florence said.

"You mean I was set up?"

"With God and Gordon Wainwright, all things are possible," she said. "In his mind, they're one and the same."

"What an idiot I was!"

"You going to stand out there all night?" she asked.

When he did not respond, she reached for his hand and drew him into the room. She snapped off the light.

"Now, if you feel like crying, cry. If you feel like cursing, curse. But face it. The fairy tale is over. The princess turned out to be vulnerable."

"Idiot . . . idiot . . . idiot . . . ," he kept accusing himself.

"If you don't want to be an even bigger idiot, instead of worrying about what's out there, take advantage of what's here."

She reached for his hands and pressed them against her breasts. He reached out to embrace her.

Their love-making was feverish. He needed consoling, and he proved himself an even better lover than she had expected. More intense. More virile. He fell asleep before she did. She lay awake, his head against her breast.

He is going to love me, even when he doesn't need me, she thought. *He will.*

With dinner cleared, Wainwright led Kitzi out onto the deck to witness the last of a glorious Pacific sunset. The sun's radiance painted the clouds a brilliant, constantly changing fiery red, which gradually turned to gray.

While Kitzi leaned against the deck railing watching evening change into night, Wainwright stood beside her and spoke in a haunting whisper.

"The secret of all acting before a camera is to do less and less, not more and more. Do not project as you've been trained to do in the theater. You have only to think, to feel. The camera will find that in your eyes, reflect and enhance it. Now, if you attempt to deceive it . . ."

The cool night air coming off the ocean made her shudder slightly. He needed no further cue to put his arm around her and draw her close as he continued. "If you attempt to deceive the camera, it becomes a very treacherous enemy. That scene you were doing this afternoon with Burt, you were *acting.*" He spoke the word as if acting were one of the mortal sins. "In films, we do not act. We *are.* We *think.* We *feel.* Remember that."

"I try," Kitzi said.

He could tell from the feel of her young body that she had become relaxed and trusting to the point of total submissiveness.

"Ah, I fear I've exhausted you by trying to teach you too much at once. Fortunately, we have two long days to work on this. You get on up to bed. See you in the morning."

He watched as she tried to make a graceful exit, though she knew she was somewhat unsteady from all the wine at dinner. He was amused.

Lovely child. Drinks a bit much. But she's young. She'll learn.

As soon as he heard her door close, he raced up the stairs and went straight to his peephole. He watched her undress, and he savored the way she leaned naked over the washbasin, her breasts delightful and firm. She washed her face clean of all makeup, studied herself in the mirror, shook her head to clear it, then started back into the bedroom, affording him the sight of graceful thighs and buttocks which were delightfully dimpled.

Kitzi slipped into bed and realized that for the first time in her life she was between silk sheets. She pulled the top sheet against her soft skin and fell asleep, lulled by the wine and the hedonistic joy of indulging herself in unrestrained luxury. And the old cliché about directors taking advantage of young ambitious actresses seemed to be just a myth. He had seemed embarrassed when he walked in on her.

She had been asleep for less than an hour when she became aware of a pleasant feeling. It was as if she were awash in warm and perfumed waters. She felt it in her breasts, and then in the warm, sensitive area between her legs. As she gave herself to it, she gradually realized what was happening. He pleasured her with his tongue and mouth. She felt herself responding to him. Part of her would have resisted were it not overruled by the more passionate part of her relaxed by wine. When the frenzy of her excitement slowly began to subside, it was replaced by a delicious pulsating response. She felt his beard work its way up her body to press against her breasts. She waited, expecting that he would venture further. He did not. He fell asleep. As content with the episode as she had been, apparently he was not even going to attempt to enter her. She fell asleep wondering about that.

* * *

Florence woke Marvin at seven.

"Go back to your room. Get showered and dressed. You brought a fresh shirt, didn't you? You've got to see Roger at nine."

Before she let him go, she kissed him.

He found Roger Stevens in his office at nine o'clock. He was tall, almost bald, with a plain but strong face, and he worked standing up, his desk at chest height. While Marvin talked, Stevens read statements of gross receipts and budgets of planned shows, and scanned contracts with stars, directors, and authors.

Marvin recited the litany which Stevens had heard too many times from too many agents representing too many stars who, because of nervousness or sheer hatred, wanted directors, costars, or even minor actors replaced.

Marvin stressed that what was needed on a New York opening night was confidence, which his client was now lacking. Another director, a new face, a breath of fresh air would be stimulating, not only to her but to the entire cast.

Stevens seemed not to be paying attention as he shuffled his papers, putting some to one side and some to the other. He did not look up until Marvin had finished. Then he said, "I already called Mike Nichols. He's busy. So I have Quintero and Sherin coming down to see the performance at the matinee today."

"Then you'll replace the director?" Marvin asked.

"I'll replace him," Stevens agreed.

"I'm sorry about this," Marvin said.

"Don't be," Stevens said. "He's a bright young man. Caught in a bad situation. I've already signed him to do another play. No reason to damage his career, is there?"

"No. No reason," Marvin agreed.

He left Stevens's office, thinking, *There are some decent people in this business after all.*

That comforting thought existed only for a moment, when it was overshadowed by another depressing thought.

Stevens had decided to change directors on his own. There was no need for me to make this trip to Washington. I could have handled this by phone. Even from California. Boy, was I set up! Florence was right. Idiot! Shmuck!

* * *

Still geared to Eastern time, Kitzi Mills woke at dawn, Wainwright still asleep beside her. Now he was not the imposing figure he had seemed the night before, but an old man with a beard, mainly white, and a wrinkled face with deep, jagged creases and, around his eyes, the wrinkles and puffiness which were the legacy of a dissolute life.

She slipped out of bed gently so as not to wake him and went to the wide, floor-to-ceiling windows. She pushed aside one corner of the draperies to look out. She could not see the ocean for the heavy mist. The deck was gray and damp from it. It was not a promising day.

She heard a rustle of bedclothes. She turned to find him waking. He opened one eye, spied her, smiled. He beckoned her back to bed. Despite her reservations, she went. He embraced her body as if to warm her. When she relaxed, he began to kiss and lick at her body, face, eyes, neck, breasts, nipples, belly, and then the softest part of her.

The ecstasy was even more intense now that she could no longer resist it. When she was spent, she wanted to reward him. She reached for his sex, found it, ran her fingers gently over it, but got no response. She continued to try until his hand reached down to stop her.

He whispered softly, "My dear, don't you think I would if I could have?"

She felt a wave of pity for him.

"I did a film once about King David. In his later years, when he was aged and cold, he asked for young maidens to warm him. This, I think, is the real sport of kings. Old kings, that is."

11

Marvin finally got Kitzi on the telephone on Monday evening. She didn't tell him what had happened, but she didn't need to. Even if he hadn't known about the betrayal, thanks to Florence, he would have sensed it in the tone of Kitzi's voice. He heard a certain distance there now, a holding back.

For the following weekends, Marvin did not need to be tricked into staying away from Hollywood. Resolving not to visit her until she told him what had happened, he invented his own office emergencies in order to stay away. And he was even more hurt to discover that Kitzi offered only token disappointment.

When he wasn't at work, Marvin felt lost. Nowhere to go but back to their apartment, whose emptiness mocked him, depressed him, imprisoned him. He found himself aimlessly wandering Broadway and its side streets.

During one night of solitary wandering, Marvin was passing the Booth Theatre on the Forty-fifth Street side of Shubert Alley. He heard his name called and turned to discover Florence Fenton in the lobby. He felt a surge of guilt. Since that night in Washington weeks ago, he had never called her.

He stepped into the tiny lobby of the Booth to greet her, "Hi, darling . . ."

"In show business, 'Darling' is for people whose name you can't remember," she rebuked.

"We're taking production photos to dress the outside of the house for the opening," she explained. "If you wait a little, I'll be free. If you don't mind taking me to supper."

"Of course not. I hate to eat alone," he admitted.

"Which, I understand, you've been doing a lot of lately," she said.

He would have resented that but for the obvious sympathy and understanding he saw in her soft black eyes.

They were in the lobby of the Algonquin, where a noisy aftertheater crowd was enjoying the supper buffet. Marvin had done his best to make casual and evasive conversation throughout dinner.

"And now," Florence asked over coffee, "what about you?"

"I haven't seen her for four weeks." He paused before confessing, "somehow, she doesn't seem very disappointed when I call to tell her I can't come out."

"Don't forget she's busy. Working hard. And must be nervous as hell, this being her first picture," Florence said.

He reached for Florence's hand, to make her look directly into his eyes. "Why are you making excuses for her when you should be doing just the opposite?"

"If I don't defend her, you will," she admitted frankly. "So I might as well appear to be a sweet, understanding woman, instead of the jealous bitch I am."

"Jealous?"

"Of course." There was no hint of apology in her eyes. "Don't look shocked, Marv. That night in Washington was an audition. I haven't auditioned many men, but you got the part. Oh, did you get the part!" she said.

Then, more softly, she confessed, "I kept waiting for you to call."

"I'm sorry," he said.

"That's what I like about you. You have a sense of guilt. Every man should have a sense of guilt. So few do." She glanced at her watch. "Good God, so late. And I have an interview early in the morning. One of those young idiot television stars in town for some publicity. I have to be there to cover for any stupidity she might dish out."

They came out of the Algonquin. With no cab in sight, he suggested they walk.

They started north on the Avenue of the Americas and passed other couples. Some street people. A derelict who lay in the entrance to a shoe repair shop. An empty rum bottle lay by his head.

"Jesus . . .," was all she said, and reached for Marvin's hand. "Scares me. That human beings can sink so low. Makes me wonder. Could that ever happen to someone like me, or anyone I know?"

"They say it's a sickness," he observed. "Who knows? Thank God we don't know anyone like that."

They walked that way, his hand in hers, until they came to the newly opened apartment building across from the George Gordon office.

"I get off here," she said.

"You live here? Right across from the office?" He was surprised.

"Yes, I live here. Right across from your office. But I didn't plan it that way," she said, laughing.

He grew suddenly serious as he said, "Do you have to go up?"

"Why?"

"Because . . . because I don't want you to leave. What I mean is . . ."

She said it for him. "You don't want to be alone again tonight," and took his hand.

They started into the marble lobby of the building. He could tell from the look of surprise on the elevator man's face that this was unusual conduct for Florence Fenton. When they reached her floor, the man held the elevator door open until Florence had unlocked her own door and they had disappeared into her apartment.

She shed her strong, forthright attitude with her businesslike attire. Once naked, her black hair loose and flowing over her soft shoulders and between her ample breasts, she was amorous and compliant. He was able to lose himself in her totally and completely.

By the time he woke, she had already showered, dressed, and left to keep her breakfast appointment. He lay in her bed, inhaling the aroma of her.

When he went into the kitchen to get some orange juice, he found a note stuck to the refrigerator door with a magnet: "As my Aunt Sadie used to say, Now that you've found the way, don't be such a stranger."

She had signed it "J.B."

He thought it was odd for someone whose names, first and last, began with F.

Until he realized "J.B." stood for "Jealous Bitch."

12

Marvin continued to stay away from Kitzi, but, ironically, Florence was assigned to fly out to California with a group of publicity and advertising people to begin planning the *Landfall* campaign. She made it a point to be pleasant and restrainedly casual when she met Kitzi. The interview was brief.

"How do you like Hollywood, Miss Mills? Or can I call you Kitzi?"

"Kitzi is fine," she enthused, smiling. Her blue eyes lit up. "As for Hollywood, I really couldn't tell you. I've been so busy. Shooting five days a week and preparing all weekend for next week's shooting."

Florence Fenton could not avoid thinking, *She's so beautiful, so*

*goddamn beautiful, and, from what I hear, talented besides. It isn't
fair for women like me to have to compete against a woman like her.
I wish she'd do something or say something that would make me
hate her.*

Instead, Florence smiled in return as she continued:
"You work every weekend, do you? No time off?"

"Gordon—I mean, Mr. Wainwright—has been very kind. He's
given up his social life to work with me on the weekends. And he's
taught me a great deal. A great deal."

I'll bet, Florence thought.

"From what I hear about your performance," Florence said, "it's
paying off. Everyone is talking Academy Award nomination."

Kitzi blushed, and Florence thought, *Beautiful isn't enough.
Blonde and blue-eyed isn't enough. Gentile isn't enough. She has the
nerve to be modest too.*

"You'll have to get used to hearing that, Kitzi," Florence continued. "We'll be using it in all the publicity."

"I wish you wouldn't," Kitzi protested.

"Why not?"

"It's tempting fate."

"Not out here," Florence said. "Out here, wishing can make it so.
Provided it's backed up with heavy advertising in the trades, of
course."

"Well, if I do get a nomination, it'll be thanks to Gordon . . . Mr.
Wainwright, I mean." Kitzi said. "He's been wonderful to me. Like
a father."

"Good! I like that. Veteran director, one of the fabled names in
cinema history, as a valedictory, is passing on his knowledge and
experience to the younger generation."

"I've learned more from him than any other person except my
grandfather."

"Your grandfather?" For some reason she could not explain, Florence was intrigued. "Tell me more. There might be some interesting
background material there."

"He was a fine man, my grandfather," Kitzi began. "Very well thought of. No, the right word is esteemed. He was a minister. Very distinguished, a white beard. Not the flowing kind, but neat, carefully trimmed. When he walked into a room, voices stopped. People turned even before they saw him. They sensed him. He had that sort of magnetism. And his eyes. He had blue eyes which had a piercing quality. You weren't likely to lie to him. Not with those eyes."

"A minister's granddaughter. Might be an angle there. I assume you inherited your blue eyes from him," Florence remarked.

"Oh, no one has the kind of eyes he had. He was the most gently dominating man I've ever seen. Except of course for Gordon . . . I mean Mr. Wainwright."

Wainwright came across the set toward them.

"Florence, will you excuse us? We have to rehearse the next shot."

"Of course," she said, drawing back into the shadows as Wainwright took Kitzi by the arm, leaning so close to her that their heads were touching as he whispered to her. Kitzi kept nodding and clung to his arm, reluctant to let go.

He owns her, Florence thought. *The old bastard owns her.* She determined to have lunch or dinner with Kitzi before she started back to New York.

That proved difficult to arrange, because of Gordon Wainwright's possessiveness. Only on Friday, when Kitzi's scenes were scheduled for late in the afternoon, did he allow Florence to take her off the lot to lunch at La Serre.

When Florence suggested a drink, Kitzi said, "Gordon absolutely forbids drinking at lunch. Says it interferes with my work."

"Some wine, then?" Florence offered.

"Wine is for weekends only. Gordon has an amazing wine cellar. Rare vintages. . . ."

Florence ordered a small carafe of white house wine with her salad. As lunch proceeded, Florence observed, or thought she observed, that Kitzi watched her closely every time she lifted her glass to take a sip. That fact lingered with her.

The talk at lunch concentrated on Kitzi's plans for when she returned to New York. Marriage. Having a child. Or two. Then combining her private life with her professional plans.

When she dropped Kitzi at the *Landfall* stage, she said casually, "Oh, I run into your agent occasionally. Marvin Morse."

Kitzi blushed again. "He's more than my agent. He's the man I'm going to marry."

"Congratulations," Florence said, smiling as pleasantly as she could manage.

The plane ride back to New York was long and tiring. Florence arrived at her apartment after ten o'clock. Her answering machine was blinking away to announce three days of messages. She put down her suitcase, tossed her purse onto the couch, dropped her coat on the way to the machine, then pressed the "Message" button.

The first voice she heard was Marvin Morse's. *"Flo, honey, call me as soon as you get back. No matter what time. Thanks."*

She reached for the phone, then changed her mind and thought, *Let him wait. I'll take my bath first, have a drink, maybe even a snack, and then I'll call him.*

She was luxuriating in a warm, fragrant bath when she decided to forget the drink and the snack and call him then. She reached for her bathroom extension. From the eager sound of his voice, she knew he had been waiting for her.

"Marv, it's me."

He asked, "How was your flight?"

"The usual," she said, waiting for him to ask about her.

"Did you see her? Get a chance to talk to her?"

"Yes, I saw her. Yes, I did get a chance to talk to her. In fact, we had lunch today."

"Really?" he said, surprised. Then, he asked, carefully, "Did you tell her that you know me?"

"I mentioned that we'd met," she said coolly.

"What did she say?"

Florence hesitated, thinking a minute before she replied, "Not much. She did go on quite a bit about Wainwright, though."

"She's raved about him on the phone. Not the monster you once described. She looks on him as a father."

"More likely a grandfather, to hear her tell it. Whatever Wainwright says, she does. He says no drinks on shooting days, she obeys faithfully. Of course weekends are different. To hear her tell it, endless bottles of fine wines, the rarest vintages."

Marvin laughed. "Endless bottles? Kitzi? She can't handle alcohol at all."

"Then she must be learning." Florence said. "Well, I've got to haul this naked body out of this tub and fix myself a drink and a sandwich."

"You're in the tub?" he asked. The image enticed him.

"If you're hungry," he went on, "I could pick up something and be right over. Chinese? Or sandwiches from the all-night deli on Fifty-seventh Street? I didn't have much dinner myself tonight."

Of course not, she thought. *You've been waiting home all night for me to call. To find out about her. Well, what you need, buster, is for me not to be so available.*

Having decided that, and luxuriating sensuously in her warm, perfumed tub, she said, "Marv, I'm awfully tired. Some other night. Maybe tomorrow night. Call me."

And she hung up.

He felt even more alone than ever. More than alone, he felt angry. Florence had actually seen—had had lunch with Kitzi. Obviously he was the only one in the business not allowed to see her. Well, no more, he determined.

He grabbed his phone, dialed. "American? I'd like a single seat on the nine o'clock to Los Angeles. Tomorrow morning. No, I mean today!"

13

American's flight 1 fought headwinds all the way across the continent. It arrived fifty-one minutes late.

By the time Marvin Morse arrived at the MGM Studios, where Gordon Wainwright was shooting *Landfall,* it was just past two o'clock in the afternoon. The lunch break over, crew, cast, and stars had begun to drift back.

The sign outside the entrance to Stage Ten was clearly marked Closed Stage. Visitors Prohibited. Marvin opened the heavy soundproof door and entered. He stood in a huge, wide space with catwalks crisscrossing high above his head. It was dark except for one far corner where there was subdued lighting. He started toward it.

Though Stage Ten was large, even by major studio standards, the set involved in this day's shooting was small and cordoned off by flats and furnishings which simulated the corner of a paneled drawing room in an elegant home. The arc lights were all dark, and only the work lights were on.

Marvin walked into the set and looked about until he was approached by a burly man in work shirt and jeans.

"Help you, buddy?" he asked.

"I'm looking for Miss Mills. I'm her agent from New York," Marvin said, and handed the man his card.

"She's having lunch."

"In the commissary?" Marvin asked.

"In Mr. Wainwright's trailer. They're rehearsing her next scene."

"And where *is* that?"

"It's the last one down the line here. But I got to warn you. Mr. Wainwright does not like to be disturbed when he's working."

"That's okay," Marvin improvised. "He's expecting me."

Marvin walked along a row of private trailers, some with their doors open, others with doors closed. The door of the last one was closed. But he could hear Wainwright's voice, so soft that the words were indistinguishable, yet the tone was mesmerizing. Marvin knocked.

It sounded as if the voice of God came at him through the locked door. "Who the hell is that?"

"It's me. Marvin Morse."

"Marvin——" Wainwright was totally baffled for an instant.

But Kitzi called out, "Marvin? What are you doing . . ."

Before she could finish, Marvin pushed open the door and saw Kitzi drawing back into a corner of the studio couch and covering her naked body with her dress. Wainwright tried to shield her by positioning himself between her and Marvin.

At the same time he called out, "Somebody! Get this man out of here! Throw him off the set. Throw him off the lot! Get him the hell out of here!" His voice echoed across the empty stage.

Marvin commanded, "Kitzi! Kitzi!"

She did not move. In moments, half a dozen of the stage crew surrounded Marvin. They seized him, grappled with him, but could not overcome him until he heard Kitzi cry out, "Marvin, please! Go! Just go!"

He stopped struggling and glared at her. The others backed away. With contempt glittering in his eyes, he turned on his heel and strode away. Actors, actresses, crew members stared at him until he left the dark stage for the bright, hot sunlight of the California afternoon. He stood there panting, drenched in sweat, burning with rage.

He returned to New York on the red-eye. When he arrived at the office, he knew that word of his disastrous venture had preceded him. He knew it from Sarah's silence and the pitying shake of her head. He knew it from the memo that lay in the center of his desk blotter. "Marvin! See me! N.C."

The conversation was brief.

"Marv, my boy," Cohn said, "take it from an older man. In this business, a successful agent thinks with his head, not his cock. Never do such a foolish thing again. You could have ruined that girl's career. More important, you could have ruined your own career."

No threats, no long recriminations, just a capsule of professional advice. Followed by "Marv, I think from now on it would be better if someone else handled Mills."

Through the next ten days, when she had the time and their busy schedules permitted, Florence Fenton nursed Marvin through his pain from the disaster he had suffered in California.

With some apprehension she awaited the eleventh day. According to daily reports from the Coast office, Kitzi Mills would have finished her part in *Landfall* by then.

Twelve days after Marvin's trip to California, Kitzi Mills arrived in New York. She went straight to the apartment. Before she slipped out of her coat, she sank down on their bed, reached for the telephone, and dialed.

When Sarah Blinkhorn answered, Kitzi asked, "Sarah, is he there?"

"Yes, yes, he's here," the old woman acknowledged coolly.

"May I talk to him?" Kitzi asked.

Sarah was tempted to reply, *What for?* Instead, she said, "Why not?" She put Kitzi on hold, buzzed Marvin, and announced, "She is on the phone." No further identification was required.

His first impulse was to slam down the phone. "Yes?" he answered, distantly.

"Marv. Can you get away from the office? Right now? Please, Marv. Please? I've got something to tell you. Something very important!" she said. Her phrases ran one into the next so swiftly there was no room for him to interrupt. "Marv? Darling?"

He was determined to refuse but he had no defenses against her. "Okay. I'll be there. Right away."

She had slipped out of her clothes and taken a warm bath and was fresh and fragrant for him when he arrived. All the speeches, the recriminations he had prepared on his way in the cab disappeared when she raced into his arms and he felt her body against him under her thin silk robe.

"Oh, Kitzi . . . Kitzi . . . ," he started to say.

She smothered his words with her kisses. In his passion he would forgive her anything.

They remained in bed throughout the afternoon and into the evening. It was long dark when he asked, "Hungry?"

"Uh-uh."

"Well, I am. And there's nothing much here. I haven't been home much since you went away," he said. "We better get dressed to go out and eat."

As he moved to slip out of bed, she reached for his hand, placed it on her belly.

"Feel anything?" she asked.

"Warm. Nice. But you were always nice there," he said, puzzled.

"Not as nice as now," she said. She realized that he failed to understand. "Idiot!" she giggled. "We're going to have a baby."

"Baby . . . we . . . are going to have a baby?" he questioned.

"Just before I left here, I went to a gynecologist. He said Yes, it's true. Isn't that marvelous?"

She felt him draw back from her. She laughed. "Silly, you don't have to be afraid. My doctor said until the eighth month it's perfectly all right to have sex. It can't hurt the baby at all."

She tried to draw him close. He became even more distant.

"Marv?"

"How do I know?"

"Know what?"

"If it's mine? Or Wainwright's?"

"Wainwright? . . . Are you crazy? It couldn't possibly be Wainwright's baby," she said, no longer giggling.

"Oh, no?" he responded.

Then there poured out of him all the angry words he had prepared for her since his return from California.

"Marv, you don't understand!" she pleaded.

"Of course not! After all, that old bastard is screwing the woman I love, and I don't understand? Or is it my approval you want? Sure, honey, go on, let him fuck you every weekend so long as you look good in the dailies! Then when you come home, I can have a little something to remember that son of a bitch by—a baby! What do we call him, Gordon Wainwright Morse?"

Throughout, Kitzi protested through her tears, "No, darling. Marvin, no. Believe me, you're wrong. It's impossible . . . it couldn't be his."

"How can I know that?" he demanded.

"It just couldn't," she repeated. "Believe me!"

"That's no answer!"

Challenged, she realized that she would have even greater difficulty explaining what happened than if she had to confess having had an affair. Yet she had no other way of convincing him of the identity of the child she carried within her.

Slowly, haltingly, protected only by the darkness, she revealed what had happened at the Malibu house that first night, and every night she had spent there.

When she was finished, he asked in a hoarse whisper, "How could you let him do that to you?"

"I . . . I couldn't stop him, I couldn't . . ."

She kept shaking her head, tears streaming down her face, but unable to explain further.

"The picture meant that much to you? More than me. More than us!" he accused.

She shook her head even more violently.

"You're a minister's granddaughter. How could you be part of something like that? How?"

She could not answer. She could not explain. Even if she had, he wouldn't have understood. No one would.

"Marv? Honey?" She pleaded to be forgiven.

Silent, wordless, he began to dress.

"At least say something! Shout! Curse! Beat me, if it would make you feel better!" she pleaded.

"That might make *you* feel better," he countered. "Not me! You made me a laughingstock. Everyone in Hollywood knows. Everyone in New York knows. I'm not allowed to represent you anymore. Did you know that? The office won't let me. Now if you have that child, who's going to believe it's mine? Who is going to believe what you just told me? Nobody! That's who!"

He was dressed and on his way to the door.

"Marvin! Don't go! Please!"

She huddled up like an abandoned child, weeping, and clutching the damp bedsheet between her thighs. She could not tell him. She could never tell anyone why she had been unable to resist Gordon Wainwright.

14

Kitzi had fallen asleep crying. It was the dull pain that woke her. Not a physical pain, but an ache in the pit of her stomach. Gradually, she became aware and remembered. Her pain grew worse.

He was gone.

She was alone.

Not only alone but with child. Her child. Not his. Not theirs. Hers. He had disowned it.

She bathed, had a light breakfast. She went out into Central Park.

Two months in California had distorted her sense of seasons. On the Coast it had been warm, almost summery; here, spring had just arrived. The winter snow had left large muddy patches. Most of the trees were still skeletons. The wind sweeping across from the east chilled her. She should have dressed more warmly.

What happens if a mother catches cold during these early months? What medication is she allowed to take? Was there something in one of the magazines, *Reader's Digest* or *Cosmo* or *Ladies' Home Journal,* about what aspirin could do to the fetus? Or did the warning about aspirin relate to stomach upset? Or ulcers?

There was so much she would have to find out if she were to keep the baby. So much.

She found herself on the east side of the park, near the boat pond, a large, oval, concrete pool some hundreds of feet long and fifty feet wide where children sailed their boats. The benches around the oval were occupied mostly by mothers with baby carriages, or well-dressed children guarded by nannies. Occasionally there was an outburst of crying, or a noisy dispute between youngsters. But, on the whole, the area was peaceful and quiet, as children enjoyed their play and adults enjoyed the sunshine of an early spring day.

Kitzi found an empty place on one of the benches facing east. She sat, eyes closed, tilting her lovely unadorned face up toward the sun while listening to the soothing sound of children at play, their giggling laughter. She opened her eyes to study the children around her. White, black, Oriental, blonde, dark-haired, brown-eyed, blue-eyed, they all seemed beautiful.

She wondered what her own child would look like. Would it resemble her, fair-skinned and blond? Or Marvin, olive-skinned and black-haired? Or would it be some combination? She was sure of one thing—the child, boy or girl, would be handsome or pretty. If only there were someone to talk to. She missed having a mother at a time like this. From childhood, she had been alone, brought up by her grandfather, a minister and a stern man of God who had expelled her mother from his house when she returned pregnant and unmarried.

Suddenly she thought, *Here am I, also alone, pregnant, and un-*

*married, with not even a father to go back to. Will my child end up
the same way? Perhaps she would be better off not being born at
all.*

She had not felt so alone since her very first day in New York. She
felt desolate, beyond weeping. Numb.

On the morning of the seventh day after Kitzi Mills had returned
from California, she was awakened by the phone. She glanced at the
clock on the bedside table. Ten-seventeen. She let the phone ring.
Usually they gave up after the seventh or eighth ring. Not this time.
It continued until she was finally forced to answer it.

"Hello?" she said, in a husky, early-morning voice.

"Kitz . . ."

It was Marvin's voice. She heard it. She felt it. In the tightening
of her breasts.

"Marv . . ." she whispered.

"I have to see you."

"Why?"

"I've been through hell the last seven days," he said.

Instinctively she was tempted to cry out, *You've been through
hell? What about me? What have I been through? Didn't that mean
anything to you?*

She exercised more control than she thought she was capable of
as she asked, "What do you want to see me about?"

"*Us,* of course!" he said. "May I come up?"

She hesitated, knowing that if he came up, the moment he embraced her, kissed her, they would start making love. Which would
solve nothing.

"I'll meet you anywhere you say, but don't come up."

"Why not? It's my apartment, too," he protested.

"Don't try to come up." To reinforce her decision she lied. "It
wouldn't help. I've had the locks changed."

"So soon?" he asked.

"It's been seven days," she pointed out. "Now where do you want
to meet? What about the boat pond in the park?"

"Okay. The pond. Three o'clock?"

"Three o'clock," she agreed.

* * *

She arrived there at five minutes to three. He was already waiting on a bench in front of the Hans Christian Andersen statue.

He saw her, rose, rushed to her, and held her tightly as he whispered, "God, I missed you!" She huddled against him, burrowing her face into his chest. While they stood that way, close, with other people staring, he said, "I know what we have to do. And everything will be all right again."

"What?" she asked, full of hope once more.

"Come." He took her by the hand, and they climbed the hill up from the pond where they could talk without being overheard or observed.

At the crest of the hill he eased her down onto the new grass and dropped beside her.

"I know I blew my top. But the thought of that old bastard . . . I went crazy. We can't ever let anything come between us again."

She nestled against him, embracing his arm. *It's going to be all right,* she thought, *it's going to be like it was.*

"I thought it all out. It wasn't your fault. Young, inexperienced. Your first film. Under the control of an overpowering figure like Wainwright. What chance did you have to resist? I blame myself for that."

He held her face before him and looked into her blue eyes. "I don't blame you. Understand? I do not blame you," he said emphatically.

When tears came to her eyes, he kissed them. He held her tightly. She felt all the pain and the tension drain out of her.

He continued, "I'll never forgive myself for what I've done to you, to both of us, this last week. We must never be separated again. We must never fight again. Or accuse each other again."

He held her. For some minutes he was silent. Until he said, "About . . . about the . . . about being pregnant . . ."

"Yes?" she asked eagerly.

"If there's a baby, every time I see it I'll be reminded of what happened. I know myself well enough to know I couldn't take that—couldn't."

She drew back slightly. Her pain was beginning to return.

"What are you saying?"

"I'm saying let's have a baby of our own."

"This is our own."

"Kitzi, nobody could believe that," he said.

"There are blood tests that can prove who the father is," she protested.

"No, Kitzi, I talked to my brother Seymour. He's just finishing med school. He told me blood tests can only prove who is *not* the father. Not who is," he explained.

"So?" she asked.

"There's only one way," he said. "You have to get rid of this baby. So we can start fresh."

"Get rid—" She could barely repeat the words. "Start fresh—"

Suddenly her pain was much worse.

He's willing to forgive and forget something that never happened. But not this child I have in me. He's punishing his own child for what he thinks Wainwright did. His child? He's given up all rights to this child. This child is mine, and mine alone. And damn it, I will not give it up! No matter what doubts I had before, I have none now!

"Kitzi? It's the only way, the best way. When you think it over, you'll see."

"I will not 'get rid' of this baby," she said firmly.

"Kitzi, I said think it over."

She freed herself from him and rose to her feet.

"Kitzi?"

"Until this morning I had my doubts. But no more. I am going to have my baby."

She started away. He got to his feet and called after her.

"Kitzi! Darling! Kitzi!"

She did not look back but kept walking. He started after her, caught up with her, put his arms around her to make her listen as he pleaded, "Honey, please."

"Let go of me!" she said furiously. With all the force of her slender body, she broke free. And started to run.

"Kitzi . . . Kitzi!" he kept calling.

She never looked back.

15

Kitzi was breathless by the time she reached the apartment. She needed something to settle her nerves. She went to the bar and mixed herself a vodka and tonic. Drink in hand, she dropped into a comfortable chair by the window and watched the children playing in the park.

Think. I have to think very clearly. I'm on my own now. Alone. No. I may be on my own, but I am not alone. I have my baby. And I am not going to give it up. People will say I'm foolish to risk my career by taking this time off when things look so promising. But I am going to have this baby. And I will take good care of it from this moment on. No more wine. No more cigarettes. No more anything that the doctor says is bad for the baby.

She took one other vow.

From now on I depend only on myself. My talent. My intelligence. I will not give myself completely to any man ever again. From when I was a child until now, too many men have manipulated me. It will never happen again. I have proved myself as an actress. On the stage. In films. I am my own woman from now on.

She called the Gordon office, asked to talk to Nat Cohn, and told him that she was not interested in any Broadway, film, or television roles for the next six months.

"Six months?" Cohn exploded in surprise and anger. "In six months they'll forget all about you. In this business timing is everything. Strike while the iron is hot. And right now you are hot!"

"Six months," she repeated.

"You have a Gordon Wainwright film in the can. It could mean an Oscar nomination! Look, darling, you're just back. You're tired. And I understand there was a little . . . a little upset with Marvin. Take a few days, take a week, and we'll talk again."

"Six months," Kitzi Mills said.

"What about the offers we keep getting? The scripts for you?"

"Find a good one for next season," Kitzi said.

"Next season?" Cohn repeated, always sure that clients had been born only to torment him. "Next season is like forever!"

"Next season," she reiterated. Before he could say anything else, she hung up.

Accompanied by Evelina Downs, the black woman who had been her dresser on Broadway, Kitzi Mills moved from her Manhattan apartment to a small house in Mamaroneck. It wasn't too far from the railroad station, so she was able to get into the city easily.

She spent her days doing exercises and reading books she had long wanted to read—books about the theater, biographies of Bernhardt, Duse, the Barrymores, and autobiographies of current stars of the British and the American stage. From time to time the office would send her a film script or a new play or the score of a musical in progress. She read them all and returned them all, sometimes with the comment.

"This would be interesting six months from now." Or "Five months from now." Or "Four months." Or "Three months from now." Though she spent hours in the kitchen watching Evelina cook, she resisted Evelina's attempts to fatten her up with her tempting cuisine. Her curiosity about Evelina's recipes and kitchen practices was so strong that the black woman asked, "Your mama never taught you to cook? How come?"

"I never had a mama," Kitzi said. "My grandfather brought me up. And cooking to him meant adding water to canned soup. Then, later, when I worked as a waitress, seeing how they handled food, I didn't want to learn how to cook. But I'm going to cook for her."

"How do you know it's a little girl, honey?"

"It's going to be a girl," Kitzi insisted. "Black-haired, brown-eyed. And very beautiful."

She was on the phone refusing one more time to sign for a new film when she experienced the first pains. She called her doctor. He told her to call back in two hours and let him know how often the pains were occurring.

When she called back, he instructed her to start for the city at once and to warn the cab driver to drive very, very carefully, avoiding New York's notorious potholes.

She'd had her small suitcase packed for several weeks. When the cab arrived, Evelina tried to help her into it. Kitzi preferred to do it by herself. Evelina climbed in and they started toward the city.

On the way, whenever Kitzi grimaced or tensed in response to her labor pains, Evelina tried to ease things by joking, "You're not going to have it here in the cab, are you? 'Cause I don't know nothin' 'bout birthin' babies, Miz Scarlett."

They both laughed, which made Kitzi's pains a bit more tolerable.

Kitzi Mills was delivered of a six-pound nine-ounce baby girl with wispy blond hair, whose wrinkled red face was quite lovely for a newborn.

Despite Kitzi's efforts to be discreet, somehow the word got out. There was mention on the scandal page of the afternoon newspaper. And a talk-show hostess listed it with other babies born to unwed stage, screen, and television stars.

At the George Gordon Agency, no one mentioned the subject in Marvin Morse's presence. Not even Sarah Blinkhorn. He ordered a dozen pink roses (Kitzi had always liked pink roses) with a card. Half an hour later he called the florist and said, "Forget the card. Just send the flowers."

Kitzi wondered about the pink roses, but she suspected they were from Marvin. She was determined, however, not to think of him that way again. She had her baby. She could now resume her career. She had her whole life before her.

Several weeks after she had returned to the apartment with her baby, Alice, Kitzi Mills called the Agency and asked who had been delegated to represent her. The choice, Sol Landau, offered to visit her to discuss what he called "future career moves."

Landau was a man well into middle age, with thinning gray hair, a parchment complexion, and rimless bifocals.

He came with flowers for Kitzi and a toy for Alice. "Miss Mills," he began, "I have made an intensive study of your career thus far.

Based on the grosses I hear from the studio, *Landfall* is doing great. We have to be in a position to capitalize on that."

"I would like to do a play," Kitzi said, coming directly to the point.

"Miss Mills, I don't have to tell you what the odds are. Especially if it's an American play, these days. Three out of every four plays fail. We think that your next career move should be a film which you carry. In fact, I brought along a screenplay for you to consider. Solid producers, excellent director, a very promising setup. Top billing. And your first million-dollar fee."

He had saved that for last, sure that it would clinch the deal.

"Read the script. And if you like it, they'd be delighted to fly you out to the Coast to meet with the director."

"I have a child now. I'm not free to move about," Kitzi said.

"Then I'm sure he'd fly East to see you," Landau promised quickly. "Read it and let me know."

The script lay on the foyer table for three days while Kitzi Mills nursed, bathed, and played with little Alice. On the fourth day, after putting Alice down for her nap, she picked up the screenplay, *End of Summer.* The script started well. It was truly a starring part. She interrupted reading only long enough to take Alice from her crib. While she nursed, Kitzi finished reading. By the time she closed the script, Alice was fast asleep. Kitzi Mills was wide awake, and thinking hard.

16

Just before six o'clock, Marvin hung up with the Coast office. He noticed that his second line was lit up, which meant a call was waiting. Instead of Sarah Blinkhorn simply buzzing to announce it, she appeared in his doorway, somewhat tentative and almost tremulous.

"Sarah? What the hell's going on?"

"She . . . she's on the other line."

"*Who* is on the other line?" he demanded.

"*She,*" Sarah said.

Marvin ventured, "Kitzi——?" Sarah nodded and withdrew, closing the door as she left.

"Kitz . . . Is that you? How are you?"

"Fine." Her voice had a guarded, cautious tone. "Marvin, I would like to talk to you."

"About the baby——?"

Before he could finish, she interrupted sharply. "About business!"

"I'll come by this evening."

"No!" she said. "I will meet you away from here. Say, for lunch tomorrow."

"Okay. Lunch. Tomorrow. Tavern on the Green all right with you?" At once he corrected himself. "No. We'd better go to some out-of-the-way place."

"Right. We don't want to be seen together," Kitzi agreed. "Remember that little Chinese restaurant we used to go to? On upper Broadway?"

"Sure. See you there at one," he promised.

He was there by quarter to one and waiting anxiously.

She was late. She apologized. "Alice was restless today. I couldn't leave before she fell asleep."

"How is she? I mean, what does she look like?"

"She's blond," was all Kitzi said. She wanted Marvin to know that the child did not have his coloring.

When he suggested a drink before lunch, she refused. "Not while I'm nursing."

They ordered food, then ignored it as she launched into the purpose of the meeting.

"Landau brought me a script. Said something about a million-dollar offer and star billing."

"I know," Marvin said.

"Kane and Rosen, the producers, are clients of the office, aren't they?" she asked.

"So is the director," Marvin added, "and the writer."

"So it's a George Gordon package. Ten percent of everything," she realized. "And they want me?"

"Not *want* you. *Need* you. You're hot, Kitzi. Everybody out there is talking about the new Wainwright film."

At the mention of that name, their eyes met for a brief instant. But Marvin continued, "Talking about your performance, I mean. If the office can deliver you for this new film, they've got a deal at Orion. Otherwise, no deal."

"If you were representing me, what would you tell me to do?"

"If I were you, I'd ask for three million," Marvin said.

"Three?" she asked, to make sure.

"Then I'd settle for two million plus five percent of the gross. But make sure it's gross. Net only means a lawsuit." He concluded, "That's the best deal you can get."

She absorbed the figures and nodded.

"Also tell them you want your own lawyer in on the deal."

"They're my agents. Why do I need a lawyer?"

"In this business, sometimes you need an agent to represent you against your own agent," he said.

"Okay. Tell me the name of an honest lawyer."

They reached the front door of her house. Marvin asked to come up and see the baby.

"She's usually still asleep at this hour."

"I'd like to see her, even if she is asleep," he insisted.

"No, Marvin. No," she said quietly. She turned and entered through the door held open for her by the uniformed doorman.

Marvin walked away and crossed to the park side of the street to start down toward the office.

She's just as beautiful as ever. More beautiful. Somehow she's no longer mine. She's a woman. She's taken control of her life. Why wouldn't she let me see the baby so I could decide for myself if she's mine or not?

Two months later, Kitzi emerged from negotiations with a deal for two million five hundred thousand dollars up front, plus seven-and-a-half percent of the gross.

When the final deal memo crossed his desk at the Agency, and Marvin read the terms, he could not resist calling her.

"Kitz, how the hell did you ever get such a rich deal?"

"I had to. I'm providing for my daughter's future," she replied, adding "That lawyer you suggested said I should meet you one more time."

"He didn't say anything to me."

"That's my job. Tomorrow. Lunch. Côte Basque. One o'clock?"

"One o'clock. I'll have Sarah make the reservation."

She appeared at Côte Basque promptly at one. She was dressed in a navy suit with sedate white trim, looking very much the woman executive. She had little time for pleasantries. Even before their food arrived she set forth the purpose of the meeting.

"My lawyer said once the deal was wrapped up I should find myself another agent. As he put it, ever so delicately, 'All agents are whores. Almost as unprincipled as lawyers. Get an agent who has only your interest at heart. Someone you trust.' "

"You want me to suggest one," Marvin assumed.

"No, I want you to *be* one," she corrected. "I want you to represent me."

He stared across the table at her, debating her motive.

She continued, "You'll have to leave the Gordon Agency. But you ought to be on your own. The Marvin Morse Agency."

"That's what you've decided?" he asked, more than a bit resentful.

"We used to talk about it. Remember? In the old days?" she reminded him. "Why do people always call it 'the old days'? When it was really our young days."

"It wasn't that long ago."

She said, "This has to be strictly business. Nothing personal. Never again personal. Agent-client. That's it."

"Sure. Of course," he agreed reluctantly. With her sitting across from him now—yet so close that he could inhale the delicate perfume she used, a fragrance which would forever be part of sex for him—her warning was necessary.

"Let me know. Soon," she said.

"I will," he said.

He returned to the office and told Sarah to hold all calls. He spent three hours playing out in his mind every conceivable scenario he could devise about his future if he left the security of a large agency to strike out on his own.

In the end, it was his feeling for Kitzi that made him decide.

"Sarah, call Nat Cohn's secretary and tell her it is urgent that I see him this afternoon!"

By quarter to six that evening, he called Kitzi.

"Kitz, can I come up and see you right away?" he asked.

"No. Just tell me what you decided," she said.

"You've got yourself an agent."

"Good," was all she said.

Three months later, when it was time for Kitzi to depart for the Coast to do the film *End of Summer,* Marvin offered to drive them to Kennedy International.

Kitzi refused. She had engaged a stretch limousine for herself, the baby, and Evelina.

She would not allow him to see the baby.

Part Two

17

End of Summer, the first film in which Kitzi Mills's name appeared above the title, and the first of which she owned seven-and-a-half percent of the gross, was a moderate box-office success. More important, she won further praise from most of the critics.

The picture proved that she could, on her own, carry a film, in a year when not many adult films ended up in the black. It also provided her with financial independence.

She moved from the apartment she and Marvin had occupied to a much larger place in the Beresford, twenty-two stories up, which faced Central Park on the east and looked south on the New York skyline.

She spoke frequently with Marvin about business. But almost always by phone. When a meeting was unavoidable, she insisted it be away from the house, in a formal setting.

He always inquired about her personal well-being, and the child's. The child was always "fine" or "great" or "splendid." As for her private life, he did not ask. He had no need to. It was too well covered in the gossip columns. Kitzi's affairs were numerous and highly publicized. Always she chose her men with great care. A well-known and quite prestigious producer of plays, who pursued her until he realized that she would never marry. A foreign director with whom she worked on a film. The surgeon whom she met at the opening-night party of one of her greatest stage successes.

She had a more lengthy and serious affair with an Under-secretary of State whom she met when she did her one-woman concert at the

Kennedy Center. That affair lasted longest. Despite his devotion, his insistence that he would secure a divorce from his wife to marry her, she refused.

When he presented her with an ultimatum—either marry or end the affair—she took him at his word and ended it with a brief but loving note and pair of monogrammed gold cufflinks from Cartier. She could not, would not, permit herself to become dependent on one man ever again.

Painful as her affairs were to him, Marvin was even more disturbed by the gossip that reached him more and more frequently concerning Kitzi's drinking. The memory of those terrible nights in Boston still lingered.

After she made the front page of the *New York Post* and three television news shows for a drunken assault on a police officer, Marvin decided it would be best to separate her from the local social scene and her drinking companions.

He searched for a vehicle that would keep her on the road and constantly busy. He found it in the one-woman concert with which she had scored so brilliantly in Washington. Because she hadn't been satisfied with any script in recent months, he was able to convince her that the tour was the proper vehicle for her at this stage of her career. He arranged a series of concerts that would keep her away from New York for seven months.

Of course, she would have to tour alone. Alice was now six, and registered at the best and most expensive private school in Manhattan.

Kitzi would have to do what so many touring stars had done before her. Evelina would care for Alice at home, then bring her to wherever Kitzi was appearing when the child had time off from school. Christmas, surely. Easter. Thanksgiving. Mother and daughter would have all the holidays together. In some hotel suite, of course. But Kitzi would make those days as festive and as colorful as if they were taking place at home.

Secretly, Marvin arranged to pay the tour's company manager a special fee each week to keep him informed of Kitzi's condition. Most specifically, he was to report if she resumed drinking.

Marvin's concern was not only professional. He felt a deep sense of personal guilt as well. For he correlated Kitzi's most recent bout of drinking with the night that he came backstage to tell her about an important change in his own life.

He thought she was entitled to hear it from him, not read about it in *Variety* or the *Times*. Marvin Morse, president of the Marvin Morse Agency, and Florence Fenton, well-known show-business publicist, were to be married.

He was never sure that what compelled him to tell her himself was the small hope that she would change her mind about marrying him. It was a secret he kept from Kitzi, from Florence, and, almost, from himself.

But he felt quite sure that after that her drinking had increased.

It increased even more while she was on her tour, which involved not only a great deal of traveling but long, lonely nights after her concerts when she came back to her hotel suite, exhausted, too tired to take advantage of all the invitations that were pressed on her by local social leaders anxious to be seen with her, the star.

She usually preferred a late supper in her suite, preceded by a relaxing drink or two. Or three. Or four. On particularly exhausting nights, when she had difficulty falling asleep, a Seconal. Or three. The important thing was sleep. To be able to withstand tomorrow's travel and to be fresh for tomorrow night's performance.

Dr. Herman Spangler, famous in show-business circles for his treatment of back pain and similar discomforts solely through the use of medically prescribed cocaine, always made sure that when Kitzi was out of New York and beyond the reach of his personal ministrations, she was provided with a sufficient supply of pills to see her through.

By the time her tour was half over, she was using vodka to wash down the pills.

When she began to miss performances, Marvin flew out to meet her in Minneapolis. When he began to talk, she exploded in a torrent of abuse.

"This whole tour was your idea. I hate touring. I hate being forced to do one-night and two-night stands. Most of all, I hate being away from Alice. I want to see her every morning before she goes off to school. I want to be there every afternoon when she comes home."

"Tell me, Kitz, what you want to do and I'll arrange it."

"Find me a new musical. A show that will keep me in New York."

"I'll do that," Marvin promised.

Things changed very little with her new production. During rehearsals, Kitzi was too busy to spend much time with Alice. Once the show opened to great notices for Kitzi, things grew worse. She woke too late to see Alice off to school every morning. And somehow, she was either never at home in the evening or too drunk to kiss the child good night before she went off to the theater.

It was one of the few nights when Marvin Morse and his wife were both free of professional obligations. They were granted the rare privilege of having dinner at home. It was a nice night to be home, to eat one of Florence's home-cooked meals, and to relax. What made it even nicer was the fact that a heavy rain beat against the windows of their apartment that faced Park Avenue.

Marvin had just sat down at the dining room table, anticipating a bowl of Florence's pea soup, when the phone rang.

"Don't answer it," Florence called from the kitchen. "I'll get rid of them, whoever it is."

"Whoever it is" turned out to be Bobbie Flynn, the young woman who was the stage manager of Kitzi's musical. Marvin took the call in the den.

"Okay, Bobbie, what is it this time?"

"Missing. She's just plain goddamn missing. Not here at the theater. Not at home. Evelina is here but hasn't the slightest idea where Kitzi might be," the young stage manager reported.

"Well, I . . . Okay, Bobbie, I'll be right there. He hung up the phone.

"Got to go," he said to Florence, who was standing in the dining room holding the two steaming plates of soup she was ready to set on the table. He kissed her on the cheek, and started out to the foyer to put on his raincoat and battered tweed hat.

"Be back," he called to Florence. "Maybe after the show. But I'll be back. Save the soup."

110

He was gone.

Save the soup, Florence thought. *That woman has a greater hold on him now than if she had married him. He'll never be free of her. Never.*

Despite the doorman's efforts, it proved impossible to flag down an empty cab. Finally Marvin said, "Forget it, Pat. I'll walk." He started into the rain, fighting the wind as he walked south.

He was drenched by the time he reached Forty-fifth Street. Water cascaded off his tweed hat and ran down his cheeks. Backstage, there was still no sign of Kitzi Mills. Evelina was in tears. Kitzi's understudy was made up and ready to go on. But Bobbie Flynn resisted making the announcement. The show was getting a bad reputation. Kitzi was missing too many performances. Marvin asked her to hold the curtain.

He went out into the rain once more and started west on Forty-fifth Street toward Eighth Avenue. At the corner he stepped into a puddle that was ankle deep. He crossed to the west side of Eighth. Out of habit, he started south, peering into every bar he passed, searching. He had made more than a few such searches in the last year. He knew he would find her. Or, if he did not, that there would be a call from the police precinct up on Fifty-fourth Street.

As he walked past the Emerald Isle Bar and Grill, he peered in through the glass of the front door. Instead of the usual line of drinkers ranged along the bar, he saw them huddled in a group. A sick feeling in his stomach told him he had found Kitzi. He went in, pushing his way through the group despite considerable drunken resistance. He found her.

She was lying on the floor, her dress up beyond her navel. She was totally exposed and writhing as if in the ecstasy of an orgasm. "Come on, boys. Come on!"

He pushed the men aside. Despite her loud protests, he lifted her from the floor and started out with Kitzi over his shoulder, kicking him, punching him. Through the rain, against the wind, up Eighth Avenue. At the corner he turned east on Forty-fifth Street, passing a patrol car with two officers who greeted him, "Hi, Mr. Morse. Again?"

111

He trudged toward the stage entrance of the theater. With the whole cast staring at them, he crossed backstage to her dressing room. There he delivered her, sopping wet and drunk, into the arms of Evelina.

"Get her ready," he said.

He spoke to the stage manager outside the dressing room. "Bobbie, go out and announce that due to the inclement weather the curtain will be a little late."

"You think she'll be ready?" she asked, peering tensely through her thick-lensed glasses.

"She'll be ready!" he said.

He went back into the dressing room to assist Evelina, who, in recent years, had become quite adept at preparing Kitzi Mills for an entrance.

In performance, Kitzi did well. She always did well. Only a few missed cues, of which the audience was not even aware. After the show, he took Kitzi and Evelina home, and continued across town to his own apartment.

Florence was still up. There was no need for conversation. It would just be a repeat of the conversation they'd had too many times before.

So she said only, "Get out of those wet clothes and into your pajamas and robe. What you need is some good hot soup."

While he changed, he called to her from the bedroom, "Once she gets onstage, she's amazing."

Florence did not respond.

"If only I could keep her onstage all the time," he said.

When he appeared, dry again and warm in his pajamas and his cashmere robe, he discovered that she had set up a small table for him in the den. There was the soup, hot, fragrant, steaming. And two chunks of French bread.

After some time, during which he ate and Florence sat there, silent, he said, "Great soup. Best you've ever made."

"I put the trees back in your shoes. But I don't think it'll help. They're ruined. What did you do, swim all the way there?" Florence asked.

"I couldn't get a cab."

Later, when they went to bed, he edged close against her warm body and embraced her. But she pulled free of him.

"It's not necessary to tip the help," she said.

He had never felt so guilty.

18

The next morning, Marvin decided to confront the problem with Kitzi. On the pretext of having a new film to discuss, he arranged to meet her for lunch.

He made a reservation at the Tavern on the Green for her convenience. Seeing her in natural daylight, in the middle of the day, was more of a shock than he had anticipated.

As soon as she was seated at the secluded table he had selected, she ordered a straight double vodka, with water on the side. She never touched the water.

"How are things?" she asked, trying to appear both sober and pleasant.

"Oh, fine, fine," he said. "Business has never been better. Have to enlarge the office. Brought in two new young agents."

"I meant your personal life, your marriage, Florence," she said.

"Oh, fine, fine. I wish we could spend more time together. But you know this crazy business."

"Yes," Kitzi said, "I know this business. It's what made me quit the tour last year."

He avoided reminding her of the real reason she had to quit the tour. She seemed impatient. "Okay, Marvin, as the old joke goes, enough of this lovemaking. What did you want to discuss?"

Deprived of the subtle manner in which he had intended to introduce the subject, he began, "There's talk. Too much talk. It's beginning to hurt."

"Talk? Such as?"

"Such as . . ." He pointed to the second glass of vodka the waiter had just served.

113

Defiantly, she did not sip this drink but drank it down in one long gulp. She glared at him. "You were saying——"

He reached across the table for her hand. She drew it back.

"Kitz, I wanted to discuss this quietly, intelligently. I didn't want to make an issue of it," he said.

"But you did!" she accused.

"Okay. I did. Kitz, years ago, up in Boston, there was a reason. That terrible disappointment. But now, you've got the world in your hands. There's no reason to drink like you do."

"How the hell would you know?" she shot back, her voice so loud that people at other tables began to stare.

"Kitzi, please . . . ," he whispered. "Hold it down. People are staring."

"People always stare at me," she declared. "Except most times they pay for the privilege."

"My God, what's happened to you? You never used to be this way."

"Never used to be *what* way?" she challenged. "Never used to drink like this? Never used to go onstage drunk? Never used to screw around with strangers? Is that what you're going to say? Lies! All lies! I am perfectly all right!"

In her attempt to prove it, she rose abruptly from her chair, but she could not stand erect. If Marvin had not reached for her arm, she would have fallen against the table and sent it crashing to the floor, shattering glasses, dishes, and the crystal flower vase.

Marvin shepherded her out of the restaurant. There was a cab waiting. She refused to get in. "Damn it, I'm only blocks from my home. I don't need a cab!"

She fought to free herself from his grasp. But he held her tightly and led her to a park bench some fifty feet away. Once they were seated, he said, "Kitzi, I beg you, get help."

"I don't need help!" she protested.

"At least do something about this for Alice's sake," Marvin pleaded.

"Alice is fine. Perfectly fine! She goes to the best school. The best summer camp. She has everything any child could want. Every advantage!"

"Except one," Marvin pointed out. "She's entitled to a mother who doesn't see the day through with a glass in her hand."

Kitzi rose. With a pretense at carrying herself regally erect, she started away from him. She had not gone more than four steps when she staggered. He raced to her side.

He surrendered her to the waiting arms of Evelina. The black woman shook her head sadly.

After she led Kitzi to her bedroom, she returned. There were tears in her eyes as she said, "Mr. Morse, I don't know how it's going to end. It's worse each time. Nights she's missing and they bring her home, the police, I mean. Times, I find a man, a strange man, in bed with her in the morning. That's no way, Mr. Morse, no way at all. Not for us who knew her like she was. And what it's doing to the child, God alone knows."

Tears glistened on her face.

"Alice . . . is she home?" he asked. "Can I see her?"

"You know how Missy is about you ever seeing that child," Evelina reminded him. She glanced down the hallway toward Kitzi's bedroom to make sure they were not being observed. Then she indicated the door to the child's bedroom.

As he approached the door, he heard music playing. He knocked.

"Mommy?" the child called out.

The door opened. Alice was startled to see a strange man. She also looked resentful. Like Evelina, she had obviously had this experience many times before.

"Yes, sir, what do you want?" she asked.

"Alice, I'm an old friend of your mother's. And also her agent."

"You must be the Marvin she talks to on the phone."

"Yes," he said, "I'd heard so much about you, I just wanted to see what you looked like."

The child braced herself for his inspection. He stared down at her. She was a pretty child. Blonde. Fair-skinned. Her mother's cleft chin. She stared up at him through soft brown eyes.

He realized that she did not resemble him in coloring. And she had been fortunate to inherit her mother's beauty. Yet somehow he felt an undeniable attraction to her.

19

In the weeks that followed, Kitzi's drinking and her erratic behavior grew not better, but worse. She had missed so many performances that the Shuberts threatened to close the show.

More times than he wanted to count Marvin had had to carry or drag a drunken Kitzi Mills into her dressing room only minutes before the curtain was scheduled to go up.

The ritual was always the same. He would set her down before her lighted makeup mirror while Evelina would put down a glass of colorless liquid that pretended to be water. At the same time the black woman would shake her head sadly and glance toward Marvin.

Drunk as Kitzi was, the exchange which was reflected in her three-sided dressing-table mirror did not escape her notice.

"Damn you, Evelina, you got something to say *about* me, say it *to* me!"

Evelina did not respond.

Kitzi commenced work on her long blond hair. She dipped her comb into the glass on the table, ostensibly to wet her hair and make it more manageable. But it was a charade in which all three of them conspired. Her routine was always the same. Kitzi would dip her comb into the vodka and use it to dampen her hair. Then, as if forgetful, and clearing her throat each time, she would take a sip of the liquid. Before she had finished her hair, she had dipped the comb half a dozen times, had sipped a dozen or more times, and the glass would be empty.

She was ready to go onstage.

She rose from her chair. Both Marvin and Evelina dared not move, but each was poised, ready to spring to Kitzi's side if she wavered too much. To defy them, she forced herself to stand erect and straight—too straight, for she seemed rigid and unnatural for a woman who was normally extremely graceful.

"Okay, darlin'?" Evelina dared to ask.

"Better than okay! I am perfect!" the star shot back and started for the door. Marvin reached to open it for her. She forbade it. "I can do that myself!"

He stepped back to allow her free access. She reached for the doorknob, misjudged it on her first try, finally found it, and opened the door, allowing the sound of the repeated overture to flood into the room.

Evelina watched from the wings as Kitzi went through her first scene, which ended with her song "Love Is All." Evelina held a glass in her hand. Clear, colorless liquid, which Kitzi would need when she came off. She only had time for a costume change and two gulps of the stuff.

In the back of the house, leaning against the wall just behind the last row of orchestra seats, stood Marvin. He watched critically, trying to detect the flaws in her performance. Soon he became aware that he was not alone.

"Hi, Wally," Marvin greeted in a whisper too soft to disturb the audience.

Wally Presser did not reply but took up his position as a critical observer. He was of more than medium height with the fleshy face of a man used to living well, eating well, and drinking well. His blue, expressionless eyes were fixed on Kitzi Mills with the same concentration as the follow spot which held her in its beam as she moved with grace and elegance through "Love Is All." Presser listened intently, like a physician trying to detect any sound or sign of a serious illness.

The number was over. Kitzi exited with a lingering look back at the audience. The people loved that smile, that fetching smile. Only the most jaded theatergoers could resist it. The applause, from a full Saturday-night house, was deafening.

Marvin glanced at Presser. The boss of all Shubert theaters appeared disappointed that he had found nothing to criticize. Without a word to Marvin he turned, pushed his way through a number of standing-room patrons, and left the theater. Marvin caught up with him in the lobby.

"Wally? What do you think?"

"Not bad," was all the praise Presser could afford.

The curtain was coming down on act one. Marvin raced down the side aisle to the backstage door. He was determined to be in the wings when Kitzi came off. He brushed by Bobbie Flynn's desk, past the light board, and almost collided with two stagehands who were waiting to make the set change for the opening of act two.

Kitzi came off to very strong applause. She appeared animated but was actually breathless as Marvin put his arms around her to shepherd her to her dressing room.

Evelina was ready to embrace her with a large bath towel. When Kitzi drank heavily, she had a tendency to perspire profusely. This night was no exception. Evelina stripped off Kitzi's clothes, toweled dry her slender body, and, with an apologetic look at Marvin, handed her a water tumbler of vodka.

Kitzi sipped it slowly. It seemed to revive her. She sat there, naked except for the towel, sipping and smiling. As if unaware of Marvin's presence, she dropped the towel, rose and, standing completely naked, said, "Okay, Evelina. Act two."

Marvin stared at a body he had seen in the nude many times, made love to many times. Considering the abuse to which it had been subjected, it was still a fabulously sensual body. With a greater sense of propriety, Evelina said softly, "Mr. Morse, please?"

He went back out to the rear of the house to mingle with the audience and to eavesdrop on their reactions. Had they detected how drunk Kitzi was? Did they know that she had missed two cues but covered well? Or that she had cut a whole page of dialogue from her third scene in act one?

All he could hear was praise, extravagant praise. *She's getting away with it,* Marvin reassured himself. *Give her an audience and she comes on like gangbusters, drunk or sober.*

The second act came off, if not flawlessly, then without any discernible fluffs. This time she had all her lines. She missed no cues. If her dancing was slightly off, no one but the choreographer would have noticed. Marvin felt much better as he pushed down the aisle against the departing audience, hearing their praise. And the frequent comment, "God, there's only one Kitzi Mills. She's fantastic!"

He found her sitting before her dressing table. Evelina, behind her, was toweling her dry. Kitzi breathed deeply, then exhaled all at once, letting her body go limp. She repeated that several times. Until she noticed Marvin in her mirror.

"Hi, sweetie. Surprised to see you come by tonight," she said, sounding very casual.

The peculiar nature of her remark did not strike him at first. Kitzi held out her hand to Evelina. When Evelina did not respond, Kitzi snapped her fingers impatiently.

"Evelina, my glass!"

"Glass?" the black woman repeated, still puzzled.

"We don't have to play games in front of Marvin. Get the glass! Fill it! I have to do my hair."

"Really, Kitz," Marvin intervened, "you don't have to do your hair. Why don't we go to some quiet, out-of-the-way place for a little supper?"

"Supper? What the hell are you talking about? I have a show to do!" she exclaimed furiously. "Evelina!"

Marvin looked to Evelina. Evelina looked back at him, frightened now.

Very gingerly, Marvin said, "Kitz . . . Honey . . . you've already done the show."

"Done . . . ," she started to say, looking at him in the mirror to see if he was joking. Instead, she saw the look of concern and shock on his face. "What the hell's the matter with you, Marvin?"

He dropped beside her chair, resting on one knee. He took her hand, looked into her face. "Kitzi, listen to me. You did the show. Don't you remember? In the first act you cut a whole page of dialogue—the third scene, where you always get those laughs. Tonight you cut it. . . . Don't you remember?"

"You're out of your mind!" she accused him fiercely. "I never cut dialogue. Never! Now, get out. I have to make up for my entrance."

Behind her, Evelina shook her head sadly. It was evident to both her and Marvin Morse that Kitzi had just delivered an entire per-

formance from sheer habit, ingrained through hundreds of performances. She had come off stage with no memory of what she had done.
She had suffered a total blackout!

Blackout.

The word struck Marvin with sudden and terrifying significance.
"Blackout" was the word that his brother Seymour had used. When
Kitzi's drinking and pill-taking had become a problem, Marvin had
turned to his brother. Seymour had stressed that he was no specialist
on alcoholism, but there were certain signs to watch for. The tendency to forgo food for the nonnutritive calories of alcohol. The habit
of drinking alone.

But most significant of all, and most symptomatic of advanced
alcoholism, was the blackout, when the alcoholic came to his senses
with no awareness of where he had been or what he had done or said.

It was now clear, if it hadn't been already, that Kitzi's condition
had deteriorated to such a degree that he had to take drastic steps.
As he watched her execute her ritual of drinking vodka while doing
her hair, he directed a meaningful glance at Evelina to urge her to
join him outside the dressing room.

They huddled in a corner of the corridor.

"Evelina . . ." he began.

"I know, I know," she said. "And this wasn't the first time."

"What do you mean?" he asked, seizing her by the shoulders until
she winced. "Tell me."

"Forgetting like that. She's done it before. Not knowing where
she's been or what she's said."

"When did it start?" he asked.

"Weeks. . . . ," the woman said. "Mr. Morse, you got to do
something."

"I will," he said.

Despite his apparent decision, his mind was torn by conflicting
possibilities. *Put her in an institution? Impossible. It would kill the
show and might even make her uninsurable for future shows or films.
Call in a specialist? Might as well go straight to* People *magazine with
the way doctors like to brag about their famous patients.*

There was another way. Difficult. Both for the alcoholic and the
person trying to save her. He would have to be firm, tough. For

forty-eight hours, or longer, he would have to put out of his mind every tender feeling he had ever had about her, all the love he had had for her. He would break her of this habit once and for all. Cold turkey! Starting tonight!

"Evie, let's get her home!"

20

Once they were back at the Beresford, Marvin took Kitzi to her bedroom, at the same time calling to Evelina, "Go through every cabinet, closet, the wine cellar, the refrigerator, every place where a bottle of vodka, whiskey, or wine can be hidden. Pour them down the sink. Every goddamned one! We are putting an end to her drinking tonight. *Now!*"

"You black bitch, you touch one of those bottles and I'll kill you! You hear me?" Kitzi shouted at the top of her powerful voice.

Marvin saw the door at the end of the hall open slightly. From behind it, the face of terrified, twelve-year-old Alice peered out.

"What are you doing to my mother?"

"Alice, she's perfectly safe. Go back into your room and stay there. No matter what you hear. Understand?"

The child stared at her struggling mother, who continued to curse Evelina and Marvin Morse.

"Alice, do as I say!" Morse ordered.

"Don't you hurt her," the child warned.

"Alice, darling, please? I'm trying to help her. Believe me," Marvin said.

It wasn't until Evelina reassured the child with a nod of her head that she finally withdrew into her own room.

Kitzi continued shouting until Marvin finally succeeded in forcing her into her bedroom.

He locked the door. He turned to face her. She had thrown aside her coat and was standing before him in only her slip.

"What the fuck are you staring at?" she defied him. "Thinking maybe you'd like to screw me, like in the old days? Well, think again, Jew-boy!"

She made an effort, an alcoholic effort, at assuming a posture and attitude of great dignity. She wove slightly, unable to control her movements, yet determined to play the star.

Finally she capitulated. "Ah, shit! Let's have a drink!"

"There isn't anything to drink. Not now, not tonight, not ever again," he said firmly.

She stared at him, trying to affect a superior smile but managing only a twisted imitation.

"Marvin . . . I . . . would . . . like . . . a drink," she said, spacing her words carefully to help with her enunciation, which even she recognized was faulty.

"Kitzi, honey, I'm sorry. It's going to be rough for a day or two, but no more booze. No more pills. We're going to get you over this once and for all. Do you understand? It will be hell, but we're going to lick it."

"Who do you think you are, telling me what to do? I don't work for you! You work for me! Or did! You're fired. So get out!"

She stood there reeling, weaving, yet determined to dominate him.

"You heard me! Get out! I said, Get out!"

With the cunning of an alcoholic, she pretended to turn away from him but lunged for the door. He caught her. She struggled. She scratched his face, drawing blood the length of his cheek. Still he held her, until she collapsed in his arms. He carried her to the bed.

At least she was asleep now. Passed out. Evelina returned.

"Poor child, what she's doing to herself," the woman said. "She hardly eats at all."

"She will," he said. "We'll make her. You watch over her. I'll go see what's in the fridge."

He started for the door but stopped. Kitzi had begun to stir and make sounds. Strange sounds. Unintelligible sounds. Then she began to shout. She drew her body up into a defensive attitude as she slammed herself against the headboard. At the same time she struck out as if to fight off an attacker. She twisted and writhed. She started to cry out.

"No! Don't! I don't want to die! I don't—Don't touch me!"

She jumped up so suddenly that if Marvin had not seized her, she would have hurled herself out of bed. He embraced her, held her, soothed her.

"Easy, Kitz, it's me. Nothing to be afraid of. I'm here. You're safe. You're in your own bed. Easy . . . easy . . . baby."

But neither his words nor his strong arms reassured her. She twisted, turned, tried to hide her face from whatever was attacking her in her demented hallucination.

Evelina hovered over them, crying and whispering, "Honey, we're here, you're going to be all right. Nothing to fear. Nothing. . . ."

Kitzi relaxed. She breathed evenly again. Marvin set her down gently. He looked to Evelina, who was wiping the tears from her eyes with her bare fingers.

"Oh, Mr. Morse . . . Mr. Morse . . . ," was all she could say.

"Don't worry. I'll sit here and watch." That reminded him. "I should call Florence and tell her I won't be home. You keep watch. I'll make the call from the living room."

He felt guilty for waking his wife at two o'clock in the morning, but started to dial anyway. Midway, he interrupted himself. Better not to wake her. He changed his mind once more and dialed again. He expected it would ring a number of times. Florence was a sound sleeper.

To his surprise, his second ring was interrupted by a pickup. Florence did not sound like a woman who had been awakened.

"Flo . . . you still up?"

"I was watching a late late movie." He knew that was not the whole truth. "What happened, Marv? Where are you?"

"She's having a bad night."

"Again?" More a comment than a question.

"She's a sick girl, Flo."

"How can a woman of thirty-two, a star, still be a girl?"

"Honey, please try to understand," he said.

"Understand? Haven't I been understanding enough about her since the beginning?"

"Flo, I'm making her quit. Cold turkey. It isn't easy on her. But it's the only way."

He was interrupted by a sudden shrill, desperate outcry from

Evelina. "Mr. Morse! Come quick!" The woman sounded as if she were struggling physically.

"Flo, I got to go!"

Without bothering to hang up he bolted from the room. His wife's voice could be heard from the dangling phone. "Of course. She calls. You got to go."

He raced into the bedroom. "There!" Kitzi was shouting. "There it is! Can't you see it? That . . . that thing. . . . It's . . . it's a rat! Coming through the wall. Get it! Kill it before it kills me!"

All the while Evelina was moaning and weeping, "Oh, God, oh God, help this poor child. Help her."

Kitzi cried out, "Kill the fucking thing! Somebody kill it!" With that, her body went completely stiff. It convulsed in a seizure. She began to foam at the mouth. Her body, rigid as it was, contorted into weird positions.

Though it was hardly more than a minute until she relaxed again, it seemed a much longer time. When she went limp in his arms, Marvin carried her back to her bed. He covered her perspiration-soaked body with the light sheet. As he sat down next to the bed, the seizure took possession of her body once more and she became rigid, convulsing, thrashing the bed with involuntary but powerful movement.

He embraced her to keep her from injuring herself. She twisted, turned, twice almost escaped his hold. Her body battered against him, stiff, strong, uncontrollable. Her head was perched at a bizarre angle. She began to gasp for breath. She seemed to be suffocating. He held her head erect, allowing her to breathe more easily. In moments the seizure had ended. He still held her, feeling it might not be over. When he felt more confident, he set her down. With his eyes fixed on her, he reached for the phone.

"Mr. Morse?" Evelina asked. He did not answer but dialed a number he knew very well. He waited through seven rings before he received a response.

"Seymour? Marvin."

Evelina could not hear what Seymour said. But Marvin replied, "No, Seymour. It's not me. It's not Florence. It's Kitzi. I'm trying to get her off the booze. And she's reacting very strangely. Could you come over? Right away? I'm afraid. Very much afraid. Please, Seymour. Please! And hurry!"

21

"Tell me exactly what happened," hastily clothed and disheveled-looking Dr. Seymour Morse said. "What you did. How she reacted. Everything!" At the same time, he took Kitzi's pulse and tested her blood pressure.

"I know she won't taper off," Marvin said. "So with her, there can be only one way. Cold turkey."

Seymour turned on his brother, glaring at him. "Are you crazy? You're trying to detox her by yourself? Cold turkey?"

"What did you want me to do? Expose her to a hospital? Or a drying-out tank? You know what lousy publicity that can mean."

"Publicity? Is that what you were thinking about?" Seymour rebuked. "Idiot! Don't you know that making an alcoholic go cold turkey can kill her?"

As Seymour removed the blood-pressure cuff from Kitzi's arm, her seizures began again. She went rigid, and her body began to thrash the bed once more. Seymour dropped down beside her. He held her tightly and her tormented body beat against him, her arms flailing the air, her legs rigid. While Marvin and Evelina watched, the seizure passed slowly. Her body went limp once more.

Seymour set her down as he said, "That's the most dangerous part. Clonic seizures. Sometimes they can cause a fracture of the spine."

"You mean all the time I was holding her . . . ," Marvin started to ask, but he was afraid to draw the obvious conclusion.

"That's right," Seymour said. "Clonic seizures can do that. That and suicide are the two things you have to be alert for." He turned to Evelina. "Ma'am, get me some sheets. Not the softest you have, certainly not silk, but the strongest."

Once Evelina left to carry out his request, Seymour turned to his older brother. "Marv, I know how you feel about bad publicity. I read the columns too. There have been hints. Not only about booze. But pills too. And cocaine. Which, I must assume from her condition, is true."

Marvin conceded by nodding.

"I think it's necessary to hospitalize her."

"I'd rather not——" Marvin started to say.

"Marv, this isn't a case of 'rather.' You may not have any choice. The next few days will tell."

Evelina was back with an armful of plain white cotton sheets. "This is the strongest we have."

Seymour folded them so they were full length but only two feet wide. He prepared three sheets in this way. He threw the end of the first across the bed over Kitzi's body, breast high, tucking his end deep under the mattress. At the same time, he said, "Ma'am, take care of your end." Evelina tucked it in, as deep under the mattress as it could go, thus pinning Kitzi Mills's body in place. They used two more sheets, one across her midriff and the other across her legs.

"Not the most effective restraints," Seymour said, "but the best we have. If things get any worse we'll hospitalize her. Even there, the usual restraints may not work. We may have to use leather straps and cuffs."

Before he finished, Kitzi tried to stir. But the restraints appeared to control her. Her head turned, and from her mouth came a stream of greenish vomit. Her body began to shake and tremble, causing the bed to shake.

Seymour stared down at the patient, then opened the black bag he had brought with him. Evelina returned to clean up the vomit. Marvin stood by watching helplessly as Seymour filled a hypodermic with a colorless liquid. He indicated that Evelina hold Kitzi as still as she could. He selected a place on her arm, just above the upper restraint. He swabbed it clean, inserted the needle, and pressed the plunger as he remarked to his brother, "Atavan. Ten milligrams. Should keep her quiet for a while. Now, we have to talk."

As the brothers started from the room, the doctor called back to Evelina, "Ma'am, get me a bottle of liquor. Her favorite, if you have it."

"We don't have any," Evelina said.

"An alcoholic's apartment. And no liquor? What are you trying to pull?" the doctor demanded.

Marvin interceded. "I had her pour it down the sink. All of it. Got rid of it. Once and for all!"

"What!" the doctor demanded, outraged.

"It was the only way to keep it out of her hands."

"Get some! I don't care where or how! Get some! Unless you want this woman to die!" he commanded.

"Die?" Marvin echoed in shock.

"Yes! Die! She's got to be detoxed slowly. What was she drinking?"

"Vodka," Marvin said.

"Then get me some vodka!"

"At this hour?"

"Ring some neighbor's bell. Do something! But get it!"

"Home! I'll get it at home!" Marvin said, starting for the door.

The cab waited for him downstairs at his apartment house. Florence, in nightgown and robe, could only stare as he searched through their bar. He had slipped two bottles of vodka into his coat pockets, and taken two more in hand when she asked, "Marv, what's going on? Are you crazy? Why do you need so much vodka? Is it for *her?*"

"Yes, it's for *her,*" was all he would say.

"Why? Hasn't she got enough?"

"Flo, please, not now. We're trying to save her life."

"We?"

"Seymour and Evelina and I. We're trying to keep her alive!"

As he raced for the door, Florence's words followed him. "She's crazy, and she's making all the rest of us crazy!"

The elevator was waiting, door open. Marvin rushed in. "Down, José. And fast!"

The cab was waiting, door open. Marvin bounded in. "Back to Central Park West and Eighty-first!"

As if conducting a laboratory procedure, Seymour measured out the vodka carefully. Two ounces, as near as he could estimate.

"Okay," he said, starting for Kitzi's bedroom. They found Evelina sitting by the side of the bed, wiping Kitzi's perspiring face. Seymour looked down at her.

"God, how can she still be so beautiful?" he said. "Look, my dear, hold her up so I can get this into her."

Tenderly, Evelina raised Kitzi's head. The doctor held the glass to her mouth.

"Kitzi, drink."

She opened her eyes, seeming startled by the closeness of a man she hardly knew. She became aware of the glass. He tilted it. She opened her mouth. She drank. She seemed more at ease. Evelina gently lowered her head.

"Just to make sure," Seymour said as he prepared another hypodermic of ten milligrams of Atavan. As he injected it into her, he added, "I should hospitalize her."

"Sy, the publicity," Marvin warned again.

"One of you will have to stay the night with her."

At once, Evelina and Marvin both volunteered.

"And we ought to call in a nurse. I know an excellent woman for cases like this."

"I told you, Sy, as little publicity as possible."

"Then both of you stay. Now, here's what you do. Every two hours for the next six you give her two more ounces of vodka. I'll mark the glass. Then, starting at, say, ten o'clock in the morning, go on an every-three-hour schedule. After that, on a four-hour schedule."

"How long——" Evelina started to ask.

"Three days—four. Until her body stabilizes enough for me to do a complete physical. After that, we have to decide——"

"Decide what?" Marvin asked.

"She needs treatment."

"Sy, three times I've arranged for her to dry out. It doesn't work."

"It'll work or she'll die," the doctor said simply. He gathered up the tools of his trade and dropped them into his black bag. "If she goes into clonic seizure again, call me at once!"

The sun was just beginning to appear over the tops of the buildings on the East Side. Marvin turned from staring directly into it to peer through the window that faced south. From this window, twenty-two floors up, Marvin Morse could see the building where he had first met Kitzi Mills.

The offices of the George Gordon Agency were still there. He could almost make out the window of the small office where he had first seen Kitzi Mills—Katherine Millendorfer—more than twelve years ago!

He had never suspected then that he would now be debating the steps to take to save her life.

Seymour's words were stamped on his mind as if they had been burned there.

It'll work, or she'll die!

22

Marvin listened very attentively to Dr. Stover, an elderly physician Seymour recommended who was considered by many in the field to be the leading clinician on the treatment of patients suffering from chemical dependency. Stover advised that one no longer treated alcoholics or addicts by force. The patient had to be convinced to accept treatment willingly.

"She won't seek treatment," Marvin warned.

"I don't expect that she will at first," Stover conceded. "That's where we come in. You, I, anyone and everyone who can have any impact on her."

"God knows I've tried," Marvin said. "She has an answer or an excuse for every argument I make."

"That's the trouble with alcoholics. They are so clever at defending, evading, hiding, pretending, and lying. Being an actress, she must have learned the art of denial and evasion better than most. But we have to try. When can we confront her?"

"I'd better talk to Alice first."

"Alice?"

"Her daughter," Marvin identified.

"Age?"

"Twelve."

"Bright?"

"Oh, yes. And sensitive," Marvin said.

"Anyone else who is close to Miss Mills?"

"Evelina, her dresser, friend—her mother, almost."

"No other family?" Stover asked.

"Her last remaining relative was her grandfather. But he's gone."

"So we have very few people to rely on."

"Does that make it impossible?" Marvin asked, sensing that the only potential cure was slipping through his fingers.

The doctor thought a long moment before replying. "What we cannot do by weight of numbers, we must accomplish by the force of what we say. Talk to her daughter."

Marvin appeared at Alice Mills's private school the next afternoon. He introduced himself to the Dean. As subtly as he could, he explained the situation to her. He discovered that he need not have been so circumspect.

"I am aware of the problem, Mr. Morse. Painfully aware."

"All I intend to do," Marvin said, "is talk to the child. Tell her what we plan to do. And what her part in it must be."

"You may use my office," the dean said.

"I thought that since the weather is as nice as it is, I'd take her out into the park."

"As you wish. If any of us can be of assistance, please let me know."

Marvin Morse and twelve-year-old Alice Mills started into Central Park, walking south along the East Drive. Since it was spring, the drive was closed to vehicular traffic. They encountered only a few runners, a few cyclists. At first, Marvin avoided direct mention of the subject. They drew close to the boat pond and the adjacent refreshment stand.

"Ice cream, Alice?"

"No thanks."

"Hot dog? Soda?"

"No thanks," she said. Then she asked, "Are we going to walk forever?"

"Tired, darling? Want to sit down?"

"I'm not tired. I meant, why are we here like this? You said you want to talk to me. But you don't. Are we going to just keep walking?"

"Alice . . ."

The child looked up at him. On her pretty face, so reminiscent of her mother's, was a look of great concern. Her blond hair fell loose to her shoulders, framing her face and serving as a contrast to her deep, sensitive brown eyes. Marvin could not avoid thinking, *Not Kitzi's blue eyes, not Wainwright's gray eyes, but brown like mine.*

"Alice," he began once more, "we have to do something about your mother. I guess you know that she is not well."

"She drinks too much," the child said straightforwardly. "Half the time she doesn't know what she's doing. And she forgets. She tells me something in the morning and then repeats it five or six times during the day, never knowing that she's told it to me before. And she——"

The child stopped talking suddenly. She stared down at the boat pond below, at the children playing by the water.

Marvin did not prod her. What she had to say she would say voluntarily.

"Sometimes . . . You won't ever tell her I told you, will you?"

"Anything you tell me, she'll never hear from me."

"Sometimes . . ." The child had difficulty continuing. "Sometimes, she falls down. I mean, I come into her room, and she's lying on the floor. Not even knowing it. I try to get her up. I didn't used to be able to, but now I can. I help her up and get her to bed. When she wakes up, she never even knows what happened."

"I know what you mean," Marvin said, taking the child's hand to comfort her.

"No, you don't," Alice contradicted. "I get scared. Very scared. Maybe the next time that happens and I try to pick her up she won't move. She'll be . . . dead. That could happen, couldn't it?"

He was determined not to dissemble. "Yes, Alice, it could happen."

131

"Then where would I go? I don't have anybody. I mean, the other girls in school have fathers and mothers and grandfathers and grandmothers. I don't have anybody. What would they do with me? Who'd want me?"

He put his arm around her shoulder. "I'd want you, Alice. You could become my little girl."

She settled into his embrace. "Mother always tells me, 'Don't you worry, baby, you're well provided for.' What does that mean when there's nobody? Times I think I'll try to find out who my father was. We have kids in school who were adopted. Some of them talk about finding their true mother. But they say you've got to be older to do that. Twenty-one or something. Maybe when I'm twenty-one I'll find out who my father is. And if he's still alive I'll go find him. And I'll say, 'Here I am. Now you be my father.' "

"Alice, honey, these things . . . will you be able to tell them to your mother?"

The child looked up at him, her eyes betraying great reluctance.

"What if, by telling her, you could make it possible for her to get better? To stop drinking?"

"You mean, she could . . . she might?" the child asked.

"It's—it's possible. But to do that we have to convince her to want to."

"We?" Alice asked.

"You, Evelina, me, Dr. Stover."

"Dr. Stover?" The child tensed at the unfamiliar name.

"He's a doctor who's going to help us convince your mother."

"Will I have to say things like this in front of him?" Alice considered.

"Nobody outside that room will ever know what you said," Marvin promised. "Do you think you can be honest with her? Stop hiding your feelings?"

"It would hurt her, hurt her a lot,"

"It might hurt her now, but she'd be better off later."

"What if it doesn't work?" the child asked directly.

"If it doesn't work——" Marvin was at a loss, so he said, "It *has* to work. It must work. Do you think you can do it?"

The child was silent for a time before she replied, "I . . . I think so."

132

"Good girl!" Marvin said.

Walking out of the park, Alice clung to his hand.

"What do you think my father was like?"

"To judge from you I'd say he was a very handsome man," Marvin replied.

Thinking he was joking with her, she smiled up at him. "No, really, what do you think?"

Before he could answer, the sad import of her question became clearer when she said, "I hope he wasn't like some she brings home now. I hope I didn't get to be born just because she went out and got drunk."

"No, you didn't," Marvin assured her.

"How can you be sure, if you didn't know him?" Alice said, looking up at him, her intensity demanding an answer.

23

On Dr. Stover's instructions, Marvin had arranged for a bed at The Retreat and had phoned Tony Frascati, who offered his private jet. He instructed Evelina to pack a suitcase. For if this confrontation were to succeed at all, it must be acted on quickly.

Dr. Stover approached the moment with great reservations.

"Usually there's a husband, plus other relatives, a clergyman, a boss. The sheer force of numbers helps. Has her life been so solitary, so cut off from close relationships? Isn't there some man, even if he's her lover?"

Marvin avoided addressing Stover's question directly. "Between her career, which is too demanding, and her devotion to Alice, she really didn't have much time for anyone else."

The hour set was nine o'clock that evening. Marvin and Dr. Stover arrived together. Evelina was already there. Alice was waiting. Kitzi was still asleep, under the influence of a sedative Seymour Morse had prescribed.

Alice was sent to wake her.

"Mom . . . Mommy . . . They're here."

Kitzi stirred, turning from her side to lie on her back, stare up at the ceiling, ask, "Alice? Baby? What time is it? Why aren't you in bed? Don't you have school tomorrow?"

"Yes, Mommy, but Uncle Marvin said for me to stay up. And they're here."

"Who's here?" Kitzi sat up abruptly, trying to blink away the effects of the sedative, for she suddenly felt threatened and afraid. Her nightgown had opened so that her left breast was exposed. She carefully buttoned the gown in an act of uncharacteristic modesty. She always strove to be proper in the presence of her daughter.

"Who is here?" she repeated more slowly and carefully.

"Mr. Morse. Evelina. And another doctor. An old man," Alice said.

"Another doctor?" Growing more tense and suspicious, Kitzi reached to the chair for her robe. She rose from her bed, drawing the red velvet gown around her. "Another doctor," she repeated, growing more angry and defensive. She started out of the room, saying, "Come, darling! I don't know what Marvin is up to, but I am going to put a stop to it!"

"Mommy, please . . . ," Alice begged as she trailed alongside her.

Kitzi burst into the living room, where they were assembled.

"What the hell is going on here?" she demanded.

"Kitzi, what is going on here is that the people in this world who love you most want to talk to you."

"About what?" she demanded. At the same time, she reached to draw Alice close to her. It was obvious that she needed the child for solidarity and courage.

Dr. Stover took over.

"My dear Miss Mills——"

"Who the fuck are you?" Kitzi demanded.

"Kitzi, this is Dr. Arnold Stover. He is a specialist in chemically addictive diseases."

"Then what's he doing here?"

"He's here to help save your life," Marvin said.

"I don't need any help from anybody! Especially doctors!" She turned to Alice, who clung to her side. "Do I, baby?" When Alice did not respond at once, Kitzi insisted, "Do I?"

But for Marvin's beseeching eyes, Alice might have agreed with her. Instead, the child drew away from her mother and said, "Mommy, I think Mr. Morse is right."

Kitzi stared at her daughter in surprise, then turned to glare viciously at Marvin.

"So you've turned her against me. Trying to get at me through her. You bastard!" She began to weep.

Dr. Stover gave Evelina a signal. The black woman, who herself was on the verge of tears, went to Kitzi and put her arm around her. She led her to one of the easy chairs by a corner window that looked out over Central Park. It was where Kitzi sat when she was determined to avoid facing uncomfortable situations or people.

She sat staring out the window. Her hands pressed between her thighs. As a vague afterthought, she said softly, "Thank you, Evelina. I can always depend on you." She reached for the black woman's hand.

"Tell her," Marvin said.

Evelina looked to him, her eyes pleading, *Must we?* He nodded firmly, reinforced by Dr. Stover.

"Missy, we've come to the time of truth. You've got to do something to help yourself. 'Cause there's no one else can do it. You've got to go away to where they can do for you all the things that need doing. But you've got to want to go."

Kitzi withdrew her hand angrily and turned away from Evelina.

"Won't do any good to try to avoid me, Missy. If you don't go, I am through here. I am no longer going to be waiting up for you. I am no longer going to clean up your vomit. No longer going into that bedroom and find your bedsheets still wet from some damn man you brought home. I can't do that any longer. I am a decent woman. I am a religious woman. I can no longer abide your sinning like you do. So either you decide to go, or I go."

Evelina drew back from Kitzi, the tears that filled her eyes starting to overflow them. She turned to the wall. Marvin could see her body shake from crying. He moved close to Kitzi. Looked to Stover, who nodded.

"Kitzi . . ."

Kitzi expressed her anger by turning sharply from Marvin to stare out the window, though in her fury she saw nothing.

"Kitzi, you must listen. Whatever else anyone knows about you, I know it all. They have my name on file at the Fifty-fourth Street police station. When Kitzi Mills is found drunk or disorderly, call Marvin Morse. Damn it, Kitz, every time my phone rings late at night I dread picking it up because I wonder what you've done now? And it's been getting worse and worse, more and more frequent. I can't take it anymore. Florence can't take it anymore."

"That bitch!" Kitzi exploded, revealing that she had not only been listening but had been greatly affected by what she had heard.

"She's not a bitch, Kitzi. She's put up with her share of this, too. If she were here, she could tell you the times I have been called away because of you. Times when *she* needed me. But she knew that when it comes to Kitzi Mills, there's nothing I wouldn't do. But no more, Kitz. No more. I can't assist or preside over the final and utter destruction of a human being."

He paused, waiting, hoping that she would respond. She did not, except to draw her robe tighter around her as if to ward off his rebukes and his threats.

"Kitz, something else you have to know," Marvin continued. But she turned away even further. He reached out and seized her by the shoulders so that she had no choice but to face him. She shut her eyes and kept them shut. He reached to her dimpled chin and lifted her face. He stared down at it. Still she would not open her eyes to him.

"Kitzi, I got word from the Shuberts."

"Fuck the Shuberts!" she said, trying to break free of his grip. He held her fast.

"After what happened last Saturday night, Wally said they will no longer book a Kitzi Mills show in any Shubert house."

"There's always Nederlander."

"No more, Kitz," Marvin said. "No more. Because they can't get insurance on you." These days, with musicals running four and five million, who's going to take the risk without insurance?"

"I don't need them. I don't need you," Kitzi said, then started to shout, "I don't need anybody! *Anybody!*" She turned to stare around the room until her eyes fixed on Alice, who cowered beside the grand piano as if to hide. "Except you, baby. Alice . . . baby? Alice!"

The child moved from the piano, taking one tentative step toward her mother, who held out her arms to embrace her. Alice looked to Marvin to ask permission. Marvin shook his head.

The child took another step toward her mother but refused to come close enough to be embraced by her.

"Mommy," the child began hesitantly, "Mommy, please do like they say. So things here can be like they are other places. I mean, like in my friends' homes. I don't have any real friends anymore. Other girls sleep over. Not me. Because I can't invite any girls here. 'Cause if I do I don't know how you'll come home. Or if you'll come home. I don't know when I open the door if I will find you okay. Or will you be on the floor? Passed out?

"You know when I did invite girls over? When you were on the road. Or out in Hollywood making a picture. All my friends envy me because my mother is a Big Star. They all think I have such an exciting life. That I meet so many celebrities. They don't know that the only kind of men I meet are the kind you bring home. And when those men see me in the morning, they get dressed in a hurry and leave. Then later when I start for school I can't stand for the elevator man to look at me, or the doorman. They all feel sorry for me. I don't want people to be nice to me because they're sorry for me. I don't, Mommy. I don't."

The child was in tears now.

Marvin put his arms around the child. "Kitz, either you go out there, or I will take legal steps to have you declared an unfit mother. I'll take Alice away from you."

"You wouldn't!" she protested. "You couldn't. No judge would ever do that!"

Evelina pleaded, "Missy, please, if you don't go out there, I will have to go into court and tell some judge all the things I've seen. Everything you put this poor child through. I don't want to do that."

"Mommy, please?" Alice asked, weeping freely now.

Kitzi beckoned to her. The child went to her and hid her face in her mother's breasts.

"My baby . . . my baby. . . ." Kitzi had begun to weep as well.

Marvin asked softly, "Kitzi?"

Kitzi pressed her face against the child's golden head but did not respond at once.

"Evelina's packed your bag. I'll have Tony Frascati's private jet at La Guardia tomorrow. You won't have to face any other passengers. Kitz?"

Kitzi Mills finally nodded. As he had done so many times in years past, Marvin handed her his pocket handkerchief to dry her eyes. She wiped away Alice's tears first, then her own.

She smiled as she said, "I've got a collection of your handkerchiefs. Almost a drawerful. Monogrammed. I'll keep this one, too."

By seventeen minutes past ten o'clock the next morning, Kitzi Mills and Marvin Morse were in Tony Frascati's private jet as it took off from La Guardia Airport.

Part Three

. . . Kitzi Mills pushed open the tall, bleached-oak-and-glass door and stepped into the quiet reception area. At the front desk, she hesitated, then announced softly, "I'm Kitzi Mills. I think you're expecting me."

24

"**M**iss Mills," the receptionist said. "Yes, Mrs. Armbruster said she would like to see you the moment you arrived." The woman pressed a call button.

An attendant, informally dressed in khaki slacks and a flamboyant sports shirt, appeared. He took Kitzi's suitcase and said softly, "Follow me, Miss Mills."

She started behind him, down a short hallway to a thick, bleached-oak door. He knocked and opened the door to a large office. Behind the desk stood Norma Armbruster, whom Kitzi recognized at once. She had seen her on television many times, being interviewed about the work of The Retreat.

She was a slender woman, tall and quite handsome. *Good bone structure and clear green eyes,* Kitzi noted. *And she had once been an alcoholic herself. Hard to believe.*

"Well, Miss Mills, I've been expecting you. Sit down, please. Coffee?"

"No, thank you," Kitzi said, as she lowered herself into a bright tweed chair, thankful for the support of the arms. She tried to conceal her shakiness by gripping them, but the trembling of her hands became so uncontrollable that she gave up. She was aware that Norma Armbruster had observed every detail of her condition.

"Welcome to The Retreat," Mrs. Armbruster began. "Where we have no locked doors. No barred windows. Everything is open. You could walk out of here at any time and no one would stop you. Of course, once you leave, you can never come back. But we do have our rules, and our routine. Your day will be filled with lectures, films, reading, group sessions——"

"How many sessions are there?" Kitzi interrupted, betraying her resistance to engage in that activity.

"Two group sessions every day. Morning and afternoon. After the second session, you have an hour for recreation. Walking, jogging, running, swimming. To help you rehabilitate your body, which has endured considerable damage from alcohol and drugs. In early evening, we have study time, quiet time. A time to reflect on the day. A time to write in your journal."

"Journal?"

"Miss Scott, your dorm supervisor, will explain. We fill your days and nights with group sessions, lectures, and books, all about one subject: how to kick your habit. Before you kill yourself or anyone else."

She was no longer smiling.

"Our entire program is designed to accomplish three things: To make you believe that you can be helped. To show you what your habit has done not only to you but to others. And to show you the steps you must take to control your sickness. Because, in the end, only you can do it for you."

"You said 'steps,' " Kitzi questioned tremulously, while thinking, *Try, try to stop trembling in the presence of this woman. She may reject you as hopeless.*

"Alcoholics Anonymous has twelve Steps to Sobriety. We've adopted the first five of them as our criteria for determining when a patient is well enough to leave."

"Five steps . . ." Kitzi repeated vaguely as she sat there, trying to control her shakes and desperately needing a tall, strong shot of vodka, or, at the least, a pill.

Norma Armbruster had presided over the admission of many patients. She knew exactly how Kitzi Mills felt.

"I know the challenge, Miss Mills. It seemed impossible to me once, too. We can only offer you guidance and an exacting schedule. The rest is up to you."

Kitzi nodded, a vague, distant look in her delft-blue eyes, surrounded by whites shot through with thin, blood-red streaks.

"Joe will show you to your dorm," Mrs. Armbruster said, concluding the arrival interview.

* * *

The attendant led the way along a concrete walk, past one low white concrete dormitory, then past a second, to reach the last one in the complex. They entered the building, stepping from hot sunlight into a cool, dark corridor. Kitzi followed until they came into a large, bright, open lounge area where a dozen or more men and women were enjoying a coffee break. As she came into view, she could sense the excitement that her arrival had created.

They're staring at me, she thought. *They recognize me. Once I pass through, they'll start gossiping about me.* She was determined to carry herself in her most queenly stage posture, to let them know that, whatever else they thought, she was a star!

Joe preceded her to a cheerful bedroom with two beds, two closets, two dressing tables. He placed her bag on the bed closest to the patio doors and said, "Don't open that bag."

"Why not?" Kitzi Mills asked.

"Your dorm counselor, Miss Scott, will be in shortly to explain."

Kitzi looked around. It was a pleasant room, not large but comfortable, of bleached desert woods, brightly colored spreads and draperies, a high ceiling. She had spent many days on the road in hotels and motels which were far less hospitable. She went to the patio doors, nervously reached for the handles, but decided that, despite what Mrs. Armbruster had said, the doors must surely be locked.

A woman's voice urged, "Go on. Open them. Step out. Take a look around."

Kitzi turned to face a dark-haired woman in her early thirties who was quite small, no more than five feet three inches. The woman smiled, her plain face warm and friendly. She was not dressed in hospital garb but in a brown-and-navy plaid skirt and a blue cashmere sweater. She looked more ready to play golf than to brief new patients. She carried an armful of books which, combined with her youthful appearance, gave her the look of a college senior.

"Go on," the young woman urged.

Hesitantly, Kitzi slid back the door and stepped out onto the concrete patio. She moved beyond the shaded area into the strong light of the afternoon sun. She looked up at the cloudless sky, at the distant mountains with their shades of desert brown, purple, and gold. She lowered her gaze to discover that as far as she could see there were no fences, no restraints. Beyond the wide green lawns, the open desert stretched endlessly in all directions.

Her fear of being imprisoned slowly dissipated. For the first time she could accept everything that Marvin had promised her about this place. She might be able to endure four weeks here.

Four weeks to freedom, she promised herself. *Four weeks to satisfy Alice.*

Yes, for Alice's sake, I could endure it. Not too great a price for a child to exact after the way her young life had been made hostage to my hectic career.

Her thought was interrupted by the woman's voice behind her. "Magnificent view, isn't it?"

"Yes. Yes, it is," Kitzi agreed.

"I'm Joyce Scott, your dorm counselor."

Smiling, she held out her hand. Kitzi shook it, and discovered how firm, strong, and warm it was, compared with her own.

"Now, let's unpack you," Joyce Scott said pleasantly. "Open your bag, Miss Mills."

Kitzi sprang the locks and lifted the lid, but before she could touch any of the contents, Joyce Scott said, "I'll do that."

She proceeded to take out each article of clothing: slacks, skirts, blouses, sweaters, delicate underthings, a robe. She examined each one thoroughly—every pocket, every pleat, every seam, every inch of every garment. Kitzi realized the woman was searching for drugs.

Joyce Scott removed all the clothes and uncovered the plastic zippered bag in which Evelina had packed Kitzi's perfumes, toothpaste, vitamin pills, calcium, and other toiletries.

"I'll have to take these," she said pleasantly, as she put the perfumes and pills back into the plastic bag.

"But that's my Joy and my Calandre. I always use those."

"The base of all perfume is alcohol. The same is true of your mouthwash. I'll take that, too."

"But I always——" Kitzi started to protest again.

"Of course. Nothing better to hide the smell of liquor than a strong mouthwash. But I've seen more than one alcoholic drink his own mouthwash. So, sorry! No perfume, no mouthwash, and no pills."

"They're only vitamins," Kitzi explained.

"When you have your physical at the hospital, Dr. Gordon will prescribe any vitamins you might need," Joyce Scott said. "Now you may start putting your things away. While you do, I will give you your instructions. There's your closet. And your chest of drawers."

Kitzi began to hang her slacks and skirts in the empty closet. As she reached for one of the hangers she felt her hand begin to tremble. She was determined not to let Joyce Scott notice. But she already had.

"Don't feel self-conscious. I've seen people with the shakes before. And far worse than yours. One thing we don't do here is try to put up a bold front. We're all in the same boat, so we don't try to fool each other."

Kitzi turned from the closet to stare at the young woman. "Yes, Miss Mills, I'm a recovering alcoholic. Have to be, to understand those who are trying to recover. Right now, you honestly believe that if you only had a drink, one single drink, it would steady your nerves. It probably would. But it would only start the cycle all over again. Dr. Gordon will give you a thorough physical and determine if you need further detoxing, in which event we will ship you over to the hospital for a few days. If not, you will do what all the rest of us have done. Tough it out for the first few days until you realize there isn't going to be any more drinking, pill-popping, or snorting. So you're asking yourself, How will I face the long days? You'll be kept busy every moment of every day. Now for your chores. You make your own bed and vacuum this room. In addition, you will be assigned another duty each day by your Granny."

"Granny?"

"The patient in charge of this dorm. You'll find him to be really quite nice. Good sense of humor. But firm. Highly intelligent. He should be. He's one of the best surgeons in the country."

"And he's a Granny?" Kitzi remarked.

"He'll assign your other duties to you."

"What kinds of duties?" Kitzi asked, her voice betraying that no matter what they were, she would resist doing them.

"Setting the dorm's table in the common cafeteria. Clearing after meals."

Kitzi felt an overpowering need for a drink. Her mouth felt dry. Her hands were icy cold, and starting to tremble more obviously.

145

Joyce Scott noticed. "We have coffee in the lounge at all hours, if you need some."

"I don't need anything!" Kitzi protested, clenching her hands at her side to keep them still. She was determined to refuse any help.

Joyce Scott searched the pocket of the suitcase, finding two play-scripts which she added to the pile of things she was taking with her.

"Those are scripts I promised to read, for possible fall productions," Kitzi explained.

"You'll have enough to read with these." Joyce Scott indicated the load of books and pamphlets she had brought. "This book about Alcoholics Anonymous. These pamphlets on sobriety, on the effects of alcoholism on the family. You'll spend your reading time on these. And on this."

She held out a large, blue-covered, looseleaf notebook, which Kitzi stared at but refused to take.

"This is your journal. While you're here, you will write in it every day. All your thoughts, fears, desires, and reactions. The purpose is to express your honest feelings. It's the only way to bring you into touch with yourself."

"I'm not very good at writing," Kitzi started to explain. "It's a challenge for me even to write a thank-you note."

"It's difficult for all of us at first, but you'll learn. Just listen to the others and you'll get the hang of it."

"You mean what I write will be revealed to those people out there in the lounge?"

"Those 'people out there' are in the same boat you are. They'll help you recover, and you'll help them."

Never, Kitzi Mills resolved. *I'm here to do my four weeks. And that's all I'll do! And if you start to pressure me, I'll just leave. Now that I'm sure there are no physical barriers or boundaries to this place, I'll just walk out one day, or one night, and keep going!*

"Now, Miss Mills, it's time for your physical examination. Immediately after that you will join us for our second group-therapy session of the day. See you there."

Kitzi dropped onto the bed, dispirited and frightened, trapped. She glared at the stack of books Joyce Scott had left. She hated them. She pretended to be not even curious about them. Finally she could not resist. She picked one up. Flipping through the pages, she made no attempt to read any of it. She knew she was going to hate it. She tossed it aside.

She picked up a slim pamphlet because the title mocked her. "Five Steps to Sobriety at The Retreat." This must be what that Armbruster woman was talking about.

She turned the title page to be confronted by a declaration in bold type: Master these five steps and you will have mastered your addiction.

She continued to read:

Step One: Admit you are powerless over alcohol and your life has become unmanageable.

Step Two: Believe that only a Power greater than you are can restore you to sanity.

Step Three: Make a decision to turn your will and your life over to God as you understand Him.

Step Four: Make a searching and fearless moral inventory of yourself.

Step Five: Admit to God, to yourself, and to another human being the exact nature of your wrongs.

Five little rules that sound like Sunday School are going to do it? If your brain's gone soft from too much booze, maybe you can believe that junk. I don't belong here. I don't know how they ever talked me into coming here. Christ, do I need a drink! With a drink I could figure out how to handle this. God? Fearless moral inventory? Admit to another human being the nature of my wrongs? I don't see anybody admitting the wrongs they committed against me! Screw 'em! Screw 'em all! Five steps or five hundred, I do not buy all this crap and I never will!

There must be some way to get a drink around here. Some attendant, some orderly, some nurse, someone I can make a deal with.

Until she realized, *I haven't seen an attendant, or a nurse, or an orderly. Just that damn counselor and that administrator. Still, there must be ways. There always are. Because I need a drink. Or at least a few Valiums. Or even one of those soothing treatments from Doc Spangler.*

25

After a thorough medical exam from an attractive, young physician, Kitzi walked slowly down the dormitory corridor. As she approached the room at the far end, she became aware of several voices raised angrily. Only the compelling thought that to win back her freedom she had better do as instructed for the next twenty-eight days forced her to push the door open in time to hear one woman cry out, "Bullshit!" Some of the others joined in with equally vigorous contradictions.

Tremulous and inadequate to confront anger, Kitzi felt a compulsion to turn and flee. But from across the room and facing her, Joyce Scott directed her to the one empty chair in the circle.

Before she started forward, Kitzi slowly surveyed the group. They seemed to possess no single characteristic in common.

One old man, who peered through old-fashioned silver-framed glasses and had an unlit cigarette in the corner of his mouth, appeared to be in his mid-sixties.

There was a small woman who, despite her over-blonded hair, seemed to be as old.

A young black man who was very tall and muscular.

A white man, mature, short, round faced, with obvious jowls, and a head so bald that it shone.

Most of the others, both men and women, were nondescript, with unremarkable physical or facial characteristics.

Kitzi's first thought was, *If they were holding an open Equity call, or this were a group from Central Casting for average crowd types, they would look like this. Except, possibly, for that one old man. Something strangely familiar about him. And that young black man. A kid, really. God, at his young age can he be so far gone that he had to seek treatment here?*

Joyce Scott was gesturing to her again, this time with more urgency. In an effort to be as unpretentious as possible, Kitzi started toward the circle. She slipped into the empty seat. She was so tense that she had to grip the sides of the chair for reassurance. She stared straight ahead, avoiding eye contact with those seated opposite her. The little blond woman looked like an adoring fan. Kitzi's impulse was to rise and flee. Instead, she gripped the chair even more tightly.

The man to Kitzi's right—rather handsome, she thought, and in his mid-forties—had evidently been the recipient of the group's criticism, for all eyes were on him, challenging him to continue.

Tense, his lips twitching nervously, Ward McGivney was groping for words. He pounded his right fist into the palm of his left hand. His struggle to express himself was so intense that Kitzi felt a need to speak out for him. But no one moved, no one spoke. He had to conquer both the moment and himself.

Finally he was able to say, "Okay, okay. . . . So what I said was . . . was bullshit. But one thing is sure. When you're in sales, drinking is as much a part of selling as selling. Especially when you sell big-ticket items. You don't get really close to your prospect until you've been drunk with him a time or two."

"More bullshit," the short, plump, dark-haired woman across from Kitzi called out. "Billions of dollars worth of goods are sold in this country by people who don't get drunk."

"Damn right!" Joe Bigelow, the small, bald man alongside Kitzi, agreed. "I traveled the whole western territory, was top man in sales for six straight years, and never got drunk with a customer."

But he lowered his voice as he admitted, "My trouble was *after*. I'd get back to the hotel. Alone. I was too shy to call the bell captain and ask him to send me a girl. So I'd just go to my room with a bottle in my sample case. Before I could fall asleep, I'd have to drink the whole damn thing."

He turned on Ward McGivney. "I wish I had a dollar for every sale you *lost* because you got drunk."

Kitzi, watching and listening, promised herself, *I'll never say a word here. Not to these vultures.*

Her body grew more rigid as she became more resistant. Joyce Scott noticed this and was not surprised. Kitzi Mills was suffering the combined stress of being physically weaned from her addiction while being exposed to new surroundings, new faces, and a new method of treatment, all of which could be very unsettling for a star in an institution where there were no stars.

149

To direct the discussion into a more fruitful channel, Joyce Scott turned to Ward McGivney.

"Ward, what brought you here to The Retreat? What made you say, 'If I don't lick this thing, it's going to kill me'?"

McGivney shifted slightly in his chair and pressed his hands into his thighs.

"All right," he said finally. He drew a deep breath. "It wasn't much different from any other morning, after any other night. I woke up in my own bed. . . . By that time, Hazel insisted we have separate bedrooms. She was sick of my coming home like I'd been doing. Drunk. Sometimes . . . sometimes I'd had so much to drink I'd wet the bed and wasn't even aware. She wasn't going to stand for it anymore. So I was sleeping in what'd been Sally's room before she moved to Pittsburgh.

"Hazel said Sally was my fault, too. Said Sally couldn't stand living with us. With me. So she got this job in Pittsburgh. Hazel said, if I wasn't out on the road so much, she'd have left too."

Bertha Shawn, the plump woman opposite Kitzi, called out, "So? What finally brought you here?"

McGivney cast an angry glance at her but continued, "Give me a chance! I was saying I got up that morning. Felt like all the other mornings. That taste. My stomach all churning. Then, like I do first thing every morning, I turn on the radio to get the news."

More softly, he admitted, "Actually, I do that to let Hazel know that I'm home. You see, some mornings I don't get home. But when I do, I turn on the radio. Because I know she's listening to find out if I'm there.

"Well, this one morning I turn on the radio and I'm taking my usual get-up drink. Hair of the dog, you know. I get the bottle this high to my lips when I hear the news on the radio . . . 'was struck by a hit-and-run driver near the corner of Laverne and Fourth streets. Brought to the Emergency Room of Mercy Hospital, the boy was pronounced dead on arrival.'

"I stand there, bottle in hand, just ready to drink when I say to myself 'Laverne and Fourth. I went by Laverne and Fourth on my way home last night. I don't remember hitting anything. Or anybody. Except maybe—you see, there are times when I do hit things—the ashcan outside the house, the fence along our driveway—and don't even know it till the next day when Hazel points it out.

"So after I have my drink—three drinks, actually—I get into my clothes. They're dry by then. I go downstairs. Hazel is at the kitchen table having her coffee. So I try to slip out the front door. But she sees me and she calls to me, 'Ward? That you?' I don't answer, just keep going. Out the side door. Back to the garage. I go over my car bumper to bumper. Every fender. Every headlight. Every door. No broken glass. No bent fenders. No paint scratches. Thank God, it wasn't me that hit that boy! I start to get the shakes from sheer relief."

Though his hands still gripped his thighs, McGivney began to tremble.

"I'm like this, holding on to the front fender, when Hazel comes into the garage. She says, 'It was the Kirschner boy. And I was afraid of the same thing, so I was in here earlier. This time it wasn't you, Ward. But next time it *will* be. I'm not going to be a part of this anymore.'

"Hazel goes into the house and starts packing. I beg her not to. She keeps packing. She slams down the lid and snaps the locks and is picking up the bag when I get between her and it. I beg. I plead. I promise."

"We've all done that," the man alongside Kitzi said sadly. "For alcoholics, the road to hell is paved with promises."

"Hazel says, 'Ward, when you've done something about it, let me know. I'll decide whether I come back.' She's gone. I sink down on the bed. I start to cry. Like a kid whose mother'd left him. That's when I decided. It was do something or die. Die alone."

McGivney leaned forward, covering his eyes with his hands. He rocked back and forward. Kitzi saw his body go rigid and then convulse. The man was crying. No one in the group spoke or moved. It seemed to her that a moment of solemn, almost religious, communion had been established between Ward McGivney and his fellow patients.

After a long silence, once his sobs had faded, Joyce Scott asked, "Well, Ward, can you say it now?" He did not reply. She repeated, "Ward? You'll feel better."

He drew himself up, wiped his eyes, looked around the circle at his fellow patients, admitted softly, "I'm Ward McGivney and I'm . . . I'm an alcoholic."

Eighteen other patients greeted him in unison. "Hi, Ward!" And they applauded him.

"Good!" Joyce Scott said. "First step. The most difficult, but the first step."

Kitzi drew back in her chair. The entire procedure had revolted her. She was sure of one thing: *I am never, but never, going to make such a confession. These others might. What do they have to lose? They're just a group of . . . they're just a bunch of nondescript Ward McGivneys. I'll be damned if I am going to put myself in the same class as them. Not me!*

I know what to do. I need a character to play for the next four weeks. A character that will enable me to protect my privacy. To keep it from being invaded. I am not going to make any tearful confessions, or indulge in maudlin breakdowns. To me, this will just be four weeks on the road. Four weeks in a new play. As a new character. By the end of the four weeks, I'll be free to leave. Free! And then . . .

Her thoughts were interrupted when all nineteen people in the group, and Joyce Scott, rose to their feet, bowed their heads, and joined hands to say in unison, "God grant me the serenity to accept the things I cannot change, the courage to change the things I can, and the wisdom to know the difference."

Kitzi glanced furtively from one face to another and thought, *Christ, they take this seriously. They mean it. They actually mean it.*

As the group finished their prayer, Joyce Scott announced, "We have a new member of our group who just joined us this afternoon." She turned to Kitzi. "Would you introduce yourself?"

If they think I am going to stand up and say I'm an alcoholic, they can go screw themselves.

Kitzi smiled, the regal smile she usually reserved for publicity photos.

"I'm Kitzi Mills. And I'm a star, thank you."

Without another word she made a dramatic exit. She returned to her room, slamming the door hard and loud to let them all know she would not tolerate having her privacy invaded.

26

Kitzi sat on the edge of her bed, pondering her next move. She pressed her hands down on the bed. That did little to steady them. She rose angrily, realizing she was not so different from Ward McGivney.

It's part of their plan. They keep you from having a drink to calm your nerves. They wear you down, till you do damn near anything, even confess to being an alcoholic like that McGivney. He made a fool of himself. And all those idiots applauded. Talk about bullshit. That is bullshit!

She repeated it out loud, aiming it at the door to defy them. "Bullshit!" she shouted. "Bullshit!"

Before she had completed the word for the second time the door was opened. A tall, distinguished man who had sat opposite her in the group now stood in the doorway. He was well over six feet, and handsome. The kind of handsome that would have made her consider him as a leading man if she were casting a play. She decided to cultivate him as a friend—more precisely, an ally. She would need allies here, thrust as she was into this group of hostile people.

She smiled, pretending to be shy and even more embarrassed than she felt. "Sorry. Nothing personal."

His own smile put her at ease.

She thought, *Good, he bought the embarrassment bit.*

He came forward and held out his hand in greeting. "I'm Brad Corell and I'm——"

Before he could say another word her mind leaped at it. *If he says, "and I'm an alcoholic," I'll scream.*

He must have read her mind, for he smiled again and said, "I'm Brad Corell, and I'm your Granny."

They shook hands. In her most seductive voice she said, "Can we close the door and talk? I mean really talk."

"First, we can't close the door. No fraternizing with the opposite sex in any room with the door closed. We would be expelled. Second, we can talk, 'really talk' as you put it, with the door open. Or if you'd like, out on the patio," he said, pointing the way.

She considered his invitation, then started for the patio. As soon as she stepped through the door she could feel the late afternoon heat blanketing the desert.

"Are they serious about that 'I'm an alcoholic' bit?" she asked. "What do you people do all day, sit around making public confessions? Is that what it's all about here?"

"That's part of it," Corell said.

She turned from looking out at the mountains and caught him staring at her in the way that men had always stared at her, even before she had become a star. She knew it was working. She was making a conquest that in some way would come in handy later.

"If that's only part of it," she asked, "what's the rest?"

"Our days are structured. Highly structured. We don't *do* anything or *read* anything or *watch* anything that isn't aimed at curing our problem."

"Brainwashing."

"Call it that if you like," Corell said, his blue eyes fixed on her in a way she found disconcerting. "I came in to tell you your duty assignment for your first week. You will set and clear our dorm's tables in the cafeteria."

"I haven't set or cleared a table since I was a waitress when I first came to New York," she protested.

"Miss Mills, we are not asking you to do any more than other stars have done here. Liz Taylor made her own bed, cleaned her room, and cleared tables. So did Mary Tyler Moore. And did it most graciously, I might add. Since you obviously need help more than they did, I would advise you to follow the rules."

"What do you mean, I need help more than they did?" she demanded.

"Attitude, Miss Mills, attitude. The ones who feel they don't need help need it most. You need it real bad."

She felt a chill run through her. This man was breaching the defense she had set up. Was reaching her in a way she had not anticipated. "Now," he went on, "since you object to setting and clearing tables, next week you will vacuum all the rooms. Or, if you prefer, you can swab the bathrooms every morning. Anything else you'd like to know?"

She could tell from the look in his steel-blue eyes that far from making a conquest, she had antagonized him. He left by way of the patio, stopping at the wall to look back at her.

"One thing I forgot. You haven't met your roommate yet."

"I can hardly wait," she replied acidly.

"Bertha."

"Bertha?" she repeated, indicating her lack of recognition.

"Bertha Shawn. The short, stocky, dark-haired woman."

"Oh. The tough one, who keeps saying bullshit," Kitzi identified her.

"Based on what I heard when I came in, you two speak the same language."

With that rebuke, he turned sharply and started away. Her first response to any situation in which she was frustrated was to reach for a drink, then reach for the phone, call Marvin, and vent her anger on him. There was no drink at hand. But she could get to a phone. She went back into her room, to where she expected the phone would be, between the two twin beds. There was no phone. She had noticed a wall phone outside the lounge. But before she reached the door, Bertha Shawn entered.

"Hi," Bertha greeted pleasantly.

"Hi," Kitzi responded, also pleasantly, for she needed information and help. "The phone out in the lounge, is that a pay phone? Can I use a telephone credit card?"

"Didn't they tell you?" Bertha asked.

"Tell me what?"

"You're not allowed to make any phone calls for the first five days."

"But I have to talk to my agent, and my lawyer. We're negotiating the movie of my show," Kitzi improvised.

"They don't care if you're negotiating an arms reduction treaty. No phone calls the first five days," Bertha said.

"You mean I can't even call my daughter?" Kitzi asked.

"Right."

"I think that's terrible," Kitzi said. "And I mean to do something about it!"

"Lotsa luck," Bertha replied.

Kitzi had started for the door when Bertha called to her, "Look, honey, don't make this any tougher on yourself than it is. Any feelings you have, write them in your journal. That's the way to get it off your chest. But don't think they're going to break the rules, or even bend them, for you just because you're Kitzi Mills. Uh-uh. Not here."

"But my daughter, Alice . . . She'll want to know how I am. I have a right to call her, a duty," Kitzi protested.

"If you could call her, what would you tell her that she doesn't already know about you?" Bertha demanded. "She's probably already seen you drunk and throwing up at night when you get home, *if* you get home."

Kitzi was furious, but too ashamed to deny the accusations.

"So if it's concern for your daughter, the best thing you can do is stay right here. Obey the rules. And work like hell on getting better."

"I understand only half of the people here ever do get cured."

"Nobody gets 'cured.' If we're lucky, if we work at it, we become recovering alcoholics. But we never get cured. It's with us all our lives."

Recovering alcoholic.

The phrase sent a chill through Kitzi. She came back toward her bed, sank down on it. *A drink, if I had a drink right now, just one. Even when Marvin called in his brother, he gave me a drink every few hours. If he were here now . . . Or maybe I could pretend that I'm having withdrawal symptoms. They'd send me over to the hospital. I'd surely get a drink there.*

Bertha Shawn sat down on the bed opposite her. "Look, don't try to think ahead four weeks, or even one week, or even five days to your first phone call. Just see this day through. It's tough. I have moments even now when I crave a drink. That's why they keep us so busy. Now, it's recreation time. Would you like to go for a swim? Or play some tennis? Or maybe just go for a walk? I'll go with you, if you like."

"Swim . . ." Kitzi considered. "Evelina packed for me. She never thought to put a swim suit in."

156

"We could find one for you," Bertha volunteered. "Nettie,—Nettie Rosenstein's about your size. I'm sure she'd lend you one."

"Okay," Kitzi finally agreed, "let's go for a swim."

Bertha's round face broke into a sad, sheepish smile. "I don't swim."

"It's never too late to learn," Kitzi said.

"Oh, I know how. I don't swim because I hate to be seen in a swimsuit," Bertha confessed. "Now, if I had a figure like yours . . ."

"Then let's go for that walk instead," Kitzi suggested.

"Look, if you'd rather swim——"

"I'd rather walk," Kitzi insisted.

They had walked to the farthest extent of the vast, meticulously cultivated lawn of The Retreat, where the land suddenly became sandy desert once more. Kitzi stood looking up at the mountains in the distance. The setting sun caught the peaks, painting them gold at their very crests in contrast to shades of purple below. In minutes the sun had sunk. The mountains were all shadows, some darker than others.

Kitzi felt the sudden cold that comes over the desert once the sun has set.

"Let's go back," Bertha said. "You're not used to the nights here. You're not dressed for it."

They started toward the low, white, red-roofed dorms, walking in silence, until Bertha said, "If you don't mind my suggesting . . ."

"I don't mind," Kitzi said.

"When we get back, it'll be quiet time."

"Quiet time?"

"Study time. Start writing in your journal. You have to turn it in tonight. Or, at the latest, before breakfast," Bertha said. "So you might as well start getting into the habit now."

"You write in your journal every night?"

"Every night."

"What do you write?"

"Things. Thoughts. At the start it was all——"

"Bullshit?" Kitzi suggested.

"Yeah, bullshit. It was everything but what I really felt. Funny, when I talk I can say damn near anything. But when I have to write it down, every word becomes important. So I tried to be very wise, very philosophical. As a result I didn't say anything that meant much."

"And now?"

"Now, I don't try to impress anybody. I just write what I feel. Some days, I'm not a very nice person. It's good for me to know that. Some days I like to pretend that I am. Those are the days when Scotty lets me have it. You can't pull any crap on her. So don't even try."

It was almost dark and quite cool by the time they reached the dorm.

27

Evening. Quiet time. Study time. Kitzi sat on her bed examining the books Joyce Scott had left for her. Across the room, seated at her own writing table, Bertha was pondering her open journal. Kitzi had been conscious for some time of the sound of Bertha's pen as she wrote furiously.

Kitzi wondered, *Is she writing about me. What did she say about me? And why did she stop just now?*

Kitzi resumed studying her books. *Alcoholics Anonymous,* the large blue official book of that organization. She leafed through it out of a sense of duty, despite rejecting in advance what it might say.

She turned from the books to be confronted by her journal. She opened it. She was looking at plain lined looseleaf paper. She had not owned a book like this since high school.

Bertha said all they wanted were her honest thoughts and feelings.

She stared at the blank page, shut the book angrily, and was about to put it aside when Bertha glanced in her direction again.

"Scotty doesn't like a blank book," Bertha said by way of friendly advice.

"I can't think of anything to write."

"Don't think. Just write," Bertha advised. "And don't try to be perfect. That's a sign that you're faking."

"I haven't written anything but autographs and thank-you notes for so long, I've forgotten how," Kitzi said. "Almost everything I say is written for me."

"Well, get into the habit. Because you'll have to do it. Every night. Either that or get up before six in the morning and do it."

Bertha resumed writing. Kitzi opened her journal once more, stared at the blank page, and decided she had better make a try.

She started to write, slowly. She wrote less than a dozen words, tore the page out, crumpled it.

"If you don't like a word or a sentence, cross it out. But if you keep ripping out pages you'll never write, and pretty soon you'll have no pages left."

"Damn it, I'm trying! I'm trying!" Kitzi shouted. She slammed the book shut and flung it at the wall. The book exploded, looseleaf pages scattering across the room. Bertha said nothing, only stared. Kitzi glared back.

"I don't have to stay here, you know! There are other places to dry out!"

"I know," Bertha said softly. "I've been there."

Her confession encouraged Kitzi to venture, "Was it so terrible for you your first day here? Did you feel that if you didn't have a drink you'd go out of your mind? That being dead couldn't be worse?"

"Worse," Bertha said. "You see, with me it was also cocaine."

"Oh?"

"When you first come here, you think that no one else in the world feels as terrible as you do. Here we learn we all have the same fears and needs. That's what these journals are for. To learn about ourselves. So, Miss Mills, much as you might hate to do it, try. Now let's gather up those pages. Okay?"

"Okay," Kitzi finally said.

Each from her side of the room started to collect the far-flung pages.

While they did, Bertha said, "I should let you do this by yourself. But I feel sorry for you. Having this public image, the big talented star. With me, I'm nobody, so I don't have an image to keep up. With me, it's just family, my two kids. But you . . . Miss Mills, I wouldn't want your burden for the world."

They met in the center of the room. As Bertha handed her pages to her, Kitzi said, "Thanks. Now would you do something else for me?"

"Like what?"

"Call me by my first name."

"Okay, Kitzi," Bertha agreed.

"No. Katherine. That's really my name. Katherine Millendorfer. If I have to start from the beginning, I'd like someone to call me Katherine again."

Puzzled, Bertha nodded. "Okay, Katherine. Now try to write. Okay?"

"I'll try, I'll try."

She inserted the pages into the looseleaf journal and flattened out the wrinkled top page. With determination, she started.

> During the flight, and for the first hour or two here, I was very frightened. I didn't know what to expect. But now I realize this is where I belong. I just hope I have a constructive attitude so I can make the most of my time here in the next four weeks.

There, she thought, *that should make a very good first report.*

She turned off her light, slipped into bed, and called softly, "Good night, Bertha."

"Good night, Katherine."

They both intended to fall asleep at once. But they were restless. Each could hear the other turning from side to side, until Bertha asked, "What's it like? Really like?"

"What?"

"To be beautiful, to be famous, to have every man in the world itching to get you into bed," Bertha said. "Me, I'm not exactly Miss America. When Al proposed to me, I was so relieved I said yes before he even finished the question. I used to dream that one day I would be beautiful. Then men would desire me. I've always liked that word, "desire." But I don't think any man ever really desired me. Grope me, yeah, screw me, yeah. But desire me, like in the novels and in a girl's dreams? No chance."

She stopped talking. Kitzi held her breath, curious but not wishing to pry. After some moments of silence, Bertha said, "What the hell, I've already told them in group. I might as well.

"You see, after my daughter Nancy was born, sex with Al became less and less. Then nothing. I thought, Well, that's natural. The honeymoon doesn't last forever. I've heard lots of women say that after a kid or two that old flame burns down pretty low. But what I didn't know, what I found out one day, five years ago just by accidentally picking up the extension phone, there was someone else."

"Another woman," Kitzi assumed. "I know the feeling."

"Not this feeling you don't," Bertha corrected. "Another man."

"Another . . ." Kitzi stopped short of repeating the word.

"You can say it. Another man. *M-a-n.* Man! That's when my real drinking began. I used to think I was drinking to forget him. When I got here, I discovered I was drinking to forget me."

"Where are your children now?" Kitzi asked.

"With my mother and father. That's why I have to make it here," Bertha said. "I've got to make up to them for what the last five years have been like. They'll never come home from school and find me dead drunk on the kitchen floor, never again."

They were both silent. Long minutes later, Kitzi heard the deep breathing and a faint snore that told her Bertha was finally asleep.

28

There was a knock on their door at six-thirty A.M. Kitzi woke with a start and was about to call out, "Hold the curtain, I'm not finished making up," when she realized where she was and, a moment later, why she was there.

As she dressed, she remembered that Corell had assigned her to set tables in the cafeteria for breakfast.

She took up her blue journal and started on her way to the cafeteria, stopping only long enough to drop her journal on the desk in Joyce Scott's office, where it became one among twenty blue journals.

* * *

By the time she had set down the last napkin, the last fork, knife, and spoon, Bertha was at her side, urging, "Meditation walk. Let's go."

They walked around the outer perimeter of the grounds of The Retreat. High above them, in the cloudless blue sky, silent jet planes on their way east were unrolling their vapor trails. Underfoot, the grass was damp with dew. Kitzi saw a jackrabbit jump from behind some desert brush and disappear in the distance.

They walked without a word. Bertha's confession of the night before was too painful for either of them to comment upon.

Nothing was said until Bertha reminded, "Time to go back."

The members of their dorm had assembled in their part of the dining room. They formed a circle, held hands, and recited, "God grant me the serenity to accept the things I cannot change, the courage to change the things I can, and the wisdom to know the difference."

Kitzi grasped Bertha's hand and the hand of the old man who happened to be on her left.

Damn, he does look familiar. Where have I run into him before? Kitzi wondered.

She had not joined in the prayer. Once it was spoken by the others, they were free to line up, cafeteria style, and select breakfast.

Kitzi chose orange juice, French toast, coffee. At table, she found herself using more syrup than she used to, even as a child. She became self-conscious. But the man across from her, a man she had not even noticed yesterday, encouraged, "Pour it on. In the beginning, sweets take the place of booze. And with a figure like yours, you can stand it."

She cast a guarded glance at him, wondering, *Is he coming on to me? I thought that was forbidden here.*

He read her mind and hastened to explain, "I know your work, Miss Mills. After all, I should. We put up half the money for *Never Leave Me.* To get the album rights. I must have seen that show twenty times. Loved you every time."

"You're in the record business?" she asked, surprised.

"I'm with the Network. Was president of the Entertainment Division," he said, introducing himself. "Harlan Brody."

162

"Hi," she said. "Have we met before?"

"The night you cut the cast album. I still remember. You wore a white satin blouse and black slacks and had a red bandanna around your head. You looked fantastic."

"I'll never look like that again," she said softly.

"After this place, you'll look even better. I make you a promise right now. On your next show, the Network'll put up *all* the money."

Nice, she thought, *he's being too nice, trying to get me over the first shock of being here. I'll bet when the time comes his Network won't put up a dime. They'll ask, "Can that lush carry a show any longer?"*

But Kitzi smiled as sweetly as she could. "I'll ask my producers to give you first crack at my next show."

The morning lecture involved The Retreat's entire patient group. Sixty patients from three dorms, equal numbers of men and women, ranging in age from the early twenties to that one man in her own dorm who looked to be in his sixties. Kitzi took her place, sitting with Bertha in the second row. She hardly dared look around, sensitive to the fact that she had already been recognized by several patients from the other two dorms. There had been whispered comments about her. She was relieved when Mrs. Armbruster introduced the guest lecturer, Dr. Henry Sloane.

Sloane was trim, in the manner of a highly trained athlete, with a tanned complexion that bespoke many hours in the sun. He had a deceptive smile, coming as it did from his lean, dour, angular face. He was smiling when he said, "Good morning. I'm Henry Sloane, and I'm a recovering alcoholic."

"Hi, Henry," everyone in the group called back, everyone except Kitzi.

"Well, now, the reason I've been invited here today was to cover the medical aspects of alcoholism. You've all been warned about cirrhosis of the liver. The irreversible damage that is deadly.

"But just as bad is what alcoholism does to your heart. Alcohol attacks the nerves that regulate and control the heart, giving rise to irregular heartbeats and eventually to fibrilation that is very often fatal. It also attacks the heart muscle itself. Ever had those flutters, those skipped beats, those rapid beats, when it feels like your heart is running away with itself? Of course. We alcoholics have all had them. Well, those are only warnings. The real damage goes on silently."

Kitzi looked around cautiously, to see if any other patients shared the same suspicion she had. This doctor had evidently been instructed to deliver this particular lecture today because it was her first full day. He was describing exactly what she had experienced not once but many times. He was obviously trying to frighten her.

She would deal with him as she did when confronted by anyone with unwelcome news. Attorneys who advised her to live up to contracts. Producers who pleaded for extensions of successful runs. Directors who insisted that she adhere to the script. Playwrights who criticized her treatment of their material. She let them talk, argue, shout, and rave. She just tuned out.

Tune out, and stay tuned out, she resolved. So she did. Until the phrase "brain damage" intruded on her consciousness. She could no longer resist listening.

"So," Sloane continued, "everything I've said about the effect of heavy drinking on the liver, heart, pancreas, kidneys, blood vessels, and the body's immune system almost pales beside the destruction of your brain cells. Because, unlike most other organs of the body, no form of exercise, diet, or medication can restore brain cells. The longer you indulge in heavy drinking, the more of your brain you destroy."

Now Kitzi was staring at him intensely. He caught a glimpse of that and addressed his next remarks to her.

"Now, some of you may be thinking, He's saying all this to scare me. Damn right! If it takes fear to make you reconsider the way you've been living, then I want you to be afraid. You have good reason to be afraid. But only if it makes you determined to quit. Once and for all, and forever. Now, let's join in our serenity prayer."

With that, the meeting disbanded. Each group returned to its own dorm, ready to plunge into their first group session of the day.

Kitzi attended, listened, but continued to remain aloof.

As she proceeded down the corridor toward her room, she was interrupted by the announcement on the loudspeaker: "Miss Mills, please report to my office at once."

She recognized Joyce Scott's voice.

* * *

She found the counselor seated at her desk, the stack of blue journals before her. Without a word of greeting, she gestured Kitzi to be seated.

From Joyce Scott's posture and attitude, Kitzi knew that the young counselor was displeased. "This journal you turned in."

"Yes?" Kitzi responded, pretending enormous interest and expecting a glowing response.

"Pure, unadulterated garbage!" Joyce Scott said.

"What do you mean——" Kitzi started to protest.

"I mean, Mills, that nobody, but nobody, feels like this on their first day," Joyce Scott said. "What are you trying to do, score brownie points? Be honest! You hate being here. You hate our rules and our restrictions. You think everything we do is ridiculous. Infantile. The serenity prayer we say, you think that's bullshit. Well, we don't. Now if I were grading this paper I'd give you an F. But since I am understanding and sympathetic, I am going to tear up this page and give you a chance to start over again. When you hand this in tomorrow, I want the truth. That's all. Just the truth."

She ripped out the page, slapped the book shut, and shoved it across the table at Kitzi.

Not since Kitzi had been an unknown and striving young actress had anyone dared talk to her that way. She snatched the journal angrily and left the room.

29

Evening. Kitzi had survived her first full day at The Retreat. Only twenty-seven more days to go. If only she could leave. It would be easy. All she had to do was walk. Just walk. Out of her dorm. Past the buildings of The Retreat. Beyond the grounds. And she would be free. Better than free. She would not be permitted back. All the pleading by Alice, by Marvin, by Evelina, by the doctors, could not reverse that.

Once out, she could have that drink she needed so desperately. She could taste it. She could feel it warm its way down her throat, which was now as dry and grainy as desert sand.

Help, freedom, relief from her overwhelming thirst was as close as the lights she could see from her patio at night. The lights of houses. Homes. Where they would be flattered and delighted to greet Kitzi Mills and offer her a drink. And another drink. And the whole bottle. All she had to do was walk out of here.

It was simple. Too simple. Much as she needed that drink, and all the ones that would follow, she could not betray them. Not Marvin. Not Alice. She could not face her child and say, "I just walked out."

But, with the delusional shrewdness of an alcoholic, she contrived another way. A way in which she would become the victim and get herself expelled. She had been warned that sexual hanky-panky was out. There were three or four men who would jump at making it with her. But that would mean getting some other poor bastard kicked out. She decided not to add them to her list of victims.

There was another, simpler and subtler, tactic.

Joyce Scott kept pressing her for more revealing entries in her journal. Okay. She'd let her have it, after which Scott would have no choice but insist that she leave. Kitzi could already savor that first drink. Vodka. On ice. Straight. Cold and straight. Yet warm and comforting. She wrote,

> I have been here exactly thirty-seven hours and I hate this place. You lie about it being free and open, no fences, no walls, no locked doors. This is worse than any prison. There is no letup. You are rushed from one activity to the next—lectures, films, group therapy, books, writing dumb reports like this. Mind control is what this is.
>
> A Communist psychiatric prison must be like this. Keep repeating the same thing over and over until you have no mind of your own but accept everything they say.
>
> That damn serenity prayer. I have spoken many lines of dialogue in my career but only when I've felt they were honest and believable. I do not believe that prayer. I will not say it. Besides, I do not believe in God. So how is that damned prayer going to help me?
>
> Worse, yesterday they told me I couldn't make a call

out of here for five days. Five whole days. Now, after thirty-seven hours, I know why you don't let people call out. Because they'd call a friend, a relative, someone, and say, "Come take me out of here!"

And what makes five days a magic number? By that time do you have the inmates so brainwashed that they have no will of their own? They can't even call for help. They just give up and say, "Do anything you want with me."

Well, not me!

So, my dear Miss Scott, if this is your game, I say fuck it. That's right, fuck it! And fuck you!!!

Though it was late, long past bedtime, she slipped out of the room quietly so as not to wake Bertha. She went down the hall until she reached the dimly lit lounge. She was surprised to find two other patients still awake. One man. One woman. They were both drinking coffee. Kitzi had been here only thirty-seven hours, but had already discovered that recovering alcoholics drink coffee, lots of coffee. And many smoked, some chain-smoked. The only ultimate and forbidden vice was alcohol.

Kitzi went past the lounge to Joyce Scott's office. She tried the door. It was unlocked. She entered the dark room and put her journal down squarely in the center of the desk so the counselor would be forced to see it first thing in the morning.

On her way back she stopped in the lounge. She needed a cup of coffee herself. She sat down, as far from the other two as possible, and sipped her coffee.

Soon the female patient, the fiftyish woman with the blond hair, finished reading. She took her empty cup with her, starting toward the counter. As she reached Kitzi, she stopped. She was a slender woman, fifty or possibly a little younger. It was hard to tell. Liquor had done things to her face. Kitzi had noticed her earlier in the day and thought, *Good bone structure. She must have been quite lovely in her day.*

The woman spoke in a whisper. Not that she could have been overheard, but in institutions people tend to whisper late at night.

"Miss Mills?"

Kitzi tensed. "Yes?"

"I saw you yesterday at supper for the first time. I wanted to tell you how much I admire you."

Oh, God, not another fan. Next she'll be telling me her mother took her to see me when she was a mere child, and she's older than I am, almost twenty years older. The curse of achieving success in show business at a young age.

She was braced for the extravagant praise to which she was usually subjected after a performance or even a chance encounter in some store when she shopped for clothes.

"Miss Mills, may I call you Kitzi?"

"If you like," Kitzi said, thinking, *Four weeks of this would have driven me crazy. I can't wait for Scott's reaction.*

"I've been here six days now," the woman said. "Yesterday I had my first call out. I called my husband and pleaded, 'Joe, come and get me. I can't take it.'"

"I know how you feel," Kitzi said, comforted that she was not alone.

"But then this evening I called him again and I said, 'Joe, forget what I said last night. A woman joined us yesterday afternoon. A great star. If she can come to this place and want to get cured, then I can stick it out.' You gave me the incentive I needed to stay on and lick this thing. Thanks, Kitzi."

Kitzi was at first aghast, then merely embarrassed. "You know my name, but I don't know yours."

"Nettie. Nettie Rosenstein."

"Glad to meet you, Nettie."

"Now I've got to get some sleep. Granny listed me to do the wake-up chore tomorrow morning. See you then."

Thank God that's over, she thought. I'm not the Statue of Liberty. I am not Eleanor Roosevelt. Or Nancy Reagan. I'm just an actress, who also happens to sing and dance. Damn well, I might add. But I've troubles enough of my own without being responsible for others. I'll be glad to get out of here. Miss Scott, wake up! Wake up early! And read my journal first thing!

The man who had been sitting at the far end of the lounge closed his book and picked up his empty coffee cup.

As he drew close to Kitzi, she realized he was one of the two men who had seemed familiar to her yesterday. He walked with a slouch and had a cigarette butt hanging from the side of his mouth. She judged him to be in his early sixties.

Hardly worth reforming, she found herself thinking.

As he passed her, he glanced down. "Good night, my dear." When she evidenced her puzzlement, he said, "Chamberlain. August Chamberlain."

She realized at once why he had seemed so familiar. He was a foreign correspondent for the *New York Times.* He said no more. Just rinsed his coffee cup before he started off down the corridor to his room.

She was alone. She sipped her coffee. Now it was too tepid. She debated taking a fresh, hot cup. Decided not to. She rinsed her cup and started back to her room.

She entered. She could hear Bertha's shallow breathing. The woman was asleep. Without booze, without pills, she was asleep.

She must be in the last stage, Kitzi thought. *If you bought all that crap about serenity, endured the masochistic exposure in group therapy sessions, wrote in that damn journal until you were totally brainwashed, you could sleep the sleep of benign idiots.*

Get up, Miss Scott. Read my journal! And do what you have to. I'm ready to leave now!

30

Throughout the next morning, Kitzi attempted to make eye contact with Joyce Scott. She kept concentrating, *Watch me, notice me, react to me!* There was no sign that Joyce Scott had read her journal. But before the day was over she would. She must.

At lunch, Joyce Scott approached Kitzi's table, leaned close to her, and whispered, "When you're done, would you come to my office?"

"I'm done now," Kitzi said, dropping her fork into her untouched salad.

In her office, Joyce Scott picked up Kitzi's journal.

"Quite a document, Mills," she began.

"You said to write what I thought and felt," Kitzi said, pretending innocence.

"*I* did. And *you* did," Joyce Scott said, smiling.

Her smile irritated Kitzi. This was no small matter to be treated with a smile. She wanted out. And today.

"What this really needs is more intensity," Joyce Scott said. "Needs to cut closer to the bone, so to speak."

"I don't know what you mean," Kitzi replied.

"You'd been here how many hours . . . forty . . . forty one . . . ? And you decided you didn't like our routine. So you want out. But, like all alcoholics, you refuse to take responsibility for your own actions. You want *us* to make the move. I've seen hundreds of such journals from newcomers. And most of them a hell of a lot better, I must say. So, for originality I'd give your little billet-doux about four out of ten."

"There *are* those who don't make it," Kitzi protested. "The doctor who lectured yesterday said fifty percent fail."

"If you fail, you fail," Joyce Scott said. "But, damn it, *you* are going to try. And *we* are going to try. If you want to walk out of here, be adult enough to take the responsibility. Otherwise, stick it out. Because I think you could be one of the half that *does* make it."

"You only want me here because of who I am!" Kitzi accused. "It makes this place famous. Drums up business for you."

"Mills, we don't need 'business.' Our struggle is to keep up with the demand for beds. If word about you does leak out, it won't come from us." She held out Kitzi's journal. "Here, my dear, take this. Keep writing. The important things will come. At least now you're angry enough to fight. Just start fighting the right enemy."

Unconsoled but undefeated, Kitzi took possession of her journal and started for the door. There she stopped and turned to face Joyce Scott. "I do not believe in God!"

"I know," Scott said, unperturbed.

"Then I really am faking it if I say that serenity prayer," Kitzi said.

"You don't have to believe in God," Scott said. "All you have to do is learn the Five Steps in the book we gave you. The first two are a beginning. One, admit that you are powerless over alcohol and it has made your life unmanageable. Two, believe that only a Power greater than yourself can restore you to sanity. That Power does not have to be any special God. Or any God at all. Just a power greater than you are. You have to believe that, if it's going to work for you here."

Kitzi did not respond. The defiance was in her eyes, which were brighter now since she had not had a drink in two whole days. A nod from Scott dismissed her.

On her third day when she woke up, she felt sick to her stomach. She realized that what she missed most was the security of knowing that in the bar in the foyer was an endless supply of alcohol, all she could drink. Here there was nothing. She knew now why they had confiscated her bottles of mouthwash and her perfume.

From under the window drapery a thin line of faint light began to appear. She slipped out of the bed quietly, so as not to disturb Bertha who was in deep sleep in the other bed exhaling heavily with just the hint of a throaty snore at the end of each breath.

Kitzi parted the draperies enough to peer out. Dawn was breaking on the desert. She could see the distant mountains with the light of the sun just making its appearance.

Nothing seemed to move. Not the potted cactus which decorated their little patio, nor the more distant desert vegetation. The air seemed as still as if all life had been suspended.

She slid the door back silently. On bare feet she stepped out on the cold concrete. She went to the wall at the edge of the patio and looked out at the vast desert. The light was growing stronger. The spectacle of the earth coming alive made her think, *This could be a marvelous world to live in if only I had a drink. Just one. To take the edge off. To make life bearable. Why can't I have one? I'd promise not to overdo. I'd go back to work. I'd be better than I've ever been, and God damn it, I've been good. Great! I'll be even*

171

greater. If only they would understand. If only Marvin would understand. But he never will. He's too anxious to protect his money machine. His position in the industry. Sole representative of Kitzi Mills.

Even as she thought that, she knew that the Marvin Morse Agency was large and powerful without her as a client. But she needed to punish him, until, she found herself remembering how many times Marvin had come searching for her along the West Forties, where she usually gravitated when she was drunk. She had a few favorite bars where, drunk as she was, they would continue to serve her. Then she would mount the bar to favor the other drunks with songs from her shows, sometimes until she was silenced by her own hoarseness.

Marvin would come in with that desperate look on his perspiring face, his eyes taking in the scene in one sweeping glare. He would pick her up, despite her kicking, screaming protest. He would carry her out. And, except for one occasion, no man dared to dispute him.

That one time a man who was not so drunk and who had other plans in mind for her, did challenge Marvin. Marvin put her down in a chair, because she could not stand. He attacked the man and they had a bloody fight that only ended when the police arrived. Marvin was able to explain to them so they did not make an arrest. He had picked her up again, carried her out to the street where, then too, dawn was breaking. But dawn in New York was quite different from dawn in the desert. Garbage trucks, bakery wagons, milk trucks. The smell of the city. The noise and vibration of the subway underfoot. The litter in the streets. The stray taxis. The news trucks tossing their bundles in front of newsstands and stores. Always, off in the distance, the sound of a police siren.

She yearned for the noisy smelly dawn of the city. For Alice. For the Kitzi Mills who was free to do anything she wished, including drink. Kitzi could feel her hands tremble and blamed the chill of the early desert morning, the dewy cold on her naked feet. She pressed her hands hard against the top of the low patio wall. She still could not control them.

A drink. Just one. Nothing fancy. Plain vodka would do it. Or maybe a pill and vodka to wash it down. That would be asking too much. She would settle for the drink.

Her thoughts were interrupted when she became aware of some-one stirring in the room behind her. A moment later, Bertha was at her side, disheveled from sleep but eyes alert and searching. In an instant, she relaxed and returned to looking sleepy once more.

Bertha said nothing. But Kitzi could see fear in Bertha's eyes, fear that Kitzi had decided to run away.

She resented being spied on, yet she could not deny feeling touched that Bertha was concerned about her, even terrified that she might have defected.

Resentment won out. Kitzi snapped at her, "I wasn't running away. I'll do my goddamn chores. I'll sit through the damn lectures. And the group. God, how I am beginning to loathe some of those faces. I was once in a production of *Macbeth* where the Three Witches in their ghastly makeup looked better than some of the people in this dorm!"

Bertha only yawned and said, "I got to go to the toilet." She disappeared back into the room.

Kitzi could once more feel the cold under her feet, and the damp-ness. She had to take a hot shower and get dressed for another long, long, dry, dry day.

The inevitable lecture, this time by a woman physician. When she was first informed that today's visiting lecturer would be a female doctor, Kitzi had expected someone motherly, gray-haired. She was surprised to find a young woman, with black, shining hair coiffed in a way that indicated she was in the hands of an excellent stylist. She wore a black suit and a blouse of crimson silk, just enough color to contrast with the black.

Her subject for the morning lecture was "How Women Alcoholics Differ from Men."

Kitzi was determined to listen with only a minimum of involve-ment. There would, she knew, be the usual threats and warnings associated with such lectures.

"The chief problem that afflicts the female alcoholic is the result of promiscuous sex. Whereas the male might wish to be promiscuous, alcohol usually makes him impotent.

"On the other hand, the female alcoholic, regardless of her con-dition, is always available for sex, even when she is not aware of what's happening to her. This leaves her open to the unfortunate possibility of contracting a number of venereal diseases. Nowadays, with the AIDS epidemic, that can become a matter of life and death."

Kitzi tried to shut out the rest of the lecture and was left with a random collection of facts about the percentage of women alcoholics who are also drug dependent, women who end up with bruises they can't explain from falls they can't remember, and an assortment of physical consequences of alcoholism that threaten their lives, and in many instances their unborn children.

She felt enormous relief when the lecture was finally over. Some women in the group crowded around the young physician to ask her pertinent personal questions. Curious, Kitzi could not resist joining them. When the doctor recognized her, she asked, "Miss Mills, I heard you were here. If there's any way I can help, anything you want to know . . ."

"Yes, doctor, there is something I want to know."

The woman invited her question with an eager and friendly "Fire away, Miss Mills!"

"Where did you ever get that elegant but understated suit?" Kitzi asked, a mischievous twinkle in her eyes.

The doctor stared at Kitzi for a moment, then turned her attention to another patient who had a more relevant question.

At group session, Joyce Scott permitted what she considered a decent interval of silence before she spoke.

"Shall I assume that all our problems are solved and no one has anything to say?" She glanced around the circle. "Bertha? Calvin? Ward? Nettie? We must have made enormous progress since yesterday when we all seemed to have a great deal on our minds. Mills?"

Kitzi stared back at her, silent, unyielding.

"Nothing? Not even resentment?" Scott asked.

"If resentment is what you want," Kitzi said, "I want to know what gives you the right to keep a mother from calling her daughter!"

"It's the rule, Mills. First five days, no calls out. No calls in."

"Even when you're arrested you're allowed one call," Kitzi reminded her.

"You seem very familiar with that routine," Joyce Scott said dryly. "Anything else bugging you?"

"Nothing that I care to discuss!" Kitzi responded.

"Which means there must be a great deal," Scott said. She turned from Kitzi to the lone black man in the group. "Calvin?"

Calvin Thompson was young, black, extremely tall, athletic, lean save for the muscles of his calves and biceps. Kitzi had noticed him before and been startled by his resemblance to Sidney Poitier. She was not aware that in his own milieu Calvin Thompson was much better known than Sidney Poitier. He was, or had been, one of the best young prospects to come into the National Basketball Association in the last half-dozen years.

In previous group sessions, Kitzi had not heard him say a word beyond speaking the serenity prayer with the others. Challenged directly by Joyce Scott, he shifted uneasily in his chair, crossed his long legs, then uncrossed them.

"I don't have much to say. An' if I did, wouldn't know how to say it."

"You might start like the rest of us do," Scott suggested. " 'I'm Calvin Thompson and I'm a recovering alcoholic.' "

"That's the trouble," Thompson said shyly, "I don't think I'm recovering . . . I don't think I'm doing anything here."

"Why not, Calvin?" Scott asked.

" 'Cause I can't do the things . . . I mean, you all are talking about yourself and writing about yourself . . . and . . ."

He turned to Joyce Scott, his eyes filling up with tears.

"I've been to a good college and never felt so stupid there as I do here. There, they were always easing the way for me. I didn't have to write, I didn't have to answer questions. All I did was shoot baskets. I didn't learn that there. Shit, I could do that before I ever went to college. College was just something I had to do to get into the pros.

"Here, they want me to write in that little blue book and talk, like right now. Miss Scott, you know I can't write. I don't know how to spell. As for talking, I ain't too good at that either.

"Back in college, my coach used to rehearse me. One speech, if we won. Another speech, if we lost. One time I give the losing speech when we won. Everybody thought it was a big joke.

"Funny, hell! I was just plain stupid. Guess the only time I felt worse was the day they gave me my diploma. I went up on that platform like all the rest, except I was the tallest one there. I'm thinking to myself, You are sticking out from the crowd because you are so tall, and so black, and so damn stupid.

"My grandma was there. My daddy ran off when I was little. My mama died soon after. But my grandma kept saying all my life, 'Calvin, you are going to do what your daddy never did. You are going to college.' " So she was there that day. She was so proud and full of tears when I handed my diploma to her. She held it like it was the most precious thing in the world. She took my arm, stood on tiptoe, and said, 'Son, you have made me a proud woman today. And if your mama was alive she'd been prouder still, her son graduating from college.'

"I wanted to say to her, 'Grandma, it's a lie, it's all a lie. I ain't educated, I'm just graduated. They're not the same.' But nobody asked if they were the same. Because by that time the NBA draft was on, and I was one of the first picks. They gave me more money to sign than I could count. Because counting was another thing I never learned to do.

" 'S long as all I had to do was get my hands on that ball and shoot, I was okay. But the loneliness gets to you. I mean, there you are in some strange town with nothing to do but watch television in some hotel room. A dude gets lonely. He wants looking for company. Another warm body. Somebody to talk to, or just to be with. Or, yeah, to fuck. I did a lot of that."

He looked down, embarrassed.

"One thing, when you're an athlete, you can always find chicks, at least. Until that's not enough. You want that and a real high at the same time. Kinda like a double high. That's the start. After a while, all you want is the high. The chick is just someone who brings you the stuff.

"I guess chicks have always been trouble for me. One time, when I was still in college, my third year after we beat Kansas, we went to a frat party and got boozed up. There was a chick there, drunk as a skunk and acting pretty loose. So a bunch of us guys from the team got her up in one of the bedrooms. She didn't exactly resist, and we were all so drunk. . . ."

He hesitated, groping for words that would reveal what happened yet protect him from the censure of the women in the group.

"Anyway . . . another chick walked in on us and made quite a fuss. Well, the way it was, they caught me just short of what the judge said . . . Well, they couldn't prove what he called 'penetration.' So technically it wasn't rape. I got off with a warning. Besides, the big game, the one against Indiana, was coming up. So it got all hushed up.

"But somehow somebody got word to my grandma. She came out to the school. She walked into the gymnasium right in the middle of practice. When Coach Coles said, 'Get that woman out of here!' I said, 'Hey, that's my grandma.' He said, 'If she's down for the game, let her wait till Friday night. We got work to do.'

"But she came right up to him and said, 'He's my grandson and I got to talk to him. Right now! If you try to stop me I'll pull him out of this college so fast it'll make your head spin.' She's a very strong woman, my grandma. She didn't get to be a supervisor of nurses by being dumb or weak. So Coles had no choice.

"Well, she takes me into his office and closes the door. First thing she does is slap me right across the face. 'There,' she says, 'that's to remind you that you are my grandson. And my grandson don't do the things you've been doing. When you got this scholarship here at the university, I thought, Thank God, now that boy will have a chance. He is going to grow up to be a man, a real man. But from what I hear you're not a man. You're still just a boy who can shoot a basketball. And because you can you've been getting away with murder. Or just short of murder. Calvin, you got to start being responsible for yourself. Because you won't be able to shoot a basketball all your life. And I don't want any shiftless bum on my hands ten years from now!'

"Then she reaches to the coach's desk and picks up a book. It was one he'd written himself on how to play the game. She opens that book and says, 'Calvin! Read!' So I start reading. Not fast. Not very good. Hardly at all. She sat there, this strong woman, and she starts to cry. 'Your mama, least she could read well. Never had the chances you had, but damn it, she could read and write above her station.'

"She went out on that practice floor and right in the middle of things she marched up to Coach Coles, holding my hand, and she says, 'Unless this boy has tutoring starting right now, he don't play another game for this university.' 'Course, two days away from the Indiana game, Coles would promise anyone anything to keep his starting five. So he promised. When I asked my grandma to stay and see me in that game, she refused, saying, 'I'm sorry you ever discovered that a basketball is round and that it's supposed to go through a hoop.'

"Later, when I was drafted by the NBA, she didn't care so much about the money, but I have the only contract in the league that calls for a private tutor when we're playing home games. 'Course, that turned out to be a joke in a way. The team got me a young tutor. Good-looking chick, too. We didn't study much. She became pregnant. She wanted to get married and I didn't. So she didn't have the baby. And we broke up.

"After that, I . . . I started drinking more. And snorting more. Until one of the guys on the squad, he found a hot connection for real pure stuff. I went at it harder. I felt great. I was out there on the floor playing my heart out. I had more energy than before. But for a shorter time. I started having a bad second half. Then a bad second quarter. Even though it felt great when I was out there, I wasn't scoring. I had my moves. I got to the basket. But somehow the ball wasn't going in. A doctor told me later that it was the coke. It made me think I was feeling great but my timing was off. Way off.

"They sent me to be tested. It showed. They sent me for rehab. Didn't work. So I was out. Done. My grandma arranged for me to come here. And . . . and she's paying for it. 'Cause I don't have any of the money left. It all went for the pure white stuff."

He sighed softly before he said, "I guess I'm a victim of circumstances. If I'd never had a basketball in my hands, if I'd had to depend on my brain instead of my muscles, I coulda' made it. My grandma, she's not dumb. Nor was my mama. I must have some brains. Just nobody asked me to use them."

"Bullshit!" Bertha said, not loudly but very, very firmly.

"Bertha, please . . . ," Kitzi started to say.

The chunky little woman persisted. "Self-pity is one thing we got more of than anything else around here. I had it too. We all consider ourselves victims. But it's only an out. The easy way."

She turned on Kitzi. "I'll bet when *you* start to open up, we'll get the same crap. 'I was a victim, don't blame me, pity me!' Well, not here."

She turned back to Calvin Thompson. "Okay, so you're black. That's tough! Blame the whole world. You're only the poor victim. But who tried to rape that girl. You did! So put the blame where it belongs!"

August Chamberlain leaned in to confront Thompson eye to eye. "Bertha's right. Your grandma was right. You had great chances and blew 'em. Right up your nostrils. As for being overpaid and spoiled and not having to be a grown-up human being because you were a superb athlete, what about Bill Russell? The Doc, Julius Erving? Jabbar and Oscar Robinson? Great players, well paid. They turn out to be highly intelligent individuals, great businessmen. So if it's pity you want, not around here. Thompson, you're a disgrace to your people, and most of all to your grandmother. I'd like to meet that woman and offer her my condolences in person. You're a poor excuse for a man, Calvin Thompson. So don't seek sympathy or forgiveness. Not from us!"

The rebuke, coming from such a paternal figure as August Chamberlain, reduced young Calvin to tears. He hid his face and turned away. His sobbing soon became the only sound in the room.

Kitzi stared around the circle. If there was any sympathy among them for the young ex-athlete, it did not appear on their faces. She alone understood him. She knew the loneliness of being out on the road, bereft of familiar surroundings and people. She knew the solace that a bottle or some white powder could provide.

If no one spoke up for this young man, she would. She aimed her reply at old Chamberlain.

"I think what I have just seen here is . . . is savage. That's the only word that can describe it. No one has tried to help this young man. All you have done is condemn him."

"Now, hold on—" Ward McGivney started to say.

She used the power of her stage voice to override him. "You've all had your say, now I'll have mine! People don't know what it means to be a star. You've got the whole world staring at you. And they always want perfection. Unfortunately, we can't always give them that. When it's over, better than anyone, you know when you've fallen short. But by then you're alone. The lies of your stage manager or your agent or your coach don't help. It's just you and that damn mirror. You can either cover it up or take a drink. And another, and another. Until what you see in the mirror doesn't rebuke you anymore. If the rest of you had been stars, like Calvin once was, you'd know the feeling. And you wouldn't be so brutal with him."

She stood up, crossed the open area of the circle, looked into Calvin Thompson's face.

"I don't know about the rest of these people, but I'm sorry for you. Very sorry." She started out of the room.

"She's only been here a few days," Ward McGivney said.

"Despite her obvious show of sympathy for Calvin, it's herself she's sorry for," Joyce Scott said, as Kitzi closed the door behind her.

31

At dinner time, Kitzi said nothing to any of her fellow patients. She chose very little food from the selections the cafeteria offered. She picked a table where only one other person sat, a matronly woman from a suburb of San Francisco. Heiress to a farming and real estate fortune, she had a longtime habit of drinking the best wines, the not-so-best wines, then, finally, any wines she could get hold of.

The woman gave every indication of wishing to engage Kitzi in conversation. Kitzi did not encourage her.

Speaking just above a whisper to make them coconspirators, the woman said, "Miss Mills, I think you were so right this afternoon."

Instead of responding, she set down her fork brusquely and left the table. She raced down the corridor to her room, entered and slammed the door to shut out this world in which she was imprisoned against her will. Her impulse was to pour herself a drink. She was desperate for a drink. Just one.

She had been determined not to let the people here get close to her. Talk to her. But by defending Calvin Thompson she had encouraged them, opened herself to their advances. Well, she would never speak again in those group sessions. Not even to defend someone else. She had lived the better part of her life exposed to public scrutiny, to drama critics, film critics, columnists, audiences, and she had survived it all, the good and the bad. But to reveal herself to these people in a small room where you could hear their breathing, smell them, be subject to their scrutiny—that was too much, even when they were honestly compassionate. Far too much.

There was only one way. She had to find the quickest way to a drink. Quickly meant *now*. She took a sweater from her closet to protect her from the night air. As for the rest of her clothes, they could send them back. Or burn them, as far as she was concerned. She slipped into a soft, red cashmere and started toward the patio doors. She paused to consider. It would make a much more dramatic exit to leave a note.

She searched for a sheet of paper on which to write. She found none. But there it was, her blue notebook. What more fitting symbol than this book in which she was supposed to write all her thoughts and feelings.

Well, Miss Scott, one last thought!

So as not to be misunderstood, since she had grown careless with her handwriting, mainly from scribbling so many hasty autographs, Kitzi Mills began to print in large block letters: "I HAVE HAD ALL I CAN TAKE OF THIS FUCKING PLACE. I AM LEAVING. NO. I HAVE LEFT."

She signed it with a bold flourish, "Katherine Millendorfer." Unused to writing out her full and original name, the "-dorfer" had to be printed down the side of the page. She slammed the book shut defiantly. Reconsidering that it would be bolder and more defiant, she opened it for Bertha, short, chubby, impossibly optimistic Bertha, to see.

She went to the patio doors, pushed aside the draperies, and slipped through the open doors into the darkness. She inhaled the night air. It was fragrant with the perfume of desert trees and vegetation. Ahead of her, a huge, full, orange-colored desert moon was rising up from the horizon. The light was so bright she could feel it. She stepped off the patio and onto the grass, realizing that she would not be free until she felt the sand. Once on sand, she would have committed the one unpardonable sin for which she would be barred from this prison forever. She broke into a run, her sandals padding along the close-cropped grass for what seemed an endless stretch. Ahead of her, two white-and-glass buildings, their windows dark, gleamed in the strong moonlight. The medical office buildings and laboratories, closed for the night. She would head for them. Instead of desert sand, concrete would mean freedom. The important thing was to escape and get a drink. Any kind of drink.

She remembered the one time—she had guarded this secret from everyone—she had accepted a drink of cheap wine from a derelict who lay in a storefront alcove with a bottle clutched to him. He had recognized not who she was but what she was, so he offered to share it with her.

She would accept that drink again—right now! She raced toward the empty parking lot and was almost to the edge of the soft lawn when she tripped on something. It seemed a snare, deliberately set to trap her. She fell forward, half on the grass, half on concrete, scraping her palms. The gardeners had fenced some freshly sodded lawn with twine on pegs to keep people from trampling it. One of the pegs had tripped her.

She took a moment to catch her breath, then rose to her feet, conscious of the scrapes on her hands. She looked about her and wondered where she should go. To her left was a roadway, a main artery, to judge from the number of headlights that went flashing by. To her right was darkness, desert, and the distant moon, which seemed smaller now that it had risen somewhat.

The road, she decided. If she did not succeed in getting a lift, there were houses there. Refuge. A drink. Who would fail to take in an attractive woman in obvious distress, with bleeding hands, who was lost in an unfamiliar place? What would be more civilized or natural than to offer her a drink to calm her nerves?

Yes, the roadway. She started in that direction. From her first step she realized that more than her hands had been hurt when she fell.

She had twisted her right ankle. Despite that, she tried to run. Unable to, she limped along.

The pain became too great. She sank down to the concrete and massaged her right ankle.

Frustrated, desperately feeling her thirst, alone, lost, she began to cry. She kept brushing away the tears with the palms of her scraped hands. She was utterly and finally defeated.

Whether it was minutes, or longer, she would never know. She heard her name being called from the darkness.

"Katherine," a female voice called. "Katherine, are you there? Is that you?"

She tried to hide by pressing flat against the concrete. Soon someone stood over her.

"Good God, what have you done to yourself?" she heard Bertha ask.

The woman helped Kitzi to her feet and studied her face in the dim light of the moon. She saw smudges of blood where Kitzi had tried to wipe away her tears with her wounded hands. "Oh, Katherine!" Bertha exclaimed, like a mother who has discovered her child has been misbehaving. "Come with me. We'll take care of it."

Kitzi resisted. "Did you read my note?"

"Why else would I have come after you?"

"How did you know where I was?"

"You left the patio doors open. The rest was obvious," Bertha said.

"I could have run that way, out into the desert."

"Oh, no," Bertha said confidently.

"Why not?"

"There are no drinks in the desert."

"I'm not going back," Kitzi said.

"Oh, yes, you are!" Bertha insisted.

"You know the rules: once you run away, you're not allowed back," Kitzi replied.

"No one knows you're gone, so you're going back!"

"You're off grounds, too. You could be kicked out," Kitzi reminded.

"Yes, I could," Bertha admitted.

Kitzi stopped, stared into the eyes of the doughy-faced little woman, and realized the risk her roommate had taken for her. She said no more but surrendered herself to Bertha, who pulled Kitzi's arm around her shoulder and assisted her back to their room.

Kitzi sat at the foot of her bed while Bertha used wads of wet Kleenex to wipe the blood from her face and from her bruised hands.

"There we are," Bertha said, as each step of the cleanup was accomplished. "There we are . . ."

"Thank you," Kitzi said. "I appreciate your taking a risk for me, just days away from your finishing here."

"It's okay," Bertha said. "Now, tear that out of your journal!"

"What?"

"That note you wrote. Running away. Ridiculous. Very, very transparent, as our dear psychiatrist Dr. Woolman would say if he found it. Scotty would have laughed. Once she got over being angry, that is."

"If I hadn't fallen I'd be gone by now, long gone," Kitzi protested.

"Oh, no. Anyone who really wanted to run wouldn't have left that note. Certainly wouldn't have left that book open. It just cried out to say, 'I can't take it, I'd like to run away, but I can't.' You're hooked. You know that there's some hope here. A chance. A fifty-fifty chance. You really hate the part of you that loves to drink. And right now it's bigger than you are, more powerful than you are. But somewhere inside of you there's a part that keeps saying, 'I'll beat it, I'll lick it, somehow I'll lick it. I'll be the Kitzi Mills I used to be so proud of.' That little spark of hope is what made you do what you did. Now, look, you're cleaned up. No one knows what happened. Let's forget about it. And you better start writing your day's notes in your journal!"

32

Kitzi sat in the small pool of light from her table lamp, her open journal before her. She could hear Bertha's gurgling breathing as the little woman slept. Her mind was a muddle of conflicting thoughts and fears, just as craving a drink was. She needed it, desperately. Yet she feared it as well. She remembered too vividly what those mornings were like. Feeling so sick, retching over the toilet bowl until she felt her stomach would be torn out of her. And Alice, lurking outside the bathroom, frightened and begging, "Mommy? Mommy, shall I call someone?"

Then, after suffering the pain and the nausea, Kitzi would curl up in bed, in the chill dampness of her own sweat. She would lie there, trying to breathe regularly, normally. Soon she would feel Alice climb cautiously onto the bed, slip under the covers, and press her little body into her mother's belly, to warm her with her body heat.

She could not write down those memories. It would mean giving away that part of herself which she had kept secret from everyone. Though not aware of it yet, what she feared most was that once she began to reveal herself in her journal, it would be only a matter of time before she might be tempted to do so in the group. Then would come the inevitable onslaught from her fellow patients. So she wrote down a single sentence: *"I would feel more like a patient and less like a prisoner if I could make a single phone call to my daughter."*

"Was that all?" Joyce Scott asked the next afternoon. "This one sentence, this one thought, was that all that yesterday produced?"

"All that had any meaning," Kitzi replied.

"That group session that you walked out on yesterday meant nothing?"

"I think it was a brutal display of sadism on the part of the other patients. I wouldn't be surprised if underneath it all there was a form of racist jealousy."

"Racist?" Scott asked, leaning a little closer in Kitzi's direction.

"Yes, indeed! We are both stars. Both of us earn enough to make the others jealous. They're a little more willing to forgive me because I am white. But he's black. So they say, 'Million and a half dollars a year just to drop a round ball into a round basket? Black boys like him used to be lucky to get jobs shining shoes in some barbershop. Not being stars, signing autographs, and doing endorsements on television and getting their picture in the sports pages.' That's why they lit into him yesterday. I felt sorry for him."

"So that's what yesterday meant to you?" Joyce Scott commented. "Not that they were trying to help him by stripping away his defenses, the little lies he set up to excuse himself for his cocaine habit."

"Attacking a man, especially so young a man, when he's most vulnerable, is not what I consider helping," Kitzi said. She became aware that her hands were trembling. She clenched her fists to conceal it. Joyce Scott noticed.

"So my hands are shaking. So what?" Kitzi said defiantly.

"Good question. *What?* Or should it be, *Why?*" Joyce Scott said.

"I did not come in here to play games," Kitzi responded.

"So this is still a game to you," Scott commented. "I don't want to sound melodramatic, Mills, but if this is a game to you, you should be aware that the stakes are your life."

"Curtain, act two," Kitzi said sarcastically.

"Act two, my ass," Scott said sharply. "You haven't gotten that far yet. And unless something changes drastically, you never will. To me, and to The Retreat, so far, you are a failure. We have them. More frequently than we like to recall."

"Yes, I know. Fifty percent make it, fifty percent don't," Kitzi reminded.

"Mills, if you fail, as far as you are concerned that's a one hundred percent failure rate. Total. Complete. Self-destruct!" Scott said.

"Read me the litany," Kitzi defied. "Producers won't hire me. The Shuberts won't give me a theater. They won't insure me, so I can't make pictures. I'll become a 'once famous star of stage and screen.'"

"If I thought threats would do you any good, I'd make them. But they won't help. Because, even aware of those threats, you can't help yourself. Step One of the first five steps you have to embrace before we can consider you a recovering alcoholic, is to admit that you—no, *we*—are powerless over alcohol and our lives have become unmanageable."

"No, Bertha didn't tell me. And I didn't spy on you. I was returning from a staff meeting at the hospital last night. I was crossing campus and saw it all."

Kitzi groped for something to say. She found nothing.

Joyce Scott reminded her softly, "Bertha's one of the people here that you think is 'jealous' of you. Let these people help you, Mills. Help them a little, too. We're all in this together."

"You want me to stand up and say, 'I'm Kitzi Mills and I'm an alcoholic'? I won't do it!"

"No. Of course not. You treat this place, us, like part of some play you're in. Group sessions are just scenes in that play. When you don't like what goes on, you just leave. This is life, though, Mills. Real life. Your life. You can't walk away from it by making a dramatic exit. Or pouring yourself another drink!"

"Are you quite finished, Miss Scott?" Kitzi asked, a chill in her voice.

"Yes, I'm finished. You're free to go."

There was nothing to do but to leave the room and end this upsetting session. As for her phone call to Alice, it was two days away, forty-eight hours. She would tough it out.

33

By the time Kitzi slipped into the room, her group had joined hands. Bertha made room for her as they intoned, "God grant me the serenity to accept the things I cannot change, the courage to change the things I can, and the wisdom to know the difference."

She was aware of Bertha glancing at her, hoping to see her join in. Kitzi refused. To her those words meant surrender, and she was determined never to surrender and be dependent on anyone or anything as much as she had once been on Marvin.

Her rebellious thoughts were interrupted by the voice of Walter Riordan. Except for the serenity prayer, he had not spoken a word in the four days Kitzi had been here. He was thin, sallow, and old-looking though he was only thirty-seven. He had the look of a loner. His eyes were pale green and watery behind his glasses.

He startled them all by suddenly blurting out, "Higher Power? God? Give your life over . . ." He had obviously been struggling with the concept of Step One for all the days he had been here and was just now able to verbalize his feelings.

"There's something else. Maybe even stronger than that Higher

Power. Fear. Fear of dying. You have to come face to face with death."

Out of respect for the man's torment, no one said a word.

"I wasn't like—like some of you—one of those all-the-time drunks who couldn't get up every morning without taking a few jolts. I could go days without a drink. That's how I kept my job. A damned good job, too. I am an important man. In a very important manufacturing firm. I had control. Over the job. Over myself. I knew the danger. So I didn't drink. Except when I wasn't going to be under scrutiny. Then I would go on benders. Real benders. One year I was drunk for my entire vacation, twenty-eight straight days. My wife had to tell me later. Because I didn't remember a thing.

"But I got by. I prided myself on being the one alcoholic who could control it. I only got drunk when it didn't betray me.

"But there was something else going on that I never figured on. I've got a stressful job. I'm a damage control man. When something goes wrong with our equipment anywhere in the world, I'm the guy they call. I can diagnose most troubles on the phone. But sometimes, at a moment's notice, I have to fly to wherever the trouble is and straighten it out. So, being under stress, I'm always popping aspirin. After a while, you get to be an aspirin junkie. The minute your phone rings, you're popping a pill.

"It's harmless, so what the hell, you never think of it. But as the doctors explained to me later, aspirin is an acid, eating away at your stomach all the time. By itself it's not necessarily dangerous. Until you start drinking and popping aspirin at the same time.

"I was on my way back from Hamburg, where we had a big installation that ran into trouble. One of their engineers had gone against the manual, done some crazy thing. I wasn't sure I could get it straightened out at all. So I was on a food-free diet of straight aspirin for damn near two days. But I got that equipment working again. I was a big hero. They insisted on toasting me with champagne before they drove me to the airport to catch the plane back to the States.

"Once I got on that plane, I figured what the hell, why not continue? Since the firm always sent me first class, I felt an obligation to drink. Just to use up my allotment. That old, 'so long as it's paid for' syndrome. I just kept on drinking. Scotch first. Then wine with dinner. Champagne after dinner. Then the stewardess was coaxing, 'The bottle's already open, you might as well.' It's those 'might as wells' that do you in.

"Two hours out of Gander, which was our checkpoint I woke. I was in pain. A real burning pain in my stomach. Felt like I was on fire. I buzzed for the stewardess, to ask for some Alka Seltzer or anything else they had. Before she could come I felt something warm filling my mouth. Blood.

"The stewardess came to my side. The cabin was dark. Everyone else was asleep. She put on my overhead light. I looked up into her eyes. Her terrified stare told me I was in danger, I mean life-and-death danger.

"She said, 'Don't panic,' which is always a sure sign there is damn good reason to panic. 'I'll get you an ice pack.' She was gone. Not to the galley. But up front toward the cockpit. In moments she came back with the captain. Meantime, I'm trying to swallow the blood. But I am choking on it. They speak in whispers I can't even hear. She goes off to get something. The captain says to me, 'Don't worry, I'll set her down in Gander in sixty-two minutes.' He went forward to make arrangements.

"I lay there. She came back with an ice pack. She undid my pants, pulled up my shirt, pulled down my shorts, and placed the ice pack against my stomach. 'This'll slow the flow of blood. And don't worry, you'll be in Gander before you know it.' "

Riordan stared around the circle, asking each of them, "Have any of you ever had to face your own death for sixty-two minutes? I mean, you are dying. They know it. You know it. Messages are crackling through the night sky. 'Flight 429 has a passenger on board who is hemorrhaging from the mouth. He's losing blood at a dangerous, maybe fatal, rate.' It's like a goddamned movie. Except it isn't. It's real. And it's you.

"You keep thinking, What'll they tell Helen? How will they explain it? 'He died from loss of blood.' 'We did all we could.' How do you explain to a thirty-four-year-old widow and mother that her thirty-seven-year-old husband died of a hemorrhage? This man she drove to the airport and who seemed in such good health only ninety-six hours before?

"And all the others. My mom, my sister Marcia. The men and

women at the office. 'Walter Riordan suffered a fatal hemorrhage, due to too much aspirin and too much alcohol.' They'll be shocked. 'He was so nice, always in control. You mean he was really an alcoholic?'

"None of that meant anything. I only had one desire. To be able to say good-bye to Helen. To have those last minutes. People who expect death should have that right. But guys like me, bleeding to death thirty-five thousand feet up in the air, an hour out of reach of any help, we don't. I thought about making a deal with God. What I'd do if He kept me alive until I reached Gander.

"I blacked out before the plane landed. It was touch and go for a few days. They gave me six transfusions. By that time Helen was up there. She knew. I mean, she knew what happened and why. Because she had been discussing me with our doctor for some months. She made me promise to do something about it. I decided to come here. I'm scared all over again. I don't know if I'm up to it. I listen. I read. I write in my journal. I'm even resigned to turning over my life to the care of God, or any other Power. But I still don't know if I can make it. The doctors say that in a few months my body will have recovered completely from the effects of the hemorrhaging. They say I was lucky I didn't suffer brain damage through loss of blood pressure."

Joyce Scott, who had listened attentively throughout, said, "You've taken a first big step by telling us. It'll be easier from now on. Walter, come right out and say it now."

The thin, pale man considered for a moment, then drew a deep breath and said, "I'm Walter Riordan, and I'm an alcoholic."

Except for Kitzi Mills, they responded, "Hi Walter!" and they applauded. "We love you, Walter!" some of them called.

Revolting, Kitzi thought, *absolutely revolting!*

To her added dismay they joined hands again and began to recite the serenity prayer. That meant the session was over. She joined hands, but she remained silent.

Scott noticed and thought, *Mills is still not able to open herself to others or to join with them. Unless she can, and soon, she will leave as addicted as when she came.*

Something drastic must be done.

34

As Kitzi was setting the tables for dinner, she was summoned to Joyce Scott's office. She found the counselor behind her desk, on which lay a long, narrow band of black satin. Kitzi was curious. Joyce Scott noticed but didn't explain.

"Sit down, Mills."

Uneasy and tense, Kitzi tried to interrupt, "I haven't finished my chores——"

"Someone else will," Scott said. Kitzi sat down. "You've been here four full days. You tried to run away. If you hadn't been stopped, that would have been the end of my responsibility for you. The fact is you are still here. So you *are* my responsibility. I can only help you if you open up. Share your feelings. What happened to you in the past that you can't trust anyone enough to share confidences with them?"

Kitzi did not respond. She shook her head almost imperceptibly.

"Who betrayed you? Disappointed you? Made you build up this impenetrable wall?"

A single thought flashed through Kitzi's mind. The words came to her lips. She said nothing.

"No matter what anyone else may have done to you," Joyce Scott said, "we have to undo it. You have to learn to trust other people. Especially the people here in your dorm. We have a method for developing trust."

Scott picked up the black satin band. She held it out to Kitzi, who did not take it.

"Put it on." Kitzi stared at it but made no move. "I will put it on for you, if you wish."

Scott's voice sounded threatening.

Kitzi finally brought the black band to her eyes and tied it. The black satin blocked out all light.

"You will wear that for the next forty-eight hours."

"No, I won't!" Kitzi protested.

"You will. We'll do what we can to make sure you don't stumble, fall, or hurt yourself."

"But if I can't see . . ." Kitzi started to protest.

"A guide will act as your eyes. You will have to depend on that guide, trust him, have faith in him. After forty-eight hours of that, if you can't trust another person, then I will write you off as one of our failures."

Kitzi sat there in darkness, anxious to tear off the blindfold. But all she said was, "Who's my guide?"

"Since you were so defensive in his behalf, I thought you might trust him more than anyone else, except possibly Bertha. But Bertha would be too easy on you. So I selected Mr. Thompson."

"Calvin?" Kitzi asked.

"Yes, Calvin. Until you go to bed and after you come out of your room in the morning, Calvin will be your constant guide. You are to keep that blindfold on at all times."

Kitzi had played blind women twice in her career, once onstage and once in a film. But both times she wore no blindfold. She had only acted.

But now . . .

Before she had too much time to dwell on it, Scott called toward the door. "Calvin! Come in, please?"

Kitzi heard the door open. Heard his steps approach.

"Calvin, you're in charge of Mills for the next two days. Take over."

"Miss Mills . . . ," she heard him say. "Let's go."

She felt his hand take hers. She rose to her feet.

"How we going to do this?" the young black man began to consider. "You could put your hand on my shoulder." She ventured out with her right hand in his direction and found his arm. But his shoulder was so high above her that she had to rise to her toes to make it. "That's not going to work, is it, Miss Mills?"

"Not unless I walk around in ballet slippers," she said, more to put the young man at ease than to encourage herself.

"Tell you what, just grab my arm, right here," he said, as he placed her hand on his bicep.

Feeling a good deal less than trust, and a great deal of anger about what she considered an unusually demeaning form of punishment, Kitzi allowed herself to be guided from the room.

In the dining room, the patients were talking about almost everything but the lectures, group sessions, and other activities which made up their structured days. Kitzi could hear them as Calvin led her toward the door. Then she heard the sudden silence that filled the room once she appeared.

They're staring at me. This is Scott's way of humiliating me. Christ, maybe they're feeling sorry for me. I don't want anyone to feel sorry for me! Damn you! Start talking! Start eating! Do something besides stare at me!

Calvin Thompson felt her hesitate at the door. "Miss Mills, you just hold on and we'll get you some dinner."

He led her along the cafeteria line and described the food. Thus they selected her meal. As she made each choice, she instructed him on exactly how to arrange the food on her plate.

"Treat the plate like a clock, Calvin. It's all right to call you Calvin, isn't it?"

"That's my name," the young man said.

"All right then, Calvin. Put the peas at six o'clock on the plate. The potatoes at three o'clock. The broccoli at nine. The beef at twelve. I'll know my way around from there.

Following her instructions with great care, he arranged her meal for her, including a bowl of salad and a cup of hot coffee.

Once he had led her to a small table for just the two of them, he went back to select his own dinner. When he returned, he found her sitting there but not eating.

"Miss Mills?" the young man asked. "Did I do something wrong?"

For the first time since she had arrived, Kitzi had to ask someone to assist her.

"Calvin, would you . . . would you please cut up my food into bite-size pieces?"

"Sure, Miss Mills." When he had, he watched as she began to eat, and was surprised at how well she did.

"You learn real fast, Miss Mills."

She smiled, raising her head as if to look across at him. "I spent two whole weeks learning how to do this for a film I made once. *Dark Night, Bright Morning.*"

They ate in silence, except for those moments when Calvin asked, "Anything you need, Miss Mills? More coffee? More of anything?"

The others had finished eating and left. She and Calvin were the last two remaining in the dining hall. The silence was becoming oppressive.

"Miss Mills, do you need—"

"I don't need anything. I'm fine. Just fine!" She could sense him draw back in his chair, hurt. She realized he was as sensitive as she, perhaps even more so. "I'm sorry, Calvin. I didn't mean to be so brusque. Actually, I'm not so fine. I'm not fine at all. And I could use another cup of coffee." Before he could rise she added, "Damn it, I could use a drink! A big glass of straight vodka on ice! About so tall." She estimated it with a high reach of her hand.

"Me too," he confessed. "You know, out on the road after a game it wasn't all chicks and old TV movies. There was booze, lots of it. And we'd snort a few lines. Sometimes we'd do all three—booze, chicks, and a few lines. Win, you want to celebrate. Lose, you want to make yourself feel better. No matter how the game goes, you always have a good excuse. But they say they're going to fix all that here."

"Do you believe that, Calvin?

"If I don't believe that, I got nothing. I mean, if they don't let me back in the NBA, I'm not going to play for the chicken shit they pay in the minors. And I don't think any school is going to hire me as a coach. Especially after all that lousy publicity. So I got to believe in something. To get straight enough to get taken back in the NBA. They're tough. They're going to be asking about me, 'He talks the talk, but does he walk the walk?' Am I just *saying* I'm straight, or am I *really* straight?

"Now you, Miss Mills, nobody can say you can't go back on the stage, or make pictures, just because you got strung out."

He became aware that she had finished eating. "I'll clear up," he said.

"I'll help you," Kitzi said.

194

"You don't have to do that."

"Yes, I do. Just to prove I can. You lead the way. I'll do my part."

His tray in hand, with Kitzi close enough behind so she could sense his every move, she carried her own tray to the waste area. She felt for the refuse can, emptied her plate and cup, put them aside with the used utensils.

"There. Did it," she said.

"Yep, you did it. Now we have to go to group," Calvin reminded.

"It'll be easier this way, not having to look at all those faces," she joked.

"They're pretty nice folks, Miss Mills. Least they have been to me."

"Meaning it's me, not them?" she countered quickly and resentfully.

"If you don't mind my saying so, Miss Mills, you put people off. You don't want to be here. Well, nobody *wants* to be here. But we are. So don't fight it. I can't tell you how much better it made me feel to speak up at group. You got no idea how much better it feels the first time you say, 'I am Calvin Thompson and I'm an addict.'"

"For you, maybe. Not for me." Kitzi said, closing off the subject.

35

Promptly at six the next morning, there was a knock at Kitzi's door. Bertha was showering. Kitzi had to answer. It was Calvin. She called out for him to wait as she finished dressing. The last thing she had to do was tie that damned blindfold on. She held it in her hands, debating. *What if I refused to wear it? What would they do to me? What could they do? Throw me out? Good! This is a vicious punishment to inflict on an adult.*

Calvin was knocking once again.

"In a moment," she called back.

As she was tying the black cloth over her eyes, Bertha emerged, rubbing her hair dry with a thick towel.

"Show you to the door?" Bertha asked.

"I can do it myself!" Kitzi snapped. Realizing Bertha's offer had been made with good intent, she added, "Sorry. But I'll make it."

Kitzi felt her way cautiously toward the door, found the doorknob, turned it.

"Good morning, Miss Mills," Calvin greeted cheerfully.

"Good morning," she responded dryly. She resented Calvin more this morning than she had yesterday. For this was the beginning of a full day of dependence, which she feared she could not endure.

For most of her career she had had a freedom few actresses enjoy. She could ignore a director's earnest, sometimes angry, pleading. She had been known to stomp off a stage in a fit of rage in the middle of rehearsal and lock herself in her dressing room. People would come to her door, plead, negotiate, and apologize before she would come out.

Yet here she was helpless, practically tethered to this young black giant. He led the way along the corridor to the door that opened out onto the lawn. Time for their meditation walk.

She felt the concrete of the pavement underfoot. Then the soft carpet of trimmed lawn. Calvin was very solicitous of her. He warned her of any slope in the lawn, any unusual declivity, any sprinklers that protruded above the level of the grass that could trip her.

She inhaled the fragrance of the early-morning desert. She could picture the tamarisk and palm trees which had become familiar to her. She felt angry at being deprived of one of the few things she had come to like about this place, the vista of the desert.

Before breakfast was over, Joyce Scott entered the dining room and marched directly to the table where Kitzi and Calvin were eating.

"Calvin," Scott began abruptly, "I understand you did Miss Mills's therapeutic assignment this morning."

"I had to. She couldn't see."

"The fact that she is blindfolded does not relieve her of her assignment. She may have fumbled around, but with your guidance she should have been able to do it. She will have to at lunch time."

Once she heard Scott walk away, Kitzi said, "That woman hates me."

"I don't think so," Calvin said thoughtfully. "She's trying to help you. Honest."

After morning activities, Calvin led Kitzi through her duty, indicating where the various sets of eating utensils were, then guiding her to the tables. Scott had been right. After a bit of fumbling around, Kitzi learned to manage.

At recreation time, Kitzi rejected swimming, tennis, running, or even a long walk, all impossible, as she was blind. She decided to sit in the sun so Calvin could get all the exercise his athletic young body craved.

But Calvin would not permit it.

"Give me your hand," he said.

"Why?"

"Because we're going to run. Run like the wind!" he said.

"Run? Blind as I am now?"

"Nothing bad will happen to you," he promised. "Come!"

Finally she held out her hand to him. He clasped it very tightly.

"We'll start real slow at first," he said. "You set the pace. Let's go!"

She started at a slow trot, uncertain, feeling the grass beneath her. With his firm hold on her hand, her uncertainty gradually dissipated. She felt confident enough to run faster. Calvin encouraged, "That's it, you got it. Running should always have a rhythm to it. Easy. Graceful. Long strides. Maybe a little faster now?"

She began to sweat. It felt good. Very good. She had no sense of direction. She needed none. Running this way, even clutching Calvin's hand, she felt freer than she had in some time.

"We're coming to the desert now," he warned. "It won't be so flat or smooth. Want to go on?"

"Yes!" she said emphatically.

She could feel the lawn give way to sandy desert. When she became uncertain, he gripped her hand even more tightly to give her a sense of security. Finally she was out of breath and begging to stop.

"Okay," Calvin said. "Now for my exercise."

"You mean running wasn't enough?" she asked, still breathless.

"I need to give my arms and legs more of a workout. There're no weights to lift around here, so what I'd like, if you don't mind,

I'd like to take you up in my arms and run all the way back." When she hesitated, he asked, "If there's some reason why you'd rather not——"

"No. No reason," she said. "I was just wondering what the Wicked Witch of the West would say."

"You mean Miss Scott? 'Long as you're still wearing your blindfold, I don't guess she could object."

"Okay. Let's do it!"

He swung her up in his arms and holding her against his chest, started to run across the sand back toward The Retreat. She could tell the moment he passed from sand onto grass, and she could feel his strength as he raced on. This was indeed the kind of exercise an athlete needed. She felt his sweat soak through his T-shirt and dampen her cheek. She pressed herself against him more closely. It felt good, very good, to be in a man's arms. She was almost sorry to hear him say, "We're here. Back. On your patio."

He set her down on the concrete and she gripped his bicep, waiting to be led into her room. At the door he stopped.

"Far as I can go, Miss Mills. You know the rules," he said.

"Yes," she said. "The rules. Calvin, do one thing for me?"

"Sure."

"Call me Kitzi."

"Okay. I'll . . . try. Kitzi. How's that?"

"Very good. Very good indeed," she said.

"Pick you up after study time?" he said.

"Yes, Calvin," she said, laughing a little. "We'll dine together this evening. Of course, instead of champagne we'll have a little serenity prayer." As he turned to go she called, "Calvin?"

"Yes, ma'am? I mean yes, Kitzi?"

"When I leave here, and damn soon, about the only person I will want to remember is you. You're a very nice human being. In fact, one day I'd like to meet the grandmother who brought you up."

"You will," he promised. "First weekend I can have visitors she'll be here."

"That'll be nice," Kitzi said, all the while thinking, *I'll be long gone from this place by then. That call, that call tomorrow. Alice begging me to come home. That'll do it.*

36

Kitzi's visit to Dr. Woolman's office was a brief respite from being blindfolded. The waiting room was small, but tastefully done in bleached wood and brown-and-sand-colored upholstery. The door to the office opened and Dr. Woolman said, "Miss Mills? Please come in." As soon as she crossed the threshold, he went behind his desk and made some notes on a large yellow pad.

Already he's analyzing me, she thought.

He did not look up until she said, "Dr. Woolman?"

"Yes, yes, sit down, Miss Mills, sit down." He spoke warmly, as he wrote on his pad.

As she dropped into a chair, she strained to see what he was writing. She could not contain her curiosity.

"Is that about me?"

"No," he said, but offered no explanation, which only frustrated her more.

She studied the man. He seemed to have an unusually large head— or was it his bushy brown hair that made him appear so? He wore glasses with heavy tortoise-shell frames. Bifocals, she noted. His face was clean-shaven, except for a fringe of slightly graying beard which made her recall the Amish men who lived in a colony not far from her childhood home in Minnesota.

When he had finished writing, a pleasant paternal smile spread across his face and he began, "Well now, Miss Mills. I assume you know why you're here."

She resented his indulgent, over-warm attitude.

"I am here because it's part of the routine. Group sessions twice a day. Personal psychiatric sessions once a week. Unless indicated otherwise. Then more often. So I suppose I'm here today to see if I'm the 'more often' type."

"Not exactly," Woolman said. "This first visit is for us to become acquainted. To see if we can work together."

"And if we can't?" Kitzi countered.

"There is other help available in the vicinity. But we can go into that later, if necessary. Now, tell me about yourself," he invited as he studied her as innocuously as he could.

She is fidgety, very nervous, dying for a drink, but then it's only been five days. She is trying to act the highborn lady, the star in control. Pushed a bit, she might break down altogether.

"What do you think brought you here to The Retreat?" he asked.

Oh, shit, she thought, *I don't have to go through all that, do I?* Her impulse was to reply, *If you really want to know about me, just open a bottle and let's the two of us sit around.* But she knew what was required of her, or thought she did.

"The pressure of being the star. Performing is tough enough. But carrying the responsibility of the jobs of hundreds of people . . . I guess I just couldn't take it without some help. Some way to relax at the end of the night. Then, sometimes I went to extremes, I guess."

She thought she had disposed of that part of her life easily enough.

"I mean, why are you here in this place, now, at this time?"

"I told you—I went to extremes," she said, growing more resistant than she wished to appear. She felt like a prisoner up for parole before the board which would determine her fate.

"With only one hour a week, it helps if we come straight to the point. What impelled you to come here seeking the help that The Retreat offers?"

"Straight to the point?" she echoed. "Okay, I will come straight to the point. I was not '*im*pelled' to come here. I was '*com*pelled,' browbeaten, threatened, forced, surrounded by enemies who I had thought were friends, by my own daughter. It was come here or else——"

"Or else *what?*" Woolman asked.

"They made all kinds of threats. The end of my career. There was a doctor there who kept talking about nerve damage. My nerves are as good as they ever were." To prove it, she held out her hand to show how steady it was until it began to waver, then tremble, which she excused by explaining, "I have always been nervous in psychiatrists' offices."

"You changed psychiatrists frequently, did you?"

"Frequently? Hell, I've only been to four of them in my whole life. I don't call that frequent!"

At the same time she cautioned herself, *Don't blow your top. This is a crucial interview. Play it real cool. Remember the scene in* Vindicated, *where you faced the prosecutor after you had murdered your lover? You played it so cool that he was forced to turn you free. It's time to be the cool, contained Sybil of* Vindicated.

She smiled shyly, pretending embarrassment. "I'm sorry, doctor. Sometimes one wrong word can tick off a reaction more extreme than the situation calls for."

"You've already explained about psychiatrists. Four, you said. What about medical doctors? Do you have one regular doctor?"

She laughed—lightly, of course. "One doctor? These days? When there are so many specialists? Nobody relies on any one doctor anymore. Not like in the old days back in Minnesota. God, how I wish it were. When you could rely on the good, solid, dependable country doctor who seemed to know everything."

She was confident she had handled that question well until Woolman asked, "How many internists have you consulted in the last five years?"

"How many? . . ." she repeated. *What's he want to know that for?*

"Well, there was Bauman. Of course he's dead now. Lots of show people went to him. Then there was Cremoy—or was he before Bauman?" She simulated confusion and ended by saying, "I really can't remember the order."

"But there were more than a few," Woolman suggested.

"Yes . . . yes, I guess you could say that," she agreed, still wondering anxiously, *What the hell is he getting at? What difference does it make?*

"Women who have a dependency problem—dependency on alcohol, mainly, change doctors frequently. When they think that the doctor is beginning to suspect that they are alcoholics, they leave and find another doctor."

"That's not my case!" Kitzi protested at once.

"No need to be defensive about it, Miss Mills," Woolman said. "Now what were you saying about your daughter?"

"I wasn't saying anything about her," Kitzi protested.

"I believe you said she was among those who, I believe you used the words, 'threatened,' 'forced,' and 'browbeat' you," Woolman reminded her. "What did she actually say?"

"God damn it!" Kitzi exploded, rising to her feet. "It doesn't matter what she said! The only important thing is I'm not here because I chose to be here. I came here to escape them! Their threats! Their eyes! The way they stared at me. They pitied me. Well, I do not accept pity from anyone. Not even from my grandfather when he took me in and sent my mother packing. 'We'll not have the sins of the mother visited upon this poor child,' he said, the sanctimonious old bastard. He put his arm around me but pointed to my mother and said, just as flat and cold as he could be, 'Get out, harlot!' Yes, he actually used that old-fashioned biblical word, 'harlot.' "

"Sanctimonious, you said," Woolman pointed out. "Why?"

"What do you mean, *why?*" Kitzi countered. "I just told you."

"What he did was take in a child, and expel a mother who he thought was at fault, for some reason."

"She became pregnant without being married."

"Did she also drink a lot?" Woolman asked. "Was that how she became pregnant?"

"He had no right to turn her out!"

"And deprive you of a mother?"

"Yes!" she agreed in anger.

"Even so, how would that make him sanctimonious?" Woolman asked. "If I remember correctly, sanctimonious is defined by Webster as hypocritical, having only the appearance of holiness. Is that what you meant to imply about your grandfather?"

"Look, picking apart every word I use will get us nowhere," Kitzi protested. "In fact, this hour, this whole place is getting us nowhere! Why carry on this charade? Just expel me! Or whatever you call it here!"

Woolman leaned back in his swivel chair. When he said nothing,

Kitzi tried to explain. "It won't take. Not with me. I am not going to stand up and say, 'I'm an alcoholic.' I can quit, if I want to. I have before."

"Dozens of times, no doubt," Woolman observed quietly.

"What is it with you people here? A big ego trip? You collect the scalps of the celebrities you've cured? Or claim you've cured?"

"We don't 'cure,' " Woolman corrected.

"Another one of your little fables. 'There are no cured alcoholics, only controlled ones.' Okay, have it your way. But you're wasting your time on me!"

Woolman rocked in his swivel chair as a smile spread over his huge round face. The smile annoyed her, but, suspecting he did it to evoke a response from her, she controlled her feelings.

"Miss Mills, everything you say may be true. You don't want to be here. You won't cooperate. You're going to fight us every step of the way. Yet, I don't feel discouraged about your case. In fact, I feel quite optimistic."

"After everything I said . . ."

"I understand your feelings. You're coming off alcohol. You're in a strange place that was not of your choosing. You're used to being indulged and catered to, which will not happen here. Naturally, you're resisting. On the other hand, we have something on our side. Experience. Facts. Figures."

"Fifty-fifty!" she pointed out.

"Yes," he agreed readily. "But among the fifty percent that succeed, those who were *forced* into treatment do as well as those who volunteered. In addition, women seem to recover at a better rate than men. So you will have to forgive us if we persevere in your case. We will meet for one hour a week. Unless you want to meet more often."

"Once a week will be quite often enough for me," Kitzi said. "Can I go?"

"Of course."

He watched as she crossed to the door.

I expected resistance, but not that much, he admitted. *The trouble with actors is they spend so much of their time being other people it's difficult to tell whether they're being themselves or playing a*

*part. Fascinating woman, though. Worth saving. But who knows
. . . who knows . . .*

37

The next afternoon, at the end of the second group-therapy session of the day Kitzi was tense, aloof, and hostile, thinking only, *One more hour and I'll be free to make my phone call. My baby wants me and I'll have to leave. Always make a graceful exit. Jock English was a stickler for that.*

She did feel a little bad at leaving Bertha. A nice woman, victim of an unfortunate life. And Calvin, a fine young man for whom she had developed a true affection. He had something to fight for, a chance at getting back into the NBA.

The session was winding down to a close. Kitzi thought she could sense a growing tension in the room. There was an uncomfortable silence. *Are they all staring at me, waiting for me to open up?*

The moment of silence was ended. Then Joyce Scott said, almost grudgingly, "Well, time for physical activity. I guess we could all use some. It's been a tense session."

Kitzi heard the others rise, the scraping of chairs, the movement around her. She clutched Calvin's arm. "Take me to her office! It's time for me to make my phone call. Time for me to get out of here!"

"You're not leaving, Kitzi, you can't!" he said, pressing his hand on hers to keep her joined to him.

"Yes, Calvin, leaving."

"I'm sorry."

"Don't worry about me, Calvin. I'll be fine once I get out of here."

"I meant I'm sorry I failed you."

"You didn't fail, Calvin."

"The way it was supposed to work, you were going to learn to depend on someone. That someone was me. That's what Scott said when she asked me to be your guide. But it didn't work, did it?"

"*Please,* take me to her office!"

His hand over hers, they started out of the group-therapy room and down the corridor.

Before he opened Scott's door, Calvin urged, "Change your mind, Kitzi. Please?"

"Sorry, Calvin." She withdrew her hand, despite the pressure of his. "I have to make my phone call."

"I'll see you before you go, won't I?"

"Of course." She pulled him down so their faces were level. She kissed him on the cheek. "You tell your grandma she's got a terrific grandson."

She entered the room cautiously, feeling her way. Sooner than she expected she felt her thighs come in contact with Scott's desk. Without a word she undid the black blindfold and dropped it onto the desk.

"Miss Scott, I am now entitled to make my phone call. I want to know how I do that."

The defiance in her voice made Joyce Scott aware that however well the blindfold procedure had worked in other cases, it had failed with Kitzi Mills. Kitzi could read it in her eyes.

"Don't blame Calvin. He's a fine young man. And I'm sure you'll do wonders with him. Now, I would prefer not to use the wall phone outside the lounge. It's too . . . too public."

"You may use my phone," Scott said. "I'll give you fifteen minutes."

"Thank you," Kitzi said shortly.

"You realize it's three hours later back in New York. It's seven o'clock there now."

"Yes, I realize," Kitzi said impatiently. "I've spent enough time in Hollywood!"

"Then I'll step out so you can make your call."

"You might as well hear it. It'll save time."

"If you wish," Scott said.

Kitzi lifted Scott's phone and started to dial. She had played this scene too many times on the stage and in films. The dramatic phone call. When she called the police to turn her lover in. Or when she called to get some life-or-death news from a hospital.

She could hear the call ring through. One ring, two, three. But no

205

answer. It was dinner time in New York. Where could Alice be? Evelina? Finally the fourth ring was interrupted by Evelina's soft voice, "Miss Mills's residence."

"Evelina? It's me!"

"Oh, Missy, Missy . . ." At once Evelina started to cry.

"Evelina . . . Evelina, please don't cry. I'm fine. Just let me talk to Alice," Kitzi said.

"Oh, Alice isn't here."

"What do you mean she isn't there?" Kitzi demanded, aware of the effect that information had on Scott. "Where is she?"

"With Mr. Morse."

"What about Mr. Morse?" Kitzi demanded.

"He said maybe Alice was getting lonely, living with just me, so he decided to have her to their house for dinner. She'll be back by nine. He promised."

"How dare he do that? He's trying to steal her away from me, that's what he's doing! That's why he's got me locked up here!"

"Please, Missy, I don't think that's what he had in mind at all——" Evelina tried to say before she was interrupted.

"He won't get away with it! I'll call him right now and set him straight!"

"Missy, please don't do anything when you're so angry. You know how bad you always feel afterward," Evelina pleaded.

"If someone tried to steal your child, how would you feel?" she demanded before she hung up. She was still angry when she asked Joyce Scott, "Am I permitted to make a second call, since the first one didn't work?"

"Mills, I don't think a man who is so concerned about you would do anything to hurt you or your child."

Kitzi ignored the caution and dialed. The maid answered. "I wish to talk to Alice Mills."

"They're at dinner right now. Could you call back?"

"Tell her her mother is calling!" Kitzi insisted.

She glared at Scott while she waited for Alice's voice on the phone. She was startled when, instead, she heard the deep voice of a puzzled, concerned Marvin Morse.

"Kitzi?"

"I want to talk to Alice! I have news. Good news. She'll be delighted!"

"Your treatment's coming along?" Marvin assumed with great relief. "That's terrific. I'll get her."

It seemed too long a time before she heard Alice's voice.

"Mommy? It's me!"

"Baby, how wonderful to hear your voice. Are you all right? How's school? How's . . ." She could not control herself but began to weep. She had not wanted Scott to see her so exposed, but she could not prevent it.

"Mommy, you're crying. Is something wrong?"

Behind Alice, in the doorway to the dining room of Marvin's home, Marvin and his wife exchanged concerned and sympathetic looks. Florence urged him to intervene and take the phone, but Marvin shook his head. Mother and child would have to handle this on their own.

"I'm not crying," Kitzi protested through her tears, while Scott handed her a box of tissues. "I'm not crying because I've got good news, baby! Good news!"

Alice half-turned to Marvin and Florence to announce, "Mommy says she's got good news. Isn't that wonderful? Yes, Mommy, I'm listening!"

"Baby, I'm coming home tomorrow afternoon!" She defied Scott at the same time, glaring at her through her tears. "Isn't that wonderful, Allie?" There was no reply. "Allie? Are you there?"

The child turned to Marvin and Florence, on her face a look of concerned surprise. She seemed anxious to talk but was incapable.

"Alice, what is it?" Marvin asked.

"Mommy's crying and saying she's coming home tomorrow."

"Coming home? She can't! She mustn't!" Marvin insisted. "Let me talk to her!"

"No, Uncle Marvin, I'll talk to her," Alice said with more than her usual determination, for she sensed what coming home must mean. "Mommy, you don't have to come home. I'm doing fine. I go to school every day. Now I even have friends come to the house. Evelina and I, we gave a little party for the other girls. Some boys too. And, Mommy, I don't have to make up lies anymore about why

207

you can't come to the phone. And when I go to sleep at night I know you won't be coming home so I don't have to go look in your bedroom in the morning to see if you're there. Or if you're alone. So, Mommy, please don't come home until you're all cured and okay."

"But, Alice——" Kitzi tried to protest.

"Please, Mommy, don't cry. Only *don't come home now*," the child pleaded, beginning to cry herself.

Marvin took the phone from her hand, while Florence embraced the child and assured her, "Darling, Uncle Marvin will talk to her. It'll be okay. Now, come . . . come with me."

"Kitzi," Marvin began, "if you love your daughter, stick it out for the rest of the month. Longer, if that's what it takes. But you heard her: When you come back, come back cured."

"Or don't come back! That is what you're saying! You bastard! You're trying to steal that child away from me. You had your chance! Years ago. And you rejected her! Well, you won't have a second chance!"

"Kitzi, please, you're only making things worse for her and for yourself."

"In just five days you've filled her full of lies about me. You've been teaching her things to say about me! Lies to tell some judge. You want to have me declared an unfit mother, so you can take her away from me! You won't get away with it! You won't . . ." She lost all control and broke down, weeping so that Scott had to take the phone from her hand.

"Mr. Morse, she's having a rough time. But we'll do all we can."

"*Has* she decided to come home?"

"So far, yes. And of course she's free to go if that's her decision."

"We've got to give this child time. This call tonight was like opening a wound that's just starting to heal," he said.

"I understand. We're doing all we can."

She hung up the phone, pulled some tissues out of the box, and handed them to Kitzi, who had covered her wet eyes to hide from Scott's gaze.

She was all cried out. After a time, she admitted, "She didn't want me home."

"Did she say she didn't want you home? Or she didn't want you home until you were cured?"

"I can't do it. These other people here—they're masochistic. I can't do that . . . I won't . . ."

"Mills, look at me," Scott said. "What do you think is involved in making that first simple declaration, 'I'm Kitzi Mills and I'm an alcoholic'? You're not admitting that you're a criminal or an evil person or anything except that you, like millions of others, can't take a drink without suffering terrible consequences. It's no different from saying, 'I'm a diabetic' Or, 'I have a heart condition.' "

Joyce Scott was not sure that Kitzi had heard, for she kept repeating, "Didn't want me home . . . she didn't want me home."

"Until you are cured," Scott pointed out.

When Kitzi came out of Scott's office, she found Calvin Thompson waiting for her. The question was on his face.

"Calvin . . . I'm not leaving yet," she said softly.

"Oh, that's great. Terrific!" the young man said.

She put her blindfold on, and he led her toward the dining hall.

38

The next morning at six, Kitzi woke feeling angry.

"Son of a bitch!"

Bertha, who was just slipping into her slacks, looked across the room at her. "Who is it this time?"

"All of them! Scott. Marvin. They put her up to it. I don't give a damn what they say, I have been a good mother! The sacrifices I've made——"

"Yeah?" Bertha interrupted. "Like what? Hold down two jobs? Get home, cook dinner? Then do the laundry? Sit up nights with her when she was sick?"

"Damn you, don't you start picking on me, too!" Kitzi exploded.

"The point is, honey, we've all made sacrifices. But that's not why we're here. So don't go around claiming any medals. Face it. Either you do what you're supposed to do, what all of us *non-stars* do, or you'll go right back to being what you were. An out-of-control alcoholic!"

* * *

Freed of her blindfold, Kitzi stood at the edge of the lawn, bathed in the glow of the rising sun, staring into space, seeing it all, yet oblivious to it. She became aware of someone at her side.

" 'Morning," Calvin Thompson said. "Want to walk?"

"I guess," she said. "After all, this *is* supposed to be our meditation walk, isn't it?"

They walked briskly, Kitzi trying to match the easy strides of Calvin's long legs. She was silent, sullen, staring ahead at nothing in particular. He looked at her from the corner of his eye.

My God, she is what my grandmother would call one angry woman. We're trying to help her. Why can't she realize that?

"Kitzi——"

She gave him an impatient scowl, then continued to stare straight ahead.

"Kitzi, there're lots of people here who'd like to see you get well, go back home, see your little girl again."

"Christ!" she exploded. "I just had a lecture from Bertha!"

"When I would tell my grandma to get off my back, she used to say, 'The truth never gets worn out from repeating.' "

"Your grandmother was never in a place like this!"

"No. But they coulda' used her here. 'Boy,' she would say to me, 'the world don't owe you. You owe the world. So stop complaining and start doing.' "

"Okay, Calvin, say it," Kitzi finally relented.

"The way I figure things here, we owe each other. Every success is our success. But every failure is our failure, too. Like me with you. Once you took hold of my arm, I felt, This lady needs me, depends on me. And if I do my part right she is going to get better. Now, it seems *you* don't give a damn about you but *I* do. You owe it to me to at least make a try," he pleaded.

"I think now that the greatest thing in the world would be a vodka on ice, as tall as Trump Tower," she replied, ending all conversation.

After the morning lecture, Kitzi noticed a young woman, a new arrival. She was Kitzi's height but appeared smaller. Her dark hair was pulled back close to her head, causing her thin, pale face to seem more prominent.

I've never seen her before, Kitzi thought. *She must have arrived while I was blindfolded. She's not exactly homely. Just doesn't make the most of what she has. She should do something with her hair.*

The young woman appeared shy, very ill at ease as she said, "Miss Mills. I'm so delighted——"

Oh, God, not another fan, not today.

"Yes?" Kitzi responded as affably as she could.

"I'm Laurie Coombs. I was so anxious to meet you."

"Hello, Laurie," Kitzi said politely, starting to move on.

"We . . . we have something in common," the young woman said.

Kitzi was tempted to reply, *Except for booze I can't imagine what that would be.* Instead, she said, "We do? Tell me about it."

"We both played Jennifer," the young woman said.

"Jennifer? Jennifer?" Kitzi repeated, puzzled.

"Jennifer," the young woman reminded, "in *Time Out of Mind.*"

"Oh, yes, of course, *Time Out of Mind,*" Kitzi replied, wondering, *How could I have forgotten that play, that role? Why do I keep forgetting so much these days?* She smiled as sweetly as she could, "Some day you must tell me how well you did in the role."

"It was only a college production," Laurie Coombs continued, trying to prolong this moment of contact with greatness.

"I've seen some very fine productions in colleges." Kitzi could feel her patience wearing thin.

Calvin, who was standing beside her, could sense it, too. He fixed a firm grip on Kitzi's elbow as he said, "We got a ten-minute break before group. Maybe we can all get some coffee and talk about it. Huh? The coffee's extra good today. Miss Mills fixed it herself," Calvin said, urging Kitzi toward the door, with the young woman following.

Laurie Coombs was twenty-six. She had met her husband at a small college in Iowa, where she had been active in dramatics. They were married during her senior year. For a time, she had wanted to go to Chicago and join an acting company in preparation for going to New York and Broadway. But Cliff finished his premed and had been accepted at medical school. So there was the problem of money.

Instead of pursuing drama, she had gone to work as secretary to a man who ran a small farm implements business. She worked there during the time Cliff was in med school. By the time he graduated, it was too late to pick up her career. Besides, they had to move to the city where Cliff would complete his residency.

When Cliff finally went into practice, they bought a house. Fixing it up took much of her time. When that was done, the wife of an ambitious young doctor had a great deal of time to herself. That was when the drinking began. She drank alone. And in secret. She could not risk endangering her husband's reputation. She became so skillful that even Cliff never really knew how much she drank. She would always manage to be presentable, sweet-smelling, and lovely by the time he came home. Except for those nights when he came home too late, when she always made sure to be in bed and asleep. He never discovered her secret.

All the while, her thwarted dreams became nightmares. To fill her time, she considered getting a job. Cliff objected. None of the other doctors' wives worked. Charity work at the hospital was acceptable, though. She tried that for a while but found that she missed drinking. She could not do both, so she gave up charity work.

Finally, to her great relief, she became pregnant. She now had a purpose, a reason for existence aside from serving as handmaiden to her husband's career. The only problem was that she could not stop drinking. But her skill at covering up was so great that she went through the entire pregnancy without being discovered. Her obstetrician found that, to have the desired effect, any medication he prescribed had to be in larger-than-usual doses. But he never suspected why.

The events that followed had brought Laurie Coombs to The Retreat.

Calvin brought their coffee to the small table in the corner. Kitzi sipped hers, controlled, aloof, defensive.

I can't take on anybody else's burdens. God knows I've got my own.

Laurie Coombs stared at her, eyes wide, begging for Kitzi's attention.

"When did you first know?" Laurie asked.

"Know? What? About drinking?" Kitzi asked.

"No, no, no," Laurie said. "The first time you said to yourself, 'I can be a great actress'?"

"Oh. That," Kitzi said, thinking, *Christ, is this going to be another of those high school journalist interviews? What the hell, it's been so long I might as well give her my standard routine.*

"Well," she began, "it was in sixth grade. We were doing the usual Thanksgiving play. Plymouth Rock. The Pilgrims. John Alden proposing to Priscilla on behalf of Captain Miles Standish.

"I tried out for the role of Priscilla. There was one other girl who was very good. I knew I had to beat her to get the part. So I spent nights before my mirror practicing lines, looks, reactions, movements. Especially the moment when I had to say, 'Why don't you speak for yourself, John Alden?' The line is so well known, so clichéd, I was afraid that everyone would laugh. I thought, There must be a way to avoid that. The night before the final tryouts, I found it."

Laurie Coombs was hanging on Kitzi's every word. "You found it? How?"

"It was an accident, really. No, that isn't quite true. It was a moment of inspiration. I had tried every reading of that line I could imagine. Finally, feeling I had failed, I turned away from the mirror in tears. I thought I'd never get the part. That's when it happened."

By now, even Calvin Thompson was eager to know. "What happened, Kitzi?"

"Tears," she said. "As I turned from the mirror in tears, it struck me. Why not do that? But reverse it."

"Reverse it? How?" Laurie asked.

"What if, when John Alden begins to propose to me on behalf of Miles Standish, I am so distressed, so much in love with John, that I can't bear to face him as he speaks. So I turn upstage. I let the audience see only my back. Then he waits for my answer. Which I do not give at once. Then, slowly, I turn to face him, and the audience. I have tears in my eyes. As they start down my cheeks, I say, 'Why don't you speak for yourself, John Alden?' No audience in the world is going to laugh at a moment like that."

Breathless, Laurie Coombs said. "They wouldn't dare!" A moment's pause, and then, "And that's when you knew?"

"Yes," Kitzi said, with what she thought was the proper degree of humility.

"Of course," Laurie said, "I had a moment, but nothing as inspired as that."

"Tell us about it, Laurie," Kitzi urged, while behind Laurie, Calvin Thompson nodded his head, signifying *Encourage her, Kitzi, make her talk.*

"It was nothing, really. . . ." Laurie tried to beg off.

"It can't have been nothing, if you remember it so vividly," Kitzi said.

"Well . . . ," Laurie began, then paused to gird herself for the revelation. "I was nine, going on ten. We were doing the nativity play for the Christmas pageant. We were rehearsing the scene in the stable. Little Jesus had just been born. I was supposed to wrap him in swaddling clothes. They gave me this . . . this thing. I looked at it and said to myself, 'This old stuffed stocking can't be the Baby Jesus.' Still, the teacher kept telling me how I should place it in the manger. I was trying. And failing. Until she said to me, 'Laurie, if you can't do it, I'll get some girl who can.' I didn't want to lose that part. Everyone was coming to see me.

"So I said to myself, 'Laurie, you've got to *believe* that this old stocking is Baby Jesus.' I picked up that old stocking, cradled it in my arms, and kept thinking, this is He, this is He. And somehow very soon I found I could believe it. I could even see His face. What He looked like when He was a baby. When I placed that little bundle in the manger, it was so touching that people spoke about it for days after. That was when I felt I can be an actress. I can!"

"That's the way it starts, Laurie, when you can believe, and make things real by believing," Kitzi said.

"Yes, I could have . . . if all those other things hadn't intervened," Laurie said sadly.

"I think you could have, Laurie," Kitzi said.

Impulsively, Laurie embraced Kitzi and kissed her. Then, in embarrassment, she fled the lounge. Kitzi's hand went to her cheek, still moist from Laurie's kiss.

Calvin Thompson said softly, "That was very nice, what you did."

"Was it?" Kitzi said.

"Yeah. She is so scared, so upset at being here, so new——"

"It was nothing, Calvin."

"That was what was so nice about it. Being so scared and upset yourself, to be able to give her a lift."

She glared at him for presuming she was still frightened. To avoid venting her resentment, she downed the remains of her coffee.

"Kitzi . . . ," Calvin began again. "Tell me something?"

"What?" she asked impatiently.

"That story about your playing Priscilla and John Alden and stuff? Was it true?"

She hesitated before admitting, "Calvin Thompson, you are a sneaky son of a bitch. How did you know?"

"Thing about basketball, you learn to read eyes. To know when your man is going to pass, shoot, or dribble, you watch his eyes. Sure, sometimes he can fake you out. Look left and pass right. But mostly their eyes'll give them away. Your eyes said, 'Am I helping this poor kid?' "

To dispel her embarrassment, she joked, "If I'm that obvious, I guess I need more rehearsal."

"I ain't no psychiatrist, but I think you need to know what a nice person you really are."

She laughed. "Let's go to group!"

39

The session began as always. Hands clasped around the circle. "God grant me the serenity to accept the things . . ." intoned in varying degrees of belief and acceptance, depending on each patient's stage of recovery.

After the prayer, to everyone's surprise, Laurie Coombs spoke up, shy, timid, her voice a shade above a whisper.

"I want to say it."

The others in the circle remained silent, hardly moving for fear they might frighten her and stifle an admission she needed to make. She took a moment to gather her courage.

"I . . . I am Laurie Coombs, and I'm an alcoholic."

"Hi, Laurie," all the others greeted, with the exception of Kitzi. Some of them applauded. Bertha, who sat beside Laurie, reached for her hand and patted it reassuringly.

Child's play, Kitzi dismissed the moment. *Kindergarten stuff. Never. Not me!*

Laurie continued, "When I came here yesterday, I was terrified. Alone. Cut off. From the outside. From . . . from something to drink. I was in pain. Both kinds. Physical and mental. I needed a drink so bad. Or else a pill. I got on to pills early. You see, my husband is a doctor."

That explained so much that she did not dwell on it.

"But it was the drinking. I think it was being alone so much, when Cliff was doing his residency. They have the craziest hours. Sometimes forty-eight straight hours on service. . . ."

"Bullshit!" Brad Corell, the dorm Granny, called from across the circle. "I've been here almost four weeks, and I'm ready to leave soon. But before I go, I have to say I have lost patience with women who blame their alcoholism on hard-working husbands who can't come home on time every night to comfort them. There are other things women can do in their free time besides drink. So I don't want to hear that excuse again!"

"I tried to fight it by finding things to do . . ." Laurie glared at Corell. "I registered for advanced courses at the university. I bought big, thick, textbooks. Never got to read most of them. I was drinking more by then, much more. I started cutting classes, then gave up altogether. But I still had enough . . . call it pride. Though I don't see how anyone who drinks like I did can lay claim to pride. But I always managed to make a presentable appearance when it counted."

She hesitated before she said, "But when it came to the long pull, whole weeks, I couldn't. That's why it was a mistake, a terrible mistake. I mean, when I first mentioned to Cliff, having a baby, I did it because I was sure it would stop me from drinking. I never suspected it would make things worse.

"A child. Of course. I think secretly I was hoping, too, that it would bring Cliff home earlier and more often. I was the one that suggested we have a baby. He was all for it. It would keep me occupied. Of course, after practicing birth control ever since college, I didn't become pregnant quickly. When it seemed I couldn't, the stress grew worse."

"And the drinking grew worse," Bertha added sympathetically.

"Exactly."

"And you kept promising yourself, once you got pregnant you'd cut down," Corell interposed, less sympathetically.

"That, too. Finally I did become pregnant. I went to my obstetrician. Faithfully. I got all the information. Diet. Exercise. Medications to avoid. We went over all the methods I might prefer for delivery. Just in passing, he mentioned avoiding alcohol. He never suspected. But I listened faithfully and promised myself I would follow his orders.

"For three whole days I did. Then, like drunks do, I started negotiating with myself. One drink? I looked up all the booklets on pregnancy. They all said the same thing. No one knows how much alcohol it takes to affect the fetus. So if no one knows how much, surely one drink can't do it. Just one."

Nettie Rosenstein, years beyond being involved in childbearing, shook her head sadly as she said, "One drink. There's no such thing."

Laurie continued, "There surely wasn't such a thing as one drink for me. But I still had enough presence of mind to do all the other things. Diet. Exercise. Classes on delivery method. I'd go, like all the other young women. I came away each time feeling I fooled them. They never suspected.

"But then I went into premature labor. Afterwards, Doctor Burdette told me women who drink have a tendency to premature labor. At first, they attributed everything that went wrong to it being my first delivery.

"After, I knew something was wrong when they wouldn't bring me the baby for nursing. I kept asking. The nurses told me my baby was reacting strangely. I called Cliff at the office to tell him. He hadn't made it to the delivery. He said he would call the obstetrician.

"The calls didn't help much. So after a whole day of being put off I took matters into my own hands. I got out of bed. I went to the nursery to see Baby Coombs. One of the nurses tried to steer me back to my room, but I insisted. By that time I was pretty strung out from not having had a drink in two whole days. I guess I got kind of hysterical. They called my doctor. He prescribed a sedative. That helped. But I still kept wondering why wouldn't they let me see my baby. Why?"

Laurie avoided their eyes by staring down at her hands, which she was wringing in her lap.

"Why . . . ," she repeated, grasping at some skein of continuity of a story that eluded her. "Why didn't my own doctor want me to see her before Cliff arrived. He'd been in surgery and couldn't come until evening.

"I waited until it was dark and the noise subsided outside my room. I sneaked out to see for myself. I went down the corridor to the nursery. The light was dim. All the babies were sleeping in their cribs. I went from crib to crib looking at the names and faces. I looked into each crib, read each name. No Baby Coombs. She couldn't have died. They would have told me. She had to be somewhere in this hospital. The only other place I could think of was Intensive Care. After all, I did go into labor prematurely. I went down the corridor to the Neo-Nate ICU.

"There was only a night nurse on duty and she was busy with a collicky, crying infant who was struggling wildly. I was free to go from one enclosed crib to another, peering in at little infants fighting for their lives. I studied them, studied the names on the isolettes. No Baby Coombs. If she wasn't in the nursery, she had to be here!

"I started across the room to where the nurse was tending that loud and struggling infant. I said, 'I'm Mrs. Coombs and I want to know—' I got no further. She turned to me, blocking my view of the infant she had been caring for. She said, 'Mrs. Coombs, you don't belong in here. Go back to your room!' 'I want to know where my baby is!' I insisted. She said, 'Dr. Burdette is due here any minute. I'm sure he'll explain everything. Meantime, go back to your room!'

" 'I won't! There's something wrong and you're not telling me! I insist on knowing!' The door swung open just then and Dr. Burdette came in. Cliff was with him. Burdette was stunned to see me. His first words were, 'Good God, Laurie, you haven't——' The nurse responded, 'No, doctor, I didn't allow her.'

"That was too much for me. I started to shout. I went berserk.

'What the hell's going on here? Why are you all lying to me, keeping secrets from me? Why?' Cliff put his arms around me. So tight that it hurt. He looked at Burdette. 'I think we'd better do it this way,' he said. Burdette nodded. He signaled the nurse to step out of the way so I had a clear view into that isolette. I could read the name "Baby Coombs." Then I saw it. And it *was* 'it.' There was no name for what I saw. It was a . . . a thing. The face was misshapen so . . ."

She began to weep, silently, tears trickling down her cheeks.

"It was . . . it was a small thing. Tiny. Dark in color. With what seemed like a hundred different tubes and monitors attached to its body. It was twisting, turning, writhing.

"But worst was . . . the face. It was like a doll made of clay which had been dropped on the way to the kiln. Nothing was where it should have been. The jaw, the nose . . . the eyes. I tried to turn away, but Cliff held me there. When I shut my eyes, he dug his strong surgeon's fingers into my cheeks, forcing my eyes open.

" 'Look at it,' he kept saying, 'look at it! Look at what you've done!' If Burdette hadn't intervened, I think Cliff might have killed me. Burdette led me back to my room, through the quiet, night-lit corridor. Once inside, he did not turn on any lights. When Cliff came charging in he ordered him out. Then he spoke to me.

"He tried to be gentle. As gentle as a man can be with an accusation so terrible. I won't ever forget his words.

"He took my hand. 'Laurie, what you just saw was an infant suffering cold-turkey withdrawal from alcoholism. The writhing, the retching, the shivers, the cramps, are all withdrawal symptoms. Your baby is an alcoholic. She is suffering what we call FAS. Fetal Alcohol Syndrome. Simply put, every time you took a drink, that tiny, defenseless thing took a drink. Worse, her deformities and malformations are a result of the same thing.'

"I kept shaking my head and crying . . . I asked, 'What can we do for her now?'

" 'I'll talk to Cliff about that. That's why I asked him to meet me here.'

"That's all he said. He left me to go out into the corridor to meet Cliff. I lay there in the dark, crying. Some time later Cliff came in. He sat in the chair in the corner of the room and said,

'Burdette says that it's just as well. The baby probably won't make it till morning.'

" 'These days they can do all kinds of things, with plastic surgery, with—They can do anything these days,' I protested.

" 'Burdette says it isn't only the malformations. He said babies with FAS suffer mental deficits too. Subnormal intelligence.'

" 'So it's just as well . . . ,' I repeated.

"I didn't ask Cliff for any details. Between them, Burdette and Cliff agreed to let it die. I think about that. Often. Whatever happened, I was the criminal. They were just accessories.

"Cliff tried to be kind and considerate after that. We both knew it wouldn't last. Whatever we had between us died that night in Neo-Natal Intensive Care in the hospital. I killed his daughter. There is no other way to say it. I killed his daughter. He couldn't forgive that. Neither could I."

"And now we're supposed to feel sorry for you," August Chamberlain remarked cynically, peering at her through his old-fashioned silver-framed spectacles.

Most of the times, Chamberlain seemed a perceptive, if silent, critic. When he did speak, he was always accusatory. Today he appeared even more so. Like a prosecutorial monk of the Inquisition, his lips pursed, his cold gray eyes peering through his glasses, Chamberlain proceeded to pursue Laurie, who was weeping freely now.

"Typical of most patients here, you haven't come for help. You've come for forgiveness. But it's the child we should feel compassion for, not you! So, as for your confession, I am tempted to use the most common word I hear in these sessions. It is not part of my normal vocabulary, thank you. But it is the operative word for you and your pitiful tale."

Having passed judgment on the distraught young woman, he continued to glare at her.

"Listen, Chamberlain," Harlan Brody, the television executive, intervened, "I'm as quick as anyone to condemn self-pity. But these sessions aren't arranged for you to vent your anger on us. They are to encourage us to face our own failures and get them out in the open. I don't know what's sticking in your craw, but you might do better for yourself, and us, if you yourself opened up one day!"

Chamberlain sucked at the dead cigarette in the corner of his lips, clasped his hands, steepled his forefingers, and, appearing very pedagogical, intoned, "My dear chap, any man who has spent his adult life advertising headache remedies and vaginal douches is hardly in a position to tell me what to do."

"Why is it," Brody returned fire, "that you members of the media, who always know exactly how the nation and the world should be run, make such a mess of your own lives?"

To restore the session to a more constructive course, Joyce Scott took command.

"We are not going to make any headway insulting each other. What about Laurie? What can we do to help her?"

Chamberlain continued, "Young woman, you are a child of the new generation in this country. We have come to 'understand,' to 'interpret,' to 'assess the cause,' and, finally, to 'forgive,' in a very profitable enterprise called psychiatry.

"A colleague of mine in Moscow . . . or was it Prague? . . . once said to me over a glass of vodka, 'The greatest chemists of our age are your American psychiatrists. They have discovered the means of turning guilt into gold.' Laurie, you are the end product of such nonsense. You confess a crime akin to murder and then weep until we forgive you. Well, I cannot!"

Outraged, Kitzi felt compelled to reply.

"You jerk, what the hell do you know of how a woman feels about giving birth? Even if it goes perfectly, it's an experience no man can imagine. When it turns out as it did in Laurie's case, there isn't a woman here who can't sympathize with her. 'Let he who is without sin cast the first stone,' I say."

"By God," Chamberlain said, smiling sarcastically, "I have struck a deeply religious vein where I never expected to find one. The lady quotes Bible. The 'lady' who is known up and down the West Forties and Fifties for getting smashed in bars when she should be onstage. Who is a free lay for any other drunk who can manage to get it up!"

Burned so deeply, Kitzi was groping for words with which to fight back, which only afforded Chamberlain the freedom to continue.

"Miss Mills, I have known about you for a long time. From men who work for my newspaper. They frequent those bars in the West Forties. They've seen you. Some have, as the old phrase goes, 'enjoyed your favors.' "

"What I have done," Kitzi responded, "what I have been, has nothing to do with this poor child. We're discussing her. Not me!"

"Quoting Bible hardly qualifies as discussion," Chamberlain retorted. "I have always said the shallow mind resorts to quoting others. But then, you've built a whole career on that, haven't you? Speaking words written by others, so that when people leave the theater we hear them say, 'Isn't Kitzi Mills clever?' But, left on your own, there isn't much you can say. So you quote. That's the last refuge of the untutored but pretentious and virtually illiterate mind. 'Let he who is without sin' indeed. We sinners, young and old, sit around 'understanding' each other, forgiving each other. Why? Because we're all guilty. An ideal, if somewhat amusing, situation. Who can resist it? Well, I can. So forgive me, but I beg to be excused from this particular session."

Chamberlain started toward the door. As he approached it, he appeared to falter. Calvin was half out of his chair to rush to his rescue, afraid the old man had suffered an attack of some sort. But not Chamberlain. He was only preparing for his last salvo of the session. He turned to point a long, bony, mottled finger at Kitzi.

"Just who the hell do you think you are, with the wreck you've made of your life, to sympathize with anyone else?" he accused.

Stung, pained, demeaned as she had not been since she arrived at The Retreat, Kitzi rose to her feet and said in a loud, penetrating voice, "I am Kitzi Mills. And I understand this young woman because I, too, am an alcoholic!"

40

Later that evening, as she struggled over her journal, Kitzi devoted an entire page to refighting her battle with August Chamberlain. She set down all the inspired and biting retorts she should have made in reply to his imperious and unforgiving attacks, first on Laurie Coombs, then on herself.

None of what she wrote in the journal that night did Joyce Scott accept at face value the next morning.

"Mills, you're still faking it. There's too much in here about Chamberlain. And not enough about you."

To avoid answering her, Kitzi attacked, " 'Scott,' why is it that you call most other patients by their first names and keep calling me 'Mills'?"

"Because, Mills, I feel that by now I know them. But I do not know you. Nor will I, if you don't open up."

"What that old bastard did to poor Laurie was unforgivable. There will be no bloodletting at my expense."

Scott smiled, which served to further provoke Kitzi.

"You think this is funny?"

"Far from it," Scott replied. "I was only amused by the strong similarity between you two."

"Me and . . . ?"

Still smiling, Joyce Scott replied, "And August Chamberlain."

Kitzi rewarded that observation with a sharp "Ridiculous!"

"He's hiding out here, too. And, yes, drying out a little. But we don't believe in 'drying out' patients. We go for long-term results. But that's not what Chamberlain wants. Or what you want. To you, this is like being drafted. Do your stint and get discharged so you can go back to the booze. The same with Chamberlain. If it weren't against policy, I would show you his journals. Brilliant. Witty. Very incisive. Comments about everything. The world. Politics. The staff here. The other patients. He's really a fascinating writer. The only thing missing is himself. He does make sure to include some personal bit in every day's entry. That's his way of being able to say he's writing about himself. I hope one day he'll allow me to see inside him. To discover the devil that makes him drink so. A man can't have lived as long as he has without piling up guilts and debts to other people and to himself. I would like to see his final accounting."

"Do you also discuss me with other patients?" Kitzi asked.

"I only mentioned Chamberlain to make a point with you. Your brilliance as an actress should not be used against the treatment. I thought the blindfold would work with you. Evidently it didn't. You still can't trust other people. What happened to put you so much on guard against the world?"

"The world is what happened," Kitzi remarked cynically. "When you're a star, everyone you meet wants to use you in some way. Agents. Lawyers. Producers. The media. You get to the point where you don't trust anyone. I've been there a long time. A long time."

"Too bad," Joyce Scott said. "I wish there'd been some way of capturing on film what happened to you when you took over in that group meeting."

"I couldn't let the old bastard beat up on poor Laurie. Any more than I could let a director demean and destroy a young actress who's still learning."

"Could it have been something more personal that made you become her defender?"

"If you knew directors like Jock English, who get their kicks out of abusing actors, you'd know what I mean."

Joyce Scott was silent for a moment, then nodded slightly. Kitzi knew that the session was over. She was free to perform her duty chore.

As she left the office, a single thought gnawed at her. *What did Scott mean by that last comment? Why did I come to Laurie's defense?*

41

The next group session was not immediately productive. Yesterday's confrontation prevented rather than encouraged dialogue. Even Chamberlain was silent. He sat puffing ceaselessly on one cigarette after another, with a smugness that offended Kitzi.

After a long silence, Joyce Scott looked to Kitzie. "Mills, surely you must have a problem on your mind this morning?"

The others were all staring at Kitzi, waiting to hear her reply to Scott's pointed invitation.

Her resentment at being crowded into a corner made Kitzi rebel. *All right, you bitch! Two can play this game!*

"It isn't easy to talk about this," Kitzi began, "but as you all know, after you've been here for a while and are pretty well dried out, your mind becomes clear. You remember the things you were drinking to forget. Well, that's happened to me."

To heighten their anticipation, she paused. She caught a glimpse of Scott's eager eyes.

"I assume some of you have been through 'aversion therapy.' They feed you a chemical, then force you to drink alcohol. You become so ill you really believe you're going to die. After a week of that torture, you're convinced the one thing in this world you are never going to do again is take a drink. Right?"

Bertha nodded. So did Ward McGivney and Harlan Brody. Each of them had been through the same.

"You also know that in the end it doesn't work. Once you're out, you get so desperate for a drink you feel it would be worth it, even if you *do* die. Drinking becomes more important than living."

"Well, what happened to me...." She pretended she needed time to gather the courage she required to talk about a painful experience. She wet her dry lips and continued. "I'd just come out of one of those five-day miracle cures to resume my one-woman concert tour. I was due to open in St. Louis on a Monday and play the week. When I arrived at my hotel, there was a message waiting. They wanted me for a command performance at the White House. It seems that—I think it was Leontyne Price or Lena Horne who had been sched-uled—she'd had an attack of laryngitis. And the king of Saudi Arabia and several other high officials were due to attend. The First Lady was desperate. Would I fly in and do my one-woman act on Sunday? Of course you don't say no to the White House. So, tired as I was, I agreed. I picked out two gowns that I'd wear, packed my musical arrangements, and only two hours after I had landed in St. Louis, I was on my way back to the airport."

She stared down at her hands, as if her confession were too much for her. She continued.

"I guess it began . . . well, you know what it's like on a plane. It's so damned claustrophobic. Hours with nothing to do. You try to read the damn magazines. But you can't. You run through the act in your mind.

"Did you pack all the music you wanted? All the while, those damned stewardesses are passing up and down the aisle asking, 'Champagne? Drink?' The curse of traveling first class. They literally force you to drink."

"How true," Walter Riordan agreed quietly, recalling his experience on that transatlantic flight.

"I swear to God," Kitzi continued, "I don't recall saying yes. But suddenly there was a glass of champagne on the little table in front of my seat. I was so involved in selecting my music that without knowing it I started to sip. Then she refilled my glass. I went on like that, sipping.

"They told me later there was a White House limousine waiting for me at National Airport. And two Secret Service men. They said it was good there were two of them. One couldn't have handled me. They brought me to the White House, up to the room where I was to change. Somehow, someone got me dressed. The First Lady's own hairdresser was there to do my hair. By nine o'clock, when the formal dinner was over, they were ready for me. And I—I was ready for them. Boy, was I ready!

"I don't remember going onstage. You've seen how those things are set up. The chairs assembled in almost a semicircle, facing the platform, with the musicians behind the soloist.

"Well, I . . . I needed help just to make that one small step from the floor level to the platform. I tripped but was able to right myself. To cover my near fall I said, 'One small step for a woman, one giant step for womankind.' They all thought I was cute. So I got a laugh. But I hadn't fooled the First Lady. I could tell by the look in her eyes.

"I tried to ignore her. But I knew that, worried as she was about the diplomatic and international effects, she was feeling sorry for me. Pity. That's the one thing I can't stand. Pity! I don't remember anything about that performance. Except that twice I sang songs out of the routine, so I fouled up the Marine accompanist. Poor kid. Afterwards, *he* came to apologize to *me*.

"The worst part was after my program was over. They tell me that

I took the occasion to accuse the king of being hostile to Jewish people. They tell me there was a stony silence in that room. To make matters worse, when I started off the platform, I tripped again. I would have crashed to the floor if one of the Marine ushers hadn't caught me."

She began to weep silently.

"That was the most embarrassing, . . . no, embarrassing isn't a strong enough word. I had disgraced myself, my country, and my President, in the nation's House.

"All the way back to St. Louis I kept saying to myself, 'This has got to stop. I have got to gain control of my life once more. Such a debacle must never happen again.' I think that, as much as anything, is the reason I am here now.

"Fortunately, in Washington, the press is very understanding about people who drink, since they generally drink too much themselves."

She wept softly and admitted, "That's when I knew I was powerless over alcohol, that my life had become unmanageable."

Bertha came across the circle to put her arms around Kitzi. "Kitzi, remember, we all love you. You'll feel better for having got this off your chest."

The others joined in.

She surrendered herself to Bertha's comforting arms.

August Chamberlain's crusty, smoke-afflicted voice boomed out. "Don't you idiots know a performance when you see it? Instead of embracing her, you should be applauding. She has just delivered one of her best scenes. At least one of the best I've ever seen her give."

He proceeded to clap his hands, slowly, rhythmically, and sarcastically in total derision of her confession.

"What are you going to do for an encore?" Chamberlain taunted. "Portia's speech from *The Merchant of Venice?* Or perhaps a song? 'Send in the Clowns' would be a most fitting number."

"You son of a bitch!" Calvin Thompson called across the circle. "Don't you pick on her!"

"My boy," Chamberlain said, "don't you understand? I'm doing this for her sake. This woman, charming when she wants to be, talented despite herself, had some reason to make up this story.

227

Perhaps so she can convince someone, maybe herself, that she's accomplished Step Number One. She, like me, hasn't yet brought herself to that point. May never bring herself to it. So, instead of an honest confession, like some I've heard here, she has created one. Worse, she's plagiarized it."

He turned to challenge Kitzi directly. "My dear child, and I'm old enough to call you that, I was there. The night you did that White House performance on such short notice. I had been a special correspondent for the *Times* in Saudi Arabia. I knew the king, and I was invited because of that."

He turned to the others. "She was superb that night. Sober as could be. Brilliant. True, she did almost stumble mounting the platform. She did say that line about 'one giant step for womankind.' And she did get terrific applause. But drunk? Falling off the platform? Insulting His Highness? Never happened.

"So, as I listened to her just now, I kept saying to myself, 'I was there, but I didn't see that.' Yet it does seem familiar. Then it came to me. I had witnessed that scene before in a play about a man being primed to run for the presidency. His wife had a drinking problem, and in the play she did precisely what our darling Miss Mills has just described. And who do you think played that candidate's wife? Why, none other than our own Miss Mills. It wasn't a great play. That scene was the only good thing in it. Miss Mills?" he asked, demanding either a rebuttal or a confession.

Kitzi glared at him, then looked away before she suddenly bolted from her chair and fled the room.

42

The rest of the day passed without incident. Also without a word being exchanged between Kitzi and any other patient.

In late afternoon she chose to take her brisk exercise walk alone. As she walked, she became aware of someone trying to keep pace behind her. Thinking it might be Bertha, she increased her speed. It

was the cough that identified her pursuer. Dry. Hacking. It was
August Chamberlain.

She turned to confront him and found him wheezing with every
inhalation. A dead cigarette was stuck to his dry lips.

"Miss Mills . . . ," he called, breathless, begging her to wait for
him. "Miss . . ." He was unable to complete her name.

She waited for him to reach her. Before he could recover sufficiently to speak, she had the opportunity to study him. He was tall
and spare. His clothes hung on him as if they had belonged to a
bigger, taller man. The cuffs of his gray flannel trousers broke over
his shoetops not once but twice. He looked more a homeless man
than a foreign correspondent.

"Miss Mills—I . . . I would like to explain——" But he seemed
to have run out of breath again.

Kitzi feared that he might collapse. Yet her resentment was so
great that she resisted the impulse to help him.

"Miss Mills," he began once more, "I expect you think I owe you
an apology. I don't agree. I don't know what you were trying to
accomplish. But when I heard that phony story I said to myself, 'Oh,
no. I can't let her get away with it.' I felt compelled to do what I
did."

"Are you finished?"

"No, I am not finished," Chamberlain said. "I think I would be
able to talk more freely if we just pretended to continue with our
walk. For the sake of the others," he explained. "Slowly, of course.
It's difficult for me."

Kitzi hesitated, then nodded, a single brief nod. They started to
walk, side by side, slowly. She looked up at him. His thin face seemed
somewhat less gray in the golden light of the setting sun. He stared
ahead, thoughtful, concerned. He kept wetting his lips, which remained dry in the desert air.

"You know, we two are a pair," he began. "Too intelligent for our
own good. You are a bright, skilled, talented actress. Some people
think skill and talent are the same. They're not. We are born with
talent. We acquire skill. Me? I am as much a star in my profession
as you are in yours. I've covered twelve wars and so many revolutions
that I have lost count. I am welcome in the capitals of more nations

than most diplomats. My byline on an article still fetches a very handsome price. If I had less trouble with my breathing, I could do a hundred or more lectures every year, at very fancy fees. Never did like that sort of life, though. Too much time alone. Same as you. Same as that nice young black man, Calvin. Hotels. Time on my hands. The easiest thing to do is drink.

"So in a way I am a cliché. Especially here. Our stories are not all so different one from another. In the details, perhaps. But in the broad, general outline, very much the same."

Why is this man telling me all this? If this is his confession, then it had better be made to the Group. But he seems determined to continue. I have to listen to him.

"But my drinking preceded the lecture tours. In fact, from the time I first began to work on a newspaper, it was the best part of my day. I was a twenty-year-old kid before they repealed Prohibition. I had just signed on with the old *Akron Beacon Journal.*

"In those days, when we put the paper to bed, it was routine for the men to knock off and go down to the speakeasy on the street floor of the building next door. So, being 'one of the men' at twenty, I went along to prove how much a man I really was. They got a big kick out of getting me drunk on that phony needle beer. And I went along with the joke. Then Roosevelt repealed Prohibition. The same speakeasy became a legitimate bar. Drinking became easier. And cheaper. By that time, young Gus Chamberlain had a reputation for drinking. I was having a hell of a time. Doing the work I loved and having those drinks waiting for me at the end of my trick.

"What I didn't know was that I was getting to be a real alcoholic. But a funny one. I was brighter, quicker with a sharp line, or so I thought. Main thing, I was writing. And I was good.

"Then came my big break. You know how it happens. You work, plan, scheme, hope, dream, prepare. But until that break, nothing much really happens. It was that way with you. I remember your first show. That very touching love song. Careers are built on moments like those. Well, I had mine."

Suddenly he asked, "You don't remember Governor Davey of Ohio, do you? Silly question. Of course not. You weren't even born. And he never went down in the history books. No need for anyone to remember him except me. Well, he was the subject of a Legislative Investigating Committee for election fraud and other crimes. I got the assignment to cover the investigation down in Columbus. I covered those hearings day by day. And I did a series of articles. They were good. Fresh. Different. Most important of all, I had a byline every day. With a feature on Sundays.

"Before the investigation was over, I had a call from New York. They had tracked me down in the saloon across from the courthouse where those hearings were being held. The man said he was an editor on the *New York Times.* I thought it was a joke. But when he started talking job and money, I knew it was the real thing. Would I like to come to New York, go to work for the *Times?* I accepted immediately."

He noticed Kitzi shivering in the cool, early-evening air.

"We should go back, I guess," he said, a mixture of guilt and regret in his voice. At the same time, she could tell that he was begging for the chance to continue.

"No," she said, "it's all right. I'm fine. Please go on."

Thankful for the reprieve, he nodded. He paused to light up a cigarette, asking between draws, "You don't mind, do you? The hell of being an addictive personality." He took two deep draws.

"Of course New York was exciting. But the real action was over in Europe. The Soviet Union. Stories about prison camps. Enforced starvation. Kulaks being slaughtered. And in Germany a guy named Hitler. Nobody really believed what he was saying or writing. It was all too fantastic. Nobody. Except one old man on the Overseas Desk. We would spend our off hours in a bar down Forty-third Street. He would lament, 'Oh, if only I were younger. August, you're young. Full of energy. I'm going to send you overseas. You do what I'd have done if I was able.'

"That's the way I went from being a journalist to being a foreign correspondent. In the news business in those days, that was like being Phi Beta Kappa. Today every damn paper, network, and local TV station has 'correspondents.'

"I was in Paris the day the Nazi-Soviet pact was announced. That surprised the whole world. But to us, in the bar at the Ritz, it meant the Russians had guaranteed the Nazis that their Eastern Front was safe. And so it began. I was in Paris, comfortably dug in. The Maginot Line would hold off the Nazis. When it collapsed, I managed to get across into Portugal. I cabled Lorimer to let him know where I was. He cabled back, 'By any means you can, get to Moscow.' I thought he was crazy. The action wasn't there. But he was a wise old bird. He knew that eventually the Nazis had to turn east.

By the time it started, I was in Moscow. At first the Germans rode through western Russia as they had through Belgium, Holland, and France. Like a hot knife through butter. In Moscow we lived on a day-to-day, moment-to-moment basis. Drinking vodka and praying for snow. If anything was going to stop that Nazi machine it was Father Snow. Then, of course, there was Stalingrad."

Chamberlain pulled the now-dead cigarette away from his lips and lit a fresh one. One draw, a second draw, then he let that one go out too. The comfort of having it there was all that mattered.

"With what was going on, I didn't have the patience to just sit there in Moscow. The handouts from *Pravda* sounded too melodramatic, too heroic, to be true. So I wangled my way down to Stalingrad. When I got there, I saw it all. And it *was* true.

"The fighting. From behind shattered buildings. Some of it hand-to-hand. One day a building would be reduced to rubble by Nazi artillery. The next day the rubble itself became a military objective. What was lost tonight was retaken by dawn. And lost again. With the river at their backs, the Russians had to hold fast or die. They did a lot of both.

"I kept writing dispatches, and the Russians made sure they got back home. The Communists wanted my stuff to appear in the States. It would guarantee American aid. Soon my name was known all over the States. My reports from the Eastern Front were being used by hundreds of papers. I was quoted on the radio evening news.

"What finally stopped the fighting at Stalingrad was the failure of resupply for the Nazis. After the surrender, I was given the special privilege of accompanying the first Russian staff that surveyed the ruins of the Nazi army. It was the beginning of the end of the invincible Nazi war machine.

"When my cable reached the *Times* and was reprinted in full, all four thousand words of it, I was a hero in two capitals, Washington and Moscow. I was assigned to the Russian armies that started moving west against the crumbling German defense. The Germans fought hard, much harder, to stave off the Russians than they did to fight the Allied forces in the west. They knew something the Americans and the British didn't—Russia's plans for the future.

"I was the first American to enter Berlin. With the Russian forces, of course. The Germans were all in hiding. At Stalingrad, there had been the relief and the joy of victory. Here, in Berlin, there was nothing but cowering silence."

Chamberlain realized, "It's getting dark. We'd better go back now." Kitzi nodded. They started the long walk across the soft green lawn toward the dorms, where lights could be seen in the windows.

He must be wanting to tell me something more, she thought. But Chamberlain said nothing until they had entered the front door of the dorm.

"I'm confused," he said suddenly. "I hadn't meant to go on about myself. It was you I wanted to talk about. Maybe I will find the thread somehow."

With that, he started down the corridor to his right. Kitzi watched him, thin, stoop-shouldered the cuffs of his trousers brushing the carpeted floor. He was reaching into his pocket for his pack of cigarettes as he disappeared into his room.

43

That night, Kitzi had tossed in bed for more than an hour until she realized she was disturbing Bertha. She slipped into her robe and left the room.

When she reached the lounge, she discovered three pools of light. Three floor lamps, under one of which sat Nettie Rosenstein, knitting an afghan. The little woman looked up at Kitzi, smiled, held up her handiwork, and whispered, "For my daughter-in-law. She's pregnant again."

"Nice," Kitzi said. "Lovely colors."

On the other side of the room, under another lamp, Harlan Brody was writing furiously in his looseleaf journal. He was so involved in his work that he didn't notice Kitzi until August Chamberlain's hacking cough disturbed him. He looked up, saw Kitzi, smiled briefly and resumed writing intently.

As Chamberlain turned to find a fresh cigarette in the pack alongside, he spied Kitzi. He pointed his lean forefinger at her and whispered with great urgency, "You and I . . . what I started to say earlier . . ."

Kitzi stared at him, puzzled.

He smiled. "You're as confused as I seem to be. Perhaps it would be best if you read it for yourself." He passed his journal to her. "My handwriting is execrable. Too many years spent at typewriters. But if you can work your way through the chicken scratches, maybe you will understand what I was trying to say."

She hesitated to take the journal. "Is it all right? I thought this was only for Scott to see."

"They make us share our thoughts and feeling in group. Why not this?" He urged the book on her.

She started to decipher handwriting that reminded her of her daughter, Alice's. Chamberlain lit up a fresh cigarette, waving the smoke away from her.

> I know this journal is supposed to be a self-revealing document exposing a patient's thoughts and feelings. But this one time I feel compelled to write about another patient's thoughts and feelings, since she seems unable to do so.

Kitzi glanced up at him, but he directed her back to the page, commanding, "Read on."

> I understand her perfectly, because we are the same, she and I. Too taken with our own importance to admit to anything greater than ourselves. Hence, the outlook for our recovery is quite dim. In my case, that is a small loss. In fact, one doctor advised me to keep drinking so I would be less depressed by my eventual demise.

I'd be willing to settle for that. But others are not. So I must make the gallant fight. Who knows, I might even lengthen my life somewhat.

But our Miss Mills, *my* Miss Mills, is a quite different case. I call her "My Miss Mills" since I feel a proprietary interest in her, having followed her career almost from its start. More than once Miss Mills and I happened to appear in the same city at the same time, she in a show, me giving lectures as the nation's leading Kremlinologist. Faithfully, I would attend her performances. Once I even got to my own lecture late so I could stay through her matinee.

It was more than her talent and beauty that held me. She was to me a reminder of someone else who had great meaning for me at one time. Still does. But that is not relevant to this journal.

Since she arrived here and we have been in daily contact, I have come to learn more about her as a person. Despite the fact that she is the most secretive of all the patients here, I discover we are much alike.

We may make the first step in this process. We may admit that, Yes, we are powerless over alcohol, and our lives have become unmanageable. But it is that very tricky second step that defeats us. Belief in a Power greater than ourselves. Believe in God? I am the beginning of the generation that killed God. She is at the tail end of it. But it is more than that. She and I, by virtue of the work we do, must have complete confidence in ourselves. We must believe that we control our own destiny. For people as self-centered as we to hand our lives over to any other Power is quite unthinkable. As for a Power greater than ourselves, impossible.

Another thought that keeps insinuating itself into my smoke-ridden brain. A thought even less acceptable to me. Perhaps we are both frauds. I, as much an actor as she is. And if, at this late stage of things, we were to recognize that and turn to this Higher Power, He or She would reject us both. Certainly me. And, after more than half a century of denying His existence, why would he take cognizance of us now? To avoid that rejection, I choose to reject Him first. Small loss. I have little time left.

Ah, but Miss Mills is quite another matter. She has, if she mends her ways, a full lifetime ahead of her. I wish there were some way I could help her find her way past the stumbling block of Steps Two and Three, so she could decide to turn her life over to the care of God, with the inevitable proviso, "as we understand Him."

I am the one least able to aid in that process. But you, Miss Scott, can surely do more than you have to encourage her. So this overlong entry in my journal is a plea on behalf of Miss Mills. Do something! Or, if you can suggest anything that I can do, please, please tell me.

Kitzi Mills lowered the book. Chamberlain could see that she had tears in her eyes.

"I didn't know anyone felt this way about me," she confessed softly.

"At first I thought it was out of respect for your talent. By the third day I felt, No, it's because she is the daughter I might have had. By the fifth day I realized that it is because you remind me of *her.*"

"Her?"

"It was an accident. A bit of bureaucratic bungling. In countries where the bureaucracy is everything, bungling has its most tragic consequences. By the time a mistake is discovered it is too late to correct it."

He turned away to light another cigarette, but Kitzi knew it was because he would rather not reveal what was evidently a most painful personal event in his life.

"I am sure they did not intend to kill her. It was some ignorant camp commandant. The pity of it was I had already secured the papers for her release. But, as I said, by the time a mistake is discovered—"

He broke off suddenly, ground out his cigarette and said, "It's late. I'm keeping you up much too long. Six o'clock comes terribly early in this place."

He rose to leave. Kitzi reached out to take his hand. He said, "You are the first person who's touched me since I arrived here. I guess it's because I'm so aloof. But it is nice to feel the warm touch of another human being."

"*She,* that woman you speak of, was she in love with you, too?"

"Yes," he said sadly. "Yes, she was. You see, it was all a mistake. Not being in love. That was the most wonderful thing that happened to me there or anywhere. The mistake was that I rushed to Budapest in 1956. The Soviets misinterpreted . . . they thought . . . it doesn't matter now what they thought."

He paused, then continued.

"It was during the outbreak of the Hungarian rebellion. A group of us American correspondents piled into a car and started for the border. We knew we wouldn't be permitted exit to Hungary. So we said our destination was Vienna. Of course, from there it was easy to cross over into Hungary and make our way to Budapest.

"I sent my first dispatch from Budapest within hours after we got there. The city was still in the control of the freedom fighters then. In Moscow, they took my dispatches to be extremely hostile."

He withdrew his hand from Kitzi's to reach for his cigarettes. The pack was empty. He crushed it, saying, "I have a carton in my room. My poor roommate—he's been very understanding about it. Personally, I would have thrown me out a long time ago."

He stifled a cough, then said, "You must excuse me for taking so much of your time. I know you came here to write your own entry."

He started shuffling toward the corridor. Alone. She felt so sorry for him that she called, "Would you like a cup of coffee? Decaf?"

He turned to glance back at her and smiled. "Now you're feeling sorry for me."

"Yes," she admitted. "Yes, I am."

"Good!" he replied. "People always deny feeling sorry for someone else. As if it were impolite. Well, I like being felt sorry for. So I will have that cup of decaf."

The others had left the lounge. Only Kitzi and August Chamberlain remained, sipping coffee, staring at each other.

He smiled. "Whom do I remind you of? Your father? Your grandfather? God knows I'm old enough."

"Surely not my grandfather," she said. "I think he's the real reason I can't take that damned Step Two. He was a minister. He brought me up after my mother left. She didn't exactly leave. He drove her out. She was pregnant and unmarried."

"So you've had your share of the 'righteous' life," Chamberlain said.

"Lots of preaching yes. But as for a righteous life . . ." She never completed the sentence.

"My father was a harnessmaker," Chamberlain said. "When I was born he was making gear for horse-drawn Army artillery, to get them ready for what we now call World War I."

Chamberlain sipped his coffee, unconsciously feeling his pockets for those cigarettes he missed so.

"Yes," he said, "in my lifetime we have gone from horse-drawn artillery to mechanized artillery to computerized nuclear artillery. And we're not one damn bit wiser or closer to peace now than we ever were. We just get better at killing."

Suddenly he blurted out, "They should have known by that time that I could be trusted. I *had* to head for Budapest. My paper, my syndicate, would have been asking, 'What the hell's wrong with Chamberlain that he's not there to cover the biggest story of the year?' It must have been someone in the Kremlin, or the KGB, who was looking to even a personal score with me. They used my trip as a pretext. That's all they ever need, a pretext. The flimsiest excuse will do.

"She was so beautiful. So graceful," he said. "She moved like the wind. With no effort. She was a dancer, in the ballet." He stopped and smiled apologetically. "How rude and thoughtless of me to go on so about a woman to another woman. Especially about another performer to such a great actress as you."

He looked down into his cup, holding it so that the rising vapor curled slowly upward toward his pale gray eyes. Kitzi realized that he would say no more about her. The memory was too painful.

"Is that when you started drinking excessively?"

"I was a pretty good hand at it long before that. In fact, she used to joke about it. Said I was born to be a Russian, I was drunk so much of the time. After Hungary, there was a lot of time between stories.

With the KGB keeping us confined to Moscow, we hadn't much else to do but sit around and drink."

He abruptly changed the subject. "Did you come here because you were scared of dying? Like Riordan after that stomach hemorrhage on the plane?"

"No," she said.

"Me neither," he admitted. "Didn't come here out of fear. Or even wanting to. But they ganged up on me. My news syndicate. My lecture agent. Two doctors. All surrounded me and said it was either come here or die. Well, they couldn't let me die. After all, I was making money for all of them. So they forced me, which makes me think it won't work for me here. In fact, if I knew where there was a bottle of Russian vodka right this minute, I'd go for it. Pay any price for it. I'm just marking time. Like a man with a terminal illness."

Kitzi tried to encourage him. "I was told that the ones who are forced to come here do as well percentage-wise as those who come on their own."

"At best, it's only fifty-fifty."

"Better than nothing," Kitzi said, wondering even as she spoke, *Why am I encouraging him when I don't really believe it?*

"That damn group!" he exploded suddenly. "If it wasn't for that, I might have a chance. But I will not grovel before that bunch. I am not like them. I am possibly the leading authority on the Soviet system in the Western world. Not some goddamned shoe salesman or housewife."

He stared down into his cup, which was empty now. "I think I could stand a refill."

"I'll get it," Kitzi said, up and out of her chair at once. She brought back the last of the decaf. He sloshed it about in the cup but did not drink. Instead, he asked, "What was it Scotty was trying to pry out of you when you invented that White House story?"

Kitzi shrugged.

"It must have been important. You were so intent on evading. Then you launched into that preposterous tale." When she did not respond at once, he continued, "One day you'll have to tell someone."

"You're making too much of it," she finally said. "It was simply a request to have my daughter come visit before the end of my third week."

"Which Scott refused," he realized. "They are very strict here." Then he asked, "Why is it necessary for her to come now instead of two weeks from now?"

"They're trying to steal her away from me," Kitzi said.

" 'They'? 'Steal'?" he asked in such a way that she was forced to protest.

"Do I sound paranoid?" she demanded. "I may be an alcoholic, but I am not insane! Or as bad as some of the others here. I never drove a car when I was drunk. Never even came close to killing or even endangering anyone. Never drank so much that I started to hemorrhage . . ."

"Ah, yes," Chamberlain said, "aside from our own special sins we are all innocent. That poor young woman, Lily, was it?"

"Laurie," Kitzi corrected.

"Yes, yes, Laurie. I'm sure she had no intention of harming anyone, least of all her unborn child. The difference between life in here and the world outside is that to be convicted of a crime out there they have to prove intent. Here, intent is not necessary. Crimes are considered crimes based on the damage and injury they do to others. A much wiser measure of judgment. Who among us deliberately intends to harm anyone else? But, unfortunately, we do, we do," he said sadly.

He patted his pocket for the cigarettes which were not there. "I have a carton in my room. I'd better go. Good night, my dear."

He started padding softly down the corridor in his old-fashioned carpet slippers. She watched him until he disappeared into his room.

Kitzi looked about her. The dorm was totally quiet. Everyone, it seemed, was asleep. She gathered up both their cups and rinsed them out. Still restless, she took up her journal and started for the back patio to sit and think for a while.

The moon, which had been low to the horizon and deep orange when it first rose, was now high in the sky above her, clear and sharp.

The night air was cool. She pulled her robe tighter about her and leaned back on one of the deck chairs, staring up at the sky to consider what old Chamberlain had said.

He said we two are alike. We refuse to expose ourselves to others. Poor Laurie. Thank God I don't have her sins on my conscience.

And yet, at the very end, was the old man hinting at something? Was he trying to tell me that what I have done to Alice unintentionally is not unlike what Laurie did to her child? Has my drinking become as much a part of Alice's life as Laurie's was to that helpless, deformed little girl?

By the bright light of the desert moon, she began to write in her journal.

44

Joyce Scott sat at her desk debating which of the stack of blue journals she would tackle first this morning. There were those of the patients in the dorm who were close to the end of their fourth week. All wondered what would happen *out there.* How would they react the first time someone offered them a drink? How would their friends and business associates react when they did not fall into the old pattern of one drink, then another and another? Some people resent a recovering alcoholic. Worst fear of all, would their families keep a sly watch, like the KGB or the CIA, to see whether the patient was sneaking a drink on the side? After years of lies, pretenses, excuses, would anyone ever believe them again?

Scott could almost write their journals for them.

There were the others too. Those facing the impending first visit by husband or wife, children, parents, close friends, lovers. Also with the same litany of concerns and fears. Justified fears. How does one confront that first moment of meeting?

Once a patient had gotten that far, Scott did not have the same concerns she did for those who had yet to cross the first barrier. Those, like Kitzi Mills or August Chamberlain, who could not accept those first Five Steps.

The ones who resisted longest were usually the highly intelligent ones. Their intellect and creative ability were their own worst enemies.

That thought recommended Kitzi's journal as the first one to read this early morning. It was on top of the stack, the last one presented. Typical Mills. Intent on editing her thoughts, she always lingered longest over her entries.

Scott opened the blue looseleaf binder and settled back in her chair, prepared to read what she knew would be inventive, full of evasions, explanations, and excuses, but interesting nevertheless. The first line made her sit up.

Miss Scott, I owe you an apology.

A new ploy from Mills, Scott assumed. She read on:

I apologize for asking you to break the rules on my account. I apologize for my reaction to your refusal to allow Alice to visit. I apologize as well for that fraud I tried to perpetrate on the group. I realize now that the reason I came to Laurie's defense is that she and I have both inflicted serious damage on our children. However, I have an opportunity she does not have. I can still make amends. I want to start by apologizing to you.

That was the entire entry, written in shaky script, with some words trailing off the page, as if the author had written with an uncertain hand, by a failing light.

I must talk to Mills at once, Joyce Scott decided.

"Mills, your latest effort shows progress," Scott began. "But you are still looking for special consideration. Everything in here should be shared with the group. Why do you choose every way but the right way?"

"Surely there can't be just one right way," Kitzi protested.

"We've discovered that there are lots of ways if you want to fail. But only one way to make it work. Admit your failure. Confess the harm you've done to others. And start fresh."

"It's . . . it's the God part," Kitzi protested.

"Nobody's saying you have to believe in any one god. Look

around. We're all here. Catholics. Jews. Christians of all denomina-
tions. Atheists. Some who never thought much about religion."

"Just say I'm one who had too much of it as a child."

"Oh, yes," Scott said, recalling Kitzi's earlier writings. Your
grandfather, the minister. Was he remote? Aloof? Too judgmental?
Too demanding?"

To avoid a specific answer, Kitzi found it easiest to say, "All those
things."

"If you can't believe in a God Power, what *are* you going
to depend on? Yourself? You've already failed yourself," Scott
pointed out.

Scott closed the journal and handed it back. "I appreciate your
effort, Mills. But stop asking for special privilege. Share this with the
group."

Kitzi had sat through most of the session, determined to make
the great effort required. But always some other member had something to say. Calvin Thompson had received a letter from his
grandmother promising that the first time he was allowed visitors
she was determined to come. But he felt guilty about the trouble
he was causing her.

Bertha expressed her fears about meeting her children again.

During a brief lull, Kitzi thought, *Now, while they're all quiet and
attentive, I will declare myself.*

But before she could, August Chamberlain spoke up.

"I wonder," he began, "if the rest of you realize that what *you* fear
others might welcome with open arms?"

At first no one, not even Kitzi, knew what he was talking about.

"I would change places with any one of you. Especially you,
Bertha." The woman looked across at him through wet, puzzled eyes.
"Yes, I would like to experience those feelings of apprehension.
'What are they going to say when they see me?' Because not all of
us can expect visitors.

"Well," he continued, "I have no family. Or even close friends. So
I have no one's eyes to look into and wonder, 'What do they think
of me? Do I look any better to them?' Believe me, dear Bertha, I
would exchange your fears for my lonely certainties."

Kitzi became aware of Joyce Scott's eyes on her, urging, *Now, Mills, now!*

"I . . . I am still far from having to worry about visitors," Kitzi began hesitantly. "But in a way that's part of it. I am longing—No, longing is too fancy a word. I'm desperate to see my daughter. But I can't. Until this morning I've been saying to myself, 'Their damn rules won't let me.' That's not true."

She hesitated, unable to continue. Calvin reached out to her. She clutched his hand.

"It's not that *they* won't let me or that Miss Scott won't let me. The truth is, my daughter doesn't want to come here. And she doesn't want me to come home. 'Don't come home until you're cured' is what she said."

Having made the first painful confession since her arrival, Kitzi waited, expecting a response.

Little Nettie Rosenstein spoke up softly. "What if your son said to you, 'I never want to see you again!' I got drunk and vomited in front of all the guests at his party the day he graduated from Harvard Law School. To this day my son hasn't spoken to me. He even took a job with a big law firm in Washington to get away from me in Cleveland."

Kitzi tried to explain. "I know what I have to do to have my daughter visit me. Admit I'm powerless over alcohol. Christ, everyone here admits that the moment they sign in. It's the other steps . . . the Power greater than ourselves . . . and Step Three . . . turning our lives over to the care of God. I can't because I don't know how."

"I had trouble with that one, too." Harlan Brody spoke up. "Then one day, right in the middle of group, when someone was talking about being able finally to make Step Three, it dawned on me what my trouble was. I never did believe in God. Baptism, Sunday school, church. Taking my own kids to Sunday school. That wasn't religion. That was just being social." He paused to gather his thoughts. "But somehow it happened, though. Gradually, without my realizing it, it did happen. I think I absorbed that from the rest of you. I realized I had to give up the stubbornness. The pride. That feeling of 'I don't have to depend on anyone else.' We have to give that up, if we're going to make it here."

He spoke this last with considerable regret. He was warning Kitzi, Start now, work at it now, admit it now, else you won't make it. She could read that in his eyes.

45

"How do I look?" Bertha asked as she turned from the mirror to ask Kitzi's opinion. Kitzi's instant reaction was, *God, if only she would lose fifteen pounds. If she'd do her hair differently. And that makeup. Some women have a knack for making their worst features most prominent.*

Hope glistening in her eyes, Bertha asked, "Will they be able to see the difference? Katherine? Tell me the truth. How do I look?"

"You look fine!" Kitzi said, with far more enthusiasm than she felt. "But——"

Bertha's face collapsed. "All my life there's been that 'but,' " she lamented. "For my high school graduation, my mother made me a white dress. It was a Catholic academy, and we had to wear white as though it was your first communion. But we couldn't find one to fit me. I was even fatter then. So my mother made me a dress. When I put it on, I modeled it for my father. He looked up from his racing form and said, 'Nice, but it would look even nicer on a skinny girl.' All my life!"

"But," Kitzi continued, "we can make you look even better. Let's go to work." She led Bertha to the bathroom and dropped the cover of the toilet seat. "Sit down!"

Kitzi draped a towel around Bertha's neck. She looked down at the chubby woman, as so many makeup artists had looked at her when she would appear for early-morning makeup calls in Hollywood.

"Now, let's see. First . . ." Kitzi began to work as she talked. "First, we are going to redo your entire eye makeup."

Using her Albolene cream, she removed every trace of the untidy eye makeup Bertha had applied. Then she removed all the makeup, lipstick, blush, pancake, everything.

"What are you doing?" Bertha asked, beginning to panic. "They'll be here any second!"

"Just sit still and be quiet," Kitzi ordered, working quickly and professionally. *Soften everything,* she thought. *Don't accent her eyes or any one feature. Especially don't draw attention to her jaw, which is too wide. Give her whole face a warm, soft, motherly appearance. They're not coming to see a beauty queen, they're coming to find their mother, their new mother.*

Kitzi used on Bertha what she used for her own daytime makeup. Bertha kept asking anxiously, "How does it look? Are you almost done? Will it take much longer? They'll be here any minute. Maybe they're here already."

"Just a few seconds," Kitzi said, working as swiftly as she could. She stood back, examined the results of her quick work, and nodded.

"How is it?" Bertha asked apprehensively. "How do I look?"

Kitzi motioned her to get up and see for herself. Bertha got to her feet and stared into the mirror over the washbasin.

"Oh, my God! Is this me?" she asked. "I look . . . I look almost beautiful."

"You do look beautiful. No buts." Kitzi insisted. "Now, let's do something about those clothes."

"They're the best I have," Bertha protested.

"Too much, honey. Too much. We have to simplify," Kitzi said, thinking, *She's wearing not her best but her busiest. She's calling attention to her size.* "Where's that simple black skirt you wore two nights ago? The night we went to that Alcoholics Anonymous meeting in town? You wore a pink blouse with it."

"Oh, that one. Sure," Bertha said, starting for her closet to search for it.

She brought it out for Kitzi to inspect, still insisting, "I kind of like this dress I have on. It's silk. It's festive."

"Too busy," Kitzi insisted. "Don't you want them to see *you?* The *new* you? Instead of concentrating on your dress? Come on, now, get out of that dress and into this skirt," Kitzi ordered.

As Bertha changed hurriedly, she asked, "What'll I do for a blouse or a shirt?"

"I'm thinking, I'm thinking," Kitzi said, as she looked through

Bertha's closet. *Trouble is,* she realized, *they tell us to bring so few clothes with us there isn't much to choose from.*

"Hurry, hurry," Bertha kept urging. "That visitors' class'll be over soon and they'll be here."

"Let's see . . . let's see . . . ," Kitzi said. "I think I know."

She went to her own closet and, one by one, pushed back her small collection of shirts until she reached a thin white silk crepe blouse with a delicate black design tipped with touches of red. Worn outside Bertha's skirt it would hide her bulges while covering her chubby arms. It would not only camouflage most of Bertha's shortcomings but add a touch of red to pick up and enhance her lipstick. Kitzi held the garment up against Bertha.

"Take a look," Kitzi said, leading her to the mirror.

"Oh, that's lovely. But . . ."

"I know what you're going to ask, 'Will it fit?' " Kitzi anticipated. "It's loose and easy. And I think it'll fit just fine. Try it!"

"I meant, it's yours, not mine."

As Bertha started to slip into it, she noticed the label. "Oh my God! Ferragamo! This must have cost hundreds of dollars."

"It didn't cost me a dime," Kitzi lied. "I wore it in my last film and they gave me the entire wardrobe when the shooting was over."

Bertha slipped into it. The cut of the blouse was full enough to accommodate her.

"Oh, it looks lovely," Bertha said as she admired herself in the mirror.

"Good! Then it's yours," Kitzi said. "Just wear it over your skirt, loose and easy."

The woman admired herself in the mirror. "I'm Bertha Shawn. From Queens, New York. And here I am in California in one of Kitzi Mills's blouses."

At that moment there was a knock on their door. "Oh, my God!" was all she said.

"Just a moment," Kitzi called. "Now, Bertha, smile. You are going to be just as sure of yourself as you try to make me feel when I get panicky. Come now, let's see that smile."

Kitzi pinched Bertha's cheek tenderly to relax her face. "That's better. Smile, honey, smile! And no tears. You don't want them feeling sorry for you. You want them to love and admire the new you!" Kitzi coached. *Just as,* she recalled, *Marvin did for me in Boston, especially after they had cut my one big number.*

There was the knock on the door again. Kitzi took one last look at Bertha, then called, "Come in!"

The door burst open, reflecting the great expectations and eagerness of the two young people to see their mother.

"Mom!" twelve-year-old Nancy Shawn called out. She started toward Bertha. Then she stopped and stared. "Gee, Mom, you've never looked so pretty. Or so thin." Bertha smiled and looked over at Kitzi. Mother and daughter embraced. Meantime, fifteen-year-old Alfred Shawn, Junior, still awkward and gangly, stared at his mother, ashamed to display affection in the presence of a stranger. But at his mother's invitation—"Al?"—he raced into her outstretched arms and kissed her.

"Mom, you look great. Just great. Super!" he said. He awkwardly confessed, "All the way out, on the plane, we kept wondering what it'd be like . . . what you'd be like. I never expected you'd look so . . . so super. Did you, Nancy?"

"Never." She looked at her mother and asked, "Love that blouse. You get it out here?"

Bertha smiled. "Yeah, yeah, got it out here."

"I'd better leave all you Shawns to enjoy each other," Kitzi said as she withdrew. Just before she closed the door, she saw both children embrace their mother. Nancy started to cry as she said, "Mom, I missed you so. I missed you so."

Kitzi Mills started down the corridor, complimenting herself on her tactful exit, leaving Bertha's family to enjoy their very private and emotional reunion.

Suddenly, she stopped. She realized, *It wasn't their emotions I was concerned with, but my own. I was envious. Almost greedy to have Alice embrace me as Nancy embraced her mother.*

Later that morning, group session began on a more serious note than usual. Harlan Brody accused Kitzi of being too much the actress, and even of coolly viewing the others as if they were actors in a play. "I always get the feeling," he said, "that you are thinking that you

could play the scene or deliver our lines better than we could ourselves. Can't you suspend your disbelief long enough at least to help
yourself."

Kitzi did not respond. She gripped the edges of her chair to avoid
fleeing the room. Finally she said, "Some of us come by our disbelief
with more evidence than others."

"Let's hear your evidence, Miss Mills," said Chamberlain, a
slight smirk playing on his lips and a cigarette dangling from the
corner of his mouth. Kitzi felt a sudden sense of betrayal. She
would not be confronted by this old cynic with whom she had
shared confidences.

"Your evidence, Miss Mills, your evidence," Chamberlain urged.

"Damn you," Calvin shot back in defense of Kitzi. "Stop calling
her Miss Mills in that way you have of being nasty without using
nasty words. You do that to all of us. I think you do it to keep us
from telling you what we think of you." Chamberlain smiled at
young Calvin until the giant squirmed in his chair.

"And precisely what *do* you think of me?" the old man asked.

"I know one thing," Calvin said, with trepidation, for he sensed
that he was venturing into a battle for which he was ill equipped.
"You don't like yourself very much."

"Which, of course, makes me different from everyone else in this
group," Chamberlain said with a cynical smile. "You, for instance.
Tell us how proud you are of Calvin Thompson."

Calvin looked ready to attack Chamberlain, but only said, "We
know why I don't like myself. But how come, with your great brain
and all your education, you don't like what you are? How come?"

"'How come?' the young man asks," Chamberlain responded.
"Well, Calvin, any question put so succinctly and so directly deserves
a like answer. No, I am not proud of what I have become. If you must
know the truth, I despise what I have become. And that goes beyond
my drinking. I traded in my integrity for money, for fame, for
reputation.

"The irony is, the more dishonest I am, the greater my reputation
becomes.

"No matter how small a tremor shakes the Soviet Union—it might
measure a measly three on the diplomatic Richter Scale—my busi-

ness increases by thousands, hundreds of thousands. And why? Because I am as welcome in Moscow, or Hanoi, or Beijing, as I am in Washington or New York. Sources, my boy, it's all in my sources. No one has the sources I have. But there is a price to pay. Oh yes, there is a price to pay. . . ."

He seemed to have lost his train of thought. *Or,* Kitzi thought, *he has gone much further than he intended to.*

Chamberlain seemed almost to read her mind. "But let's you and I put aside our personal feud and ask Miss Mills my original question: 'What evidence?'"

He turned to Kitzi. "Miss Mills?"

She could not respond.

"Miss Mills?" Chamberlain repeated, this time without a hint of sarcasm or challenge.

"The evidence . . . ," she started to say, but then stopped. "Did I . . . I must have told all of you about how I was raised by my grandfather. My mother came back . . . She was . . ." she stopped. "This is too complicated."

Calvin's sympathetic eyes implored her to continue. She forced herself to go on.

"I want to say one thing straight out. I'm a bastard. Born out of wedlock. My mother conceived me after she had left home. When she returned to my grandfather's home, he refused her but took me in. My grandmother pleaded with him to take my mother in as well. He was adamant. Holding himself out as a man of God, my grandfather had forgiveness in his heart for others. But not for his own daughter. My grandmother wept every day after he did that—secretly, of course. I was the only one who ever knew. She died when I was six years old. I don't give a damn what doctors say, you *can* die of a broken heart. She did.

"We didn't know how to reach my mother when Grandma died. That day, he took me in his arms and said, 'Now, there's just the two of us, my dear, just the two of us.'

"I used to think that if he had taken my mother in his arms that way when she came back, there would have been three of us. Possibly even four, for I believe my grandmother would not have died when she did."

Kitzi was silent for a moment before concluding, "That's why I said, 'Some of us come by our disbelief with more evidence than others.' Now, I think it's almost time for lunch, and I have my chores to do."

She was on her way out of the room when Chamberlain caught up with her.

"Is that all, my dear? Is that all?"

She avoided his eyes and started down the corridor toward the cafeteria. He watched her go, his hand automatically groping for his pack of cigarettes.

46

Three days later, August Chamberlain was laying his belongings out on his bed. He was interrupted by a soft knock on his open door. He turned to find Kitzi in the doorway, not daring to step over the threshold. House rules.

Chamberlain half-smiled. "It's all right, provided we keep the door open." He chuckled dryly. "Personally, I would prefer it if you closed the door. Then I could tell everyone I was kicked out of here for having an affair with Kitzi Mills. Couldn't do my reputation any harm. Though it wouldn't do much for yours." He was chuckling, pretending to enjoy himself. But she noticed that his fingers were actively feeling for a cigarette that wasn't there. She wished she had one to offer him.

"Is it true, what I heard?" she asked.

"I don't know what you mean."

She joined him at the bed, picking up pieces of clothing and folding them more neatly than he had, handing them to him so he could pack them away. The activity made it possible for him to talk without looking into her sympathetic blue eyes.

"What did you hear? That I went across to the hospital yesterday for some more tests? Dr. Gordon sent for me."

"And?"

"Damn, I could use a cigarette!" He broke away to search in the jacket of his traveling suit which still hung in the closet.

"They said you have to go back to New York for some kind of treatment."

"True," he said, finally finding an almost empty pack and lighting up. "Seems my lifestyle has finally caught up with me."

"Scott said you were leaving because you might need lung surgery. Is that true?"

He turned to her, held both of her hands tightly, looked down into her eyes, and said simply, "Yes, it's true."

"Do they think it's bad?"

"I don't give a damn what *they* think. I know it's bad," he said. "And why not? I earned it. Drinking like I have, smoking like I have. I have no one to blame but myself."

"Will there be anyone—I mean——"

"You mean, is there anyone back there to share this miserable business with? I'm afraid not. Which may be the best way. After all, what consolation would there be in tormenting another human being? God, I've seen it too often. The patient, his wife. Lying to each other, about how he's feeling better each day, when he's not. She lying to him about how much better he's looking. The biggest liars, of course, the doctors. Ever notice how they seem deep in thought when they examine you? Then they make those sounds as if they had made some very encouraging discovery about you. 'Uh-huh. H'mmm. Aha.' All the while thinking, 'How shall I tell this poor bastard that he has cancer of the lung but still make it sound less deadly than it is?' "

"Are they sure you've got lung cancer?" Kitzi dared to ask.

"They pretend they're not. They talk about a 'shadow' on the X-ray. A 'hot spot' on the scan. 'Could be one of a number of things, Mr. Chamberlain.' 'Can only be sure after we go in.' Christ Almighty, I could make this diagnosis with a flashlight! I knew it when they called me back to 'discuss the situation.' I knew it even before. I knew it——"

He broke off in a burst of coughing. When he recovered, he said, "Funny thing, I once did a commercial. Yes. Me. The war was still on. Korean War, that is. They photographed me with a bunch of

Equity actors made up to look like GI's. I was the quintessential foreign correspondent. The brave man who covers the war at the front. Of course, I have a Chesterfield in my mouth, the smoke trailing up. I am offering the boys my pack. They're all smiling and delighted to have that smoke. I forget what the copy said, but the idea was that a good smoke at the right time is the best thing in the world for your nerves. Something like that. And now, a little late in the game, we discover that's not quite true. Is it?"

He turned away, saying gruffly, "Why the hell am I telling you, burdening you, with all this?"

"Because you don't have anyone else to tell?"

"I still have a few friends back in New York." It sounded like a childish boast. He realized that. "I really don't. Most of the guys I came up with are gone. Died. Or retired. But there's Cochran. Eddie's still in New York, last I heard. He'll come visit me in the hospital and we'll talk over old times. We were just kids then. Wet-behind-the-ears reporters, living in the reflected glory of Ernie Pyle and Quent Reynolds and Ed Murrow. They made the title War Correspondent mean something. Of course, once I got to Moscow . . ."

By now he had closed and locked his two-suiter.

Kitzi tried to lift it off the bed. But he said, "I can still do that." He hefted the bag down to the floor.

"Promise to let me know how it goes?" she asked.

He turned to her and placed his hands gently on her shoulders. She looked up into his eyes. "How about we exchange promises?"

"If there's anything *I* can do for *you*——" she began to respond, when he interrupted.

"There's something you can do. It's a little late for me. But promise you'll do it for yourself."

"What?" she asked.

"Give them a chance," Chamberlain said. When it was apparent she did not understand, he continued, "Here. The group. Scott. Woolman. Open up. Take that big step. The one that says, 'There's a Power greater than ourselves, and if we accept that and give ourselves over to it, we can beat this damn thing.' "

"You mean . . . God?"

"Don't call it God!" he urged. Now there was a hint of desperation in his voice, as if he had a lot to say and too little time in which to say it. "It doesn't matter what you call it. Call it a Power. Call it Family. Why not? These people here are like your family. They see you at your best and your worst. They're trying to help you, and each other and themselves. Give them a chance."

"You never really did," she accused.

"Of course not," he said. "It's too late for me. But you have time. And talent. A life to live. The best of it can be ahead of you. Me—what the hell! So, promise!"

When she didn't respond, he continued, "Look, if not for yourself, do it for me?"

"For you?" she asked, puzzled.

"Yes. I would like to leave here with the assurance that I have been able to help at least one person in this world," he said solemnly. "I don't have much to show for my time on this earth. Reputation, maybe. But there's a big difference between reputation and worth."

He paused, debating whether to continue. Then he said suddenly, "What the hell! If not now, when?"

He took on the furtive look of a man who would have preferred not to be under scrutiny.

"Sources," he began, as if it were an irrelevancy. "Maintain your sources. Play the game. They tell you there's no censorship on American correspondents in Moscow these days. Of course they don't censor your dispatches word for word like the old days. That's too gauche. What they do now is very simple. They make you censor yourself. Just step over the line and next you know you're not only kicked out on some trumped-up charge, but your syndicate or your paper or your network office is closed down. No more access to the Soviet Union. Well, with the competition that goes on between newspaper syndicates and networks, who wants to risk that?

"So, we're all whores. We report only what we're sure won't bring reprisals from the Soviets. Their own special form of excommunication. An ideal word for the processs—*ex-communication.* It is a nice tidy arrangement, an unspoken form of censorship. Clearly understood and adhered to by all the parties involved.

"Ah, but if you play the game their way they reward you handsomely, with beats and inside information. Always with the propaganda laced in, of course. You get to travel more freely. Once they know they can depend on you, you have all sorts of special privileges. Hanoi. I was one of the very few who were invited to Hanoi during the fighting. Met with the top leaders, was given tours of war damage, statistics—their statistics, naturally. So I was good for a whole new series of articles, speeches, and another book. The life of an on-scene Kremlinologist is not only interesting, but can be very, very profitable.

"And the fools over here lap it up," he said, shaking his head. "It's amazing. You wonder how long it can go on. Of course, once—just once—I overdid it. It was a special set of economic figures the Soviets wished to have circulated in order to get some low interest loans over here. I used those figures verbatim in an article on the latest Five-Year Plan. But some damn expert over here complained to the *Times* that the figures were false, deliberate misinformation. They were very upset in the New York office.

"But they were eager to retain their office in Moscow, so they couldn't recall me. Or even reprimand me openly. So they did a sly bit of business. They wrote me a long, long letter about how my reporting was becoming transparently pro-Soviet. I was using Soviet-cooked statistics without exercising a newsman's discriminating judgment. I was spreading the party line. But instead of sending that letter by the usual mail, because it would undoubtedly be read by a Soviet censor, they convinced the State Department to include it in the diplomatic pouch. It reached me untouched by Soviet hands.

"Well, that was a challenge to me. Any sudden shift in my reporting would be obvious to the Soviets. It would also end my special status, my access to exclusive sources. How to handle it?

"So I thought of a very clever way to reveal the pressure New York was exerting on me. I wrote a letter defending my dispatches. Declaring that unless I was free to report the news as I saw it, I might feel forced to return home. However, I sent my letter by ordinary Soviet mail knowing it would surely be read by a censor before it was allowed to leave the country. And the Soviets would discover the pressure I was under. Well, that was the last time New York dared to rebuke me. I had solidified my position with the KGB.

"I outlasted all the other correspondents there. Old ones left, new ones came. But August Chamberlain stayed on. I had inside sources. I was the dean of Moscow reporters.

"My income increased ten times over. I lectured to groups of industrialists on business opportunities, economists, the Union League Club. Once, I lectured to a group of women in Beverly Hills on the life of the average Russian housewife. These women didn't even know how the average American housewife lives. Oh, those were jolly times. First-class flights. Posh hotels. All the vodka I could drink. Then every few years, when my inspiration began to run low, or there was a crisis stirring in some part of the world—Africa, Southeast Asia, Central Europe—I would go back for a refresher. The Russians were always glad to see me. I was so dependable.

"That's the game. The way it's played. And nobody plays it better. I often wonder what I would have done if, when I came back home, there hadn't been all those offers waiting. What if I had just resumed being what I used to be, a damn good newspaperman? Of course, we never do know, do we?"

He looked into her eyes. "Child, what would you have been if you hadn't become an actress?"

She shrugged.

"We can fantasize. Dream. Speculate. But we never know. So I must go on pretending to be a respected expert with a drinking problem. Instead of a fraud who needs his drinking problem. And they thought they could cure me here. Ridiculous!"

"Then why did you come?" Kitzi asked.

"To hide out," he said, with a cynical smile that revealed his yellowing teeth. He turned more serious. "Not quite. One night, I had been drinking and I fell asleep with a lit cigarette in my hand. It could have been fatal. So, my doctor insisted, before I kill myself, I had better come to this place. I don't know why he was so intent on saving me. I'm not worth it," Chamberlain said. "It's late for me. But promise you'll do it for yourself. Take the big step. Knowing that you did would help to see me through what's coming. The surgery. The slow deterioration. The inevitable end. It would help me if I could say to myself, 'I did one thing to justify my existence. I helped Kitzi Mills become a great star once again. Become the mother she needs to be.' *Promise me.*"

"All right. I promise," she said quickly.

"Not that easily, child," Chamberlain said. "I want you to mean it. I don't want this to be an easy lie you'll tell to humor an old man you're never going to see again. Say it because you mean it!"

She was silent for a moment before she said, "August Chamberlain, I promise you that I will trust these people, depend on them, ask for their help, and accept them as the Power greater than I am alone."

He patted her cheek lightly. She took hold of his hand, pressed it against her cheek, then kissed it. She stood on tiptoe and kissed him on the lips.

"Good luck, Gus," she whispered.

"Thanks," he said softly.

There was the muffled sound of a rubber-tired cart outside the door. Joe, the houseman, came into view to report, "Car's waiting, Mr. Chamberlain. Can I take your luggage?"

"There it is," Chamberlain indicated the single battered bag and his portable typewriter.

"That all?" Joe asked.

"In my profession we always travel light," the old man said.

"Can I walk you to the car?" Kitzi asked.

"I would be honored."

He held out his arm for her to take. Kitzi took it. Together, they started out of the room and down the corridor.

Joyce Scott and several other members of the staff were waiting to see Chamberlain off. Kitzi was the only one he permitted to see him right to the open door of the limousine.

There he stopped, held her hand and said, "Remember! You promised!"

He slipped into the car and pulled the door closed behind him. The dark-tinted glass, meant to protect him from the strong desert sun, obscured his face sufficiently so that Kitzi would never be sure if the old man was weeping.

She turned and started back into the cool confines of The Retreat.

She did not fall asleep easily that night. Instead, she slipped out of bed and went into the lounge, where she began to write in her journal. She reported the events of her day, her conversation with old Chamberlain, her sorrow at seeing him go under such circumstances, and her fear. . . . But she crossed out the word "fear" and instead wrote:

> I know that he is not going to make it. Worse, he knows it. He is ready to die now. I am sure if they offer him the choice, surgery or not, he will say no. He'll just choose to smoke his life away. What little there is left of it.

She wrote one last line.

> If he had been my grandfather, I think my life would have been different—very different.

47

The next afternoon when Kitzi had her session with Dr. Woolman, she was still suffering the sad effects of Chamberlain's departure.

He detected it as soon as she walked into his office. He knew that without any prodding from him, today she would talk freely. It had been a week of important events in the lives of her group, some events happy and encouraging, some quite sad.

She began rather casually, talking about Bertha's impending release, the abrupt departure of Nettie Rosenstein, who, quite near the end of her stay, could not see it through and had fled.

Throughout, Woolman listened silently, thinking, *So much about the others. What is she avoiding today?*

In the middle of talking about poor little Nettie, Kitzi began to cry. The tears rolled down her cheeks. She tried to catch her breath but could not. Woolman edged the box of tissues toward her, and she groped for them blindly, used several, but continued to cry. When Woolman's silence became an oppressive demand, she said suddenly, "He's going to die!"

Though he knew, Woolman asked, "Who is going to die?"

"Chamberlain."

"Why does that disturb you so?" Woolman asked.

"He may seem nasty and tough, but he really is a sweet old man. And now he's going to die."

"We're all going to die," Woolman said, "and, as you said, he *is* old. There's no cause for such undue grief. Or is there?"

She looked across at him, her eyes wet and teary.

"What does it have to do with your grandfather?"

"I didn't say it had anything to do with him—" she began to protest.

"I had to ask. An old man faces death, and there are not only tears, but I can feel the heart being torn out of you. Why?"

"He's going to die alone. No wife, no child, nobody."

"Is that the way your grandfather died?" Woolman asked directly.

"I . . . I don't know. I wasn't there."

"Then as far as *you* are concerned, he did die alone."

"Did Miss Scott tell you about my journal?"

"No," the doctor replied.

"Then how did you know about my grandfather and Chamberlain?"

"When the illness of a man old enough to be your grandfather, causes such tears, I make what is an obvious deduction. Now, since we've both seen the connection, suppose you tell me about it."

She tried to make her confession sound as simple and innocuous as possible.

"I was in rehearsal for my second show when word came that he was in the hospital. They said it was very grave. That he wanted to see me. I didn't go."

"You chose your career over your duty to him?"

"I could have gone. But I didn't."

"Why not?"

"I didn't want to see him," Kitzi said plainly.

"Understandable. After all, he was the one who robbed you of the mother you needed so desperately," Woolman suggested.

"Yes," Kitzi said quickly.

Too quickly, Woolman realized. *I shouldn't have given her such an easy way out.* "Have you ever gone back?"

"Once. Years later. My one-woman concert series was booked into Minneapolis. It was only an hour's drive. I went and found his grave.

It was a slab of gray stone. With only the dates he was born and died, and a simple inscription, 'He tended his flock with love.' "

"Tell me, that night, did you get drunk?" the doctor asked.

She glared at him angrily, then the hostile look slowly drained from her face as she said in a whisper, "Yes. But out on the road, when you're alone, it's easy to get drunk every night."

"When Chamberlain left the other day, did you also have a strong desire to get drunk?" Woolman asked.

"No, strangely enough, no," she said, for she hadn't thought of that before.

"There must have been something special, very special, about August Chamberlain that you shed the tears for him you denied your grandfather."

"Nothing special. Except that he made me promise, for his sake, to become more a part of this place, and the people here. To look on them as my family. As my Greater Power."

"Ordinarily, Miss Mills, I am against deathbed promises. I call them blackmail," Woolman said. "But in this instance I find myself very much for it. Next week, Miss Mills?"

Joyce Scott picked up the journal with the name "Kitzi Mills" on the front cover. She opened it to the last entry and began to read.

> This is the most difficult thing I have ever had to write. Something has happened to me since August Chamberlain left here two days ago.
>
> He made an earnest plea to me to plunge into the treatment that is being forced on me. My own father, whoever he might be, and however much he could have loved me, could not have been more concerned with my welfare.
>
> So I have decided to try. For his sake.
>
> One day soon I would like to be able to call him and say, "I've done it! I'm on my way!" I would like him to know that before he dies.
>
> So I have thought about this more seriously than ever before. I have discovered that, of the Five Steps, I have accepted the first one.

If I did not admit that I am powerless over alcohol, I wouldn't be here. As for Steps Two and Three, believing in a Power greater than myself to restore me to sanity, and deciding to turn my will and my life over to Him, or It, old Gus has pointed out the way.

The group, the dorm, the people here will have to be that Power for me. I can't believe in any other. I had too much of it in my childhood. My grandfather was a religious tyrant. Secretly, I used to think of him as the Avenging Angel. But I will accept the group, with all its faults, as being my Greater Power.

Which brings me now to the point at which I have to take Steps Four and Five, and I have so little time left to take them.

I need help. I desperately need help.

Joyce Scott leaned back in her chair. *I have seen patients come and go. Most times I can detect those who will make it and those who won't. But Kitzi Mills baffles me. If I am any judge, she is about to decide now whether she can be helped or not. She must make her breakthrough now, or else be lost.*

She placed a call to Dr. Woolman, explained the situation, and sought his advice.

"Scotty, people think that we psychiatrists are good at prying secrets out of our patients. No such thing. We can probe, search, suggest, question, coax, guide, steer, but until the patient is willing to give up her secrets we are powerless. I agree with you that Chamberlain may have had a beneficial impact on her. Do what you can. And so will I."

48

Kitzi was vacuuming the lounge when Bertha found her.

"Mother Superior wants to see you," she said, using their name for Joyce Scott whenever either of them was ticked off by the counselor's strictness.

"I have to finish. You know how she is about half-done assignments."

"This time I have orders to relieve you," Bertha said. "Besides, this is another of those things I'm doing for the last time. I'll be so glad to get home. And so scared, too," she confessed.

"Don't worry, honey," Kitzi said. "I'd like to be as far along as you are." She gave Bertha a quick hug and started toward Scott's office.

"So, while this latest entry in your journal seems a big step forward, it also exhibits a certain holding back. There's an important part of you that's not in here."

"I've gone as far as I can with the Greater Power concept," Kitzi pleaded.

"You say the group will serve as your Greater Power. Okay." But *you* listen to *their* secrets. *Their* self-recriminations, *their* fears, *their* crimes against others. You never reveal your own. You're not truly a member of the group. You're just a voyeur passing through. So if I were to accept your journal at face value, believe that you have accepted Steps One, Two, and Three and are willing to turn your life over to some Power outside yourself, that should bring you to Step Four, a searching and fearless moral inventory of yourself. And Step Five, admitting to your Greater Power, to yourself, and to another human being, the exact nature of all the wrongs you've committed. Unless you can do that, you haven't really accepted the first three steps."

"I meant what I wrote in there," Kitzi insisted.

"Mills, your journal, for all its good intentions, only *tells* us. Now you have to show us."

"I'm not like the others. When they leave here, who will remember their confessions? I'm a celebrity. I'll give them something to talk about for the rest of their lives. Every time my name comes up, wherever they are, they'll say, 'I know her. Why, I once heard her say. . . .' "

"Bullshit!" Scott said. "Do you think anything you might confess will achieve more notoriety than dancing half-naked on a bar in a saloon on Forty-fourth Street? Then asking any man in the joint to come up and screw you? Stop inventing evasions. Or else I suggest you leave this place now!"

"I haven't said anything about leaving. Or even thought about it. . . . Not after the first few days."

"Of course not," Scott agreed. "Here you can play your little game. You can act being a woman who wants to conquer her drinking habit. Without really doing it. Just think of the marvelous scenes you've played. With Calvin. With Chamberlain. Scenes about this fictional character, Kitzi Mills, who is pretending to seek a cure."

"That's not what I do!" Kitzi protested.

"I think your first phone call to Alice was the same. Except that time it was Kitzi Mills starring as The Mother. What did you expect, an Academy Award?" Scott demanded. "Mills, it's time to stop playing roles and confront the problem. *You!*"

Scott shoved the journal across the desk with such finality that Kitzi knew the conference was over. She picked up the book and left.

Scott consulted her watch. Nine thirty-six Pacific Coast time, twelve thirty-six New York time. She dialed a long-distance number.

"Mr. August Chamberlain? He's in the private pavilion, I believe."

She waited. Finally came the gruff, dry voice she had grown accustomed to hearing the past few weeks.

"Chamberlain here."

"Scott here," she replied. "How's it going?"

"Oh, fine, fine," he replied. "More tests. Which I pass with very high marks. They say they've never seen such a perfect case of lung cancer before."

"Seriously, August," Scott urged.

"They want to operate. They can't promise anything. But they think that's better than doing nothing."

"And you?" Scott asked.

"I sit here puffing on my cigarettes and asking myself, What's it like? I've never had a lung removed before. How does it feel? Do you go around with a half-empty chest? Do you have to breathe twice as fast to get the same amount of oxygen? Does all that empty space make you wheeze? Is there an echo?"

Scott knew the old man was terrified but trying to conceal it.

"I don't know," he continued in the same vein. "The old news-hound says, How are you going to write about it unless you experience it? So maybe I will opt for surgery."

She could hear him strike another match for a fresh cigarette before he continued.

"Now, Scotty, let's get down to business. Did you talk to her?"

"Yes," Scott admitted.

"Were you tough with her, as I suggested?" the old man asked.

"Right to the point of saying open up or get out."

"Good!" Chamberlain said, but the word was interrupted by a spell of coughing. He recovered to say, "You'll keep me apprised. I'm very fond of her. She's a special person. She has quality. Look, if I go for that operation, I'll be out of touch for a few days. But you keep calling. Promise?"

"Promise," Scott agreed.

"And don't let up on that girl!" were his last words.

"I thought you would want to know," Scott said to Kitzi.

"Did he say for sure he was having surgery?" she asked.

"He hadn't quite made up his mind."

"He should have it," Kitzi insisted. "I've heard of cases . . ." She did not finish, for she realized she sounded like a desperate relative who refuses to accept the truth. "I'll call him. I'll talk to him."

"I think he would like that."

She had to use the wall phone outside the lounge so she felt self-conscious. The phone was answered by a female voice, recognizably black, and from one of the islands, Kitzi judged by the musical lilt.

"Mrs. Johnson speaking."

"Mrs. Johnson, I'm Kitzi Mills. A friend of Mr. Chamberlain's. How is he? Where is he?"

"Mr. Chamberlain is on his way up to the operating room, ma'am. He will be there for some time. I'll only be waitin' here to get a call from the recovery room."

"Then he *is* having surgery?"

"Oh, yes. That man needs it bad, real bad, from what I heard."

"Did you hear anything else?" Kitzi asked.

"Such as?" the nurse asked, protective of her patient's privacy now.

"His condition, his chances," Kitzi replied.

"Oh, his condition is fine, very hopeful." The nurse was quick to respond until honesty forced her to modify her exuberance. "Considerin' the man and his age . . . and his diagnosis. But these days . . ."

"When he comes out of the anesthetic, will you tell him that Kitzi Mills called to inquire about him? Kitzi Mills." She repeated.

"Oh, I know your name well. He talks about you quite a bit, ma'am."

"And . . . and tell him that I love him," Kitzi added.

"That too, ma'am," the nurse assured her.

"Oh, about him," Kitzi felt compelled to warn the nurse, "he seems like a very irritable old man. He hates to be fussed over, so he's likely to say some nasty things. Pay no attention. He's really very nice underneath."

"Most patients say they don't like being fussed over. But they do. Anything else, ma'am?"

"No. Just thank you, and tell him. Please?"

She hung up the wall phone and started toward Joyce Scott's office.

The counselor was gathering up a pile of journals to return at the session when Kitzi burst in on her.

"I would like to be excused from group this morning!" she declared.

"Did you talk to him?" Scott asked.

"No, he was on his way up to surgery."

"Good. Now, what about you and the group——"

"I would like to be excused. I think he needs someone to . . . to pray for him while he's up there."

"Pray?" Scott asked skeptically, forcing Kitzi to explain.

"He's up there under anesthesia. Defenseless. Unable to intercede for himself. I think it would be good to have someone ask . . . ask for help on his behalf."

"I understand," Scott said. "Do you think that the entire group might want to join you? They're all very fond of old Gus."

"I guess I claimed him for my own. Or else he made me feel that way."

"It might be a little bit of both," Scott suggested. "But you decide. Alone? Or in the group?"

Kitzi needed a moment to ponder that. She confessed, "They'll think it's strange—me, of all people, asking to hold a prayer meeting."

"Who better than a minister's granddaughter?" Scott suggested.

"Okay. I'll do it in group. But it has to be now, while he's up in the operating room."

49

When they had all gathered in their usual circle, Scott announced, "This morning, before we proceed to our usual session, Mills has something to say to us."

All faces turned to Kitzi. She knew they were eagerly awaiting a confession from her. She hoped they would not be disappointed.

"Three days ago, August Chamberlain left here for medical treatment back in New York. Today, right this minute, he is up in surgery being operated on. I want to ask you to . . . pray with me that he comes through it in good shape."

There was only a brief hesitation before hands were joined around the circle and everyone lowered their heads.

"Dear God," Kitzi intoned softly, "take care of that old man. Make sure that the surgeon's hand is steady. Make sure that what he has to do really works. That what he finds makes it possible for Gus to go on living. And make sure—"

"Bullshit!" came the voice from one of the lowered heads.

For an instant, no one in the room dared even breathe. Then Ward McGivney raised his head slowly to stare directly at Kitzi Mills.

"This is like everything you've done since the day you arrived here!" he accused. "It's a performance. Did you write it out and then rehearse it in your room before you decided you were ready to give us the world premiere? *Prayer for Divine Intervention,* starring Kitzi Mills!"

"That's not true!" she exclaimed, turning to Scott for support. The counselor chose not to intervene. "I asked to do this alone. Miss Scott suggested you might like to join. After all, he is part of us." "But you're not. Never were," McGivney said. "Why Gus being so sick has scared you, I don't know. But you must be terrified for him to be calling on God. You, of all people! So I say bullshit!"

Kitzi turned to Scott. "Tell him it was your idea to have the group join."

"Yes," Scott agreed, but continued, "however, that does not negate what Ward has just said. You'll have to answer that for yourself."

"Yes!" McGivney persisted. "You come crawling back—the fugitive seeking sanctuary in a cathedral, begging, 'I need help, comfort. Take me in! Help me to pray. Protect me.' Protect you from what, Mills? What are *you* afraid of?"

"Stop picking on her!" Calvin intervened.

"Calvin, you're not doing her any good by helping her cover up and hide," Joe Bigelow said. "It's okay for us to spill our guts. But not her. We should have known the first day when she said, 'I'm Kitzi Mills and I'm a star!' Not an alcoholic. Not a druggy. A star. I knew then she'd never make it. I even wrote it in my journal." He turned to Scott. "Didn't I?"

Bertha Shawn joined in. "I can confess now that some nights I deliberately stay awake, hoping that since she won't talk in group, maybe she'll talk in her sleep. But no, she's not the type to talk, even in her sleep. She's got it all neatly tied up in a package, with red ribbons around it. She doesn't trust anyone. Not even me. And I've tried to be her friend. Once I even——" She ceased abruptly.

"Once you even *what?*" McGivney insisted.

Bertha looked to Kitzi, seeking permission.

"Tell them!" Kitzi replied. "I'm not ashamed."

"One night, soon after she got here, she took off. Was on her way back to disaster. I forced her not to. Otherwise she wouldn't be here now. She'd be God knows where, drunk, or being screwed by some man she doesn't know, or even dead."

267

"I don't have to listen to any of this!" Kitzi replied.

She was halfway out of her chair, in the direction of the door, when Harlan Brody intervened.

"Kitzi! Sit down!"

Slowly she sank back into her chair.

Brody continued, "I sit here observing this. Feeling very defensive about her. I say to myself, this started out to be a simple prayer for a very sick old man. How did it suddenly become an attack on the person who asked us to pray?"

Kitzi felt justified, but Brody continued.

"Until she said, 'I don't have to listen to any of this.' Then it became clear even to me. She has never been part of us. Sure, she does her chores. Attends the group. Hands in her journal. Consults with Dr. Woolman. But that's like floating above the water. She never gets wet, does she? Never opens up to the rest of us, like the rest of us do.

"I know her, yet she's a stranger to me. What's Kitzi Mills hiding?" he asked, as if discussing her in her absence.

"Could it be she has a child and she's never been married?" Bertha asked.

"Big deal! These days that's par for the course in show business," McGivney responded.

"We know she likes to be considered the Good Fairy, like in *The Wizard of Oz,*" Bigelow said. "The gracious lady always coming to the aid of those in need."

"A female St. Jude, the hope of the hopeless," McGivney added. "Asking us to pray for old Chamberlain. God must be sitting up there now laughing and saying, 'Look who's down there praying. Asking for help for an old man named August Chamberlain, when she should be asking for help for herself. She needs it more than he does.' "

Calvin leaned forward in his chair to plead for Kitzi. "Maybe she's doing penance. My grandmother told me that women used to in the old times. Tend the sick. Do menial and degrading chores. Become serving nuns. To make up for past sins. Maybe there are some sins too terrible to confess in public. I say let her be."

"Is that what you're suggesting we do now, Calvin?" McGivney asked. "Just let her be? Let her die?"

"What do you suggest, Ward?" Corell countered. "We drop to our knees? Hold a revival meeting, pray for her to come forward and accept Jesus?"

"It would give her a chance to play Mary Magdalen," Joe Bigelow taunted.

Joyce Scott was silent throughout the exchanges that shot back and forth across the circle. She had her eyes fixed on Kitzi Mills, especially on her throat, where one faint blue vein pulsated with increasing frequency under her pale skin. She was not surprised when Kitzi finally responded.

"We are here because Gus Chamberlain is up in the operating room right this minute. He needs our prayers!" Kitzi insisted. "Now!"

"She's right. Let's all pray for old Gus," Harlan Brody seemed to agree "whose life does not depend on us, but on what the surgeon does and what he finds. But Kitzi Mills, who is right here, right now, and about whom we *can* do something—let's not talk about her." He turned to Kitzi. "How come this call to prayer? From you, who can't even accept God as a greater power? Was prayer a little act you performed for your father, before he patted you on the behind and shooed you into bed? Not something you ever believed. Just Daddy's little girl doing what would please Daddy? What a fraud you are. I'm ashamed of you, Kitzi!"

She could ignore or deny the attacks from the others. But not Brody's. He was her friend, the man who had promised to back her next musical, do the album, who had such plans for her. And now this attack? She could feel her throat tighten as she fought to hold back tears. She bolted from her chair and started for the door. Before she reached it, she heard steps. Then strong arms surrounded her, and held her so tight she could not breathe. She heard Calvin's voice whisper in her ear.

"Kitzi . . . don't! Please don't run."

She clung to him, giving way to the tears she had fought to suppress. As his grandmother had when he was a little child, he whispered, "Cry it out, baby. Cry it out. Then be strong and carry on."

"Mills," Scott called to her. "We're waiting."

269

Finally Kitzi pressed her fingers into Calvin's muscular biceps. It was her way of telling him that she had recovered sufficiently to continue. He took her hand and started back to the circle. He pulled out his handkerchief and wiped her eyes dry. Then he stepped aside, exposing her to the group.

50

As if there had been no interruption, and in reply to Harlan Brody's question, Kitzi began, "No . . . no, not my father. I never knew him. I hardly knew my mother. Only saw her once after I was four years old. We got a call . . . my grandfather, that is. She was sick. They expected she was going to die. Did he want to see her one last time?

"It was raining that morning. I remember that. He was getting dressed in his one good black suit. The one he wore to preside over weddings and funerals. I wore my good dress. Dark red velvet. It was a gift, second-hand. From one of his parishioners. When I first came there . . ."

She could not continue. The memory was too painful. She looked across the circle into the eyes of Bertha, Calvin, and Scott, all silently encouraging her.

"It was raining. . . . Oh, yes, that dress. When I first came there, to my grandfather's house . . . actually, my mother brought me. She had been writing to him. Maybe the first thing I ever remember . . . she was talking to him on the phone. A public phone, open, like the one we use in the corridor. She was crying, begging him to take us in. By that time she was drinking heavily. She couldn't keep a job. She tried . . . tried the street. But she couldn't bring herself to do it. So she was begging, 'Take us in, help us.' I don't know what he said, but she said, 'No, never!' She hung up. She took me in her arms and started down the street. It's strange. As many times as I've thought of it, I can't remember what happened after that. Except that days later we were on a bus. Heading for grandfather's.

"I had never been there before. Since my mother never married, to him she was an abomination in the eyes of the Lord. He would save my soul. But she was lost forever. She had to leave. I remember he said something about 'living down the shame she'd brought on his house.'

"I watched the front door of the little rectory close on her. I'll always remember the skimpy, yellowing, white-lace curtain on the window of that door. It hung there, limp, worn, with a loose thread at one corner. I was staring at it when he took my hand and said, 'Come, child.' He led me up the stairs. I looked back, trying to see through the glass. To see where she was going. But he tugged at my hand and said, 'Forget about her!'

"I stared down at the steps, at the old carpet. I could see the backing through the worn spots. I didn't know then but I should have. That was the way my life was going to be from then on. Everything was going to be worn, old and threadbare. Once, years later, I did a British play in which I had the line, 'We lived in genteel poverty.' I knew damn well what that meant.

"Like that red velvet dress. Mrs. Cunningham was the lady who came in once a week to tidy things up. She didn't get paid. It was her service to the church. She had a granddaughter just a little older than I was. The dress had been hers. A lovely dress. Red velvet, with a little white lace collar and cuffs. Whenever I was particularly unhappy I would go into my closet and comfort myself by feeling that soft, rich velvet.

"I wore that dress the day we went to Minneapolis to see my mother for the last time. It was an institution that had been built almost a hundred years before. Brick and red stone with few windows. It looked like a fort, not a hospital for the mentally ill. I remember walking down what seemed endless corridors, dark corridors. Hearing weird noises. Moans of pain. Sounds of demented people. Angry commands. Twice, sounds of someone being beaten and crying out in agony.

"I looked up at the woman who was leading us. I could see from her eyes that she was uneasy about what we were hearing. I could also see my grandfather, grim, determined, his face set for the ordeal. But his eyes gave him away. He felt sad, very sad. When we came to the door of the little room he said, 'I better go in first.' He was in there for what seemed a long time to a six-year-old. When he came out, his eyes were dry but his face was not so stern any longer. He made a little gesture with his hand indicating I was to go in."

Without being aware, Kitzi performed that gesture now, as she talked.

"I was too frightened. So he took my hand and led me in. The room was small and dark. There was one small window, but it was high and faced out on a brick wall. She was lying in bed, looking even worse than I could ever remember her looking, no matter how drunk she got. She was holding out her arms to me."

Again unaware, Kitzi simulated the gesture, holding out her arms, the look on her face a plea, a desperate plea.

"I wanted to go to her. I couldn't move. I was too frightened. She kept saying, 'My baby, my baby . . .' Still I couldn't move. Worse, I couldn't look at her. I buried my face in my grandfather's old black coat. I felt his hand press my head against his thigh. It wasn't that I didn't love her. I was frightened by the way she looked.

"I've said to myself a thousand times since that day that I should have gone to her, embraced her, kissed her. She was dying. All she wanted from me was one last sign of love. I was the only one she could turn to. But I didn't . . . I couldn't. I will never live long enough to erase that memory.

"Sometimes, in my dreams, I replay that scene. And it ends differently. With her in my arms, dying. A decent ending. Instead of her dying alone in that small dark room."

She turned away from them, her eyes focusing somewhere beyond them.

"I think about her often. I use her. In parts I've played. I try to imagine what she went through, how she must have felt, and I use those feelings.

"Sometimes . . . sometimes it comes too close. I mean, when . . . when two weeks ago I made my first phone call. I called Alice. And she said, 'Don't come home, Mommy. Get better, get cured, Mommy.' When I was the little girl, I rejected my mother completely.

"Six days later, the phone in the rectory rang one morning. I was on my way to school. I was passing the door to my grandfather's little office when I heard the phone. It rang three times. When he didn't answer, I did. This voice asked, 'Reverend Millendorfer?' I said, 'No, but I will go look for him.' But I couldn't find him. So I went back and asked the lady if there was any message. She said, very simply, 'Tell him that Rebekah Millendorfer passed away late last night. We need instructions about the disposition of the body.' The disposition of the body. I had heard people talk about burial. Many times, when I was little, I watched from behind a tall tombstone in the church cemetery while my grandfather presided over a burial. I watched them lower the coffin into the grave. So I knew about that. But I hadn't heard about 'the disposition of the body.'

"All I knew was that she had died. I stood in that room with the high ceiling, and the drab, dark wood walls, with only my grandfather's certificate of ordination and two holy pictures hanging there. I knew I should cry. But I didn't. I felt empty. Sick to my stomach from fear. But I couldn't cry. I didn't know what I was supposed to do. Go to school? Or not go to school? I was so torn between wanting to cry and not being able to that I just stood there, frozen, dry-eyed, my books in my arm. I still remember the sweet, fresh-ironed smell of the cotton dress I was wearing.

"He found me that way. He was just returning from having sat up most of the night with a sick parishioner who had died that same morning. He knew there was something wrong the moment he saw me.

" 'What is it, Katherine?'

" 'They called . . . a woman . . . she called. She said Mommy was dead. And they wanted to know about the—"the disposition of the body." She called her "the body." ' '

"He took the books from my arm. He sat down, drew me to him, held me on his lap. He put his arms around me, held me close. Then he took me upstairs, put me down on the bed, left me there. He went downstairs. I know he called the hospital. Because when he came back up he said, 'I gave them the instructions.' He sat down on the bed, reached out to me, and began to cry. The only time I ever saw him cry. He must have loved her very much. He had been punishing her and himself all the time he refused to take her back. I felt so sorry for him. He put his arms around me and drew me close. And we cried together. Until . . ."

Kitzi faltered.

"We . . . were crying . . . and I—he—all I knew, I could feel his cold hand on my leg in a way I had never felt it before. Slowly it worked its way up until it reached my thigh. It began searching until it found me. I was too young then even to have any hair there. I was soft and smooth. He began to gently play with me. I started to draw back, but he held me tighter. And that thin hand kept slowly playing there. He had a way that told me it was not the first time he had done something like that.

"By then, I was beginning to feel warm there. I didn't try any longer to push him away or draw back. I turned my face away. Whatever it was, it was a sin, and I didn't want to see it. But I felt it. I felt—yes, I felt very soft and tingly. My whole body was warm all over. I didn't know what he was doing. Finally I looked down. I saw him, his head between my thighs, drawing me closer and closer to his mouth. I found my body pushing upward to him, until I felt all of me suddenly explode. He must have felt it too because it stopped then. He lay beside me, holding me like a precious thing he owned. He whispered, not to me but to himself, 'Oh, Rebekah . . . Rebekah. . . .' He was calling for her. Weeping for her. Then I knew why this was a long time habit with him."

A painful quiet filled the room. No one dared interrupt. They knew there was more to come.

Kitzi remained silent, distant. She brushed away tears which were not on her cheek. She tried to gather the strength and the will to resume. For a long time it appeared to elude her.

51

"Child, you can't wear red velvet to your own mother's funeral," Kitzi said suddenly. Then, by way of explanation, she began again, "It was Mrs. Cunningham said that. 'Child, you can't wear red velvet to your own mother's funeral.'

"She took me by the hand and rushed me over to her son's home. There she went through all the clothes in her granddaughter's closet, looking for some dress fit for a funeral. She picked one out. It was too big for me, but she said, 'It'll have to do.' She took me back to the rectory, ironed that dress, and made me put it on. Then she pinned up the hem because there wasn't time to sew it. That's how I went to my mother's funeral.

"It was raining that day. At the cemetery there were a dozen people, maybe fifteen. They all had umbrellas, so it was like one big black canopy over the gravesite. Reverend Henderson, from a nearby town, came to officiate, since it was not considered right to place that burden on a bereaved man like my grandfather. Henderson said some nice, meaningless things about my mother. He spoke mostly about poor old grandfather in his grief. And about me—'a motherless child' he called me. He said what a comfort my grandfather and I must be to each other now.

"Before the workmen began shoveling the earth onto the coffin, my grandfather dropped a rose on it. Then the shoveling commenced. I could hear the earth dropping onto the wooden coffin. Someone took me by the hand to pull me away. But I wanted to stay on, to explain to her why I wasn't able to go to her that last day when she held out her arms to me. They dragged me away. I remember hearing some woman say, 'Strange child. She couldn't even cry for her own mother.' "

Kitzi lowered her eyes, no longer staring into space but into their eyes. "You understand that I wanted to cry. I was just too stunned. Too much had happened to me. I did cry later. Days later. But by that time I didn't know if I was crying for her or for myself. Because . . . because what happened after we got the word about my mother . . . began to happen often, almost every night. It got so I would try to fall asleep before he came to my room. But after a while I didn't try to fall asleep. I just waited for him. It was something that had to happen before I was allowed to go to sleep.

"Then I knew why she ran away. Why she took to drinking. Why he threw her out when she became pregnant. It wasn't that she was pregnant. It was because she had been unfaithful to him. He could never forgive that. Till the last day I saw him, he always referred to her as 'sinful' and 'debauched.' It was his favorite word. He used it in sermons all the time. 'Debauched.'

" 'Fornication,' he would accuse from the pulpit. The word took on such a sound of evil from his mouth that I would sit there cringing, and promising myself it was something I would never do. Once I dared to ask him what fornication was. He said, 'You won't want to know, child.' But when I insisted, he said to me, 'It is a dirty, immoral, debauched business. It is when a man has his way with a woman not his wife. When he invades her with his . . . his . . .' He groped for a word, then said, 'He puts his private part into hers.' He must have suspected what I was thinking, because he said, 'It's not like the two of us, child. What we have is love and consolation. I would never do any such thing to you. Make sure no other man does, either,' he warned.

"They tell me . . ." She hesitated before she admitted, "they tell me that when I am drunk and encourage any man to take me, I say, 'Come on, boys, let's fornicate.' That's the word they tell me I use. Fornicate.

"He was not trying to teach me morality. He was saying not to be unfaithful to him. Like my mother had been. When I got to be twelve and boys started walking me home from school, he would become very angry. There was never a boy he didn't have a harsh word for. Either about the boy or his family. He seemed to know everyone's secrets, every family's. So soon there were no boys. Not many girlfriends either. He wanted me for himself alone."

Kitzi became aware that she was twisting her fingers nervously. She deliberately clasped them. She held her hands rigidly in her lap.

"Before you ask why I didn't do anything about it, didn't tell someone—well, I did. One day, it after I discovered that I had become a woman because of the bloodstains on the bedsheet, he said it was time for Mrs. Cunningham to have a talk with me. She came to the house, up to my room where I was waiting for her. She was a gentle Christian woman. She tried to explain to me about menstruation and pregnancy. In the language of her own youth, she called it 'the curse.'

"I listened very carefully because this was quite frightening to me. But I also realized that this might be my chance to ask the question

276

I had not dared to ask anyone else. So, very cautiously, and without mentioning any man, I began to ask her about what had been happening between my grandfather and me.

"I will always remember her looking down at me. 'What did you say, child? Do what?' I tried to describe it as best I could. I can still see the look of horror on her face. 'You filthy, filthy child! To even think up such a thing! I'm afraid I shall have to tell your grandfather about this!' I begged her, 'Please don't tell him!'

"After that, I never told anyone else. Until now. I don't know why I told you today. I think about it more often than I like. I even wonder if I did anything to seduce him. Sometimes I've even thought that maybe I enjoyed it more than I let myself admit. I don't think it was that.

"Because, around that time, when I was twelve, I took to sneaking some of the communion wine. That's when my drinking began. It helped make it easier for me to give in to him. Since he never kissed me anyplace but there, he never knew I drank. I started hating the thought that I was becoming like my mother. Then I started hating her. She knew what he was. Why did she bring me back, leave me with him? Why?"

Bertha consoled her softly. "She had no choice. Where else? Who else?"

Kitzi shook her head slightly, still immersed in her own thoughts and recollections. Softly she said, " 'How could you let Gordon Wainwright do something like that?' Marvin kept asking. I couldn't tell him . . . I couldn't . . ."

Instantly, she fell silent. She realized that she had never mentioned the name Gordon Wainwright in the group, in her journal, or in her sessions with Dr. Woolman. They were staring at her. Waiting. She owed them an explanation. She was unable to continue.

To protect her, Brad Corell said gently, "We've forgotten all about old Gus Chamberlain. We were going to pray for him."

"Yes," Kitzi was relieved to agree, "let us do that. Please, someone?"

Corell clasped his hands, brought them to his lips, and thought for a moment before he began. "Dear God, please hear this prayer in the spirit in which it is intended. One of us is at this moment undergoing crucial, dangerous surgery. We ask that You see him through this physical ordeal and grant him a safe recovery. Because we love this gruff, cynical, crusty old man, despite all his sins. To some of us he is a gadfly, constantly calling us to account for our frailties. But to others he is the kind, noble, and caring grandfather whom we all wish we'd had, but never did."

He raised his eyes slightly to glance in Kitzi's direction. She realized that her concern for old Gus had enabled her to dispel, finally, the burden thrust on her by her own grandfather.

She could share now the feeling others in the group had experienced when they had been able to reveal their deepest, most painful secrets. The wall between her and the group had been breached, shattered. She was willing now to accept them as her Greater Power. She breathed deeply and freely.

"Maybe now you can understand why I could not accept God as my Greater Power. My grandfather's hypocrisy . . . his speaking the word of God, accusing others of sin and debauchery, yet all the while . . . . How could I turn my life over to God?"

"You're blaming God for one man's sins," Bertha pointed out.

"God was there. In that church. In that simple, spare rectory, with the bare wood floors, the worn old carpet, the tattered lace curtains, the holy pictures on the walls. He was all around me, yet He never reached out His hand to protect me. And you want me to believe in Him? I'll take my chances with this group. You've been very kind to me, very kind."

"Shall I accept the plaque on behalf of the whole group?" Harlan Brody asked sarcastically.

Kitzi turned to him, startled and resentful at his impertinent question.

"Kitzi, darling, I won't be able to leave here feeling any sense of peace until I once hear you get off the pity pot. Stop feeling sorry for yourself."

Bertha reached across to take Kitzi's hand. "Honey, I've been trying to tell you ever since you first came here to stop accusing others and excusing yourself. 'Poor me, poor me. What I need to make up for the way life has treated me is just one drink. Just one.' We wily old drunks, we know there's only one drink, as long as it's as big as the Atlantic Ocean. There may be a million excuses for becoming an alcoholic. But there's no good excuse for remaining one! You have to accept what you are and say, With help, I'm not going to be that way anymore."

"I wish old Gus were here now," Corell said. "I'd rather he told you himself. One time we were half-jogging, half-walking around the perimeter. He was wheezing, of course. Suddenly, out of the blue, he said, 'Goddamn psychoanalysts!'

"When a man does that, all you have to do is shut up and eventually he'll tell you all about it. Which, between wheezes, he did. 'Ruined,' he said, again suddenly. 'Two whole generations. Ruined. From lying on couches and being encouraged to tell anyone who'd listen—for a fee of course—what was wrong with their parents. People compare psychoanalysis with Catholic confession. Ridiculous. In confession you tell someone about your own sins. But in analysis you keep trying to put the blame on other people.'

"Then he said, 'If I weren't so stubborn, I might consider Catholicism.' After a while, he grunted, 'No, wouldn't work for me. It's the mistakes of others that attract us journalistic vultures. We feast on them. While remaining totally blameless and innocent ourselves.'

" 'Brad,' he said as he grabbed me by the elbow, since he was breathing too hard to make it on his own, 'Shakespeare said it all. The fault is not in our stars but in ourselves. I only wish I had what it takes—courage, or fear—to open up and admit all *my* faults.'

"Kitzi, if he were here now, instead of being there and under anesthetic, that's what he'd be telling you. Up to now you've done well enough blaming others. Your mother, your grandfather, Gordon Wainwright. Maybe they share the blame. But the drinker, the alcoholic, the pill-taker, is not any one of them. It's you. Take that fifth step. Admit to us, or anyone, all the wrongs you've committed by being a drunk." He pleaded again, "Kitzi?"

Kitzi did not respond, except to shake her head and stare at the floor, avoiding his eyes.

"Kitzi?" Calvin begged.

She rose and fled the room. He followed her.

52

In the corridor, Calvin caught sight of Kitzi just in time to see her slip into the little chapel.

It was a small room. Quiet, dimly lit, a place intended for private meditation. Six benches, three on each side of a narrow aisle, faced a nondenominational altar made of dark wood. The floor was carpeted in deep brown broadloom. There was a single light on at all times, just above the altar. It was encased in red glass.

The room reminded Kitzi of the church at the other end of the short hall that led from the rectory. She did not wish to be reminded of that time or that place right now. Her wounds were too fresh.

Still, she stood at the door, inhaling the fragrance of the wood paneling. The stillness was so compelling that it had a presence. She realized why. Since she had arrived at The Retreat nineteen days ago, she had been accorded virtually no solitude. She felt that she had been holding her breath, unable to relax, for all that time.

She sighed softly and slipped onto the bench nearest the door. She breathed slowly, deeply, drinking in the silence. All her thoughts were with old Gus. She could almost see the operating room—the team of surgeons, anesthetists, nurses—old Gus lying there covered, and instead of that perpetual cigarette in his mouth, a tube.

Once he had confessed to her that he wanted to give up smoking and drinking. But it was so much a part of the way he typed that he felt it would destroy his ability to work. So he never tried. Which led to even more smoking and more drinking. He, too, had experienced blackouts, and sometimes he couldn't remember what he had written.

"The last two chapters of *Glasnost, Myth or Masterstroke*—I don't remember writing those. When I read them in galleys I said to myself, 'Christ, this is damn good stuff. I wish I had been there when I wrote it.'"

Old Gus. August Chamberlain, to grant him his distinguished byline. What a wonderful grandfather he would have made for a couple of youngsters. In his own crusty way, making wry little jokes, he would have had fun with them. And given them a great deal of fun, too.

If he's still alive when I get back to New York I'll take Alice to see him. He'll love her. And she'll like the idea of having a grandfather. All the other kids talk about their grandfathers.

But now he's lying on the operating table. God knows if it will do any good. But if it does, when I get back . . .

Thinking of going home . . . is that a good sign? Does it mean being cured? Before my confession today I hadn't thought of going home. Now, is it that I would rather not face the others here?

She slipped off the bench onto her knees. She spoke in a whisper. "It's been a long time. And I'm out of practice. But I know how to make deals. So I'll make a deal with You. You save Gus and I'll beat this thing. I swear, I'll beat it! Just give me a sign by saving old Gus."

Then to her own surprise, and as if the voice came from someone else, she heard herself say, "Bullshit! Who the hell do I think I'm fooling? Gus's chances are so bad that I'm looking for an easy way out! So I can go back to drinking. I can say I'm grieving for old Gus, because God reneged on the deal we made. More bullshit. God never made a deal. I made a deal. A one-sided deal. Old Gus would have been the first to point that out. And he would have been right."

She rose from her knees. Just before slipping out, she turned back to the bare wood altar and whispered, "Sorry about the language."

She was on her way to the afternoon lecture.

The lecture was interrupted by a knock on the door. Such an intrusion was rare, but this knock had unusual and persistent urgency. Calvin went to the door. Mrs. Armbruster was there.

"There is an emergency call for Miss Mills. She may take it in my office."

Kitzi started toward the door, stopping only to ask Mrs. Armbruster, "Is it about Alice?"

"They didn't say."

She raced down the corridor to Armbruster's office. She lifted the receiver.

"This is Kitzi Mills. Who is this calling?"

"Ma'am," the soft, melodious black voice from the islands replied, "it is I. Lucille Johnson. I want you to know that Mr. Chamberlain is now in the recovery room."

"Then he's okay? I mean, he came through the operation all right?" Kitzi barely succeeded in asking before the tears started down her face.

"He is right now cussing me out, giving me orders, and asking for a cigarette."

"That's old Gus," she said, wiping back the tears and smiling. "You won't give him a cigarette, will you?"

"He so much as tries to reach for one I will put him in restraints," the nurse informed her.

"Lucille, when he's able to talk, will you have him call me?"

"Sure thing, ma'am."

Kitzi hung up, determined to rush back to lecture and inform everyone. Instead, she sank into the chair alongside Armbruster's desk and sobbed. Just before the lecture broke up, Kitzi returned to the room and told them the news.

They were all delighted. Ward McGivney said, "Nothing could kill that old son of a bitch. He wants to be around to report World War Three."

It was late afternoon. The sun had already set behind the scrubby brown mountains to the west and was casting its last rays against the mountains on the east. The air was cooler, lighter. There was a refreshing breeze.

Kitzi came out on her patio to find Calvin Thompson in running shorts, lying on the lawn stretching his long, muscular legs to relax his hamstrings, as he always did before starting on his run. He had been working for some minutes, for his chest, shoulders, and arms were glistening. His face, too, reflected his exertions, but he smiled at Kitzi when she appeared in her sweat suit.

"Mind?" she asked, indicating that she wished to join his calisthenics.

Without interrupting his rhythm, he smiled his permission. She lay down beside him and began to follow his routine. It felt good to stretch, to strain, to summon muscles she had not used for several weeks. Early in her career, when she had danced more, she was compelled to follow a daily routine of exercise. In recent years, when her drinking had grown worse, she had abandoned that along with so many other habits.

Now it felt good. And with Calvin Thompson alongside, it felt more comfortable, and easier than it would otherwise have been. Soon she was sweating too.

"When we get done with this, we're going for a run. Not just a jog but a real run," he said.

"Okay," she agreed.

Soon he was up on his feet, insisting, "Come on, Kitz. Let's go!" He reached down, took her hand, and yanked her to her feet.

They started toward the edge of the neatly manicured lawn. His long, easy, slow stride challenged her to keep up with him. Soon she was breathing heavily. Too vain to give up, she persevered. Halfway around the perimeter of the huge lawn, she finally surrendered and slipped to the grass, drawing deep breaths, then exhaling slowly. Calvin continued, stepping up his pace now that he was on his own.

He had disappeared from view beyond the Administration Building. Kitzi lay on the ground, tossing handfuls of grass up in the air to test the direction and the strength of the breeze. She felt like a child again, alone, as she used to be so much of the time.

In her childhood, her guilty secret had made her a recluse. She had kept to herself, read books, daydreamed—mainly about running away from that bare, cold rectory one day. Running away to the city. Running away to become an actress. Mostly, running away from him. She had spent many spring and summer days out on the lawn behind the church. She would lie on her back, staring up at the blue sky. In those times, too, she would toss handfuls of grass into the air and watch them be carried off by the wind.

She felt young again. She rose to her feet, wiped the sweat from her face with the heels of her hands, and started a slow run back to the dorm. She did not want to be late for her session with Dr. Woolman.

53

Joyce Scott was closing Kitzi Mills's journal.

"Mills, evidently your confession lifted a great burden from you. The follow-up in your journal is very promising."

"Thank you," Kitzi said as she reached for the book, assuming the meeting was at an end.

"There is another matter——" Scott said.

"Oh?"

"On Dr. Woolman's recommendation, it's been decided you can invite your daughter to visit and spend the weekend with you."

"Thank you," Kitzi said, her relief evident in her eyes as well as her voice.

"Don't misinterpret this. Your daughter coming to visit is not a goal, but only one move toward reaching the goal—being able to take Step Five."

"I understand," Kitzi said. "I'll call her immediately!"

"It's only eleven o'clock here. That means it's two o'clock in New York. Won't she be in school?"

"Of course, you're right. I'll wait till after we have lunch. She'll be home by then," Kitzi said.

Kitzi had selected a cup of tea and a small salad. But Calvin noticed that she hadn't eaten any of it. She kept her eyes on the wall clock in the dining room. It was finally one o'clock. Four o'clock in New York. Even if Alice had had some after-school activity, she would be home. Kitzi raced to the wall phone outside the lounge. Troubled by her remoteness through lunch, Calvin followed.

She dialed. Gave the operator her credit-card number. Waited. She heard the phone ring. Once. Twice. Three times. Alice not there? Evelina not there? Something was wrong.

She began to tremble at the frightening thoughts that flooded her mind. Alice had been in an accident and Evelina was at the hospital with her, taking care of her. She was so badly hurt, that they kept the news from her for fear she would leave The Retreat and fly home. Marvin would do something like that. In times past he had kept bad news from her to protect her. Well, she did not want to be protected. Not if her daughter was in danger. She should be the first to know, not the last.

The phone continued to ring. Alice! Evelina! Someone! Answer the phone!

She finally hung up, leaning against the wall to keep from shaking. Until then Calvin had kept a discreet distance from her. But realizing how close to collapse she was, he went to her, picked her up and carried her into the lounge. He poured a cup of hot coffee, let her sip it slowly.

"Kitzi? Bad news from home?"

"No one there. Something's wrong, terribly wrong," she said, beginning to weep.

Calvin put his arm around her. "Please, Kitz, maybe they're just out. You said you live right across from Central Park. It could be a nice day and Alice is out playing. She might be having a lot of fun right now while you're crying."

He used his handkerchief to wipe away her tears. "I bet if you call an hour from now she'll be there."

"It's after four. She should be there now!" Kitzi insisted.

"Okay, tell you what," Calvin said. "Let's give her another hour and then call again. If she's not there, I'll call my grandma and have her go down and see if there's anything wrong. How about that?"

Through her gasps, Kitzi agreed. "Okay. Good. We'll do that. Thanks, Calvin."

He took both her hands and held them as he began, and she joined him, "God grant me the serenity to accept the things I cannot change, the courage to change the things I can, and the wisdom to know the difference."

Whether it was the warm and comforting touch of his hands, or the words themselves, she felt reassured for the moment.

After the afternoon lecture, Kitzi and Calvin raced from the auditorium to the phone.

Kitzi trembled so that Calvin had to take the credit card from her hand and place the call for her. He pressed the receiver to his ear and listened as he heard the first ring, second ring, third ring. *God, please make somebody be there,* he kept insisting to himself. *Can't you see the shape she's in?*

Meanwhile, Kitzi kept her gaze fixed on his big, handsome black face, which was striving to appear pleasant and unconcerned. By the fifth ring, his forced smile began to diminish.

"Guess they may still be out," he started to say when, to his great relief, he heard the ring interrupted.

A child's voice said, "Hello? Hello? Sybil?"

"No, Alice, this is a friend of your mother's. She wants to talk to you." He placed the phone in Kitzi's hand and wrapped her fingers firmly around it.

"Alice? Honey? How are you, darling?" Kitzi asked.

"Fine," the child said. "I thought it was Sybil calling. She was supposed to call me about having a sleep-over here Friday night. Evelina said it was okay, long as it wasn't a school night."

"That's wonderful dear, except that I have great news!" Kitzi enthused. "A big surprise!"

"Yeah? What?" The child sounded apprehensive. Surprises from her mother were usually a source of embarrassment or emotional pain.

"Friday you are flying out to see Mommy!" Kitzi announced. She waited eagerly for Alice's response. For an instant there was only silence.

Then, "You all right, Mommy? I mean, you're not . . . not saying that because you've been drinking again, are you?"

"Of course not!" Kitzi protested. "I've never been better. You'll be surprised how terrific I look and feel!"

"Honest?" Alice asked, still unwilling to believe completely.

"Honest!" Kitzi said. "I'll call Marvin. I'll have him arrange for your ticket and a car to take you to the airport."

"Can Evelina come too?" the child asked.

"No, dear, it'll be just you and me," Kitzi said, beginning to feel shaky again now that the child's enthusiasm was far short of what she had anticipated.

"I'll have to call Sybil . . ."

"Well, call her," Kitzi insisted.

"She'll be disappointed," Alice said.

"Call her. Tell her!" Kitzi instructed.

"All right, Mommy, I will."

"And where were you all afternoon? I called and called."

"I was out."

"What do you mean, 'out'?"

"I was downtown with Aunt Florence."

What right does that woman have to call herself my child's aunt? I'll call that bastard Marvin and tell him that's got to stop at once! A child wouldn't know any better, but Marvin should! Or was it his idea?

But she didn't betray her anger to the child.

"What were you doing out with Mrs. Morse, honey?" she asked, pretending only casual interest.

"Shopping," Alice said.

"Shopping? Shopping for *what?*" Kitzi demanded. This was an unforgivable intrusion into her relationship with her daughter.

"Two dresses. A new blue sweater. Light blue. Aunt Florence says you'll like that shade of blue."

"How could you need clothes?" Kitzi protested. "You can't have grown that much in just three weeks."

"It's for my trip, Mommy." Alice tried to assuage her mother's anger.

"Trip? They're taking you on a trip?" Kitzi demanded. "Without asking me? Where are they taking you?"

"They're not taking me. They're sending me. But they said it would be *two* weeks from now."

"Where?" Kitzi insisted.

"Out to see you," Alice said. "Only they didn't say this Friday. That's why I asked Sybil for a sleep-over. Uncle Marvin thought it would be a week from Friday. So Aunt Florence said, 'We've got to get her a new outfit.' And Uncle Marvin said, 'It's a long weekend, better get her two outfits.' "

"And that's where you were all afternoon?"

"Where did you think I was, Mommy?"

"Out in the park, playing—having fun," Kitzi said weakly. "Sorry about your sleep-over. But you can do that next week, can't you, honey?"

"Okay, Mommy."

"I can't wait till Friday," Kitzi said, hoping to hear a similar response from her daughter.

"Mommy . . . are you sure you're all right?"

"Yes, angel. Mommy is fine, just fine. And I'll be waiting for you. Waiting."

She hung up the phone much less happy than she thought she'd be.

54

Kitzi's call came in at five-thirty New York time. At the moment, Marvin was on one of his other lines, haggling with a television network business affairs executive over the fee for a guest appearance of one of his stars. While he was being subjected to one of Eddie Steinhardt's harangues, Sarah Blinkhorn appeared in the doorway making frantic gestures. Marv tried to wave her off. But the old woman continued to gesture while explaining, "She's on. Line six."

Marv put his hand over the mouthpiece. "Sarah, I'm negotiating a deal!"

"*She* is on! Line six!"

" 'She'?" Marvin started to inquire, but immediately he knew. To Sarah, Flo was always *Mrs. Morse. She* was only one person, and always would be. *Kitzi.*

At once he said, "Eddie, call you back."

"Call me back?" Steinhardt complained. "I have orders to button up the deal today."

"I'll call you back!" Marvin was beginning to lose his temper.

Marvin reached to press the button for line six. His hand hesitated in midair. "Sarah? How'd she sound?"

"Better than last time," the woman said.

"Last time she sounded terrible."

"So I'm right. This time she sounds better."

"A little? A lot? Sarah?" Marvin asked.

"She's not drunk, if that's what you mean."

He glared at her. He hated the word. He hated the sight of Kitzi in that condition. Because he always felt a certain guilt. He would have to determine her present condition for himself. He pressed the button for line six.

"Kitz? Hi! How are you?" he asked, prepared to analyze the quality of her response.

She spoke deliberately, articulating each word with care. Her voice was the voice of the mature Kitzi Mills, vibrant and entirely distinctive.

"Marvin, I am fine. I am getting along quite well here. In fact, the reason I am calling is that this Friday I will be allowed to have visitors."

"This Friday?" Marvin was surprised. "I thought it would be next week at the earliest."

"They are making an exception," she explained.

"Terrific!" Marvin responded, greatly relieved. For when he lifted the phone he had anticipated a cry for help, possibly even word that she had run away from The Retreat and was stranded somewhere.

"It's not only for Friday but for the weekend as well. For the regular family training sessions." She sounded bitter when she said, "It seems families have to be 'trained' to deal with people like me."

"Tell me what you want me to do," Marvin said. He was becoming annoyed by Sarah, who insisted on standing in the doorway to eavesdrop. He waved her out. She did not budge. "Name it, Kitz, and you got it."

"See if you can arrange for the school to give Alice time off, without penalizing her. And arrange for her to fly out. Marv? Please?"

"I'll talk to the school. Would you want Evelina out there, too?"

"No. It's just for families. I want her, Marv," Kitzi pleaded. "I need her."

He detected that she was on the verge of tears.

"Okay, Kitz. I'll get her out there," he promised. Then, more softly, "Kitz, how is it, really? You can tell me."

"I'm trying. But sometimes they ask impossible things."

"Such as?"

"Believing in God. It almost sounds like a cult. You know me, Marv. I can't play a scene unless I believe it."

"Kitz, the others, do they believe it?"

"They believe," she admitted.

"Then it can't be so fake, can it? Kitz?"

Having never told him about her grandfather, even during their breakup over Gordon Wainwright, she was forced to be evasive now. "I guess it's because of my childhood. So much religion that I got fed up with it."

"Try, honey, try!" he encouraged.

He could hear the change in her voice as she replied, " 'Honey.' You used to call me that in the early days."

"Yes, yes, I guess I did. Now, don't you worry. Alice will be there Friday afternoon," he promised.

Once he hung up, his hand rested on the phone as he considered, *Why did I call her honey? Was it because of the way she sounded? Sober. And dependent. And fragile. Does she sound now like the woman I used to love?*

To divert his thoughts he snarled at Sarah. "You don't have to listen to every conversation I have with her!"

Ignoring the rebuke, Sarah asked, "Shall I arrange for first-class tickets?"

"Tickets?" he questioned, emphasizing the plural.

"You're going to let that kid travel alone?" Sarah asked.

"Sarah! One ticket! First class! Window seat!"

"These days, with airlines in the shape they're in, what if she misses connections?"

"Sarah! One ticket! First class! Window seat!"

"Yes, sir!" A form of address only resorted to when the two had reached a standoff.

It was past six-thirty. Flo had agreed to meet Marvin for dinner at Saito, a Japanese restaurant they both favored when they wanted to avoid the usual haunts of show people. When he arrived, he found she was not there. He called her office to discover that she was at the last run-through preceding the first preview of a new musical for which she was doing the publicity. It had been scheduled to start at one o'clock. It should have been over by five, five-thirty at the latest. If Florence was this late, something seriously wrong, or extremely important, had detained her.

When Marvin slipped into the back of the house, he discovered the two stars onstage, subjects of a still photographer at work with lights, reflectors, and other equipment not normally used in making production photos. Florence was standing in the aisle, giving directions to the stars and the photographer.

Marvin drifted down the aisle and soon discovered that Florence had succeeded in wangling a cover story from *People* magazine. This was the shoot for the story, the theme of which was "Finally, a new *American* musical." Leave it to Florence. He settled into an aisle seat.

When she finished staging the shot, Florence allowed the photographer and the interviewer to take over. She slipped into the aisle seat just in front of Marvin. He leaned forward and whispered, "I may have to go to the Coast on Friday."

Without taking her eyes off the stage she whispered back, "The Donna Avalon deal?"

He could have lied. An easy lie. He was tempted to. He could even have justified it to himself: Why subject Florence to any unnecessary pain? But she deserved the truth.

"Alice. Kitzi's allowed to have a visitor this weekend. I should take her out."

Florence stiffened visibly but said nothing. Instead, she rose and started down the aisle toward the stage to handle a question put to one of her stars which had not evoked a satisfactory answer. Marvin was relieved. The episode had passed with less difficulty than he had feared.

They stopped for a late supper at Patsy's on West Fifty-sixth Street. The place was almost empty, since the theater crowd had dined and already departed. The late supper crowd had not yet arrived. Having been introduced to the place some years ago by Tony

Frascati, Marvin was always received there as an honored and respected guest. He chose a quiet table in the rear.

They were enjoying their dinner when Florence said suddenly, "When I bought her those outfits, I thought it was a week from Friday."

For an instant Marvin was taken unaware. Then he realized. "They're very strict out there, about phone calls, about visiting. So when they say visit, you visit."

"And they said 'visit'?" Florence remarked.

"Actually, it's considered a big step forward. To be allowed to have visitors. Especially ahead of time."

"Terrific," she remarked sarcastically.

"Flo, darling, you have to understand——"

She slammed down her fork so hard that the waiter hurried to the table, asking, "Something wrong with your food, Mrs. Morse? Would you like something else?"

"No, everything's fine, Guido," Florence replied. More softly yet more firmly she said, "Let's get out of here!"

They walked west across Fifty-seventh Street, fighting the crowd that was emerging from Carnegie Hall after a concert. As they were passing the Russian Tea Room, Marvin suggested, "You must be hungry. Shall we stop in?"

"I've been hungrier," she said, "Let's get a cab."

55

When they got home, Florence went directly to her bathroom. Marvin could hear her drawing her bath. She had not said a word in the cab on the way home. Usually, by the end of a busy day, she was extremely talkative, unburdening herself of all the complaints she'd had to repress by virtue of her profession. Her clients could be undiplomatic, rude, loud, sarcastic, and hostile. It was Florence's job to be sweet, gentle, peacemaking, and convivial. She was excellent at her job, but she needed that release at the end of the day.

Whenever Florence's complaints reached a pitch that he could not dismiss as the usual bitching everyone in the industry does, Marvin would say, "Flo, if it takes this much out of you, give it up! God knows we don't need the money."

"Give it up?" she would respond, each time in the same surprised tone, as if the idea were being mentioned for the first time. "What would I do with my time? How many dinners can I cook? And then wait for you to come home, and you're always late. I'm not a Hadassah lady. Or one of those charity types. What the hell would I do with my time?"

"It's not too late for a . . . ," he would start to say.

There she would always interrupt. "No, Marvin, I know myself too well. What if after I had a child I wanted to go back to work? My own publicity agency. I get offers, you know. The Shuberts, the Nederlanders, they're always asking, 'Flo, when are you going into business for yourself?' The child would become a burden. I wouldn't want to be that child. Or that mother. So no thanks."

"Flo, you're not getting any younger."

"Maybe I'm too old already. Late thirties," she would say.

The discussion usually ended on that note.

Tonight, though, she was silent. Marvin sat in the living room catching the last ten minutes of a television special in which Chrissy Bruce, one of his clients, was featured. But his mind was on Flo.

Damn it, how long does a bath take? She's been in there for hours! Why am I getting the silent treatment?

He tossed aside his copies of *Daily Variety* and *The Hollywood Reporter* and headed for the bathroom. He pushed the door open and started, "Look, Flo, I think——"

Though the steamy fragrance of her bath filled the room, she was not there. In the bedroom, he could barely make out her silhouette. She was lying in their bed, facing away from him. He lay down beside her, put his arm around her.

"Sweetie . . . ," he said.

She did not respond. He embraced her, pressing against her body until they began to feel each other's desire. They made love more hungrily than they had for some time.

* * *

After, they both lay on their backs in the darkness, aware of the sounds of late-night traffic rising up from Park Avenue.

"Hungry?" he asked.

"No. You?"

"Not really," he said.

Neither of them could remember falling asleep. But they rose early, as usual. She was in the kitchen first, starting the coffee, setting out the juice. He came in, his hair still wet from his shower. He tried to kiss her on the back of the neck, but at the same instant she turned to him so his kiss landed awkwardly on her eye.

They both started to talk at once.

"Look, Flo," he said, "if it's going to create a problem——"

She said, "Marvin, let's face it——"

They both stopped. There was a moment of silence, both of them intent on speaking, both curious and wanting to listen.

This time she deferred to him.

"Flo, if it's going to create a problem, I won't go. After all, airlines can transport kids safely. They do it all the time, and they rarely lose any. I'll call and find out how they handle the plane change in Chicago. Okay?"

"No," she said.

"I thought that's what you wanted," he said.

"What I want, Marv, is for you to take her out there," she said. Surprise prevented him answering at once. "Otherwise you won't rest until she's safely back here. And if, God forbid, anything were to happen to her, you'd never forgive yourself. So go. Do it. And get it over with."

"If that's what you think . . . ," he started to say.

"That's what I think," she said quickly.

They were having their second cup of coffee when he looked up from the entertainment section of the *Times* to say, "I want you to know I appreciate it. Not many women would be so understanding and sympathetic."

"What makes you think I'm being understanding? *Or* sympathetic?" she asked. "Maybe I'm just being practical and realistic." A woman accustomed to dealing with crises every hour of every day,

Florence Morse was not given to easy tears. But now her eyes misted up before she could speak.

"Sweetie?" he urged.

"Don't call me that! 'Sweetie' is for clients. What did you used to call *her?* Not 'Sweetie,' I'm sure!"

"Flo, please . . ."

"No!" she interrupted firmly. "You said you want to discuss it. Okay, let's discuss! Do I want you to go out there? Yes! Is it because I am understanding? No! Why, then? Because I can face a fact that you can't."

"What the hell are you talking about?"

She rose from the table so abruptly that she knocked over her coffee cup and sent it shattering on the floor. She was on her feet, staring down at him, weeping now, and talking at the same time.

"These last few weeks, seeing that child with you as often as I have, one thing is very clear. She's your child, Marvin. Yours! She may be blond, but she has some of your features. She has your movements. She's going to be tall and long-legged, like you. When I see you two at the table together, I know it. I think you're the only one in the world who *doesn't* know it!"

"Flo, I went through all that twelve years ago!" Marvin said.

"Gordon Wainwright is not the father of that child!" Florence declared.

Marvin experienced the unsettling feeling that she was in possession of knowledge that he was not.

"Flo?"

"Gordon Wainwright couldn't have been the father of that child. Or any child. The old bastard was impotent! That's what made him such a son of a bitch in his last years. All that pussy out there for him, and he couldn't take advantage of it. The frustration was driving him crazy. He had the desire, but he had lost the ability. So he got his jollies out of playing with young girls, giving them orgasms in the only way he could. At least he had that to comfort him. He was still able to scheme and plot his little seductions. But father a child? Not in a million years!"

"I didn't believe Kitzi. Why should I believe you?" Marvin demanded hoarsely.

295

"Two reasons, my dear. One, I have nothing to gain by telling you. Two, I know. I was there."

"You were there? When Kitzi was . . ."

"Before Kitzi. When my firm first took on his publicity, they sent me out there to meet with him.

"I got invited to the Malibu house, and he came to my room in the middle of the night, like he did with all the others, before and after. We compared notes. The man was impotent! The only thing he used in bed was his tongue. That guy couldn't have gotten a hard-on in a harem."

"You knew all along," he said softly.

"Yes," she admitted.

"You never said anything."

"Should I have?" she asked.

"It would have made many things very clear," he said.

"Not as clear as they are now." He looked across at her. "It didn't work," she admitted. "I thought it might. I had so much to offer you. Love. Need. And I wanted as much as anything to be a good wife. And I have been. You must admit that. Along with my career I have given you a good life. Given you a refuge from the crazy business we're in. Given you my love, me—all of me."

She hesitated before admitting, "All of me, except one thing. No child. No son to carry on your name."

"You've always said what kind of life would it be for a child? Me, traveling a lot of the time. You with your crazy hours, going out on the road to do publicity for shows," he said, to ease her guilt.

"Excuses, Marvin. Excuses," she replied. "But excuses and reasons are not the same. The reason, the real reason, I didn't trust it."

"Didn't trust what?" Marvin asked, puzzled.

"Us. Our marriage. I was never able to convince myself that I could make it work. There was too much of you in her, and too much of her in you. You're not even aware of it. But the mere mention of her name does things to you. Sometimes I toy with the idea of walking into the living room when you're going over some papers and just saying 'she' to see what you would do. To everyone else in the English-speaking world, 'she' is just another third-person pronoun. To you it's a way of life. Part of your mind and your heart, in a way that no other woman ever can be. Not even me.

"So I'm not being noble, or understanding. Go with your daughter. See that she's safe. And see *her*. Maybe now she's more the woman you first fell in love with. If she is, feel free. I had my shot and it missed."

"Florence, no. I have never asked you, never even considered a divorce," he protested.

"Then consider it now," she said. Reluctantly, she added, "These last few weeks, seeing you and the child together, I have been having some very evil thoughts. That Kitzi would somehow disappear, or die. Then there would just be the three of us. She's a lovely child. I would have liked to have had one just like her," Florence said.

Later that day, when Marvin arrived at his office after several outside meetings, he instructed Sarah, "Get *two* tickets. First class."

"I already have," old Sarah said.

56

Kitzi stood before the full-length mirror which hung on the inside of her closet door. She turned slightly to her left, then to her right, to see how her tailored slacks fit. Very well indeed. Her hips were slimmer now, her belly flatter. Almost three weeks without a drink, without a binge, had taken off a good deal of the bloat. The daily routine of walking and jogging had tightened up her muscles. She slipped into a red-and-gray cashmere sweater which added even more color to her face, already tanned by exposure to the desert sun.

Alice will like it. Kitzi thought. Then she realized, *She must like me. Must forgive me. For everything. I'll know the moment I see her, the look on her face. I'll know when she embraces me . . . if she embraces me.*

She turned from the mirror to ask, "Well, Bertha?"

Bertha Shawn interrupted packing to examine her roommate.

"Wow! Looks terrific. Good colors for you. And you look great. Boy, when I think of what you looked like the day you first got here . . . ," Bertha said.

"What *did* I look like? Was I pale?"

"Hell, 'pale' doesn't even begin to describe it. And did you have the shakes! That first night when you tried to write in your journal, I couldn't concentrate for the noise you made every time your shaking hand tried to put pen to paper. Even after what I'd been through I thought, Christ, I feel sorry for her. And now—now you're beginning to look human again."

She'll like me, she will, Kitzi reassured herself. "Those first few minutes you're alone, what do kids say? What did yours say?"

"Nancy looked around at the dorm and said, 'It's not like I imagined. It's kind of nice.' I asked her what she meant by 'not like I imagined.' She couldn't even bring herself to tell me. That's when I realized that while I was having a tough time of it here, she was having an even tougher time back home with all her scary thoughts. I knew then what I'd done to her. I'll cut off my right arm before I reach for a drink again," Bertha said.

After the slightest pause, she admitted sadly, "Of course, I won't. I'll have moments of weakness, when a drink is the most important thing in the world. But I won't give in. I won't!"

Suddenly remembering what Kitzi had asked, she said, "You look terrific. The right word is . . . radiant. How about that? Isn't that what the critics used to say about you?"

Kitzi laughed and corrected, "My press agents. 'Kitzi Mills, radiant star of stage, screen and television. . . .' "

"You know the hell of it," Bertha said. "It's not what we do to ourselves. It's what we do to the next generation. Your grandfather, your mother, now you. And what you've done to Alice. One generation infects the next. If we could make a clean break. Hey," she continued in a brighter, if forced, vein, "we keep talking this way and it'll take all the joy out of her coming."

"Yes, she ought to be here any minute," Kitzi said. "And you've got your packing to do. I wonder who'll move in to take your place. Some terrified, trembling woman?"

"No doubt," Bertha said, as she folded and placed her clothes in the suitcase.

"I'd better go out there and wait for her."

As she started to the door, Bertha said, "Wait!"

She went to Kitzi, embraced her, pressed her face against Kitzi's.

298

"Just as I thought. You're trembling again. Don't. Be strong, because she'll be trembling. She's going to need your support. Make her know that you're fine, even if you have to act the part."

Then Bertha released her, and said, "You're on, kid. Break a leg."

Kitzi waited in the reception area. Through the amber-colored windows of the tall, bleached-oak doors, she kept watch on the circular driveway.

Four cars and two limousines had driven up and released their passengers, but no sign of Alice. Kitzi waited. One more taxi. One more big limousine. Still no sign of Alice. The phone on the reception desk rang. Instinctively Kitzi rose to answer it, thinking, *She's not coming. Something's wrong. She got sick at the last minute. She threw up just before she was supposed to get on the plane. She doesn't want to come here. She doesn't want to see me.*

She reached the side of the desk in time to hear the receptionist say, "There are still a few more expected, so I wouldn't start the visitors' class just yet."

Kitzi relaxed for the moment. As she turned back to her bench, she noticed a long white limousine draw up. She recognized Tony Frascati's big stretch limo. She waited for the door to open. Alice emerged timidly. Instead of heading for the tall doors she looked back, waiting. Out stepped Marvin. Alice reached for his hand. Instead of taking it, he gestured her toward the door, urging her to go on without him. The child hesitated, then started forward. She reached the door, which seemed much too tall and heavy for her to manage. She looked back. Marvin made a gesture to urge her through the door. Alice pushed hard. The door opened.

She stepped into the cool, shaded reception room, looking around quickly to find Kitzi. When she did, she called, "Mommy?" But the child did not move. As Kitzi approached, Alice scrutinized her mother carefully. Only then did she start toward her. Kitzi closed the distance between them much more quickly, taking Alice in her arms so anxiously that she lifted her off the floor.

Immediately she could feel what Bertha had warned. The child was trembling. Kitzi set her down, dropped to one knee, looked into her eyes.

Henry Denker

"It's all right, honey. Nothing to worry about. Everything's going to be all right now."

"Isn't Uncle Marvin allowed in here?" the child asked.

"Yes," Kitzi said, but she was disappointed at the child's dependence on him. "Let's ask him in."

Alice led the way to the door, making Kitzi wonder, *Why could he give her in just weeks the security she should have been getting from me all these years?* The answer was just as immediate. *Because he's not a drunk like you, Kitzi Mills.*

At the open front door, Alice called, "She said it's all right." Marvin approached. Alice took his hand and pulled him into the room.

What will he say? What will I say? Kitzi wondered. *Will he notice the difference from the day he brought me here? Whatever he says, will he mean it? Or will he just be humoring me like people do the mentally ill or the terminally sick?*

He was obviously no more prepared for the moment than she was.

All he said was, "Sorry if we're late. But the plane change in Chicago is always tricky. We took off late."

Just that. Nothing personal. She responded in kind.

"That's okay. As long as she got here safely."

She grasped Alice's hand. "Come, sweetheart, I'll show you Mommy's room." She started away, but looked back. "Marvin? Coming?"

They started down the corridor toward the bright sunshine at the end, toward Kitzi's room, where Bertha was standing in the open doorway. As they drew close, Bertha stared at Alice. "My! No wonder your mother was so anxious to see you. What golden hair. Just as pretty as your mother. No. Prettier. And where did you get that lovely dress?"

"Aunt Florence bought it for me," Alice said proudly.

Sensitive to Kitzi's feelings, Bertha exclaimed, "I always say it's not the dress, it's the girl who wears it makes the difference."

Joyce Scott came down the corridor, announcing, "All relatives are to meet in the auditorium for the first orientation talk. Let's gather as quickly as we can. It'll give you more time later."

"Go on, baby," Kitzi coaxed. "Go with Miss Scott. She'll show

300

you the way." But as she released the child to Scott, Kitzi asked, "Don't you think she's a little young for a lecture like that?"

"If she's old enough to suffer the effects of her mother's alcoholism, she's old enough for the lecture," Scott replied. She took Alice by the hand. "Come on, dear, let's go."

Kitzi and Marvin watched the pair go down the hall until they disappeared around a corner. Kitzi felt compelled to say something to dispel the silence created by Scott's rebuke. She turned to Bertha and, a bit awkwardly, said, "This is my agent, Marvin Morse."

"Morse? Is *that* your last name?" Bertha asked, pretending surprise. "I thought it was 'that sonofabitch.' I guess you two need to be alone." She started out into the sunlight of the patio.

They both felt awkward now. Kitzi felt a duty to explain.

"A person in my condition tends to blame everyone but herself."

"I understand," Marvin said.

"No, you don't!" she shot back. "You had no right! No right at all! None!"

"No right to do what?" he asked.

Down the corridor, Calvin Thompson and Laurie Coombs, who had been conversing, were interrupted by Kitzi's loud voice. They turned to stare in her direction.

Much more softly, she said, "I think we'd better continue this someplace more private."

"Out there?" Marvin asked. "Go for a walk?"

"Okay," she agreed, no less angry than she had been.

57

They slipped out the door onto the patio, then off toward the far edge of the green lawn that touched the raw desert. Kitzi looked up at the mountains that reflected the afternoon sun. She said nothing until they reached the edge of the grassy area.

"I love these mountains. I never thought I would. But I do," she said.

301

Henry Denker

"You said I had no right," he reminded.

"You took her away from me. In just three weeks," she said, more in sadness now than anger.

"We tried to make the separation less difficult. It wasn't easy for her, alone in that big apartment with only Evelina. Evelina's a fine woman, but she's not Alice's mother."

"And I suppose Florence is!" Kitzi exploded, sounding more hostile than she had intended.

"Florence is not her mother. And she knows she isn't."

"She had no right to go out and buy her that dress!" Kitzi insisted. "That child has a closet full of clothes! Lovely things. Expensive things. From the best shops on Madison Avenue. Florence was only doing it to point out that I . . . that I . . ." She did not complete the sentence.

"Look!" she went on. "I know what I am. What I've been. But Florence didn't have to rub my nose in it. Rub my child's nose in it! She's shrewd. She has her own subtle way of doing it. She never said a harsh word against me, did she?"

"No, she didn't," Marvin said. "Should she have?"

"She didn't have to. All she had to do was to be nice, sweet, indulgent, go on shopping sprees with Alice and let the child draw her own conclusions. Much more effective than saying, 'Your mother is a drunk and a slut and a . . . a . . .'" She ran out of derogatory terms for herself. "Your 'dear' wife is not in the public relations business for nothing!"

She began to cry. After a moment, during which Marvin handed her his handkerchief to dry her eyes, she said, "You should have stopped me from saying those things. You know how I am when I get uptight. I strike out at everyone. Alice looks fine. The dress is lovely. Maybe that's what I resented. I should have bought her a dress just like that. Thank Florence for me."

"Sure," Marvin said.

"You won't tell her what I said about——"

"Not a word," Marvin promised.

They stared at the shifting pattern of afternoon sunlight on the mountains.

"Kitzi. I've been calling out here, from time to time," he said.

302

"Almost every day, from what I hear."

"They say you're coming along," he said.

"I'm trying," she said.

"They say you might make it by the end of the four weeks. Five, possibly," he said.

"Okay, Marvin, I know you. I know when you've got something up your sleeve that you want to force me to do. But you want to make it seem as if I wanted to do it. What is it this time? A film? Or a musical? I don't know if I ever want to sing again. Or act."

"Okay," he said. "It's just that I was asked to ask you——"

"Christ! It's never your idea! All right, what did someone ask *you* to ask *me?*"

"It came from the White House," Marvin said.

She turned to look up into his face. The son of a bitch was still handsome. His black, curly hair was graying. But he was still lean-faced, and with those dimples. She was determined to resent him, but she found it difficult. She could not be sure he was telling the truth.

"Marvin Morse, is this something you cooked up?"

"No. The request came directly from the White House."

"And?"

"Four weeks from this coming Sunday there is going to be a command performance at the White House to kick off the President's drive against drug abuse. If you're up to it, and because you could be such a symbol that it is possible to beat a dependency habit, they would like you to appear. Sing two numbers and an encore . . ."

"Symbol . . . ," she considered. "One hell of a symbol I am! I haven't beaten anything yet. I can tell you, but don't you tell them. I go to bed nights still craving a drink. A symbol? Me? Not very likely."

"I said four weeks from now," Marvin reminded. "They say you're doing well. Especially this last week. Some kind of a breakthrough, they said."

She thought, *What would he say if I told him about that "break-through." What would he think? Would it remind him of Wainwright and start that all over again?*

"Yes," she said softly. "There was a sort of breakthrough. I'm glad they think that signifies progress."

303

"They said they think now you're going to make it." Then he admitted, "At the outset they thought you were going to be part of the wrong fifty percent. So, what do I tell the White House?"

"I'll think about it and let you know," she said. She was still troubled. "You won't tell Florence what I said about her, will you?"

"I promised I wouldn't," he reassured.

"Tell her . . . Tell her it was very nice, very thoughtful, to spend so much time with Alice. Tell her I love that dress. Tell her—"

She smiled sheepishly. "Here am I telling you, of all people, what to tell someone else. You'll know what to tell her. You always know what to tell someone to make them feel better."

He looked down into her face. *This place has done wonders for her. Her eyes seem as blue as they were that first day in my office. Her skin is clear and fresh again, youthful. She seems fifteen years younger. She's the girl that Mama, may she rest in peace, once called too beautiful. "Marvin," she said that day they met, "only angels look like that, not a real person."*

Later, he watched Kitzi and Alice together. He saw the look of motherly pride as other patients stopped by the dining room to meet the child and compliment Kitzi.

He also detected Kitzi's fragility. Beneath the smiles and the doting, she could barely control her trembling. That vein in her ivory-skinned throat betrayed her. He feared that at any moment her composure could give way and she might break down and cry.

It's too much for her, he thought. *Or is it my presence? Should I have sent the child alone? Would that have been easier for her?*

Bertha came by their table to say good-bye. She was going back home to her own children.

They embraced and kissed. Then, still in each other's arms, Bertha said, "Katherine, I'll never forget you. And I'll be watching. Every time you're on television, I'll be watching. When you're in a new show, I'll be there. Opening night. And you better be there, too!" She laughed. She patted Alice's cheek. "My, you'll be a heartbreaker when you grow up."

Too embarrassed to reply, the child could hardly manage a smile. She blushed.

Blushed beautifully, Marvin thought. He felt proud of the child's modesty.

When Bertha had left them, Kitzi turned her attention back to Alice.

"What did they tell you in that class, honey?" she asked.

Marvin grew tense as he awaited Alice's answer.

"About how some people . . . she called them drug, uh . . . drug something."

"Drug dependent?" Kitzi supplied.

"Yes. That. And that alcohol was one of those drugs. That it was not a sign of being bad, but being sick. And the worst thing to do for such a person was to help them lie."

The child looked at Marvin. *Did I say the wrong thing?* He reached for her hand. Encouraged, the child continued.

"That it's the family's duty to make them face the truth. To tell them we love them and we are going to help them. And . . ." She hesitated.

"And?" Kitzi urged.

"And since I'm your family, I'm the one who has to do that. They didn't say how to do that. But there's another class tomorrow."

"Of course, darling. You'll learn how tomorrow."

She embraced the child, glancing over her head at Marvin. Her eyes thanked him for bringing her.

Still in Kitzi's arms, Alice asked, "Mommy, when *are* you coming home? They didn't say that in the class."

"Soon, baby, soon. Mommy still has a few things to straighten out before they say it's all right to leave."

"Will it be before Parents' Day?" Alice asked. "Will you be able to come to school with me?"

"When is that, baby?"

"It's the tenth of next month."

"Only two weeks?" Kitzi asked. "I . . . I don't know, baby. I don't know." Marvin noticed Kitzi's hands begin to tremble.

This is all too soon., he thought. *She's going to have a relapse. It was a mistake for Kitzi to ask to see Alice so soon. And for The Retreat to agree. This whole venture was a mistake, a dangerous mistake.*

305

"We have to leave now," he said. "They said not to make the first visit too long. But we'll be back."

"Where are you staying?" Kitzi asked, trying to appear as matter-of-fact as she could.

"The new Marriott. It's fantastic," he said. "I'll ask if you're allowed out for dinner. We'll take you there. Right, Alice?"

"I hope she's allowed to go," the child responded.

Kitzi walked them to the front doors, her hand firmly clasped in Alice's. There, she knelt to kiss the child good-bye. She rose to face Marvin.

"Thanks for bringing her, instead of just sending her. I was so worried."

He took her hand. "Kitz, you're doing fine. Looking great. Keep it up and you'll make both dates. Parents' Day and the White House."

"This time I'll get up on that stage without tripping," she said, smiling, making a joke of the slight embarrassment of her last appearance at the White House.

He hadn't meant to kiss her on the lips. It was intended to be a typical show-business kiss, a bare brushing of lips on cheeks, if there was any contact at all. But, by miscalculation or chance, their lips met. The kiss was longer than either of them intended, and more intense. As she pulled back from him she looked up at him.

Did you feel it, as I felt it? Did you mean it? Or was it a kindness to an unfortunate woman you once loved, because she needs all the support she can find?

"You'd better go." Kitzi said. "It's time for Alice's dinner."

She waved at them as they got into the long white limousine. She waited until it drove off.

Inside the cool, quiet car, Marvin and Alice both sat silent, neither wishing to venture the first comment. Alice finally spoke.

"She looks different."

"Different? How?"

"When she doesn't drink, she's beautiful."

"She'll be that way from now on, Alice," he assured.

"That's not what they said."

306

"Who said?" he asked, ready to defend Kitzi.

"In the class. They said people like her are always in danger. Any day, any night, they might go right back to drinking all over again."

"They only said 'might,' didn't they?" he asked.

"Yes."

"Well," he tried to reassure her, "that's a long way from saying that she will."

"If it happens——" she started to say impulsively, then stopped.

"If it happens?"

"Can I come live with you and Aunt Florence?" the child asked innocently. When Marvin did not respond at once, she pleaded, "What happens to kids who don't have anybody else?"

"Alice, listen to me. Your mommy is going to be fine. She'll be coming home in a week, two at the most. So don't worry about what happens to little girls who don't have anybody. You have somebody. Remember that!"

"Yes, Uncle Marvin," she replied. Then, some seconds later, she asked. "Wouldn't you and Aunt Florence want a little girl? I'm not much trouble, am I?"

"Your mother is coming back," he said firmly.

"Then can I at least see Florence and you?"

"Of course you can," he said.

The child's persistent questions raised doubts in Marvin's mind about Kitzi, his sense of her fragile hold on sobriety, her vulnerability. The child had a greater sense of reality than he.

58

With the visiting weekend over, with Alice gone, with Marvin gone, Kitzi felt the emptiness of her room more than she otherwise might have. Bertha was gone, too. She missed her. Missed her honesty. Her sheer determination to speak the truth, even when it hurt, if it was for the good of the cause. Kitzi had the room to herself now, at least until a new patient arrived.

Today her schedule had been slightly different due to the final visiting hours. On any normal day she would have attended group, then the community meeting, then jogged a few laps with Calvin, ending with a swim in the pool. She had been excused from those activities to spend her last few hours with Alice.

It was now study time, quiet time. A time to read or reread one of those many books. Or time to confide her experiences, thoughts, and feelings to her journal.

With events so fresh in mind, she began to write:

Yesterday Alice arrived. Marvin brought her. Anyone who sees the two of them together must know. I was afraid Bertha was going to blurt it out. You see, Alice doesn't know.

It was so good to see her. She looks fine. And she is beautiful. Was I like that at her age? I'll never know. Because by that time I lived in my grandfather's house.

She crossed out the sentence beginning with "Because by that time. . . ." She started a new paragraph.

I hope she didn't see how tense I was all weekend. I was doing my damnedest to conceal it. But Marvin knew. Every so often I would catch him staring. It wasn't the old-time stare when I would discover him admiring me, like no other man has ever admired me.

This time it was the way people secretly study the terminally ill or patients in mental hospitals. After all I've put him through I can't blame him. But it doesn't help the patient's confidence, I can tell you.

At the last there, when he was leaving, he kissed me. I kissed him too. For the tiniest moment it was like the old days. I was loved again. Not used again. But loved. There've been men . . . I've written about them before . . . too many of them. But never one like him. Or was it me? Was I so different in those days?

He said I was invited to appear at the White House. Did

he make that up just to give me a goal? Or is it true? He'd do anything for me. Even lie to me.

What Alice said, that's true, of course. Parents' Day. When she said it, I thought, this weekend was a kind of Parents' Day too. Children coming to see their failed parents. We are a sorry lot.

God, how did it ever happen? How?

She was tempted to rip out the page.

In her early days here she would have. When she realized that, she thought, *Perhaps the change takes place without your knowing it. Maybe it doesn't require the dramatic revelation that other patients experience.*

She closed the book and decided to drop it off at Joyce Scott's office on her way to supper. She went to the mirror over her chest of drawers and stared into it.

The puffiness, the pallid color, were gone. If she were preparing for a performance tonight, she would use entirely different makeup from what she had been using the last few years. Less color, to allow more of her natural skin tone to dominate. Her eyes would not need nearly so much, with their natural blue coming through so clear and shining. The desert sun had done well by her. And the exercise.

Or, she thought, *is it merely going twenty-one whole days without a drink?*

Merely? There was nothing mere about it. She still had moments of stress during the day, and at times in the middle of the night, when she craved that one drink. Just one.

But another day had passed. She was still here, still dry.

At supper, several patients came over to her table to compliment her on Alice.

"Such a beautiful child. She has your coloring. And her uncle's dimples," Joe Bigelow said. "What a family!"

He laughed. Kitzi tried to laugh with him, but she barely succeeded.

* * *

309

Henry Denker

Dr. Woolman peered at her as he lit his pipe. "The reason I advanced your hour this week was that Scotty took the liberty of showing me the latest entry in your journal. I found it extremely revealing."

Ill at ease, Kitzi tried to joke her way out of the situation. "Revealing good? Or revealing bad?"

"A bit of both," Woolman said.

"You psychiatrists are always so willing to stand squarely in the middle of the road. Doesn't your behind get sore from constantly sitting on the fence? Don't you get professional hemorrhoids?"

"The good was your reaction to your daughter. You are now more aware of the damage you've done to her. And that it is going to demand a great deal of repair."

"What about the 'bad'?"

"The bad . . . yes," Woolman said. "It's about Morse——"

Angrily, Kitzi anticipated, "You're going to say that the moment didn't occur. It was a hallucination on my part. I wanted it so much that I deceived myself. Well, you're wrong. I know him. I know myself. I know that magic when it happens."

"I wasn't referring to that," Woolman corrected.

Kitzi feared that in her protest she had exposed too much of herself.

"The invitation to the White House," Woolman pointed out.

"You think he was lying about that," Kitzi half stated, half anticipated.

"Quite the contrary," Woolman said. "By the way, what is his situation? Married? Single? Divorced?"

"Married."

"I see," Woolman replied, without revealing anything. "Now, about the White House. Let us try to put ourselves in his situation. He has this client for whom he cares a great deal, personally as well as professionally. The call comes from the White House. Would Kitzi Mills be in condition to accept an invitation to lead off the anti-drug campaign? If he were a greedy theatrical agent, he would get on the phone at once and hit you with a fast pitch that would make you commit yourself. He didn't do that, did he?"

"No," she admitted.

"He came here with that invitation in his hip pocket, saying to

310

himself, I won't mention it unless, when I see her, I believe that she *can* make it. I don't want to impose any additional burden on her."

"That would be Marvin," she agreed.

"So I think you have both an invitation to the White House and your agent's assurance that *he* thinks you can do it."

"But you said it was bad," she reminded.

"Well, the greater the opportunity, the greater the defeat if one fails."

"And you think I'm going to fail?" Kitzi demanded.

"No. But *you* do," Woolman pointed out.

"I could be in shape to sing at the White House in a week!" Kitzi defied.

Woolman shook his head slowly.

"What do you want me to do?" she asked.

"Prove that you're ready to leave here. Strong enough to leave. Take the Fifth Step."

"Admit to God, myself, and at least one other human being the exact nature of the wrongs I've committed?"

"That's how you begin making amends to the people you've harmed."

"I told you once before, I am not going to flagellate myself in public!"

"No one asked for blood. Or physical torture. Just open up. Confess your wrongs."

"Please! If there's one thing I can't abide it's being preached to!" She gave action to her words by starting for the door.

"Miss Mills! Don't leave! Not on that note."

Slowly she turned back to face him.

"I know Step Five can be painful," Woolman said. "But, unlike alcoholism, it is never fatal."

59

Kitzi returned to her room after the late morning lecture to find Joyce Scott unpacking a new arrival.

The woman appeared to be in her forties. She was actually only thirty-four, dark-haired, petite, very pale, but with good features. She was trying to conceal her shakes, but she could not hide them from Kitzi, who thought, *Poor girl, I know the feeling.*

"Mills, I want you to meet your new roommate, Ethel Chalmers. Mrs. Chalmers, this is——"

Before Scott could conclude the introduction, Ethel Chalmers interrupted, "I know! Kitzi Mills! I'd recognize you anywhere. I'm a big fan of yours."

"Thanks," Kitzi said. "But you'll discover that around here there are no fans, and no stars. We're all the same. Patients."

Christ, Kitzi thought, *did I say that? Isn't that what Bertha said to me on my first day? It sounds so familiar.*

The timid, trembling young woman appeared not nearly so frightened as she had been.

Joyce Scott had confiscated from her luggage all perfumes, mouthwash, and other articles that might contain alcohol. She was on her way out when she cast back over her shoulder, "Mills will acquaint you with the routine. And your Granny will be in to give you your assignment."

"Assignment?" the young woman asked, puzzled.

Kitzi began to explain, just as three weeks ago Bertha Shawn had explained to her.

During her explanation of hours, group sessions, and lectures, Kitzi kept thinking, *I wonder how Bertha is doing? Is she making it? Or has she gone back? God, I hope not.*

Aloud, she heard herself saying, "Don't worry, Ethel. We're like a family here. We worry about each other. Before you know it, you'll be part of the family."

How can I be so reassuring when inside I'm still shaky myself. Or is that the way the game works? You get better by trying to help someone else. I've got to call Gus. He'll get a big kick out of me trying to encourage another "inmate," as he called us.

She had to wait to use the corridor phone. Calvin was on. He was talking to his agent. Kitzi could not avoid overhearing.

"Look, Marty, I'm getting along great. I get up before six and do an hour of calisthenics. I run at least five miles a day. I'm in terrific shape. I'm not demanding my old position back. I'm only asking for a tryout."

What Marty said was obvious, for Calvin replied, half in pride, half in anger, "Pass a urine test? You can fucking well tell them I can pass any test they got! I am clean, Marty, c-l-e-a-n, clean!"

Calvin's declaration must have had the desired effect, for Kitzi heard him say, "I'm due to leave here in five days. I will meet their doctors in New York or Washington, wherever they say!"

He hung up, his face glistening. His voice had been strong and convincing. But he was scared and uncertain. He was again the gentle young man as he asked, "Kitzi, mind if I call my grandmother first and tell her?"

Calvin made his call. Fortunately, his grandmother was home to receive it. Calvin told her of his conversation with his agent.

The next Kitzi heard, Calvin was saying, "Grandma, please . . . Please? Don't cry. I know you're happy. But don't cry. Okay, go ahead. If you're enjoying it, cry."

After a few moments he was saying, "Don't worry. I'll pass. I'm clean. And I'm going to stay clean. Grandma, please, no more crying. That's better. Good girl. Good girl."

He hung up.

"She's a terrific crier," he apologized. "You should have seen her the first game I played in the NBA. She about drowned the people in the seats around her."

Kitzi kissed him on the cheek. "No matter what you say, you're very sweet."

Calvin started away. Kitzi dialed the number.

"Gus?" she asked as soon as she heard the phone lifted.

"This is his nurse."

Kitzi's instantaneous reaction was, *God, he's had a relapse! Else he would have answered the phone himself.*

"May I talk to him?"

"Just a moment," the nurse said.

He came on the phone with his usual bravado, pretending an aside to his nurse. "That Mills woman insists on pursuing me. I keep telling her she's too old for me. Doesn't stop her." Then, still pretending, he said directly into the phone, "Hello? Who is this?"

"Listen, you old bastard, don't play games with me." She, too, was pretending, because she was disturbed by his marked breathiness. "You okay?"

"Okay? I'm great!" Then he admitted, "I was doing my exercises. Breathing exercises. Something to do with lung development, keeping my chest clear, avoiding pneumonia. Besides, I figure there's no harm in breathing. First thing they teach them in medical school is to keep the patient breathing long enough to pay the bill.

"How are all the inmates?" Chamberlain went on, trying to sound casual. "And how are you? Level with me," he insisted.

"I'm okay. Really," she insisted, wavering a little.

"Kitz . . ." and he sounded more serious now, "Kitz, strange things happen to a man when he knows he's facing death. I went into this thing thinking, I don't give a damn whether I live or die. Last thing I'll want before I go under will be a cigarette and a drink. But when it actually happened, I discovered that I do give a damn. So, the last thing, Kitz, you're not going to believe what this old cynic did just before they put that ether cone over my ugly face. I prayed. Prayed to see another day. And when I came to in the recovery room, first thing I thought was, Thanks, it's good to be around. And the second thing I thought, I've got to talk to Kitz. They say only fifty percent out there make it. She has got to be one of that fifty percent! Got to! So Kitz, I want to hear it from you. Let me hear it!"

"Okay, Gus. I'll be one of the fifty percent who make it."

"Good," he said, then could not resist adding, "If they'd let me I'd light a cigarette to celebrate. But the sons of bitches around here . . ."

Kitzi could hear his nurse call out, "Mr. Chamberlain, I've warned you!"

"See what I mean," he said into the phone.

"Take care, Gus, please?" Kitzi implored.

"Sure," he said, pretending confidence, "I want to be around a while. I want to see who the next president is. How we do in Central America. Whether the Japanese buy St. Patrick's Cathedral. And if the Mets ever win another World Series. So I'll be around. And I want you to be around, too. So don't leave there without being cured. Whatever they ask of you, do it. Promise?"

"Promise."

She hung up the phone. She knew she was due in group. But feeling such relief and joy about Gus, she went down the hall to the small chapel. She knelt before the bare, bleached wood altar.

"Dear God, I want to thank You for saving old Gus . . ." she began. She stopped. *No,* she admitted, *that's not why I'm here. Gus has already done that. I'm here for myself. If I'm ever to take Step Five, You and I have to come to an agreement. You know what I'm talking about. My grandfather. You allowed him to go on doing what he did to me, and then you let him pray. Tell me why!*

He made me feel dirty and ashamed all my life. So ashamed that I never dared to feel alive except when I was onstage being someone else. Katherine Millendorfer has always been ashamed of Katherine Millendorfer. The beauty other people saw in me? When I looked in the mirror I never saw that. I saw only the little girl I really was. Dirty. Ashamed. Disgraced. Sometimes I think that's why it took so much vodka for me to get through making up.

Yet, You let him pray to You. I hated You for listening to him. I would hate you now. Except now, I need you. Like Gus needed you. And not for myself alone. But for Alice. I don't want to do to her what my mother did to me. So help me now and I'll believe in You again. I'll even forgive You for everything that happened. That's right. I'll forgive You, God. You don't get an offer like that very often, do You?

The truth is, I'm terrified. I know that unless I face You, make peace with You, I won't make it. I need Your help. But it's up to You. It's up to You!

She became aware that her pulse was racing. She could feel her heart pounding in her chest. A trickle of sweat traced the bridge of her nose.

Her mouth felt dry, cotton dry. Her tongue was suddenly too big. A drink. She desperately needed a drink. She caught herself reaching as if for a glass. She thought, *God, I'm like old Gus with his cigarettes, reaching for them without being aware. We addicts are all alike, all alike.*

It wasn't supposed to happen this way, she knew. When you came close to God, you were supposed to be helped. Not left desperately wanting a drink.

She started from the little chapel, knowing she was late for group

315

and would be called on to explain. But how could she, without being considered demented?

At the door she stopped long enough to look back, as if expecting a reply from the altar.

There was none, of course.

60

"If it was a prayer, it was very unconventional," Kitzi admitted to Dr. Woolman.

"The important thing is that you acknowledged His existence, even if only to reprimand Him."

"What now?" she asked.

"Let it happen," Woolman suggested. "Start being honest with yourself. What wrongs have you committed? What harm have you done to others because of your drinking? To your daughter? Your friend and agent? People whose careers you've hurt in some way?"

"All that?" Kitzi asked forlornly.

"You know the list better than I do," Woolman said. "Of course, to properly complete the fifth and final step, you'll have to confess your wrongs, not only to God but to another person as well."

"To you," she assumed.

"I'm a professional. That would be too easy. Select someone else in whom you can confide, and with whom you will be completely honest. That will be more painful than talking to me. But I believe that kind of pain is part of the process."

At afternoon group, Kitzi felt compelled to speak first.

"I talked with Gus Chamberlain earlier today."

"How is he?" Calvin asked.

"Is he okay?" Laurie Coombs asked.

"Has the operation succeeded?" Joe Bigelow wanted to know.

"The operation must have gone well. He sounds like his nasty old self," Kitzi reported.

"Did they say anything about his prognosis?"

"He didn't say. But I think it's good."

It was evening. Quiet time. It had been a full day, a taxing day. Both Kitzi Mills and Ethel Chalmers were at their desks, writing in their journals. Or trying to. Both did a great deal of writing and then crossing out.

"Doesn't it ever get easier?" Ethel asked.

"It does, after a while," Kitzi assured. "Of course, some nights, when you have a particular problem, it's more difficult than usual."

"Can I tear out the things I don't like?"

"Sometimes the less you like it, the better it is to get it said. Scott'll explain that to you."

"Some of the things that I think are pretty terrible. There's my husband, my three kids, all the promises I made to them, and the only thing I can think about is a drink," the woman confessed.

"Write it down. That won't shock anybody around here," Kitzi said.

She started a new page in her own journal, writing, "What happened this morning, my call with Gus, my session with Dr. Woolman . . ." She crossed that out and started again. Then she crossed out what she had just written, tore out the page, and ripped it into bits.

"I'm going out to the lounge for a cup of coffee."

The lounge was almost empty. In the far corner, curled up on one of the sofas, deeply involved in reading one of the prescribed books, was Laurie Coombs. She was so immersed in the book that she groped vaguely for her coffee cup and almost upset it when she finally made contact. She looked up, greeted Kitzi with a slight wave and a smile, then resumed reading.

Kitzi poured herself a cup of coffee, found a place on one of the couches, and opened her journal. She made several attempts at writing but finally quit. She was content to sip her coffee and just think.

Of all her thoughts and remembrances, the one that surfaced most often was Gus's voice, gravelly, breathy, as he pleaded, "Promise me you'll be one of the fifty percent who make it!"

She took up her journal once more and wrote, *"Miss Scott, I have an important request to make."*

* * *

"Special visiting privilege for Mr. Morse?" Joyce Scott asked. "One reason we do not like to depart from the rules, as we did for your daughter Alice, is that it only leads to more requests. Is there some special reason why you wish to see Mr. Morse?"

"Yes," Kitzi said.

"This can't be handled by phone?"

"I don't think my treatment here can be completed without seeing Mr. Morse," Kitzi said.

Scott's puzzled look required an explanation.

"I think I may be ready for Step Five."

"Sarah!" Marvin Morse called from his private office. "Sarah! Where the hell is that woman?"

"Here the hell," Sarah said, stepping through the doorway to deliver a steaming cup of coffee. "Here. Not too hot. Not too cold. Just like you ordered. So you don't have to yell."

"Never mind the coffee. The tickets! Did you get our tickets on the Concorde?" Marvin asked.

"Got the tickets," the old woman assured him. "Got the river room at the Savoy. Got the limo to JFK. Got the Rolls from Gatwick. Got the supper reservations in the Grill. Anything else?"

"Did you check with Florence?"

"Checked. *She* is all packed. *You* are all packed."

"Oh," he reminded her, "don't let me forget to call Alice before we leave."

"I will not forget to not let you forget to call the child," Sarah assured him as she left the office.

61

It was four o'clock in the afternoon. Marvin had taken care of the important East Coast calls. The West Coast calls would have to await his return from London. Any producer or studio that wanted one of his clients would want him or her even more eight days from now. In show business, frustration makes the heart grow fonder. And more extravagant.

He seized his tan cashmere topcoat from the closet and his battered old tweed plaid hat, and was on his way to the door when he found himself confronted by Sarah.

The apologetic look in her eyes alerted him.

"Sarah?" he asked in a tone that demanded, *What have you done this time?*

"I tried to explain you're on your way to London. She said it was important. She wanted to talk to you for just a minute."

"*She?* Kitzi?"

Sarah nodded. He turned back to his desk, Sarah calling to him, "I told her you were in a rush!"

He lifted the phone.

"Kitzi! You all right?" he asked, fearful that she was not, which would account for her unexpected call.

"Marvin, I have to see you."

"See me . . . You mean, come to New York? Before your twenty-eight days are over?" He was terrified that she was about to flee The Retreat.

"No. I have to see you out here."

"Can it wait eight days? I'm on my way to London."

When she responded, he detected the deep disappointment in her voice. "Okay, I'll wait," she said, and hung up.

Disappointment? Or fear? He wondered.

"Sarah! Get Dr. Woolman for me!"

She knew the number well. She dialed at once. In moments she reported, "He's off the grounds. Out to lunch."

"Damn!"

"Mrs. Morse and the limo are waiting downstairs," Sarah reminded.

"Okay, okay," he said. He thought and decided. "I'll only be gone eight days. Eight days can't make that much difference."

They were in the elegant departure lounge which British Airways reserves for Concorde travelers. Florence could tell that Marvin was troubled. After seven years of marriage, she had learned all the signs. He would rub his left thumb against the slight dark bristle of beard that shadowed his face by late afternoon. The dimple in his right cheek always seemed deeper due to the tension in his jaw. And he was noticeably silent. At such times it was best to leave him alone. She assumed some important deal had gone wrong at the last minute.

So she thought, until he lifted the phone alongside his armchair and made a credit-card call to a number in the 619 area. She had too many clients in that part of California not to recognize the desert locale.

Florence's immediate reaction was denial. *It doesn't have to be her! Tony Frascati. Dinah Shore, Kirk Douglas. There are a dozen people he would have reason to call in the desert. It doesn't have to be her.*

But she knew that it was when Marvin asked, "Dr. Woolman, please? Marvin Morse calling. It's urgent."

In moments, Woolman was on the phone.

"Doctor, earlier today I received a call from Miss Mills. She wanted to see me." He tried to avoid Florence's eyes but could not. Nevertheless, he continued, "She sounded extremely disappointed when I said I was on my way to London. What is her condition?"

"I think . . . I hope . . . she's on the verge of the final breakthrough. It could be crucial."

"Does she need me?"

"If she called, she needs you."

"Can it wait eight days?" Marvin asked.

"One never knows. I've seen patients come this far, and, for one reason or another, pass that point without making it. They just leave. And eventually go back to drinking."

"Doctor, if I come out there, would it help?"

"Based on my last session with her, yes!"

Marvin hung up the phone slowly and turned to Florence. "Dr. Woolman said——"

Florence interrupted, "Don't explain."

"I have to explain," he insisted.

"No. You don't even have to apologize. Just go!"

"Florence, honey, please . . ."

"She has her addiction. You have yours. Is there anything you want me to do in London?" she asked, trying to conceal her hurt by appearing businesslike.

"See the show. See if it's worth bringing over. If Carrie Engelhardt is up to the role. The Shuberts like her."

"If you hurry," Florence said, "American has a six o'clock to Los Angeles. You can be there tonight."

"I better get going," he said, gathering up his coat, hat, and attaché case. He kissed her on the cheek, which was all she offered. "I'll make it up to you," he whispered.

"Of course," she said.

Both knew he never could.

Marvin caught the six o'clock into Los Angeles. He rented a car and drove down toward the desert. In less than two hours he pulled off the Interstate. In fifteen minutes he was at Tony Frascati's house.

Marvin pulled up just as one of Tony's dinner parties was breaking up. Tony was still in the doorway waving good-bye to his guests. As the last car pulled away, he discovered Marvin.

"Hey, paisan! What are you doing here? You look like you need a drink! Real bad! And maybe a little supper. I myself cooked the sauce for the angel hair tonight!"

They were in Frascati's den, a large room of native stone, soft luxurious leather, and rich, deeply polished wood. On the paneled walls hung what seemed an endless number of framed gold recordings, tributes to his artistry and his international popularity. Frascati was offering Marvin a second drink when his servant entered with a bowl of steaming angel-hair spaghetti in Frascati's pesto sauce.

Frascati put aside the glass of Scotch he had offered.

"With my own recipe I always include a special Chianti Classico that could make sex go out of style. Marco!" he ordered his man.

Marvin wanted to eat so he could compliment his host, but after two mouthfuls he gave up. Marco returned to present the bottle of Chianti for Frascati's approval.

"Never mind. I have a hunch Mr. Morse will be on Scotch the rest of the night," Frascati said.

Marvin was keenly aware that Frascati had never asked about, or even alluded to, Kitzi Mills. It was part of the man's code. If you wanted to talk, you did. If you chose not to, he valued your right to privacy as much as he prized his own.

Marvin sipped his Scotch until the silence became too much even for him.

"I talked to her psychiatrist," he began. "He said this might be it. Good or bad, this might be it."

"You want to talk, okay. But you look like you could use sleep even more," Frascati said. "Here." He held out the open bottle of scotch. "This'll help. Same cottage. Same suite. Or if you'd rather just sit here and drink, that's okay too. But you look like a man who does not need company tonight. See you in the morning."

Marvin pulled into the grounds of The Retreat at nine o'clock on a bright, cloudless desert morning. The air was cool and fresh. It promised to be a crisp, comfortable day.

He was shown to Dr. Woolman's office.

Woolman said only, "I can't give you any advice, or any suggestions. This is something she must do for herself. Just listen, that's all."

Joyce Scott escorted him down the corridor to the hand-carved double doors, where she paused to say, "This is the chapel. She asked to see you in here."

That sounded strange to Marvin. He entered with considerable apprehension.

62

Kitzi was sitting on the front bench, facing the altar of the small chapel. At the sound of the door, she turned to look at Marvin. He found himself staring at what he used to call "pure Kitzi Mills," meaning that she was wearing no makeup, her opalescent skin bright and shining. A sudden stab of memory brought back those mornings when he would catch her emerging from the shower, drying herself, drops of water gleaming on her glowing skin.

There had been a marked improvement in her appearance in just the past week, he realized.

Her blond hair was tied back with a simple red ribbon. She wore a slim, tailored flannel skirt and a blue cashmere sweater. If he could forget the intervening twelve years, he would have accepted her as the young Kitzi Mills again. He went to her, kissed her. A light, side-of-the-cheek kiss.

"It was nice of you to come on such short notice," she apologized.

He realized that she was tense, in contrast to the placid physical image she presented.

A little lie might help relieve her guilt. So he said, "Fortunately, London was only a short vacation. Since it's too early for the TV season, too late for Broadway, I have plenty of time."

"Did Dr. Woolman say anything?"

"He said that was for you to do."

"Yes, yes, it is," she said, turning away from him.

She began to pace in the confined area of the modest chapel. She seemed to be steeling herself to the moment. He could remember seeing her lapse into such meditative silences before an audition, or before venturing into a new scene. She had always been the best judge of when she was ready.

She turned to him suddenly. There were tears in her eyes. "Whatever else this is going to be, it can't be a performance! If I am ever going to be honest with myself and with the world, it had damn well better be now!"

He hoped that his face did not betray his surprise and concern. For he had not been prepared for this.

"Five Steps," she continued. "That's what they demand here. It's as holy to them as the Stations of the Cross to a Catholic. Because, unless you do all five, you don't 'graduate.' I guess if they don't show you to the door as a failure, it can be called graduating. Or if you don't run out on your own in the middle of the night, as some have.

"But Step Five is the toughest. Especially for me. It demands that I admit to God and to another human being the exact nature of all

323

my wrongs. Well, with my list, this could be one of those plays the Royal Shakespeare Company brings over that run eight hours."

She tried to smile to indicate she was joking. She couldn't quite carry it off.

"Well, we've got God here. They say He likes to be talked to in places like this. That's why I asked to meet you in here. Never thought that would happen. Not you, I mean, but meeting in a place like this. My old grandfather. I never did tell you much about him, did I?"

"That he was a minister was about all," Marvin said.

"He was that. And more. A child molester."

"You never said anything . . ."

"No, I never said anything," she admitted.

"Was he ever arrested?"

"No."

"Then how do you know?"

"The best way a child can know. Or the worst."

"You?" Marvin dared to ask.

"And my mother before me."

"Oh, God," he said in a whisper.

"Remember when you confronted me, demanded, 'Why couldn't you say no to Wainwright? Run away? Leave his house? Leave Hollywood?' That's why. He was my grandfather again. I was a child again. Defenseless. Alone. Terrified. So I . . . I just let him . . . what is the phrase? I let him have his way with me. You think the drinking began in Boston twelve years ago. It began in a little wooden rectory alongside a little wooden church in a little town in Minnesota. When I got drunk on communion wine so he could do what he liked to me.

"In Boston, the drinking only resumed so I could endure being victimized again. By Edith Cullen. After that, it went on. As you know. Except for one time. Once I decided to have Alice, I did not touch a drop of liquor for seven whole months. Nothing. I did not want to infect her the way my mother infected me. I didn't want to pass on the disease."

"Kitz, you don't have to worry about her. She's a terrific child," Marvin reassured her. "You've done a great job with her."

"Have I?" Kitzi disputed. "By now I get the feeling that, sitting up there, He is getting impatient. He's saying, 'Bullshit! This is supposed to be a confession of wrongs committed. And all I hear are excuses, and sly little solicitations for forgiveness and praise.' And He's right!

"That 'great job' I've done with Alice. Marvin, if you knew. If you only knew. The times she found me on the floor, passed out. And the times she found a man there.

"Once she asked me about that. In her elegant private school, where the divorce rate is very high, kids discuss things like that. 'Mommy, most of the other girls' mothers have a boyfriend stay over. But it's always the same one. Why are yours always different?' Try to explain that to an eight-year-old child—that's how old she was then.

"And the shame. Shame made a prisoner of her. Talk about wrongs? She wouldn't dare ask a friend to stay over. Or even come visit. Because she never knew how she'd find me. What if she had a sleep-over and I came home drunk that night, with my own sleep-over, whoever the hell he was?

"I guess the closest she's come to a life that was normal and domestic has been the last three-and-a-half weeks with you and Florence. At first I thought Florence was trying to steal her away from me. Until I realized she's a warm, loving person. You're very lucky, Marvin, to have her."

I am, he thought, *but how lucky is she for having me?*

"Marvin, I haven't told anyone . . . not even Dr. Woolman. But there have been times, desperate times, when I have wanted a drink so bad I was ready to escape from here. Once, I actually did try but was brought back by my roommate. But other times, especially after the first few phone calls with Alice, when I said to myself, She sounds happy with Florence, with Marvin. If I died, committed suicide, they would take her, I'm sure. After all, she's his daughter. He must know that by now. So it would all work out. The three of them would have a good life together.

"I would argue to myself, It's the least you can do for Alice. Die. You see, always, always I find it necessary to put myself in the role of the self-sacrificing victim. Never did I think living is better than

325

dying. Somehow you don't get much attention or sympathy for living. Why is that?"

He tried to interject, but she suppressed him with a simple gesture. She had a need to tell it all, or it would never be told.

"Florence. I've hated her. For years. I kept the hope alive, much as I needed to resent you, that one day you'd come back. One day, like in some wonderful emotional third act, you'd come back to me and to Alice. But there was always Florence. I feel a great deal of guilt about her. For hating her. Resenting her. Blaming her.

"It wasn't only hating her for something she never did. She didn't take you away from me. I drove you away. She took you in. She stuck with you. Putting up with all the troubles, the inconveniences, the nights when you had to come rescue me. Or bail me out. Or cover up some nasty story that would have ruined my career.

"She must be a very patient woman, a saint. Really, what does Florence say about me?"

"No matter what you think, Kitz, she's always respected you. Your talent. And she knows talent. She's a real pro."

Despite the tears in her eyes, Kitzi smiled. "Respected me? My talent? I'll bet."

"She's always said you were the best, Kitz. No one but Streisand can match you, she said."

"Was that all she said? Nothing about the real me? The drinking me? The me who blew that whole show and cost John Firestone three million dollars? John, who helped make me a star. When the time came to pay him back, when he was down on his luck, and his real estate millions were gone, who sent him into bankruptcy?"

"Kitzi, you can't blame yourself. It wasn't a very good show." Marvin tried to ease her guilt.

"No, Marvin, it wasn't a very good show. But I have made 'not very good' shows into hits. Because people came to see Kitzi Mills. But the young Kitzi Mills. The one they remembered. Not the drunken lush who missed cues. Who sang off-key two and three times in a single number. If John were here now—poor bastard, he was a gentleman. If he were alive today, he's the one I should be confessing to."

She began to weep freely.

"I'm frightened, Marvin. The more I think, the more I talk, the more frightened I become. Because with every thought, someone else comes to mind, someone else I've harmed. Ghosts. My life is full of ghosts. The strangest one, that girl. I don't even remember her name. A dancer. Blonde. About my size. And very good. She dared to come to my dressing room. I say dared, because she was so timid she could hardly talk.

"There I was before my makeup mirror, with my trusty glass of vodka on the table. I was making up. She came in. I watched her in the mirror as she stumbled through her little speech. She had always admired me, that sort of opening. I was her idol. An all-around performer. Dancer, singer, actress."

Kitzi laughed, shaking her head and causing the tears to run even faster.

"I thought she was going to ask for my autograph. But no, she was asking for advice, help, my opinion. She wanted to audition for me. And I, being a little drunk and generous at the moment, said, 'Sure, why not? Tonight, after the show.'

"Frankly, I would have forgotten if the girl hadn't shown up in my dressing room later, still in makeup and costume. She was ready. By that time I was pretty well loaded, but I went out front, sat down in the third row, on the aisle. Seems I wasn't alone. The stage manager had waited. And some members of the cast. Her friends. All there to root for her.

"I was pretty impatient, wanting to get on to more serious drinking. The orchestra pianist had waited to be her accompanist. He had lead sheets from what looked like a dozen songs. This was going to be a real serious audition. He began to play the intro for her first number. I forget what it was. She began to sing. Not a big voice but great warmth, great charm. This kid had the quality I used to have.

"I sat there, watching as much as listening. She was beautiful. So innocent. Country fresh. Beguiling, I guess, is a word the critics would use. Some of the words they used to use about me. I thought, That's me, ten years ago. Another two years and she's ready to replace me. When producers say, 'We need a young Kitzi Mills,' there she was, two years away. Well, I may have been drunk, but I wasn't stupid. I wasn't going to create my own competition. I wasn't going to be obvious either. So I waited through three songs. By which time I knew how good that girl was.

"In the middle of her fourth number I stood up . . . God, I cringe every time I think of it now. I stood up, and in my—you know how I can play the star when I want to—well, that night I did it up brown. I stood up, wavering only a little, and I said, 'My dear child, you don't call that singing, do you?' I could tell by the look on her face that the world had just come to an end for her. But I went on, 'If you've been taking lessons, you should get your money back. That little voice is never going to get you anywhere. I'm surprised your teachers haven't told you. No, if I were you, I'd stick to dancing. But I would keep my mouth very tightly shut!'

"With that, I started up the aisle, leaving the girl in tears. Poor kid, she left the show at the end of the week. I don't know what happened to her. But I often wonder."

She was unaware she was weeping until Marvin handed her his handkerchief.

"A whole gallery of victims. So many that I can't even remember them all." She seized on the name again as if recapturing it. "Florence. You didn't tell me. What does she say about me?"

"I told you," he said.

"What does she say about me those nights after you've had Alice to dinner?"

"She feels very sorry for Alice. And for you."

"She doesn't tell you how lucky you are that you never married me?"

"No."

She stopped wiping her eyes long enough to glance at him to question if he were telling her the truth.

"No," he repeated more firmly.

"Then let *me* tell you. The luckiest thing you ever did was the day you walked out on me," she said. "Miserable as I've made you as my agent, it would have been worse, far worse, if you'd married me."

"Things might have been different if I had married you," he said.

"One thing you learn here. This isn't something that comes from unhappiness. There are people here, men and women, with perfectly wonderful families, devoted families. Yet they're drunks. It's a sickness. Not a reflection of unhappiness. We make our own unhappiness by drinking. Or drugging. Men with important jobs. Women from terrific families. I see them when they visit. So it isn't unhappiness. All I would have done was destroy your life."

"Poor Alice," she went on. "The hurt in her eyes after each drunken episode. The guilt I felt each time. I used to keep consoling myself by saying, 'At least I didn't have an abortion. I saw it through. On my own. I gave her the best start an infant could have.' But now I've destroyed it."

"She's doing fine, Kitz. She's a strong child, resilient."

"She's still so young, how can you tell?"

"That's one thing Florence and I do talk about those nights after we drop her off at your place. How much a person she is in her own right. She has definite tastes and opinions."

"Like the first time I called her from here, and she said, 'Mommy, don't come home'?" Kitzi asked, still feeling the pain of that call.

"Yes," Marvin said. "Like that time when she was mature enough to know what was best for you."

"You have no idea how great that makes a mother feel, to be told by her own child, 'Stay there until you kick the habit,' " Kitzi said caustically. "And you and Florence talked about that. How nice!"

"Kitz . . . ," he tried to mollify.

"I'm sorry," she said at once. "That's one of the troubles I have about Florence. I hate her, I envy her, and I respect her, all at the same time. You can't understand that. You love people. Or you don't. A deal is good or bad. Which makes you such a tough bargainer. Me, I'm full of mixed feelings. I used to know what I wanted. Everything was so clear in those days. They say that alcohol, after enough of it for a long enough time, does something to the brain. Maybe that's it."

"No, it isn't," Marvin corrected. "I talked to a doctor over at the medical center."

"Dr. Gordon?" Kitzi asked.

"Mrs. Armbruster said I could call. Gordon said No, no brain damage. What neurological damage there was would heal, if you stayed dry."

"Maybe it's age," she said. "Whatever it is, I'm determined to change that now. The treatment here sort of sneaks up on you. In the beginning you resist it. The lectures, the group sessions, reading, writing your own journal—you don't believe it even makes sense. You just go through it because life is easier in here than fighting the world outside. But somehow, that stuff seeps into your mind, even while you're resenting it. Until one day, for some unknown reason, you realize it's happened to you.

"Like right now. Here I am doing something I never in a million years imagined I would do, or could do. Confessing my guilts, my sins—to you, of all people. If someone had said that to me a month ago I would have said, 'Anyone, anyone but him.' Yet here we are. And here I am. In this little chapel. Me. In a church."

She smiled through her tears. "God has one hell of a sense of humor.

"When I get back, I want to see Florence," she said. "You tell her I want to thank her in person for what she's done for Alice these past weeks."

"That's not necessary, Kitzi," he said.

"An obligation like this cannot be discharged with a sweet little note, or a meaningless bottle of expensive perfume. This is something one woman has to say to another. I'll see her when I get back to New York." After a moment she decided, "No, one thing I've learned here. If you feel the impulse to do something good, do it. I'll call her. Tonight. Supper time here is nine o'clock in New York."

"She's not in New York. London," he said.

"She's in London alone and you're here . . ." She considered. "Marvin?"

"Dr. Woolman said you had to see me at once."

That provoked a fresh flow of tears. "Marvin, don't you see, every time you make another sacrifice for me, it only adds another burden. Another layer of guilt."

"Kitz, there's no need to feel guilty. I'm glad to do it, glad to do anything, if it helps you get well."

"I've harmed you most of all," she insisted. "I should have let you go. But I held you by making you my agent. Made you divide your

330

life, share it with two women. One woman gave you all of herself. The other one only took. Can you ever forgive me?"

"None of us chooses to be sick," he said.

"That's no excuse," she insisted, wiping back her tears. "I don't have to be sick. I have been well for almost four weeks. Not so well that I don't feel the same craving. But now I don't give in to it. In the beginning, those first days, I hated you for forcing me to come here. But these last few days, especially since Gus, I'm glad you did. Now, if I could only find some way to repay you. To set you free . . ."

He was tempted to tell her what Florence had said, that she had lost the battle, was ready to give him up.

"Marvin, would you mind——"

"Mind what?" he asked.

"If I told Alice who her father is. With each year she grows more curious."

"These past weeks I've been tempted to tell her myself. Florence thinks I should."

"I'll have to find the right time," Kitzi said. "And I'll have to feel strong enough myself."

"Do it your own way, Kitz," he urged. "She deserves to know. And I like to think she won't mind me being her father."

She nodded thoughtfully.

"Shall I see you back to your room?" he asked.

"No, thanks. I'd like to remain here for a while. Lately I find this little room very comforting."

He kissed her on the cheek and started for the door. She called to him.

"Marvin?" Once he turned to face her, she said, "That concert at the White House. It's not something you engineered, something you cooked up, is it?"

"They want you, Kitz, I swear. They really hope you can make it."

"I've been thinking about it, working on it. I was even thinking, . . . Remember my song—Boston, Chauncey Weems, John Firestone, that dear man? I thought I might like to sing that one. I haven't sung it in so long."

"Good idea," he said, encouraged by her attitude.

331

"You wouldn't mind?"

"Mind? I've always loved that song. In a way, it was a triumph for both of us."

"That's what I mean. To me it's always been our song."

"I won't mind. I'd love it," he encouraged.

On his way out, Marvin Morse stopped at Dr. Woolman's office. "Sorry to have imposed. I upset all your plans, didn't I?" Woolman asked.

"Glad I came. If facing the truth about herself will do it, I think she's almost home."

"We'll see," Woolman said. "At my next session, we'll see."

"She said she's seriously considering that White House recital. In your opinion, is that too ambitious a goal for someone just coming out of here?"

"You mean, will the stress cause her to go back?" Woolman phrased the question for him.

"Yes," Marvin admitted.

"How are we to know if she's well unless she can function at her normal activities?" the doctor asked. "Now, does that mean I guarantee her being able to carry it off? No. Any alcoholic can go back. In fact, most of those who leave here as cured go back a time or two before they finally overcome the habit. But we only discover that once they get out there. She's no different."

"What's your guess, doctor?"

"I have no guess, Mr. Morse. Like you, like the family of the alcoholic, I just wait and see," he said.

63

Four days after Marvin Morse's visit to The Retreat, Kitzi was packing. Ethel Chalmers, just completing her first ten days of treatment, hovered over her, offering her help.

Joyce Scott came in, bringing the plastic bag that contained all of Kitzi's perfumes, mouthwash, and vitamin pills. She also held in the crook of her arm a small wrapped package, tied with blue ribbon.

"Here," Scott said, handing her the plastic bag. "Your graduation present."

They both laughed. Kitzi shoved the plastic bag into her luggage, snapped the locks, and said, "Well, ready as I'll ever be."

She turned to Ethel Chalmers. Without a word, they embraced, like comrades in a war.

"I'll always remember you, Kitzi," the woman said. "You're an inspiration to me. Nights when I lie awake in bed, full of doubt, dying for a drink, I'll say to myself, 'She's making it. So can I.'"

"I think that's what this place does best," Kitzi said. "Lets patients learn from other patients. We know we're not alone. And that it is possible to beat it. Good luck, Ethel!"

Kitzi Mills and Joyce Scott walked down the long corridor toward the sunlight at the end.

"Mr. Frascati sent his car to take you to the airport," Scott said.

"That's very nice of him," Kitzi said. "In fact, there have been lots of nice people. Kind people." She glanced at Scott out of the corner of her eye. "Even the ones who have been tough have been nice."

At the door, Scott handed her the package wrapped in gift paper and tied with blue ribbon.

"What is it?" Kitzi asked.

"You can open it now, if you like," Scott said.

Kitzi untied the ribbon, opened the bright gift wrapping. She discovered her blue looseleaf journal. She looked to Scott for an explanation.

"It's yours to keep. You'll want to read it again. Maybe even write in it again, from time to time. When you feel the need to be truthful and honest with yourself."

Joyce Scott held out her hand. Kitzi took it to shake it but instead drew her close and embraced her.

"Thanks, Scotty. Thanks for everything."

"Just remember. You're never alone. No matter where you are, there are always some of us ready to help," Scott reminded. "And the most important thing—sobriety is a better, much more enjoyable way of life."

* * *

Kitzi slipped into the cool comfort of the big white limousine with the dark, tinted windows. She settled back into the luxurious cushioned seat. The car started away.

She was free. Not unafraid, but free.

She remembered her first day. How she had to steel herself to walk the dozen steps from the car to the Administration Building, determined to carry her own bag to give the lie to what she was, and the shameful condition she was in.

Her first group. The faces there. Bertha. August Chamberlain. Ward McGivney. Brad Corell. Harlan Brody. And Calvin Thompson. She'd had three cards from him since he left. They had all been strangers on the first day and friends by the end of the second week. Then, one by one, they were gone. Until she was the last of that group. Now she had gone, leaving behind her other faces, other names, to whom she had become a symbol of hope, one of those who had run the course. And, at least for the time being, had won.

She thought of Nettie Rosenstein, who had failed. Of Gus, who never had a chance to finish.

The group, her group, was not a unanimous success. For one reason or another, her group had had its defections, its fatalities.

There was still the danger that there might be more defections among them.

Two years, she recalled from one of the books and pamphlets she had been assigned to read. *Two years before you can be sure how well the treatment has succeeded. Two years . . . and a lifetime of very careful living.*

When she boarded the plane, she found a corsage of orchids on her seat. She picked it up to read the attached card. "A small tribute to a courageous lady. T.F."

Tears came to her eyes. Another kindness from Tony Frascati. Another one of the people to whom she owed so much. She must write to him as soon as she arrived home.

She fastened her seat belt. A few minutes of delay, then she felt the surge of the plane as it sped down the runway. Liftoff! They were airborne.

She breathed a sigh of relief. Until liftoff, she never quite believed that she was free and on her way home. She settled back in her seat, eyes closed, relaxed. She heard the voice of the flight attendant. "What will you have to drink, Miss Mills?"

She hesitated before responding, "Coffee, please."

The stout man in the aisle seat beside her said, "Double Scotch on rocks. Water on the side."

Once their respective beverages had been delivered, Kitzi watched furtively as her fellow passenger alternated between sipping his whiskey and stirring it with his forefinger to chill it.

How casual he is about it, she thought. *It seems so easy. So manageable. So tempting. If he can do it, why can't I? Because,* she reminded herself, *you are an alcoholic.*

She pushed the recliner button of her seat and leaned back. Just before she drifted off to sleep, she heard the stout man ask, "Stewardess? Miss? Can we do this again? And this time forget the water."

She refused wine with her lunch. She refused a drink after the plane took off again from Chicago. She was steadfast in her determination to be sober when Alice met her at the airport.

Now the plane was dipping over Manhattan, starting on its flight path across the East River toward Brooklyn on its way to La Guardia. It was early evening. The bridges were clogged with eastbound traffic, a string of red taillights as far as she could see.

The plane banked, leveled off, and commenced its run across the bay, finally touching down with a slight bump. She was home, safely home.

They were waiting for her at the loading gate. Alice and Marvin. She heard her daughter before she saw her.

"Mommy!"

The cry sent a chill through her, not one of fear or pain but of excitement and relief. It was like those nights when she tried out a new role in a new production and the audience approved with their applause.

She rushed to the gate, dropped to one knee, and embraced Alice, who greeted her with excited kisses, at the same time clinging to her

335

Henry Denker

until Marvin intervened, "Let's go!" People turned around to look, recognized Kitzi, and smiled. A man called out, "Hi, Kitzi, coming back to do a new show?"

The greeting, which should have encouraged her, unnerved her for the moment. New shows would have to wait. She had her life to resume first. She smiled, a bit tenuously, and Marvin took her by the arm. "Come, Kitz. The car's waiting."

All during the ride back to Manhattan, Kitzi kept looking at Alice, patting her hand, reassuring her. "It's going to be different, baby. From now on it's going to be different."

"I know, Mommy," Alice assured her in a quiet, mature way.

Kitzi could not avoid the feeling that her child was watching her furtively, trying not to be obvious while looking for symptoms, traces of the old habit. Kitzi tried to make light of it.

"You don't have to worry, darling. And you don't have to keep looking at me that way."

"Was I? Was I, Mommy? They said not to do that."

"Who said?" Kitzi asked, half-turning to Marvin to see if he was part of "they."

"It's a group, children of alcoholics. A younger group of Al-Anon," he explained.

Kitzi could not control the tears that welled up and overran her eyes.

"Please don't cry, Mommy. It's all right. I don't mind going. I learned a lot. It made me feel better to know. Instead of hiding in my room when it happened and just crying, with nobody to talk to or understand."

"Will you ever forgive me, baby?"

Alice took her hand, kissed it, and held it to her cheek for the rest of the drive.

At the house, the doorman and the elevator man were genuinely glad to see her.

"Evening, Miss Mills," the doorman greeted her exuberantly. "Welcome home."

On the way up, the old elevator man, who had a bit of a brogue, was cheery and openly delighted as he said, "Back just in time

336

for the good weather, Miss Mills. Park's coming to life. There's a new playground right across the way. 'Course Alice is a little too old for that now. But it's nice to see the little ones climbing and swinging and sliding. Kind of gives you the feeling that, no matter what, life goes on. Which to a grandfather is very comforting, Miss Mills."

"Here we are," he announced as the car stopped.

Evelina was waiting at the open door. *The doorman must have alerted her,* Kitzi realized. Evelina ran to hug her.

"Oh, Missy . . . Missy . . . So good to have you back, child, so good. I said many a prayer for you." Evelina leaned back from her, looked into her face. "And to look at you now, it worked. Oh, yes indeed, it worked. Well, come in, come in. I prepared a little snack. Coffee and sandwiches."

Evelina led the way. Kitzi Mills entered her own apartment as if it had been not four weeks but four years since she had last been there. She looked around at all the familiar objects which had been part of her life, so much a part that she had either taken them for granted or been too drunk to appreciate them.

Photographs on the foyer walls of previous productions, or of herself with celebrities from the world of politics, finance, diplomacy, taken not at her request but theirs. Original manuscripts of songs she had made famous, autographed and framed by the composers. Front covers of *Playbills* of all her plays and musicals.

As she looked at them, she said to Marvin, "They don't tell the whole story, do they?"

"We're going to rewrite the script, Kitz. From here on it's a new play. The bad part that happened was like being in a flop. You read the reviews, see the closing notice go up backstage, swear you'll never never do another play. Then, Monday morning, you start reading new scripts. Think of it that way. Because there's a new one waiting inside."

He indicated the living room. She started toward it. He and Alice followed. As they passed through the archway, Alice ran ahead of her to pick something off the grand piano.

"Here it is, Mommy. From the White House!" the child announced.

337

Kitzi held the engraved white, blue, and gold invitation. Her hand began to tremble slightly.

"Read it, Mommy, read it!" Alice persisted eagerly.

Below the formal invitation, handwritten, were the words, "Please, Kitzi, as a favor to an old admirer and fan." Followed by the President's initials.

She sank into the large, comfortable, red-velvet easy chair, from which she could see Central Park and, beyond it, Fifth Avenue. Though it was not yet completely dark, the park lights were on. She fingered the invitation. Alice awaited her reply. Marvin, too. The decision would have to be hers and hers alone.

"I'd need time to rehearse," she said.

"It's three weeks away," Marvin explained. "You could be an inspiration to a lot of people, young people."

"Me?" she asked. "An inspiration?"

"The First Lady put Tony Frascati in charge of the whole evening. You were her choice and his."

"Please, Mommy? Say you'll do it. Please? You have to!" The child threw her arms around Kitzi's waist to hug her. "Wait'll I show you——" She ran out of the room.

Marvin took the moment to say quietly, "Kitzi, if you don't feel up to it, I don't want you to be under any pressure."

Before she could answer Alice was back, carrying a child's dress of red velvet, with white lace collar and cuffs. "This is what I'm going to wear to the White House, Mommy. Isn't it beautiful?"

"Lovely, darling." As she fingered the soft, luxurious fabric, Kitzi said, "I had a dress like this once. Not new, but almost the same color." Tears came to her eyes as she remembered the worn, second-hand dress that had been given her as a child.

"Mommy? You're crying again," Alice said, the joy slowly going out of her young face.

"Memories, sweetheart, memories. Every child should grow up with only good memories. But somehow they never do. The things I've done to you . . ."

"Kitzi, no, not now," Marvin urged.

She wiped aside the tears, smiled, then asked, "Who picked out this lovely dress for you?"

"I picked it out, and Aunt Florence said I could have it."

"Aunt Florence," Kitzi said. She looked to Marvin.

"Florence gets a kick out of shopping. When we go to Europe, she might forget her passport but never her credit cards. She invented the slogan Don't leave home without them."

She caught his furtive glance, trying to see if his little joke had assuaged her guilt toward Florence.

Meantime, the child persisted. "Mommy, say we'll go!"

"Yes, baby, we'll go," Kitzi said.

"Oh, Mommy!" Alice exploded. "Now I can take the price tags off!" She hugged the dress to her and raced out of the room.

"Florence is so good with Alice, she really should have had children of her own," Kitzi said. "Wasn't she able to?"

Without explaining, Marvin said, "Somehow it didn't work out."

"Does she know? About Alice, I mean?"

"I never told her," he said. "But she knows."

"Sometimes, out there," Kitzi confessed, "I would think that the reason she's so nice to Alice is that she wants to expose me, wants to say to the world, 'I'm the kind of mother Alice deserves, not that drunk, Kitzi Mills.'"

"Kitz, you know I don't like that word," he protested.

"Truth, Marv. Out there, one thing you learn, truth. Especially with yourself."

"How much truth can you take, Kitz?"

She detected a change in his tone and in the look in his eyes. He was staring at her in a way that made her know he was about to reveal something of great importance to her. She did not feel quite as secure as she wanted to when she responded.

"If it's the truth, I can take it."

"Just before Alice and I came to visit you out there, Florence told me that she knew all along I was Alice's father."

"She knew? All along?"

"She said something else, too. If I wanted to leave her, she would understand. I was free to go."

Kitzi stared at him in that almost dark room, trying to fathom what he was saying.

"The truth is, Kitz, I don't want to be free," he said. "She's a great woman. And I am very lucky to have her love someone like me."

"I'm glad you know that," Kitzi said.

She kissed him on the cheek. She was tempted to hold his face close to hers, but she restrained the impulse. A year ago, a month ago, she would not have been able to accept the reality of this moment. "Will you be there? At the White House?" she asked.

"We'll be there. Most important, Alice will be there."

He had departed. She was alone. In her living room high above the park. She looked down at the trees, full and rich after the spring rains, their branches so thick with leaves that the new playground was almost totally obscured.

Evelina came into the room.

"Sandwiches, Missy? Coffee?"

"Coffee, Evelina," she said. "From now on there's going to be lots of coffee."

Evelina started to go.

"Evelina . . ." When she stopped to listen, Kitzi said, "Evelina, Marvin told me everything you did for Alice when I was gone. And what you did for me when I didn't know it. He also told me some of the things I said to you during that time. I want you to know I'm sorry."

"There's no need, Missy. I know it was the liquor talking."

"But there is a need," Kitzi insisted. "Part of the treatment. Admit my wrongs. Make amends. I'm sorry, very sorry."

As the darkness closed in, Kitzi stood at the window looking out. Alice slipped into the room to stand beside her. Kitzi put her arm around her daughter.

The phone rang. She slipped out of Alice's grasp.

Uncertainly, Kitzi answered, "Hello?"

"Miss Mills? Cynthia Moorhead."

Kitz recognized the voice and the name. An older character actress she had seen many times and admired. But they had never had the opportunity to work together.

"Yes, Miss Moorhead? What can I do for you?"

"I'm a member of an AA group that meets in the Forties. I received a phone call saying you were coming home today. I want you to know, if you need help, at any time, just call me. Also, we meet every Friday afternoon."

"The Retreat phoned to tell you about me?" Kitzi asked.

"You didn't think you were cured the moment you walked out of there, did you? It takes time."

"At least two years, they said, before you can know for sure," Kitzi admitted.

"Right. Well, during those two years, you have us. If you want us. And, by God, I hope you do. Because, alone, it's hell. Together, we can make it. Remember that."

"Thanks, Miss Moorhead."

"Cynthia," the older woman corrected softly.

"Thanks, Cynthia."

Epilogue

EPILOGUE

In the White House, one of the small rooms outside the ballroom had been set aside for the two female performers on the night's program. Two temporary dressing tables had been installed, each with its own mirror and lights.

Kitzi sat at one table, staring into the mirror, assessing her hair, her face. The White House had offered to provide her with a hairdresser and a makeup artist. Tony Frascati had offered to fly them down from New York. Kitzi had gracefully refused. She had always done her own. She would do them tonight.

Now the time had come. She sat there, immobile, staring into the mirror. Weeks of abstinence, exercise, and good, simple, healthful food had made a difference. The sun had made a difference. Her face was tanned and no longer drawn. Her blue eyes seemed bluer than ever in their pure white background. It was easier now to recall the young Kitzi Mills of those early days. In her mind she was running through the opening bars of her first number.

If I can just get past the first six bars, she thought. She smiled at herself in the mirror. *If I had been able to get past the first six bars of another kind I wouldn't be here.*

At that moment she heard Alice calling to her. "Mommy, you all right?" Kitzi turned to see Alice, in her red velvet dress, accompanied by Marvin and Florence.

"I'm fine, darling, just fine," Kitzi said.

Marvin noticed that she had not yet begun to make up. "You'll be on in ten minutes, Kitz." He went to the side table, which was set up with refreshments, filled a tumbler with water, and set it down alongside her. She stared at it, stared up at him.

"Water, Kitz, plain old water."

She smiled at him, dipped her comb into the water, and began to do her hair.

"Mommy, you nervous?"

"If Mommy wasn't nervous before a performance, she wouldn't be Kitzi Mills," she replied.

"I met the President, Mommy. He said some very nice things about you. Then he bent down and took my hand and said, 'You're as pretty as your mother.' The President, Mommy."

From outside the room the muted sound of the music that accompanied the tenor from the Metropolitan Opera was crescending to a climax. Kitzi knew she would be on next. She worked diligently and swiftly as she said, "You all go on out there. I'll be ready."

Alice and Florence started out. Marvin lingered only long enough to ask, "Okay, Kitz?"

"Okay!" she said.

As she was applying the last touch of makeup to her cheekbones, the attendant who had been assigned to her brought a vase to her dressing table. It was filled with roses of three colors, red, pink, and white. The music for Kitzi's introduction had just begun. She had barely time to glance at the card that accompanied the roses. "From an old admirer. Give 'em hell tonight, Kitzi. Gus."

Hastily she slipped the card into her bodice, between her breasts, and hurried out.

She heard her intro music become muted as Tony Frascati spoke over it.

"Mr. President, First Lady, honored guests, may I present our own First Lady of Show Business, just returned from a triumphant four-week engagement of the most important performance she has ever given. Miss Kitzi Mills!"

As her music came up full, she started out to the thunder of their applause. When she entered the ballroom, she discovered they were all standing to greet her. She ascended the low platform and bowed her head to acknowledge their greeting. She began to sing.

There was a smile on her face as she started out, thinking, *Just get past the first six bars.* Then, *I am past the first six bars, and this audience seems to like me.*

346

When she finished her first number, their applause was intermingled with calls of "Bravo" and "Encore." She knew then they loved her once more.

She turned to where Alice, Marvin, and Florence were seated.

"In honor of a dear and devoted friend, I would like to do a special number tonight."

She nodded to the conductor. He gave his orchestra the downbeat. They began to play the first bars of Kitzi's first solo from *Oddities*.

As soon as the audience recognized the familiar strains, they burst into applause. Kitzi gracefully slipped to the floor, once more the young ingenue, shy, reclusive, too timid to confess her love to anyone.

As she sang, Marvin watched, listened, and recalled those days of a dozen years ago—a lifetime ago, it seemed.

She's back, he thought. *Kitzi Mills, the real Kitzi Mills, the one I knew and loved, is back. As great as ever.*

Kitzi raced from the stage even before her applause had died down. She found the woman who had brought her the roses.

"A phone. I must get to a phone. He'll want to know how it went."

She dialed the number in New York. She asked for Chamberlain's room. When she was told he was no longer registered, she thought, *Hospitals these days. They can't even keep their records straight. Any wonder they're always being sued?*

"I want to talk to Nurse Lucille Johnson!" she insisted.

After what seemed an eternity, she heard the warm, melodious voice.

"Yes, ma'am, I was expecting your call."

"I want to talk to him, Lucille!"

"Oh, I'm afraid you can't do that, ma'am. Mr. Chamberlain passed two nights ago."

"Passed? You mean he . . . but I received flowers from him not an hour ago."

"Yes, ma'am. Two things he insisted on at the end. His passing wasn't to be publicly mentioned till your concert was over. And his flowers were to be there before you went on."

"Oh, God . . . Gus, poor Gus. He died alone after all."

"Oh, no, ma'am. I was with him. And you being down there to sing for the President was enough to make him happy."

"Thank you, Lucille. Thank you very much . . . for both of us."

She was hanging up the phone when she heard Alice call, "Mommy! Mommy, you were super! Humongous!"

The child raced into her arms and clung to her.